Favorite Love Stories in Large Print

Other Anthologies available in Large Print:

Favorite Love Stories In Large Print

Edited by Mary C. Allen

G.K.HALL&CO.
Boston, Massachusetts
1991

G.K. Hall Large Print Book Series.

Set in 16 pt. Plantin.

Library of Congress Cataloging-in-Publication Data

Favorite love stories in large print / edited by Mary C. Allen.
    p. cm.—(G.K. Hall large print series)
   ISBN 0-8161-5002-8
   1. Love stories, American. 2. Love stories, English. 3. Large
type books. I. Allen, Mary C.
[PS648.L6F38   1991]
813'.08508—dc20   91-13855

For Jim Beaman,
who has all my love
In memoriam

Acknowledgments

The editor gratefully acknowledges permissions to reproduce the copyright material included in this volume. In the event of any error or omission, she will be pleased to make the necessary correction in future editions of this book.

"We Are Nighttime Travelers" from *Emperor of the Air* by Ethan Canin. Copyright © 1988 by Ethan Canin. Reprinted by permission of Houghton Mifflin Co.

"The Treasure of Far Island" by Willa Cather. From *Willa Cather's Collected Short Fiction 1892–1912* published by the University of Nebraska Press.

"My Mistress" from *Another Marvelous Thing* by Laurie Colwin. Copyright © 1986 by Laurie Colwin. Reprinted by permission of Alfred A. Knopf Inc.

"A Humble Romance" by Mary E. Wilkins Freeman from *A Humble Romance and Other Stories* by Mary E. Wilkins. Copyright 1887. Published by Harper & Brothers.

Contents

Editor's Note

Recently, I've become something of an expert on the subject of love. I've talked to my friends who are married or newly in love, all of whom have different stories—about instantaneous mutual attraction, or love that only blossomed slowly over time, about hard times as well as joyous ones, about the amazing ability of love to change and yet remain immutable. I myself, at the age of thirty-seven, have recently fallen thoroughly, lastingly in love at first sight—something I'd always hoped for but up until now never really believed was possible. And I have read hundreds of love stories, both old and new, in the search for ones compelling and entertaining, moving or amusing, to include in this anthology.

Those that I have chosen span a wide variety of mood, theme, character type and situation. Some, such as Willa Cather's touching "The Treasure of Far Island" and Edna O'Brien's lovingly detailed "Courtship," portray the surprise and wonder of young love. Ethan Canin's "We Are Nighttime Travelers" deals with love at the other end of the spectrum, in a moving portrait of the rekindling of love in old age. Several others as well, including Washington Irving's classic "The

Wife" and Stephanie Vaughn's wholly contemporary "Sweet Talk"—the oldest and newest stories in the collection—are concerned with the way that marital love can triumph over adversity. Some are tragic, such as "The Furnished Room" by O. Henry and Graham Greene's "Two Gentle People," both of which portray opportunities missed. Others tend toward the comic, dealing with love between some very unlikely couples, such as the gangster and the mission worker in "The Idyll of Miss Sarah Brown," the outlaw and the arrogant young beauty in "Salomy Jane's Kiss," and the rather strange pair of lovers in Laurie Colwin's "My Mistress." At least one, "Marjorie Dawe," has a surprise ending, and two more, Mark Twain's "My Platonic Sweetheart" and Rudyard Kipling's "The Brushwood Boy" involve elements of the supernatural, with love taking place in dreams. Many of the stories include snippets of poems, and one, Wilbur Daniel Steele's haunting classic "How Beautiful with Shoes," evokes the power of poetry to awaken and disturb.

Whatever your tastes and predilections, I hope you will get as much pleasure reading these stories in Large Print as I did collecting them, and find them as entertaining and enjoyable, as moving and compellingly romantic, as I do.

Mary C. Allen
Iowa City, Iowa

The Wife

Washington Irving

> The treasures of the deep are not so
>   precious
> As are the conceal'd comforts of a man
> Locked up in woman's love. I scent
>   the air
> Of blessings, when I come but near
>   the house.
> What a delicious breath marriage
>   sends forth . . .
> The violet bed's not sweeter.
> MIDDLETON

I have often had occasion to remark the fortitude with which women sustain the most overwhelming reverses of fortune. Those disasters which break down the spirit of a man and prostrate him in the dust, seem to call forth all the energies of the softer sex, and give such intrepidity and elevation to their character that at times it approaches to sublimity. Nothing can be more touching than to behold a soft and tender female, who had been all weakness and dependence, and alive to every trivial roughness, while treading the prosperous paths of life, suddenly rising in mental force to be the comforter and support of her husband under mis-

1

fortune, and abiding with unshrinking firmness the bitterest blasts of adversity.

As the vine which has long twined its graceful foliage about the oak and been lifted by it into sunshine, will, when the hardy plant is rifted by the thunderbolt, cling round it with its caressing tendrils and bind up its shattered boughs, so is it beautifully ordered by Providence that woman, who is the mere dependent and ornament of man in his happier hours, should be his stay and solace when smitten with sudden calamity, winding herself into the rugged recesses of his nature, tenderly supporting the drooping head, and binding up the broken heart.

I was once congratulating a friend, who had around him a blooming family, knit together in the strongest affection. "I can wish you no better lot," said he with enthusiasm, "than to have a wife and children. If you are prosperous, there they are to share your prosperity; if otherwise, there they are to comfort you." And indeed I have observed that a married man falling into misfortune is more apt to retrieve his situation in the world than a single one; partly because he is more stimulated to exertion by the necessities of the helpless and beloved beings who depend upon him for subsistence; but chiefly because his spirits are soothed and relieved by domestic endearments, and his self-respect kept alive by finding, that though all abroad is darkness and humiliation, yet there is still a little world of love at home, of which he is the monarch. Whereas a single man is apt to run to waste and self-neglect; to fancy himself lonely and abandoned, and his heart to fall to ruin like some deserted mansion, for want of an inhabitant.

These observations call to mind a little domestic story, of which I was once a witness. My intimate friend, Leslie, had married a beautiful and accomplished girl, who had been brought up in the midst of fashionable life. She had, it is true, no fortune, but that of my friend was ample; and he delighted in the anticipation of indulging her in every elegant pursuit, and administering to those delicate tastes and fancies that spread a kind of witchery about the sex.—"Her life," said he, "shall be like a fairy tale."

The very difference in their characters produced an harmonious combination: he was of a romantic and somewhat serious cast; she was all life and gladness. I have often noticed the mute rapture with which he would gaze upon her in company, of which her sprightly powers made her the delight; and how, in the midst of applause, her eye would still turn to him, as if there alone she sought favor and acceptance. When leaning on his arm, her slender form contrasted finely with his tall manly person. The fond confiding air with which she looked up to him seemed to call forth a flush of triumphant pride and cherishing tenderness, as if he doted on his lovely burden for its very helplessness. Never did a couple set forward on the flowery path of early and well-suited marriage with a fairer prospect of felicity.

It was the misfortune of my friend, however, to have embarked his property in large speculations; and he had not been married many months, when, by a succession of sudden disasters, it was swept from him, and he found himself reduced almost to penury. For a time he kept his situation to himself, and went about with a haggard countenance and a breaking heart. His life was but a protracted agony; and what rendered it more insupportable was the necessity of keeping up a smile in the presence of his wife; for he could not bring himself to overwhelm her with the news. She saw, however, with the quick eyes of affection, that all was not well with him. She marked his altered looks and stifled sighs, and was not to be deceived by his sickly and vapid attempts at cheerfulness. She tasked all her sprightly powers and tender blandishments to win him back to happiness; but she only drove the arrow deeper into his soul. The more he saw cause to love her, the more torturing was the thought that he was soon to make her wretched. "A little while," thought he, "and the smile will vanish from that cheek—the song will die away from those lips—the lustre of those eyes will be quenched with sorrow; and the happy heart, which now beats lightly in that bosom, will be weighed down like mine by the cares and miseries of the world."

At length he came to me one day, and related his whole situation in a tone of the deepest despair. When I heard him through I inquired, "Does your wife know all this?"—At the question he burst

4

into an agony of tears. "For God's sake!" cried he, "if you have any pity on me, don't mention my wife; it is the thought of her that drives me almost to madness!"

"And why not?" said I. "She must know it sooner or later; you cannot keep it long from her, and the intelligence may break upon her in a more startling manner than if imparted by yourself; for the accents of those we love soften the hardest tidings. Besides, you are depriving yourself of the comforts of her sympathy; and not merely that, but also endangering the only bond that can keep hearts together—an unreserved community of thought and feeling. She will soon perceive that something is secretly preying upon your mind; and true love will not brook reserve; it feels undervalued and outraged, when even the sorrows of those it loves are concealed from it."

"Oh, but, my friend! to think what a blow I am to give to all her future prospects—how I am to strike her very soul to the earth, by telling her that her husband is a beggar! that she is to forego all the elegancies of life—all the pleasures of society—to shrink with me into indigence and obscurity! To tell her that I have dragged her down from the sphere in which she might have continued to move in constant brightness—the light of every eye—the admiration of every heart!—How can she bear poverty? she has been brought up in all the refinements of opulence. How can she bear neglect? she has been the idol of society. Oh! it will break her heart—it will break her heart!—"

I saw his grief was eloquent, and I let it have its flow; for sorrow relieves itself by words. When his paroxysm had subsided, and he had relapsed into moody silence, I resumed the subject gently, and urged him to break his situation at once to his wife. He shook his head mournfully, but positively.

"But how are you to keep it from her? It is necessary she should know it, that you may take the steps proper to the alteration of your circumstances. You must change your style of living—nay," observing a pang to pass across his countenance, "don't let that afflict you. I am sure you have never placed your happiness in outward show—you have yet friends, warm friends, who will not think the worse of you for being less splendidly lodged: and surely it does not require a palace to be happy with Mary—"

"I could be happy with her," cried he, convulsively, "in a hovel!—I could go down with her into poverty and the dust!—I could—I could—God bless her!—God bless her!" cried he, bursting into a transport of grief and tenderness.

"And believe me, my friend," said I, stepping up and grasping him warmly by the hand, "believe me she can be the same with you. Ay, more: it will be a source of pride and triumph to her—it will call forth all the latent energies and fervent sympathies of her nature; for she will rejoice to prove that she loves you for yourself. There is in every true woman's heart a spark of heavenly fire, which lies dormant in the broad daylight of prosperity; but which kindles up, and beams and blazes in the dark hour of adversity. No man knows what the wife of his bosom is—no man knows what a ministering angel she is—until he has gone with her through the fiery trials of this world."

There was something in the earnestness of my manner and the figurative style of my language that caught the excited imagination of Leslie. I knew the auditor I had to deal with; and following up the impression I had made, I finished by persuading him to go home and unburden his sad heart to his wife.

I must confess, notwithstanding all I had said, I felt some little solicitude for the result. Who can calculate on the fortitude of one whose life has been a round of pleasures? Her gay spirits might revolt at the dark downward path of low humility suddenly pointed out before her, and might cling to the sunny regions in which they had hitherto revelled. Besides, ruin in fashionable life is accompanied by so many galling mortifications, to which in other ranks it is a stranger.—In short, I could not meet Leslie the next morning without trepidation. He had made the disclosure.

"And how did she bear it?"

"Like an angel! It seemed rather to be a relief to her mind, for she threw her arms round my neck, and asked if this was all that had lately made me unhappy.—But, poor girl," added he, "she cannot realize the change we must undergo. She has no idea of poverty but in the abstract; she has only read of it in poetry, where it is allied to love. She feels as yet no privation; she suffers no loss of accustomed conveniences nor elegancies. When we come practically to experience its sordid cares, its paltry wants, its petty humiliations—then will be the real trial."

"But," said I, "now that you have got over the severest task, that of breaking it to her, the sooner you let the world into the secret the better. The disclosure may be mortifying; but then it is a single misery, and soon over: whereas you otherwise suffer it in anticipation every hour in the day. It is not poverty so much as pretence, that harasses a ruined man—the struggle between a proud mind and an empty purse—the keeping up a hollow show that must soon come to an end. Have the courage to appear poor and you disarm poverty of its sharpest sting." On this point I found Leslie perfectly prepared. He had no false pride himself, and as to his wife, she was only anxious to conform to their altered fortunes.

Some days afterwards he called upon me in the evening. He had disposed of his dwelling house, and taken a small cottage in the country, a few miles from town. He had been busied all day in sending out furniture. The new establishment required few articles, and those of the simplest kind. All the splendid furniture of his late residence had been sold, excepting his wife's harp. That, he said, was too closely associated with the idea of herself; it belonged to the little story of their loves; for some of the sweetest moments of their courtship were those when he had leaned over that instrument, and listened to the melting tones of her voice. I could not but smile at this instance of romantic gallantry in a doting husband.

He was now going out to the cottage, where his wife had been all day superintending its arrangement. My feelings had become strongly interested in the progress of this family story, and as it was a fine evening, I offered to accompany him.

He was wearied with the fatigues of the day, and as he walked out, fell into a fit of gloomy musing.

"Poor Mary!" at length broke, with a heavy sigh, from his lips.

"And what of her?" asked I: "has anything happened to her?"

"What," said he, darting an impatient glance, "is it nothing to be reduced to this paltry situation—to be caged in a miserable cottage—to be obliged to toil almost in the menial concerns of her wretched habitation?"

"Has she then repined at the change?"

"Repined! she has been nothing but sweetness and good humor. Indeed, she seems in better spirits than I have ever known her; she has been to me all love and tenderness and comfort!"

"Admirable girl!" exclaimed I. "You call yourself poor, my friend; you never were so rich—you never knew the boundless treasures of excellence you possess in that woman."

"Oh! but, my friend, if this first meeting at the cottage were over, I think I could then be comfortable. But this is her first day of real experience; she has been introduced into a humble dwelling —she has been employed all day in arranging its miserable equipments—she has for the first time known the fatigues of domestic employment—she has for the first time looked round her on a home destitute of everything elegant,—almost of everything convenient; and may now be sitting down, exhausted and spiritless, brooding over a prospect of future poverty."

There was a degree of probability in this picture that I could not gainsay, so we walked on in silence.

After turning from the main road up a narrow lane, so thickly shaded with forest trees as to give it a complete air of seclusion, we came in sight of the cottage. It was humble enough in its appearance for the most pastoral poet; and yet it had a pleasing rural look. A wild vine had overrun one end with a profusion of foliage; a few trees threw their branches gracefully over it; and I observed several pots of flowers tastefully disposed about the door, and on the grass-plot in front. A small wicket gate opened upon a footpath that wound through some shrubbery to the door. Just as we approached, we heard the sound of music—Leslie grasped my arm; we paused and listened. It was Mary's voice singing, in a style of the most touching simplicity, a little air of which her husband was peculiarly fond.

I felt Leslie's hand tremble on my arm. He stepped forward to hear more distinctly. His step made a noise on the gravel walk. A bright beautiful face glanced out at the window and vanished—a light footstep was heard—and Mary came tripping forth to meet us: she was in a pretty rural dress of white; a few wild flowers were twisted in her fine hair; a fresh bloom was on her cheek; her whole countenance beamed with smiles—I had never seen her look so lovely.

"My dear George," cried she, "I am so glad you are come! I have been watching and watching for you; and running down the lane, and looking out for you. I've set out a table under a beautiful tree behind the cottage; and I've been gathering some of the most delicious strawberries, for I know you are fond of them—and we have such excellent cream—and everything is so sweet and still here—Oh!" said she, putting her arm within his, and looking up brightly in his face, "Oh, we shall be so happy!"

Poor Leslie was overcome. He caught her to his bosom—he folded his arms round her—he kissed her again and again—he could not speak, but the tears gushed into his eyes; and he has often assured me, that though the world has since gone prosperously with him, and his life has indeed been a happy one, yet never has he experienced a moment of more exquisite felicity.

The Love-Letters of a Clodhopper

Gertrude Brooke Hamilton

"There's no use talking—the person who can read this story without feeling a lump in his throat has something wrong with his heart."

—so was this archetype of
Love Conquers All
introduced in a 1917 *Redbook*

She selected several letters from the packet and put up a lovely hand to switch on the drop-light. Its glow vivified her flowing, tawny hair, waxen skin and black-lashed, coppery eyes—illuminated the bronze appointments of her ebony writing-table, purpled the pool in her jeweled inkwell and deepened the rich window hangings of her colorful room. Below the windows the tide of Manhattan broke and thundered on the shores of Seventy-second Street and Broadway. She spread the selected letters on the ebony table and began to read:

Dear Miss Gilder.

I rec'd your most helpful letter at 5.40 today.

Please excuse pencil. The ink is froze. Also please excuse, as usual, my uphill fist and bum spelling.

My married sis, Mrs. Pink Tibberly, is in a worrie to know who you are—she has brot me some of your letters from the P. O. But I wont tell her. I want the secret to myself. Just think. for 3 fine yrs you—Zola Gilder, a new York writer and poet—writing cheering letters to me—Martin Redd, a clodhopper!

Ever since I was old enuff to day-dream I have wanted to know some one like you. But when I first writ you in the care of a magazine, because that story of yours "Just Nature" had made me blubber, I calculated I was cutting fodder to rot. That first pretty, polite letter from you I wore under my shirt for 30 days. And then I seen your picture in a magazine. Shivering snakes! I went down on my big knees to what you had writ to me! It was 7:½ months before I hunched up the nerve to fist my pen again. And you writ back. And I writ back. And dearest, we kept company in letters.

Please excuse the "dearest" for you are dear to me. I have never seen you. Calculate I never will. But I don't think you ought to blame me for loving you as much as it is possible for a man to love a woman. You are good and noble. You make the farm chunks around here look like 30 cts. You know something else besides corset covers and boys and baking biscuits. You have told me 50 fine books to read. I love, honor and adoor you.

13

If this makes you mad, I am realy and truly sorry. also please forgive me.

Have just finished reading your story "Ships That Pass In The Day." I think it the sweetest one yet—a sort of sad-sweet story. Will get the current magazine you mention. As usual, I gave the "Ship" story to my sis, Mrs. Pink Tibberly, to read.

I am very sorry to hear of your having a cold, but it is no surprise to me, as I know you work to hard. You need fresh air and buttermilk. Dearest, I haven't taken a dose of Dr.'s dope for a cold or anything else for over 14 yrs and I hope I never do again.

Does it make you mad for me to call you dearest? If it does, please tell me so and please forgive me. For I would not hurt or harm you in any way, shape or form. Please an'sr soon.

Your humble friend,
MARTIN REDD.

Dear Miss Gilder.

Yours rec'd at 6.27 this evening.

I was beginning to feel that you was mad at me because I told you I loved you. I would like for to tell you heaps of such things, but I calculate you would laugh at me and think me a fool. But honest I could just fairly chaw you up—I like and love you so well.

After I writ that last letter to you I saddled my mare Crystal Herne and rode 16 hrs straight. The coarse grass on the prairie didn't seem no coarser than me handing you —Zola Gilder—a josh word like "dearest." I drove Crystal and myself to a dripping sweat. On the way home I stopped at Tibberly farm. My married sis Pink was feeding her chickens. I grabbed the mush-pot from her, and before I knew it I was telling her who my girl was. Sis sat down hard and took off her glasses to squint at me. Her eyes are so bad now that she can't read much, so she hasn't read your current story "The Shack Woman," but she will now as fast as she can. Sis thinks I ought to worship you (which I do) bow down and say my prayers to you— which I've done.

Please excuse me for calling you *my girl* to Sis. I know you are not for me, only to dream about, but in my dreams you are my girl. I wonder if you will be mad when you read this. I had a dream last night which I would like for to tell you about.

My Dream.

The date sliped up a few notches and it was midsummer, balmy and fair. I rec'd a letter from you saying you was coming out here. I hitched Crystal to the buggy and drove S. E. along the little lane from our house to the road—then turned E. to the big road called Clinton Road in the country and Clinton Ave. in town. I followed the Road to a little hill about ½ mile long. Then I turned E. and

15

drove over a new concrete bridge—the sides big walls of solid concrete and steel. I drove on over the grade, with Salt Creek running E. at the foot of the grade. There was no houses —all farm ground and pasture. Then I left the grade, drove up a hill—and was on the prairie.

You was there waiting for me. You was just what I know you are, a tall, straight-backed girl with fairy feet and flying hair and something that smells of God about you—like the girls you write of in your stories, like your face in the magazine pictures. You come running to meet me, and as you run you threw off your fine New York clothes and underneath them you wore a print dress and under your shirt you wore that picture of me with my best yearling that I sent you 2 yrs ago.

When you got close by me you stopped, sort of shy, and said, "Howdy, Martin Redd."

And I—pretending I was stuck-up and city-ish, and wanting the laugh on you said, "Excuse me. At what hog show did we meet? I can't calculate to remember, Miss Zola."

And you hung your head and shook your flying hair over your eyes and you begun to cry.

And *man alive!* I went down on my big fool knees to you right then and there.

And you laughed quicker than you cried. You run—you was lighter than dandelion fluff—to Crystal and kissed the white star on her forehead and you jumped into the buggy and grabbed up the reins and hollered— "Giddap!"

Crystal backed in the traces and begun to skid. I got in and took the reins. Crystal reared, shyed, laid back her ears and let loose! She had us home in about 5 minutes.

Before the buggy quit swaying you was out of it, dancing by the barn, touching the head of my Holstein heifer, kissing the cat that has double-pawed kittens, wading and capering thro the S. W. field of clover, grabbing up apples and pears and biting into them and throwing them over your shoulder and running all the time to my mother, throwing yourself into her arms and crying. And all the time dancing with your feet.

For supper we chawed something. I never dreamed what. After supper I raced you to the barn. You tiptoed into it and kissed Crystal eating oats and corn in her stall. And mooed at the cows, Blossom and Lillian Russell, munching their straw, and shook your hair over the guinea fowls squeaking to get out of the barred back doors. And like a squirrel you scampered to the hay lofts. I climbed after you. You got to the highest loft and spread out your arms like a bird and sailed down 10 ft and lay there for a minute beautiful and rosy and climbed up again, and said, "Unbar the back doors of the barn,

Martin Redd. Let the crying guinea fowls
out. And show me the view."

I pulled back the wooden bars and opened
the whole back of the barn and you spun out
on your tiptoes and whirled about and
shrieked with joy at the view. You can see 5
counties—a river—and about 1000 acres of
heavy timber from the back of our barn. It is
like standing in the clouds with the angels so
high up that you can't see no people—just
spires and the tops of things. You got sort of
solemn over it and you cuddled close to my
side and your hand stole up to my breast and
lay there.

Next thing—you was laughing. I was fixing
a swing for you under the stars. It was N. E.
of the clover field where the view is high
again. You leaped into the swing and swung
up touching the trees. Down, brushing by to
quick for me to kiss you.

Next Mother was giving you a foaming
pitcher of milk to drink. You drunk and
drunk till we all laughed and loved you and
worshiped you and went clean mad about
you. Mother took you to the S. W. bedroom
that is next to hers and she give you a lamp.
It shed a sort of a glory over you. We like for
to have died from *honoring* you.

You said—looking at the flame of the
lamp, "Martin Redd, I love you—I love
Crystal Herne, and the cows and the heifer,
and the guinea fowls and the double-pawed

kittens and your Mother and your married sis, Mrs. Pink Tibberly." And sly as a little spider you spun into the S. W. room and shut the door on me. Mother and Sis run down to the kitchen and begun to break eggs and cream butter and sift flour for the wedding cake.

In the night—when I was prowling under the window of the S. W. room—I heard the sash slip up. You put a foot over the sill and jumped down.

I said, "Where are you going?"

And you changed into a farm chunk.

Dearest, I woke up blubbering.

If this dream ofends you I am truly sorry.

The robins have come and the wild duck and geese are going north but we have had several flurries of snow—about 1 inch deep last night.

How is your work getting on? I wonder if when things go wrong you would like for some big strong person to take you in his arms and make you forget worrie—past and future.

I told you about 13 months ago what I look like. I am 6 ft., weigh 170 lbs. have yellow hair and gray eyes, sound teeth, high nose and reddish skin.

Hope you are well and prosperous. Write when you can.

As ever your humble friend,
MARTIN REDD.

19

Dear Miss Gilder.

I sent you a letter some months ago. Like to never got it mailed as I was in the woods cutting timber for 2 weeks on a stretch.

We are having some cussed weather. Spring don't seem to be coming this yr. everything is covered with sleet and ice. Telephone lines is nearly all down and things in bum shape generally. I wonder how cold it gets in New York. It gets 30 below real often here, sometimes 35 and 40.

Please forgive me for that last letter. I calculate I deserve the 10 weeks silence you have handed me. Also please excuse ink blots. Time to feed the hogs.

Hope you are well and happy.

Your humble friend,
MARTIN REDD.

Dear Miss Gilder.

Yours of the 22nd arrived on Christmas Day. I am happy to hear about your good luck about your work and sorry you was to busy to write to me for 3 months.

I have lost $400. worth of hogs. That wont seem a very large sum to you.

I read your story "No King But Caesar" and thought it fine. It hits a world of women —the women in the world. As usual, I gave the Caesar story to my sis, Mrs. Pink Tibberly, to read.

Am glad you got a smile off my mare's

name. She is all right. When the mare was a baby it seemed that one of her eyes was going to be what people call *glass eye* an eye that is *white*. I decided on the Crystal partly on account of the crystal-like eye and partly for Crystal Herne. I seen her once in a play when I was in Chicago and thought her fine.

I am glad you are coming to the good money. Hope you are able to keep it up. I am not like you for I don't want heaps of coin or fame.

I wont bother you with any more.

I love you.

> Your humble friend,
> MARTIN REDD.

Dear Miss Gilder.

I went to a corn-roast in these parts last night.

The men build a big camp fire in the field. The girls bring corn and salt and marshmallows sometimes rolls and hot sausages. They sit around the camp fire and eat and tell stories. There is always a funny fellow and a girl who recites sad pieces. Once I could laugh at that fellow and the pieces always brot tears to my eyes. Last night I sat like a stiff in the crowd. I saw your face in the big camp fire. Your arms reached out to me in the licking flames. Your curling mouth laughed at the bunch I went with—guyed my friends, guyed me, sang up to the stars in the smoke from the fire and made fun of the clodhopper who had gone stargazing. It come to me in a crack that the love making was always on my side and that it wasn't getting me nowhere. I calculated I was getting tired of kisses on paper. I sort of flared up high as the camp fire and put the blame on you. You have crammed my head with 75 books and set me blubbering over your stories and writ me letters to wear under my shirt. And I'll be thirty next birthday.

This is for you *alone*. I want to work for you, to do things to please you. I want you to like the things I like and I like the things you like—to hold you in my arms evenings and tell you that same old sweet story over and over and over. I love you! You can't never marry me. What is the end of real love but marriage?

What did you learn me to love you for?

MARTIN REDD

Dearest.

I could grab you in my arms and murmur lots of things in your ear and lay your head on my shoulder—and blubber. All of which would make you justly mad!

I am tipping my hat to you for that lock of hair. It is realy beautiful hair. I have your pictures propped up in front of me as I write. The 3 I have cut from magazines. I wish I was at your side that I might stroke that

22

beautiful hair and kiss and caress you. I don't feel like telling you nothing but I love you. I wonder how you would like for me to come into your room and love you savagely, to take up your hair in my hands and bury my face in it, to look into your eyes and find nothing but purity there. But on the other hand if you was the Devil's own Daughter and your hair was coils of glittering snakes I would love you. You couldn't do nothing low or mean enuff to keep me from loving you.

I am going to ride 18 hrs. straight and think it out.

My Thoughts.

At first I thought I would come to New York and give you back your letters and only slightly smile when I saw you and then come back home after having just loved you with my eyes.

And then—dawn was on the prairie when I come to my 2nd thought—I felt my big, young body and the muscles in my arms. I thought of the $3000 I have in the Fairbanks bank in Mansfield and the 200 good acres I own. I looked at my hands—brown and hard enuff to protect any soft white hand that would trust itself to it. I thought of my married sis, Mrs. Pink Tibberly, who thinks me good enuff for any woman. And my Mother who says I am the handsomest man around these parts. And the farm chunks who any

23

one of them would jump at slinging hash for
me.

My 3rd thought was about Love.

My 4th thought was You. I read the beautiful things between the lines of your letters. I
heard you calling me. I saw you in New York
—pestered by men—fighting for your fame
and money—and all the while resting in my
big ugly arms.

For you are mine by the right of my
manhood—by the right that hasn't nothing to
do with schooling—by the right that made
Eve belong to Adam.

I am coming to New York to pick you up
in my arms and bring you back with me.
You're mine! My friend! my girl! my ideal!
my pal! my saint! my wife! Those fairy feet of
yours may run fast, dearest, but they shant
outrun your clodhopper's hoofs. Inall my
dreams you get away from me. I am going to
quit dreaming! I am coming to New York to
pick you up in my arms and bring you back
with me!

I live you so I am sick and humble from
love. My knees knock at the thought of coming into your presence. My eyes blubber. I
am like an old man with a young man's
lungs. I am feeble and powerful—glad and
blue—resolute and uncertain—shouting and
afraid—bold and hanging back.

Tell me to come. Tell me *you love me*.

MARTIN REDD.

24

Miss Zola Gilder.

I would like for to kill you for your letter rec'd today at 12.50.

I would like for to come into your room and put the marks of my fingers on your white shoulders and stamp with my feet on your feet and use my horsewhip on your beautiful back.

You begin your letter with some French that I can't read because I don't know no language but my own. You go on to say that you are not the marrying sort—that my letters have been one long, big laugh to you—that the only reason you encouraged them was to get what you call copy—that a clodhopper story you hope to sell for $500. is already in your typewriter—that love is a fairy tale that brings so much a word—that nothing funnier could be imagined than Zola Gilder jumping about in hay lofts and nestling up to a six-foot son of the soil! You end your letter with some Latin that you know I can't read. And with that you are thro.

Well so am I. Here are your letters, the lock of your hair and the magazine pictures of you, you beauty, you she-wolf.

I am glad you got a $500. laugh out of me.

I love you.

THE CLODHOPPER.

She replaced the letters in the packet and put out lovely hands to pick up a pair of crutches. Slowly

25

she got to her feet and crossed her colorful room to an electric button. She punched white light in abundance over the room. At her ebony-framed, full-length mirror she took stock of her flowing, tawny hair, well-chiseled brow, black-lashed, coppery eyes, delicate nose, idealistic nostrils and red, wistful mouth. Pulling a shimmering mass of hair over her shoulder and half turning from her mirror, she gave a slant stare at the hump on her back and at her shrunken legs and crippled, club feet. She spread her hands on her crutches and began to sob.

The telephone rang. Zola Gilder answered it.

"Mr. Martin Redd, of Illinois, calling," came the metallic voice of the hotel clerk.

"Who?" Zola gasped.

"Mr. Martin Redd, of Illinois, calling," replied the mechanical voice.

Zola Gilder's face went white. "Martin Redd—calling!" she repeated. In swift succession, panic, joy, apprehension, despair, possessed her features.

She moistened her lips, and said into the telephone: "Have Mr. Martin Redd shown up to my suite."

Her hand, as she put the receiver into the hook, went weak. Her shoulders rested heavily on her crutches. She seemed about to crumple up like an imperfect rose-petal at the end of a perfect summer.

Then the spirit that shone in her coppery eyes conquered her weakness. Resolutely she moved to the center of the room, where the light from the chandelier fell full upon her.

Outside, in the softly padded corridor, feet passed and repassed. Somewhere a room-telephone tinkled. The heavy sound of a trunk-truck rumbled by.

An elevator-door clanged. A tread, different from the rest, came along the corridor. The knock that smote her door reverberated through the suite.

With wild, uneven steps, hampered by her infirmity, she rushed to her door—and locked it.

The knock came again. It was, perhaps, the *rap-rap* of knuckles fisted to strike.

Zola leaned against the door and put her paling lips on the wood where the knock sounded. "Martin Redd," she whispered dryly, "go away! What have you come for?"

A hand wrenched the door-knob. A heavy foot struck against the satin panel of the door. It seemed as if a giant shoulder might be placed against the wood and the door might come crashing in.

Zola Gilder unlocked the door and moved back to her position under the chandelier. "Come in," she said.

Martin Redd opened the door—and was in the room. He carried a rawhide whip.

Zola Gilder spread out her lovely hands on the rungs of her crutches. "Howdy, Clodhopper," she said faintly.

Martin Redd's balked, baffled stare played on her exquisite face and hair—and on her body.

"You see," she said with a three-cornered smile, "I *would* be funny jumping about in hay-lofts."

His look of amazement increased.

She shook back her flowing hair. The movement revealed the nobility of her brow, the beauty of her eyes, the idealism of her nostrils and the redness of her mouth. "You wouldn't want to come into my room and love me savagely, would you?" she faltered.

Martin Redd took a step toward her and stood still.

Zola Gilder smiled. For the second, her face was all that a man might dream of.

Then renunciation leveled and controlled her face. "I am glad you came, Martin Redd," she said slowly. "I am glad I have had the courage to see you. I am glad to be able to tell you that I did not encourage you to obtain what I call copy. I have not written a clodhopper story. I was lying."

Her voice sank, became infinitely sweet. "Now that you have seen me, you can go back and happily marry a 'farm chunk.' Now that you have seen me, you can forget—or laugh. For it is funny!" She pulled a mass of hair over her shoulder, with brave, tragic humor, exposing her deformity. "See how far I am from the woman you have wanted, Martin. Brains I have, and soul, and beauty of face—" Her tragedy shook her.

His arms hung at his sides, inanimate as his stare.

The slow, luminous calm of the spirit challenging the physical composed her. The spirit transcended the physical. "You can never marry me," she said, sadly. Her face colored. "What is the real end of love but marriage?"

She seemed to wither. "I have done wrong in deceiving you," she stammered. "Use your whip on my—back." She hung her head and shook her tawny hair over her eyes and began to cry.

Martin Redd placed the rawhide whip on her ebony writing-table beside the jeweled inkwell.

A step took him to her.

Gently he threw away the crutches and picked her up in his arms. "Blubber on my onery shoulder, dearest," he said, in a rich voice. "Please excuse the 'dearest,' for you are dear to me."

He walked her up and down the gorgeous room, stroking her beautiful hair—kissing and caressing her.

Below the windows, the tides of Manhattan broke and thundered on the shores of Seventy-second Street and Broadway. As an automobile-siren screamed in the streets, Zola laid a hand on Martin's breast.

"You cannot marry me!" she cried.

"I fail for to see why," he answered.

"I am misshapen."

"I calculate that don't make no difference."

"But Martin, I am a cripple!"

"You're my girl." He rocked and cradled her. "You're glad you're where you are, in my big, ugly arms. Aren't you, dearest? Lay your head

29

down on my shoulder. There." The rich voice was humble. "If you will let me take you back with me, you'll do me honor. I love you."

Her hand on his breast, lighter than a snowflake, seemed to melt there. Her face on his shoulder became less the face of a child-sufferer, less the face of a brilliant recluse—more the face of a woman who would play her woman's part.

A delicate and courageous ecstasy flowed through Zola Gilder's whisper, "I could die from honoring you, Martin Redd."

A Humble Romance

Mary E. Wilkins Freeman

She was stooping over the great kitchen sink, washing the breakfast dishes. Under fostering circumstances, her slenderness of build might have resulted in delicacy or daintiness; now the harmony between strength and task had been repeatedly broken, and the result was ugliness. Her finger joints and wrist bones were knotty and out of proportion, her elbows, which her rolled-up sleeves displayed, were pointed and knobby, her shoulders bent, her feet spread beyond their natural bounds—from head to foot she was a little discordant note. She had a pale, peaked face, her scanty fair hair was strained tightly back, and twisted into a tiny knot, and her expression was at once passive and eager.

There came a ringing knock at the kitchen door, and a face of another description, large, strong-featured, and assured, peered out of the pantry, which was over against the sink.

"Who is it, Sally?"

"I don' know, Mis' King."

"Well, go to the door, can't you, an' not stan' thar gapin'. I can't; my hands are in the butter."

Sally shook the dish-water off her red, sodden fingers, and shuffled to the door.

A tall man with a scraggy sandy mustache stood there. He had some scales in his hand.

"Good-mornin', marm," he said. "Hev you got any rags?"

"I'll see," said the girl. Then she went over to the pantry, and whispered to her mistress that it was the tin-peddler.

"Botheration!" cried Mrs. King, impatiently. "Why couldn't he hev come another day? Here I am right in the midst of butter, an' I've got lots of rags, an' I've got to hev some new milk-pails right away."

All of this reached the ears of the tin-peddler, but he merely stood waiting, the corners of his large mouth curving up good-naturedly, and scrutinized with pleasant blue eyes the belongings of the kitchen, and especially the slight, slouching figure at the sink, to which Sally had returned.

"I s'pose," said Mrs. King, approaching the peddler at length, with decision thinly veiled by doubt, "that I shall hev to trade with you, though I don' know how to stop this mornin', for I'm right in the midst of butter-making. I wish you'd 'a happened along some other day."

"Wa'al," replied the peddler, laughing, "an' so I would, marm, ef I'd only known. But I don't see jest how I could hev, unless you'd 'a pasted it up on the fences, or had it put in the newspaper, or mebbe in the almanac."

He lounged smilingly against the door-casing,

jingling his scales, and waiting for the woman to make up her mind.

She smiled unwillingly, with knitted brows.

"Well," said she, "of course you ain't to blame. I guess I'll go an' pick up my rags, up in the garret. There's quite a lot of 'em, an' it'll take some time. I don't know as you'll want to wait."

"Lor', I don't keer," answered the peddler. "I'd jest as soon rest a leetle as not. It's a powerful hot mornin' for this time o' year, an' I've got all the day afore me."

He came in and seated himself, with a loose-jointed sprawl, on a chair near the door.

After Mrs. King had gone out, he sat a few minutes eyeing the girl at the sink intently. She kept steadily on with her work, though there was a little embarrassment and uncertainty in her face.

"Would it be too much trouble ef I should ask you to give me a tumbler of water, miss?"

She filled one of her hot, newly-washed glasses with water from a pail standing on a shelf at one end of the sink, and brought it over to him. "It's cold," she said. "I drawed it myself jest a few minutes ago, or I'd get some right out of the well for you."

"This is all right, an' thanky kindly, miss; it's proper good water."

He drained the glass, and carried it back to her at the sink, where she had returned. She did not seem to dare absent herself from her dish-washing task an instant.

He set the empty glass down beside the pail;

33

then he caught hold of the girl by her slender shoulders and faced her round towards him. She turned pale, and gave a smothered scream.

"Thar! thar! don't you go to being afeard of me," said the peddler. "I wouldn't hurt you for the whole world. I jest want to take a squar look at you. You're the worst-off-lookin' little cretur I ever set my eyes on."

She looked up at him pitifully, still only half-reassured. There were inflamed circles around her dilated blue eyes.

"You've been cryin', ain't you?"

The girl nodded meekly. "Please let me go," she said.

"Yes, I'll let you go; but I'm a-goin' to ask you a few questions first, an' I want you to answer 'em, for I'll be hanged ef I ever see—Ain't she good to you?" indicating Mrs. King with a wave of his hand towards the door through which she had departed.

"Yes, she's good enough, I guess."

"Don't ever scold you, hey?"

"I don' know; I guess so, sometimes."

"Did this mornin', didn't she?"

"A little. I was kinder behind with the work."

"Keeps you workin' pretty stiddy, don't she?"

"Yes; thar's consider'ble to do this time o' year."

"Cookin' for hired men, I s'pose, and butter an' milk?"

"Yes."

"How long hev you been livin' here?"

34

"She took me when I was little."

"Do you do anything besides work?—go round like other gals?—hev any good times?"

"Sometimes." She said it doubtfully, as if casting about in her mind for reminiscences to prove the truth of it.

"Git good wages?"

"A dollar a week sence I was eighteen. I worked for my board an' close afore."

"Got any folks?"

"I guess I've got some brothers and sisters somewhar. I don' know jest whar. Two of 'em went West, an' one is married somewhar in York State. We was scattered when father died. Thar was ten of us, an' we was awful poor. Mis' King took me. I was the youngest; 'bout four, they said I was. I 'ain't never known any folks but Mis' King."

The peddler walked up and down the kitchen floor twice; Sally kept on with her dishes; then he came back to her.

"Look a-here," he said; "leave your dish-washin' alone a minute. I want you to give me a good look in the face, an' tell me what you think of me."

She looked up shyly in his florid, freckled face, with its high cheek-bones and scraggy sandy mustache; then she plunged her hands into the dish-tub again.

"I don' know," she said, bashfully.

"Well, mebbe you do know, only you can't put it into words. Now jest take a look out the window

35

at my tin cart thar. That's all my own, a private consarn. I ain't runnin' for no company. I owns the cart an' horse, an' disposes of the rags, an' sells the tin, all on my own hook. An' I'm a-doin' pretty well at it; I'm a-layin' up a leetle money. I ain't got no family. Now this was what I was a-comin' at: s'pose you should jest leave the dishes, an' the scoldin' woman, an' the butter, an' every-thing, an' go a-ridin' off with me on my tin-cart. I wouldn't know you, an' *she* wouldn't know you, an' you wouldn't know yourself, in a week. You wouldn't hev a bit of work to do, but jest set up thar like a queen, a-ridin' and seein' the country. For that's the way we'd live, you know. I wouldn't hev you keepin' house an' slavin'. We'd stop along the road for vittles, and bring up at taverns nights. What d'ye say to it?"

She stopped her dish-washing now, and stood staring at him, her lips slightly parted and her cheeks flushed.

"I know I ain't much in the way of looks," the peddler went on, "an' I'm older than you—I'm near forty—an' I've been married afore. I don't s'pose you kin take a likin' to me right off, but you might arter a while. An' I'd take keer of you, you poor leetle thing. An' I don't b'lieve you know anything about how nice it is to be taken keer of, an' hev the hard, rough things kep' off by some-body that likes yer."

Still she said nothing, but stood staring at him.

"You ain't got no beau, hev you?" asked the peddler, as a sudden thought struck him.

"No." She shook her head, and her cheeks flushed redder.

"Well, what do you say to goin' with me? You'll hev to hurry up an' make up your mind, or the old lady'll be back."

The girl was almost foolishly ignorant of the world, but her instincts were as brave and innocent as an angel's. Tainted with the shiftless weariness and phlegm of her parents, in one direction she was vigorous enough.

Whether it was by the grace of God, or an inheritance from some far-off Puritan ancestor, the fire in whose veins had not burned low, she could see, if she saw nothing else, the distinction between right and wrong with awful plainness. Nobody had ever called her anything but a *good* girl. It was said with a disparagement, maybe, but it was always "a good girl."

She looked up at the man before her, her cheeks burning painfully hot, her eyes at once drooping and searching.

"I—don't know jest—how you mean," she stammered. "I wouldn't go with the king, if—it wasn't to—go honest—"

The peddler's face flushed as red as hers.

"Now, look a-here, little un," he said. "You jest listen, an' it's God's own truth; ef I hadn't 'a meant all right I wouldn't 'a come to you, but to some other gal, hansumer, an' pearter, an'—but, O Lord! I ain't that kind, anyway. What I want is to merry you honest, an' take keer of you, an' git that look off your face. I know it's awful sud-

37

den, an' it's askin' a good deal of a gal to trust so much in a fellow she never set eyes on afore. Ef you can't do it, I'll never blame you; but ef you kin, well, I don't b'lieve you'll ever be sorry. Most folks would think I was a fool, too, an' mebbe I am, but I wanted to take keer on you the minute I set eyes on you; an' afore I know it the wantin' to take keer on you will be growin' into lovin' you. Now you hurry and make up your mind, or she will be back."

Sally had little imagination, and a loving nature. In her heart, as in all girls' hearts, the shy, secret longing for a lover had strengthened with her growth, but she had never dreamed definitely of one. Now she surveyed the homely, scrawny, good-natured visage before her, and it filled well enough the longing nature had placed in her helpless heart. His appearance dispelled no previous illusion, for previous illusion there had been none. No one had ever spoken to her in this way. Rough and precipitate though it was, it was skillful wooing; for it made its sincerity felt, and a girl more sophisticated than this one could not have listened to it wholly untouched.

The erratic nature of the whole proceeding did not dismay her. She had no conscience for conventionalities; she was too simple; hers only provided for pure right and wrong. Strange to say, the possible injury she would do her mistress by leaving her in this way did not occur to her till afterward. Now she looked at her lover, and began to believe in him, and as soon as she began to believe in him—poor, unattractive, ignorant little thing that she was!—she began to love just like other girls. All over her crimson face flashed the signs of yielding. The peddler saw and understood them.

"You will—won't you, little un?" he cried. Then, as her eyes drooped more before his, and her mouth quivered between a sob and a smile, he took a step forward and stretched out his arms toward her. Then he stepped back, and his arms fell.

"No," he cried, "I won't; I'd like to give you a hug, but I won't; I won't so much as touch that little lean hand of yours till you're my wife. You shall see I mean honest. But come along now, little un, or she will be back. I declar' ef I don't more'n half believe she's fell in a fit, or she'd ha' been back afore now. Come now, dear, be spry!"

"Now?" said Sally, in turn.

"Now! why, of course now: what's the use of waitin'? Mebbe you want to make some weddin' cake, but I reckon we'd better buy some over in Derby, for it might put the old lady out;" and the peddler chuckled. "Why, I'm jest a-goin' to stow you away in that 'ere tin-cart of mine—there's plenty of room, for I've been on the road a-sellin' nigh a week. An' then I'm a-goin' to drive out of this yard, arter I've traded with your missis, as innocent as the very innocentest lamb you ever see, an' I'm a-goin' to drive along a piece till it's safe; an' then you're a-goin' to git out and set up on the seat alongside of me, an' we're goin' to

39

keep on till we git to Derby, an' then we'll git merried, jest as soon as we kin find a minister as wants to airn a ten-dollar bill."

"But," gasped Sally, "she'll ask whar I am."

"I'll fix that. You lay there in the cart an' hear what I say. Lor', I'd jest as soon tell her to her face, myself, what we was goin' to do, an' set you right up on the seat aside of me, afore her eyes; but she'd talk hard, most likely, an' you look scared enough now, an' you'd cry, an' your eyes would git redder; an' she might sass you so you'd be ready to back out, too. Women kin say hard things to other women, an' they ain't likely to understan' any woman but themselves trustin' a man overmuch. I reckon this is the best way." He went towards the door, and motioned her to come.

"But I want my bonnet."

"Never mind the bunnit; I'll buy you one in Derby."

"But I don't want to ride into Derby bare-headed," said Sally, almost crying.

"Well, I don't know as you do, little un, that's a fact; but hurry an' git the bunnit, or she *will* be here. I thought I heard her a minute ago."

"Thar's a leetle money I've saved, too."

"Well, git that; we don't want to make the old lady vallyble presents, an' you kin buy yourself sugar-plums with it. But be spry."

She gave him one more scared glance, and hastened out of the room, her limp calico accommodating itself to every ungraceful hitch of her thin limbs and sharp hips.

"I'll git her a gown with puckers in the back," mused the peddler, gazing after her. Then he hastened out to his tin-cart, and arranged a vacant space in the body of it. He had a great-coat, which he spread over the floor.

"Thar, little un, let me put you right in," he whispered, when Sally emerged, her bonnet on, a figured green delaine shawl over her shoulders, and her little hoard in an old stocking dangling from her hand.

She turned round and faced him once more, her eyes like a child's peering into a dark room. "You mean *honest?*"

"Before God, I do, little un. Now git in quick, for she *is* comin'!"

He had to lift her in, for her poor little limbs were too weak to support her. They were not a moment too soon, for Mrs. King stood in the kitchen door a second later.

"Here! you ain't goin', air you?" she called out.

"No, marm; I jest stepped out to look arter my hoss; he was a trifle uneasy with the flies, an' thar was a yaller wasp buzzin' round." And the peddler stepped up to the door with an open and artless visage.

"Well, I didn't know but you'd git tired waitin'. You spoke so about not bein' in a hurry that I stopped to pick my white rags out from the colored ones. I knew they'd bring more ef I did. I'd been meanin' to hev 'em all sorted out afore a peddler come along. I thought I'd hev Sally pick 'em over last week, but she was sick—Why, whar is Sally?"

41

"Who?"

"Sally—the girl that was washin' dishes when you come—she went to the door."

"Oh, the gal! I b'lieve I saw her go out the door a minute afore I went out to see to my hoss."

"Well, I'll call her, for she'll never git the dishes done, I guess, an' then we'll see about the rags."

Mrs. King strode towards the door, but the peddler stopped her.

"Now, marm, ef you please," said he, "I'd a leetle rayther you'd attend to business first, and call Sally arterwards, ef it's jest the same to you, for I am gittin' in a leetle of a hurry, and don't feel as ef I could afford to wait much longer."

"Well," said Mrs. King, reluctantly. "I don't suppose I orter ask you to, but I do hev such discouragin' times with help. I declare it don't seem to me as ef Sally ever would git them dishes done."

"Wa'al, it don't seem to me, from what I've seen, that she ever will, either," said the peddler, as he gathered up Mrs. King's ragbags and started for the cart.

"Anybody wouldn't need to watch her for more'n two minutes to see how slow she was," assented Mrs. King, following. "She's a girl I took when she was a baby to bring up, an' I've wished more'n fifty times I hadn't. She's a good girl enough, but she's awful slow—no snap to her. How much is them milk pans?"

Mrs. King was reputedly a sharp woman at a bargain. To trade with her was ordinarily a long job for any peddler, but to-day it was shortened through skillful management. The tinman came down with astonishing alacrity from his first price, at the merest suggestion from his customer, and, in a much shorter time than usual, she bustled into the house, her arms full of pans, and the radiant and triumphant conviction of a good bargain in her face.

The peddler whirled rapidly into his seat, and snatched up the lines; but even then he heard Mrs. King calling the girl as he rattled around the corner.

A quarter of a mile from Mrs. King's there was a house; a little beyond, the road ran through a considerable stretch of woods. This was a very thinly settled neighborhood. The peddler drove rapidly until he reached the woods; then he stopped, got down, and peered into the cart.

Sally's white face and round eyes peered piteously back at him.

"How're you gittin' along, little un?"

"Oh, let me git out an' go back!"

"Lor', no, little un, you don't want to go back now! Bless your heart, she's all primed for an awful sassin'. I tell you what 'tis, you sha'n't ride cooped up in thar any longer; you shall git out an' set up here with me. We'll keep our ears pricked up, an' ef we hear anybody comin', I'll stow you in the box under the seat afore you kin say Jack Robinson, an' thar ain't any houses for three mile."

He helped the poor shivering little thing out,

and lifted her up to the high seat. When he had seated himself beside her, and gathered up the lines, he looked down at her curiously. Her bonnet the severe taste of Mrs. King had regulated. It was a brown straw, trimmed with brown ribbon. He eyed it disapprovingly. "I'll git you a white bunnit, sich as brides wear, in Derby," said he.

She blushed a little at that, and glanced up at him, a little grateful light over her face.

"You poor little thing!" said the peddler, and put out his hand towards her, then drew it back again.

Derby was a town with the prestige of a city. It was the center of trade for a large circle of little country towns; its main street was crowded on a fair day, when the roads were good, with any quantity of nondescript and antediluvian-looking vehicles, and the owners thereof presented a wide variety of quaintness in person and attire.

So this eloping pair, the tall, bony, shambling man, and the thin, cowed-looking girl, her scant skirts slipping too far below her waistline in the back, and following the movements of her awkward heels, excited no particular attention.

After the tin-cart had been put up in the hotel stable, and the two had been legally pronounced man and wife, or, specifically, Mr. and Mrs. Jake Russell, they proceeded on foot down the principal street, in which all the shops were congregated, in search of some amendments to the bride's attire.

If it was comparatively unnoticed, Sally was

fully alive to the unsuitableness of her costume. She turned around, and followed with wistful eyes the prettily dressed girls they met. There was a great regret in her heart over her best gown, a brown delaine, with a flounce on the bottom, and a shiny back. She had so confidently believed in its grandeur so long, that now, seen by her mental vision, it hardly paled before these splendors of pleating and draping. It compared, advantageously, in her mind, with a brown velvet suit whose wearer looked with amusement in her eyes at Sally's forlorn figure. If she only had on her brown delaine, she felt that she could walk more confidently through this strangeness. But, nervously snatching her bonnet and her money, she had, in fact, heard Mrs. King's tread on the attic stairs, and had not dared to stop longer to secure it.

She knew they were out on a search for a new dress for her now, but she felt a sorrowful conviction that nothing could be found which could fully make up for the loss of her own beloved best gown. And then Sally was not very quick with her needle; she thought with dismay of the making up; the possibility of being aided by a dressmaker, or a ready-made costume, never entered her simple mind.

Jake shambled loosely down the street, and she followed meekly after him, a pace or two behind.

At length the peddler stopped before a large establishment, in whose windows some ready-made ladies' garments were displayed.

"Here we air," said he, triumphantly.

Sally stepped weakly after him up the broad steps.

One particular dress in the window had excited the peddler's warm admiration. It was a trifle florid in design, with dashes of red here and there.

Sally eyed it a little doubtfully, when the clerk, at Jake's request, had taken it down to show them. Untutored as her taste was, she turned as naturally to quiet plumage as a wood-pigeon. The red slashes rather alarmed her. However, she said nothing against her husband's decision to purchase the dress. She turned pale at the price; it was nearly the whole of her precious store. But she took up her stocking-purse determinedly when Jake began examining his pocket-book.

"I pays for this," said she to the clerk, lifting up her little face to him with scared resolve.

"Why, no you don't, little un!" cried Jake, catching hold of her arm. "I'm a-goin' to pay for it, o' course. It's a pity ef I can't buy my own wife a dress."

Sally flushed all over her lean throat, but she resolutely held out the money.

"No," she said again, shaking her head obstinately, "*I* pays for it."

The peddler let her have her way then, though he bit his scraggy mustache with amaze and vexation as he watched her pay the bill, and stare with a sort of frightened wistfulness after her beloved money as it disappeared in the clerk's grasp.

When they emerged from the store, the new

dress under his arm, he burst out, "What on airth made you do that, little un?"

"Other folks does that way. When they gits merried they buys their own close, ef they kin."

"But it took pretty nearly all you'd got, didn't it?"

"That ain't no matter."

The peddler stared at her, half in consternation, half in admiration.

"Well," said he, "I guess you've got a little will o' your own, arter all, little un, an' I'm glad on't. A woman'd orter hev a little will to back her sweetness; it's all too soft an' slushy otherways. But I'll git even with you about the dress."

Which he proceeded to do by ushering his startled bride into the next dry-goods establishment, and purchasing a dress pattern of robin's-egg-blue silk, and a delicate white bonnet. Sally, however, insisted on buying a plain sun-hat with the remainder of her own money. She was keenly alive to the absurdity and peril of that airy white structure on the top of a tin-cart.

The pair remained in Derby about a week; then they started forth on their travels, the blue silk, which a Derby dressmaker had made up after the prevailing mode, and the white bonnet, stowed away in a little new trunk in the body of the cart.

The peddler, having only himself to consult as to his motions, struck a new route now. Sally wished to keep away from her late mistress's vicinity. She had always a nervous dread of meeting her in some unlikely fashion.

47

She wrote a curious little ill-spelled note to her, at the first town where they stopped after leaving Derby. Whether or not Mrs. King was consoled and mollified by it she never knew.

Their way still lay through a thinly settled country. The tin-peddler found readier customers in those farmers' wives who were far from stores. It was late spring. Often they rode for a mile or two through the lovely fresh woods, without coming to a single house.

The girl had never heard of Arcadia, but, all unexpressed to herself, she was riding through it under gold-green boughs, to the sweet, broken jangling of tin-ware.

When they stopped to trade at the farmhouses, how proudly she sat, a new erectness in her slender back, and held her husband's horse tightly while he talked with the woman of the house, with now and then a careful glance towards her to see if she were safe. They always contrived to bring up, on a Sabbath-day, at some town where there was a place of worship. Then the blue silk and the white bonnet were taken reverently from their hiding-place, and Sally, full of happy consciousness, went to church with her husband in all her bridal bravery.

These two simple pilgrims, with all the beauty and grace in either of them turned only towards each other, and seen rightly only in each other's untutored, uncritical eyes, had journeyed together blissfully for about three months, when one afternoon Jake came out of a little country tavern, where they had proposed stopping for the night, with a pale face. Sally had been waiting on the cart outside until he should see if they could be accommodated. He jumped up beside her and took the lines.

"We'll go on to Ware," he said, in a dry voice; "it's only three mile further. They're full here."

Jake drove rapidly along, an awful look on his homely face, giving it the beauty of tragedy.

Sally kept looking up at him with pathetic wonder, but he never looked at her or spoke till they reached the last stretch of woods before Ware village. Then, just before they left the leafy cover, he slackened his speed a little, and threw his arms around her.

"See here, little un," he said, brokenly. "You've —got—consider'ble backbone, 'ain't you? Ef anything awful should happen, it wouldn't—kill you —you'd bear up?"

"Ef you told me to."

He caught at her words eagerly. "I would tell you to, little un—I do tell you to," he cried. "Ef anything awful ever should—happen—you'll remember that I told you to bear up."

"Yes, I'll bear up." Then she clung to him, trembling. "Oh, what is it, Jake?"

"Never mind now, little un," he answered; "p'rhaps nothin' awful's goin' to happen; I didn't say thar was. Chirk up an' give us a kiss, an' look at that 'ere sky thar, all pink an' yaller."

He tried to be cheerful, and comfort her with joking endearments then, but the awful lines in

49

his face stayed rigid and unchanged under the smiles.

Sally, however, had not much discernment, and little of the sensitiveness of temperament which takes impressions of coming evil. She soon recovered her spirits, and was unusually merry, for her, the whole evening, making, out of the excess of her innocence and happiness, several little jokes, which made Jake laugh loyally, and set his stricken face harder the next minute.

In the course of the evening he took out his pocket-book and displayed his money, and counted it jokingly. Then he spoke, in a careless, casual manner, of a certain sum he had deposited in a country bank, and now, if he were taken sick and needed it, Sally could draw it out as well as he. Then he spoke of the value of his stock in trade and horse and cart. When they went to bed that night he had told his wife, without her suspecting he was telling her, all about his affairs.

She fell asleep as easily as a child. Jake lay rigid and motionless till he had listened an hour to her regular breathing. Then he rose softly, lighted a candle, which he shaded from her face, and sat down at a little table with a pen and paper. He wrote painfully, with cramped muscles, his head bent on one side, following every movement of his pen, yet with a confident steadiness which seemed to show that all the subject-matter had been learned by heart beforehand. Then he folded the paper carefully around a little book which he took from his pocket, and approached the bed, keeping his face turned away from his sleeping wife. He laid the little package on his vacant pillow, still keeping his face aside.

Then he got into his clothes quickly, his head turned persistently from the bed, and opened the door softly, and went out, never once looking back.

When Sally awoke the next morning she found her husband gone, and the little package on the pillow. She opened it, more curious than frightened. There was a note folded around a bankbook. Sally spelled out the note laboriously, with whitening lips and dilating eyes. It was a singular composition, its deep feeling pricking through its illiterate stiffness.

Dear Wife,—I've got to go and leve you. It's the only way. Ef I kin ever come back, I will. I told you bout my bizness last night. You'd better drive the cart to Derby to that Mister Arms I told you bout, an' he'll help you sell it an' the hoss. Tell him your husband had to go away, an' left them orders. I've left you my bank-book, so you can git the money out of the bank the way I told you, an' my watch an' pocket-book is under the pillow. I left you all the money, cept what little I couldn't git long without. You'd better git boarded somewhar in Derby. You'll hev enough money to keep you awhile, an' I'll send you some more when thet's gone, ef I hev to work my fingers to the bone. Don't ye go to worryin' an' wor-

51

kin' hard. An' bear up. Don't forgit that you promised me to bear up. When you gits to feelin' awful bad, an' you will, jest say it over to yourself—"He told me to bear up, an' I said as I would bear up." Scuse poor writin' an' a bad pen.

Yours till death,
JAKE RUSSEL

When Sally had read the letter quite through, she sat still a few minutes on the edge of the bed, her lean, round-shouldered figure showing painfully through her clinging night-dress, her eyes staring straight before her.

Then she rose, dressed herself, put the bankbook, with the letter folded around it, and her husband's pocket-book, in her bosom, and went down-stairs quietly. Just before she went out her room door she paused with her hand on the latch, and muttered to herself, "He told me to bear up, an' I said as I would bear up."

She sought the landlord to pay her bill, and found that it was already paid, and that her recreant husband had smoothed over matters in one direction for her by telling the landlord that he was called away on urgent business, and that his wife was to take the tin-cart next morning, and meet him at a certain point.

So she drove away on her tin-cart in solitary state without exciting any of the wondering comments which would have been agony to her.

When she gathered up the lines and went rattling down the country road, if ever there was a zealous disciple of a new religion, she was one. Her prophet was her raw-boned peddler husband, and her creed and whole confession of faith his parting words to her.

She did not take the road to Derby; she had made up her mind about that as she sat on the edge of the bed after reading the letter. She drove straight along the originally prescribed route, stopping at the farmhouses, taking rags and selling tin, just as she had seen her husband do. There were much astonishment and many curious questions among her customers. A woman running a tin-cart was an unprecedented spectacle, but she explained matters, with meek dignity, to all who questioned her. Her husband had gone away, and she was to attend to his customers until he should return. She could not always quite allay the suspicion that there must needs be something wrong, but she managed the trading satisfactorily, and gave good bargains, and so went on her way unmolested. But not a farmyard did she enter or leave without the words sounding in her beating little heart, like a strong, encouraging chant, "He told me to bear up, an' I said as I would bear up."

When her stock ran low, she drove to Derby to replenish it. Here she had opposition from the dealers, but her almost abnormal persistence overcame it.

She showed Jake's letter to Mr. Arms, the tin-dealer with whom she traded, and he urged her to take up with the advice in it, promising her a good bargain; but she was resolute.

Soon she found that she was doing as well as her husband had done, if not better. Her customers, after they had grown used to the novelty of a tinwoman, instead of a tinman, liked her. In addition to the regular stock, she carried various little notions needed frequently by housewives, such as pins, needles, thread, etc.

She oftener stayed at a farmhouse overnight than a tavern, and frequently stopped over at one a few days in severe weather.

After her trip to Derby she always carried a little pistol, probably more to guard Jake's watch and property than herself.

Whatever money she did not absolutely require for current expenses went to swell Jake's little hoard in the Derby bank. During the three years she kept up her lonely travelling little remittances came directed to her from time to time, in the care of Mr. Arms. When one came, Sally cried pitifully, and put it into the bank with the rest.

She never gave up expecting her husband. She never woke up one morning without the hope in her heart that he would come that day. Every golden dawn showed a fair possibility to her, and so did every red sunset. She scanned every distant, approaching figure in the sweet country road with the half conviction in her heart that it was he, and when nearness dispelled the illusion, her heart bounded bravely back from its momentary sinking, and she looked ahead for another traveller.

Still he did not come for three years from the spring he went away. Except through the money remittances, which gave no clue but the New York postmark on the envelope, she had not heard from him.

One June afternoon she, a poor lonely pilgrim, now without her beloved swain, driving through her old Arcadian solitudes, whose enchanted meaning was lost to her, heard a voice from behind calling to her, above the jangling of tin, "Sally! Sally! Sally!"

She turned, and there he was, running after her. She turned her head quickly, and, stopping the horse, sat perfectly still, her breath almost gone with suspense. She did not dare look again for fear she had not seen aright.

The hurrying steps came nearer and nearer; she looked when they came abreast the cart. It was he. It always seemed to her that she would have died if it had not been, that time.

"Jake! Jake!"

"Oh, Sally!"

He was up on the seat before she could breathe again, and his arms around her.

"Jake, I did—bear up—I did."

"I know you did, little un. Mr. Arms told me all about it. Oh, you dear little un, you poor little un, a-drivin' round on this cart all alone!"

Jake laid his cheek against Sally's and sobbed.

"Don't cry, Jake. I've airned money, I hev, an' it's in the bank for you."

"Oh, you blessed little un! Sally, they said hard things 'bout me to you in Derby, didn't they?"

She started violently at that. There was one thing which had been said to her in Derby, and the memory of it had been a repressed terror ever since.

"Yes: they said as how you'd run off with—another woman."

"What did you say?"

"I didn't believe it."

"I did, Sally."

"Well, you've come back."

"Afore I married you I'd been married afore. By all that's good an' great, little un, I thought my wife was dead. Her folks said she was. When I come home from peddlin' one time, she was gone, an' they said she was off on a visit. I found out in a few weeks she'd run off with another fellow. I went off peddlin' agin without carin' much what become of me. 'Bout a year arterwards I saw her death in a paper, an' I wrote to her folks, an' they said 'twas true. They were a bad lot, the whole of 'em. I got took in. But she had a mighty pretty face, an' a tongue like honey, an' I s'pose I was green. Three year ago, when I went into that 'ere tavern in Grover, thar she was in the kitchin a-cookin'. The fellow she run off with had left her, an' she'd been trying to hunt me up. She was awful poor, an' had come across this place an' took it. She was allers a good cook, an' she suited the customers fust-rate. I guess they liked to see her pretty face 'round too, confound her!

"Well, little un, she knew me right off, an' hung on to me, an' cried, an' begged me to forgive her; and when she spied you a-settin' thar on the cart, she tore. I had to hold her to keep her from goin' out an' tellin' you the whole story. I thought you'd die ef she did. I didn't know then how you could bear up, little un. *Ef* you 'ain't got backbone!''

"Jake, I did bear up."

"I know you did, you blessed little cretur. Well, she said ef I didn't leave you, an' go with her, she'd expose me. As soon as she found she'd got the weapons in her own hands, an' could hev me up for bigamy, she didn't cry so much, an' wa'n't quite so humble.

"Well, little un, then I run off an' left you. I couldn't stay with you ef you wa'n't my wife, an' 'twas all the way to stop her tongue. I met her that night, an' we went to New York. I got lodgin's for her; then I went to work in a box factory, an' supported her. I never went nigh her from one week's end to the other; I couldn't do it without hevin' murder in my heart; but I kep' her in money. Every scrap I could save I sent to you, but I used to lay awake nights, worryin' for fear you'd want things. Well, it's all over. She died a month ago, an' I saw her buried."

"I knowed she was dead when you begun to tell about her, because you'd come."

"Yes, she's dead this time, an' I'm glad. Don't you look scared, little un. I hope that Lord'll forgive me, but *I'm glad*. She was a bad un, you know, Sally."

57

"Was she sorry?"

"I don' know, little un."

Sally's head was resting peacefully on Jake's shoulder; golden flecks of light sifted down on them through the rustling maple and locust boughs; the horse, with bent head, was cropping the tender young grass at the side of the road.

"Now we'll start up the horse, an' go to Derby an' git merried over agin, Sally."

She raised her head suddenly, and looked up at him with eager eyes.

"Jake."

"Well, little un?"

"Oh, Jake, my blue silk dress an' the white bonnet is in the trunk in the cart jest the same, an' I can git 'em out, an' put 'em on under the trees thar, an' wear 'em to be married in!"

Salomy Jane's Kiss

Bret Harte

Only one shot had been fired. It had gone wide of its mark—the ringleader of the vigilantes—and had left Red Pete, who had fired it, covered by their rifles and at their mercy. For his hand had been cramped by hard riding and his eye distracted by their sudden onset, and so the inevitable end had come. He submitted sullenly to his captors; his companion fugitive and horse thief gave up the protracted struggle with a feeling not unlike relief. Even the hot and revengeful victors were content. They had taken their men alive. At any time during the long chase they could have brought them down by a rifle shot, but it would have been unsportsmanlike and have ended in a free fight instead of an example. Besides, their doom was already sealed. Their end, by a rope and a tree, although not sanctified by law, would have at least the deliberation of justice. It was the tribute paid by the vigilantes to that order which they had themselves disregarded in the pursuit and capture. Yet this strange logic of the frontier sufficed them and gave a certain dignity to the climax.

"Ef you've got anythin' to say to your folks, say it *now* and say it quick," said the ringleader.

Red Pete glanced around him. He had been run to earth at his own cabin in the clearing, whence a few relations and friends, mostly women and children, noncombatants, had outflowed, gazing vacantly at the twenty vigilantes who surrounded them. All were accustomed to scenes of violence, blood feud, chase and hardship; it was only the suddenness of the onset and its quick result that had surprised them. They looked on with dazed curiosity and some disappointment; there had been no fight to speak of—no spectacle! A boy, nephew of Red Pete, got upon the rain barrel to view the proceedings more comfortably; a tall handsome lazy Kentucky girl, a visiting neighbor, leaned against the doorpost, chewing gum. Only a yellow hound was actively perplexed. He could not make out if a hunt was just over or beginning, and ran eagerly backward and forward, leaping alternately upon the captives and the captors.

The ringleader repeated his challenge. Red Pete gave a reckless laugh and looked at his wife.

At which Mrs. Red Pete came forward. It seemed that she had much to say incoherently, furiously, vindictively to the ringleader. His soul would roast in hell for that day's work! He called himself a man, skunkin' in the open and afraid to show himself except with a crowd of other "Ki-yi's" around a house of women and children. Heaping insult upon insult, inveighing against his low blood, his ancestors, his dubious origin she at last flung out a wild taunt of his invalid wife, the insult of a woman to a woman, until his white face grew rigid and only that western American fetish of the sanctity of sex kept his twitching fingers from the lock of his rifle. Even her husband noticed it and with a half-authoritative "Let up on that, old gal," and a pat of his freed left hand on her back, took his last parting. The ringleader, still white under the lash of the woman's tongue, turned abruptly to the second captive. "And if *you've* got anybody to say good-by to, now's your chance."

The man looked up. Nobody stirred or spoke. He was a stranger there, being a chance confederate picked up by Red Pete and known to no one. Still young, but an outlaw from his abandoned boyhood of which father and mother were only a forgotten dream, he loved horses and stole them, fully accepting the frontier penalty of life for the interference with that animal on which a man's life so often depended. But he understood the good points of a horse as was shown by the one he bestrode, until a few days before the property of Judge Boompointer. This was his sole distinction.

The unexpected question stirred him for a moment out of the attitude of reckless indifference, for attitude it was, and a part of his profession. But it may have touched him that at that moment he was less than his companion and his virago wife. However he only shook his head. As he did so his eye casually fell on the handsome girl by the doorpost, who was looking at him. The ringleader too may have been touched by his complete loneliness, for *he* hesitated. At the same moment he saw that the girl was looking at his friendless captive.

A grotesque idea struck him.

"Salomy Jane, ye might do worse than come yer and say good-by to a dyin' man, and him a stranger," he said.

There seemed to be a subtle stroke of poetry and irony in this that equally struck the apathetic crowd. It was well known that Salomy Jane Clay thought no small potatoes of herself and always held off the local swains with a lazy nymphlike scorn. Nevertheless she slowly disengaged herself from the doorpost, and to everybody's astonishment lounged with languid grace and outstretched hand toward the prisoner. The color came into the gray reckless mask which the doomed man wore as her right hand grasped his left, just loosed by his captors. Then she paused; her shy fawnlike eyes grew bold and fixed themselves upon him. She took the chewing gum from her mouth, wiped her red lips with the back of her hand, by a sudden lithe spring placed her foot on his stirrup, and bounding to the saddle, threw her arms about his neck and pressed a kiss upon his lips.

They remained thus for a hushed moment— the man on the threshold of death, the young woman in the fullness of youth and beauty— linked together. Then the crowd laughed; in the audacious effrontery of the girl's act the ultimate fate of the two men was forgotten. She slipped languidly to the ground; *she* was the focus of all eyes, she only! The ringleader saw it and his opportunity. He shouted: "Time's up! Forward!" —and urged his horse beside his captives. The next moment the whole cavalcade was sweeping over the clearing into the darkening woods.

Their destination was Sawyer's Crossing, the headquarters of the committee, where the council was still sitting and where both culprits were to expiate the offense of which that council had already found them guilty. They rode in great and breathless haste, a haste in which, strangely enough, even the captives seemed to join. That haste possibly prevented them from noticing the singular change which had taken place in the second captive since the episode of the kiss. His high color remained as if it had burned through his mask of indifference; his eyes were quick, alert and keen, his mouth half open as if the girl's kiss still lingered there. And that haste had made them careless, for the horse of the man who led him slipped in a gopher hole, rolled over, unseated his rider, and even dragged the bound and helpless second captive from Judge Boompointer's favorite mare. In an instant they were all on their feet again, but in that supreme moment the second captive felt the cords which bound his arms had slipped to his wrists. By keeping his elbows to his sides and obliging the others to help him mount it escaped their notice. By riding close to his captors and keeping in the crush of the throng he further concealed the accident, slowly working his hands downward out of his bonds.

Their way lay through a sylvan wilderness, mid-leg deep in ferns, whose tall fronds brushed their horses' sides in their furious gallop and concealed the flapping of the captive's loosened cords. The peaceful vista, more suggestive of the offerings of nymph and shepherd than of human sacrifice, was in a strange contrast to this whirlwind rush of stern armed men. The westering sun pierced the subdued light and the tremor of leaves with yellow lances; birds started into song on blue and dove-like wings, and on either side of the trail of this vengeful storm could be heard the murmur of hidden and tranquil waters. In a few moments they would be on the open ridge whence sloped the common turnpike to Sawyer's, a mile away. It was the custom of returning cavalcades to take this hill at headlong speed with shouts and cries that heralded their coming. They withheld the latter that day as inconsistent with their dignity; but emerging from the wood, swept silently like an avalanche down the slope. They were well under way, looking only to their horses, when the second captive slipped his right arm from the bonds and succeeded in grasping the reins that lay trailing on the horse's neck. A sudden vaquero jerk which the well-trained animal understood threw him on his haunches with his forelegs firmly planted on the slope. The rest of the cavalcade swept on; the man who was leading the captive's horse by the riata, thinking only of another accident, dropped the line to save himself from being dragged backward from his horse. The captive wheeled and the next moment was galloping furiously up the slope.

It was the work of a moment, a trained horse and an experienced hand. The cavalcade had covered nearly fifty yards before they could pull up; the freed captive had covered half that distance uphill. The road was so narrow that only two shots could be fired, and these broke dust two yards ahead of the fugitive. They had not dared to fire low; the horse was the more valuable animal. The fugitive knew this in his extremity also, and would have gladly taken a shot in his own leg to spare that of his horse. Five men were detached to recapture or kill him. The latter seemed inevitable. But he had calculated his chances; before they could reload he had reached the woods again; winding in and out between the pillared tree trunks, he offered no mark. They knew his horse was superior to their own; at the end of two hours they returned, for he had disappeared without track or trail. The end was briefly told in the *Sierra Record:*

Red Pete, the notorious horse thief who had so long eluded justice, was captured and hung by the Sawyer's Crossing Vigilantes last week; his confederate unfortunately escaped on a valuable horse belonging to Judge Boompointer. The judge had refused one thousand dollars for the horse only a week before. As the thief who

65

is still at large would find it difficult to dispose of so valuable an animal without detection the chances are against either of them turning up again.

Salomy Jane watched the cavalcade until it had disappeared. Then she became aware that her brief popularity had passed. Mrs. Red Pete in stormy hysterics had included her in a sweeping denunciation of the whole universe, possibly for simulating an emotion in which she herself was deficient. The other women hated her for her momentary exaltation above them; only the children still admired her as one who had undoubtedly "canoodled" with a man "a-goin' to be hung"— a daring flight beyond their wildest ambition. Salomy Jane accepted the charge with charming unconcern. She put on her yellow nankeen sunbonnet—a hideous affair that would have ruined any other woman but which only enhanced the piquancy of her fresh brunette skin—tied the strings letting her blue-black braids escape below its frilled curtain behind, jumped on her mustang with a casual display of agile ankles in shapely white stockings, whistled to the hound, and waving her hand with a "So long, sonny!" to the lately bereft but admiring nephew, flapped and fluttered away in her short brown holland gown.

Her father's house was four miles distant. Contrasted with the cabin she had just left it was a superior dwelling with a long lean-to at the rear, which brought the eaves almost to the ground and made it look like a low triangle. It had a long barn and cattlesheds, for Madison Clay was a great stock raiser and the owner of a quarter section. It had a sitting room and a parlor organ whose transportation thither had been a marvel of packing. These things were supposed to give Salomy Jane an undue importance, but the girl's reserve and inaccessibility to local advances were rather the result of a cool lazy temperament and the preoccupation of a large protecting admiration for her father, for some years a widower. For Mr. Madison Clay's life had been threatened in one or two feuds, not without cause, it was said, and it is possible that the pathetic spectacle of her father doing his visiting with a shotgun may have touched her closely and somewhat prejudiced her against the neighboring masculinity. The thought that cattle, horses and quarter section would one day be hers did not disturb her calm. As for Mr. Clay, he accepted her as housewifely though somewhat interfering, and being one of his own womankind, not without some degree of merit.

"Wot's this yer I'm hearin' of your doin's over at Red Pete's? Honeyfoglin' with a horse thief, eh?" said Mr. Clay two days later at breakfast.

"I reckon you heard about the straight thing, then," said Salomy Jane unconcernedly, without looking around.

"What do you calkilate Rube will say to it? What are you goin' to tell *him?*" said Mr. Clay sarcastically.

Rube, or Reuben Waters was a swain supposed

to be favored particularly by Mr. Clay. Salomy Jane looked up.

"I'll tell him that when *he's* on his way to be hung, I'll kiss him—not till then," said the young lady brightly.

This delightful witticism suited the paternal humor, and Mr. Clay smiled; nevertheless he frowned a moment afterward.

"But this yer hoss thief got away arter all, and that's a hoss of a different color," he said grimly.

Salomy Jane put down her knife and fork. This was certainly a new and different phase of the situation. She had never thought of it before, and strangely enough, for the first time she became interested in the man. "Got away?" she repeated. "Did they let him off?"

"Not much," said her father briefly. "Slipped his cords and goin' down the grade pulled up short, just like a vaquero agin a lassoed bull, almost draggin' the man leadin' him off his hoss, and then skyuted up the grade. For that matter, on that hoss o' Judge Boompointer's he mout have dragged the whole posse of 'em down on their knees ef he liked! Sarved 'em right, too. Instead of stringin' him up afore the door or shootin' him on sight they must allow to take him down afore the hull committee 'for an example.' Example be blowed! Ther' 's example enough when some stranger comes unbeknownst slap onter a man hanged to a tree and plugged full of holes. *That's* an example, and *he* knows what it means. Wot more do ye want? But then those vigilantes is allus clingin' and hangin' onter some mere scrap o' the law they're pretendin' to despise. It makes me sick! Why, when Jake Myers shot your ole Aunt Viney's second husband, and I laid in wait for Jake afterwards in the Butternut Hollow, did *I* tie him to his hoss and fetch him down to your Aunt Viney's cabin 'for an example' before I plugged him? No!" in deep disgust. "No! Why, I just meandered through the woods, careless-like, till he comes out, and I just rode up to him, and I said—"

But Salomy Jane had heard her father's story before. Even one's dearest relatives are apt to become tiresome in narration. "I know, dad," she interrupted; "but this yer man—this hoss thief— did *he* get clean away without gettin' hurt at all?"

"He did, and unless he's fool enough to sell the hoss, he kin keep away, too. So ye see ye can't ladle out purp stuff about a dyin' stranger to Rube. He won't swaller it."

"All the same, dad," returned the girl cheerfully, "I reckon to say it, and say more; I'll tell him that ef *he* manages to get away too, I'll marry him—there! But ye don't ketch Rube takin' any such risks in gettin' ketched, or in gettin' away arter!"

Madison Clay smiled grimly, pushed back his chair, rose, dropped a perfunctory kiss on his daughter's hair, and taking his shotgun from the corner, departed on a peaceful Samaritan mission to a cow who had dropped a calf in the far pasture. Inclined as he was to Reuben's wooing from his

69

eligibility as to property, he was conscious that he was sadly deficient in certain qualities inherent in the Clay family. It certainly would be a kind of *mésalliance.*

Left to herself Salomy Jane stared a long while at the coffee pot, and then called the two squaws who assisted her in her household duties to clear away the things while she went up to her own room to make her bed. Here she was confronted with a possible prospect of that proverbial bed she might be making in her willfulness, and on which she must lie, in the photograph of a somewhat serious young man of refined features—Reuben Waters—stuck in her window frame. Salomy Jane smiled over her last witticism regarding him and enjoyed it like your true humorist, and then, catching sight of her own handsome face in the little mirror, smiled again. But wasn't it funny about that horse thief getting off after all? Good Lordy! Fancy Reuben hearing he was alive and going around with that kiss of hers set on his lips! She laughed again, a little more abstractedly. And he had returned it like a man, holding her tight and almost breathless, and he going to be hung the next minute! Salomy Jane had been kissed at other times by force, chance or stratagem. In a certain ingenuous forfeit game of the locality known as "I'm a-pinin'," many had "pined" for a "sweet kiss" from Salomy Jane, which she had yielded in a sense of honor and fair play. She had never been kissed like this before—she would never again—and yet the man was alive! And behold, she could see in the mirror that she was blushing!

She should hardly know him again. A young man with very bright eyes, a flushed and sunburnt cheek, a kind of fixed look in the face and no beard; no, none that she could feel. Yet he was not at all like Reuben, not a bit. She took Reuben's picture from the window and laid it on her workbox. And to think she did not even know this young man's name! That was queer. To be kissed by a man whom she might never know! Of course he knew hers. She wondered if he remembered it and her. But of course he was so glad to get off with his life that he never thought of anything else. Yet she did not give more than four or five minutes to these speculations, but like a sensible girl thought of something else. Once again, however, in opening the closet she found the brown holland gown she had worn on the day before; she thought it very unbecoming and regretted that she had not worn her best gown on her visit to Red Pete's cottage. On such an occasion she really might have been more impressive.

When her father came home that night she asked him the news. No, they had *not* captured the second horse thief, who was still at large. Judge Boompointer talked of invoking the aid of the despised law. It remained, then, to see whether the horse thief was fool enough to try to get rid of the animal. Red Pete's body had been delivered to his widow. Perhaps it would only be neighborly for Salomy Jane to ride over to the funeral. But

Salomy Jane did not take to the suggestion kindly, nor yet did she explain to her father that as the other man was still living, she did not care to undergo a second disciplining at the widow's hands. Nevertheless she contrasted her situation with that of the widow with a new and singular satisfaction. It might have been Red Pete who had escaped. But he had not the grit of the nameless one. She had already settled his heroic quality.

"Ye ain't harkenin' to me, Salomy."

Salomy Jane started.

"Here I'm askin' ye if ye've see that hound Phil Larrabee sneakin' by yer today?"

Salomy Jane had not. But she became interested and self-reproachful, for she knew that Phil Larrabee was one of her father's enemies. "He wouldn't dare to go by here unless he knew you were out," she said quickly.

"That's what gets me," he said, scratching his grizzled head. "I've been kind o' thinkin' o' him all day, and one of them Chinese said he saw him at Sawyer's Crossing. He was a kind of friend o' Pete's wife. That's why I thought yer might find out ef he'd been there." Salomy Jane grew more self-reproachful at her father's self-interest in her neighborliness. "But that ain't all," continued Mr. Clay. "Thar was tracks over the far pasture that warn't mine. I followed 'em, and they went round and round the house two or three times, ez ef they mout hev bin prowlin', and then I lost 'em in the woods again. It's just like that sneakin' hound

72

Larrabee to hev bin lyin' in wait for me and afraid to meet a man fair and square in the open."

"You just lie low, dad, for a day or two more and let me do a little prowlin'," said the girl with sympathetic indignation in her dark eyes. "Ef it's that skunk, I'll spot him soon enough and let you know whar he's hidin'."

"You'll just stay where ye are, Salomy," said her father decisively. "This ain't no woman's work—though I ain't sayin' you haven't got more head for it than some men I know."

Nevertheless, that night after her father had gone to bed, Salomy Jane sat by the open window of the sitting room in an apparent attitude of languid contemplation, but alert and intent of eye and ear. It was a fine moonlit night. Two pines near the door, solitary pickets of the serried ranks of distant forest, cast long shadows like paths to the cottage and sighed their spiced breath in the windows. For there was no frivolity of vine or flower around Salomy Jane's bower. The clearing was too recent, the life too practical for vanities like these. But the moon added a vague elusiveness to everything, softened the rigid outlines of the sheds, gave shadows to the lidless windows, and touched with merciful indirectness the hideous debris of refuse gravel and the gaunt scars of burnt vegetation before the door. Even Salomy Jane was affected by it and exhaled something between a sigh and a yawn with the breath of the pines. Then she suddenly sat upright.

Her quick ear had caught a faint "click, click"

in the direction of the wood; her quicker instinct and rustic training enabled her to determine that it was the ring of a horse's shoe on flinty ground; her knowledge of the locality told her it came from the spot where the trail passed over an outcrop of flint, scarcely a quarter of a mile from where she sat, and within the clearing. It was no errant stock, for the foot was shod with iron; it was a mounted trespasser by night and boded no good to a man like Clay.

She rose, threw her shawl over her head more for disguise than shelter, and passed out of the door. A sudden impulse made her seize her father's shotgun from the corner where it stood—not that she feared any danger to herself but it gave her an excuse. She made directly for the wood, keeping in the shadow of the pines as long as she could. At the fringe she halted; whoever was there must pass her before reaching the house.

Then there seemed to be a suspense of all nature. Everything was deadly still; even the moonbeams appeared no longer tremulous. Soon there was a rustle as of some stealthy animal among the ferns, and then a dismounted man stepped into the moonlight. It was the horse thief—the man she had kissed!

For a wild moment a strange fancy seized her usually sane intellect and stirred her temperate blood. The news they had told her was *not* true; he had been hung and this was his ghost! He looked as white and spiritlike in the moonlight, and was dressed in the same clothes as when she saw him last. He had evidently seen her approaching and moved quickly to meet her. But in his haste he stumbled slightly; she reflected suddenly that ghosts did not stumble, and a feeling of relief came over her. It was no assassin of her father that had been prowling around—only this unhappy fugitive. A momentary color came into her cheek; her coolness and hardihood returned; it was with a tinge of sauciness in her voice that she said:

"I reckoned you were a ghost."

"I mout have been," he said, looking at her fixedly. "But I reckon I'd have come back here all the same."

"It's a little riskier comin' back alive," she said with a levity that died on her lips, for a singular nervousness, half fear and half expectation, was beginning to take the place of her relief of a moment ago. "Then it was *you* who was prowlin' round and makin' tracks in the far pasture?"

"Yes; I came straight here when I got away."

She felt his eyes were burning her but did not dare to raise her own. "Why," she began, hesitated, and ended vaguely. *"How* did you get here?"

"You helped me!"

"I?"

"Yes. That kiss you gave me put life into me, gave me strength to get away. I swore to myself I'd come back and thank you, alive or dead."

Every word he said she could have anticipated, so plain the situation seemed to her now. And every word he said she knew was the truth. Yet her cool common sense struggled against it.

"What's the use of your escapin' ef you're comin' back here to be ketched again?" she said pertly.

He drew a little nearer to her, but seemed to her the more awkward as she resumed her self-possession. His voice, too, was broken as if by exhaustion as he said, catching his breath at intervals:

"I'll tell you. You did more for me than you think. You made another man o' me. I never had a man, woman or child do to me what you did. I never had a friend—only a pal like Red Pete who picked me up on shares. I want to quit this yer —what I'm doin'. I want to begin by doin' the square thing to you." He stopped, breathed hard and then said brokenly, "My hoss is over thar, staked out. I want to give him to you. Judge Boompointer will give you a thousand dollars for him. I ain't lyin'; it's God's truth! I saw it on the handbill agin a tree. Take him and I'll get away afoot. Take him. It's the only thing I can do for you, and I know it don't half pay for what you did. Take it; your father can get the reward for you if you can't."

Such were the ethics of this strange locality that neither the man who made the offer nor the girl to whom it was made was struck by anything that seemed illogical or indelicate, or at all inconsistent with justice or the horse thief's real conversion.

Salomy Jane nevertheless dissented, from another and weaker reason.

"I don't want your hoss, though I reckon dad might; but you're just starvin'. I'll get suthin'." She turned toward the house.

"Say you'll take the hoss first," he said, grasping her hand. At the touch she felt herself coloring and struggled, expecting perhaps another kiss. But he dropped her hand. She turned again with a saucy gesture, said, "Hol' on; I'll come right back," and slipped away, the mere shadow of a coy and flying nymph in the moonlight, until she reached the house.

Here she not only procured food and whiskey but added a long dust coat and hat of her father's to her burden. They would serve as a disguise for him and hide that heroic figure, which she thought everybody must now know as she did. Then she rejoined him breathlessly. But he put the food and whiskey aside.

"Listen," he said. "I've turned the hoss into your corral. You'll find him there in the morning, and no one will know but that he got lost and joined the other horses."

Then she burst out. "But you—*you*—what will become of you? You'll be ketched!"

"I'll manage to get away," he said in a low voice, "ef—ef—"

"Ef what?" she said tremblingly.

"Ef you'll put the heart in me agin, as you did!" he gasped.

She tried to laugh, to move away. She could do

neither. Suddenly he caught her in his arms with a long kiss, which she returned again and again. Then they stood embraced as they had embraced two days before, but no longer the same. For the cool, lazy Salomy Jane had been transformed into another woman—a passionate clinging savage. Perhaps something of her father's blood had surged within her at that supreme moment. The man stood erect and determined.

"Wot's your name?" she whispered quickly. It was a woman's quickest way of defining her feelings.

"Dart."

"Yer first name?"

"Jack."

"Let me go now, Jack. Lie low in the woods till tomorrow sunup. I'll come again."

He released her. Yet she lingered a moment. "Put on those things," she said, with a sudden happy flash of eyes and teeth, "and lie close till I come." And then she sped away home.

But midway up the distance she felt her feet going slower, and something at her heartstrings seemed to be pulling her back. She stopped, turned and glanced to where he had been standing. Had she seen him then she might have returned. But he had disappeared. She gave her first sigh, and then ran quickly again. It must be nearly one o'clock! It was not very long to morning!

She was within a few steps of her own door when the sleeping woods and silent air appeared to suddenly awake with a sharp "crack!"

She stopped, paralyzed. Another "crack!" followed, that echoed over the far corral. She recalled herself instantly and dashed off wildly to the woods again.

As she ran she thought of one thing only. He had been dogged by one of his old pursuers and attacked. But there were two shots and he was unarmed. Suddenly she remembered that she had left her father's gun standing against the tree where they were talking. Thank God! She might again have saved him. She ran to the tree; the gun was gone. She ran hither and thither, dreading at every step to fall upon his lifeless body. A new thought struck her; she ran to the corral. The horse was not there! He must have been able to regain it and escape *after* the shots had been fired. She drew a long breath of relief, but it was caught up in an apprehension of alarm. Her father, awakened from his sleep by the shots, was hurriedly approaching her.

"What's up now, Salomy Jane?" he demanded excitedly.

"Nothin'," said the girl, with an effort. "Nothin', at least, that *I* can find." She was usually truthful because fearless, and a lie stuck in her throat; but she was no longer fearless, thinking of *him*. "I wasn't abed; so I ran out as soon as I heard the shots fired," she answered in return to his curious gaze.

"And you've hid my gun somewhere where it can't be found," he said reproachfully. "Ef it was that sneak Larrabee and he fired them shots to lure me out, he might have potted me without a show a dozen times in the last five minutes."

She had not thought since of her father's enemy! It might indeed have been he who had attacked Jack. But she made a quick point of the suggestion. "Run in, dad, run in and find the gun; you've got no show out here without it." She seized him by the shoulders from behind, shielding him from the woods and hurried him, half expostulating, half struggling, to the house.

But there no gun was to be found. It was strange; it must have been mislaid in some corner! Was he sure he had not left it in the barn? But no matter now. The danger was over; the Larrabee trick had failed. He must go to bed now and in the morning they would make a search together. At the same time she had inwardly resolved to rise before him and make another search of the wood, and perhaps—fearful joy as she recalled her promise!—find Jack alive and well, awaiting her!

Salomy Jane slept little that night, nor did her father. But toward morning he fell into a tired man's slumber until the sun was well up the horizon. Far different was it with his daughter; she lay with her face to the window, her head half lifted to catch every sound, from the creaking of the sun-warped shingles above her head to the far-off moan of the rising wind in the pine trees. Sometimes she fell into a breathless half-ecstatic trance, living over every moment of the stolen interview, feeling the fugitive's arm still around her, hearing his whispered voice in her ears—the birth of her new life! This was followed again by a period of agonizing dread—that he might even then be lying in the woods, his life ebbing away, with her name on his lips and she resting here inactive, until she half started from her bed to go to his succor. And this went on until a pale opal glow came into the sky, followed by a still paler pink on the summit of the white Sierras. Then she rose and hurriedly began to dress. Still so sanguine was her hope of meeting him that she lingered yet a moment to select the brown holland skirt and yellow sunbonnet she had worn when she first saw him. And she had only seen him twice! Only *twice!* It would be cruel, too cruel, not to see him again!

She crept softly down the stairs, listening to the long-drawn breathing of her father in his bedroom, and then by the light of a guttering candle scrawled a note to him, begging him not to trust himself out of the house until she returned from her search. Then leaving the note open on the table she swiftly ran out into the growing day.

Three hours afterward Mr. Madison Clay awoke to the sound of loud knocking. At first this forced itself upon his consciousness as his daughter's regular morning summons, and was responded to by a grunt of recognition and a nestling closer in the blankets. Then he awoke with a start and a muttered oath, remembered the events of last night and his intention to get up early, and rolled out of bed. Becoming aware by this time that the knocking was at the outer door and hearing the shout of a familiar voice he hastily pulled on his boots and his jean trousers, and fastened a single suspender over his shoulder as he clattered downstairs. The outside door was open, and waiting on the threshold was his kinsman, an old ally in many a blood feud—Breckenridge Clay!

"You *are* a cool one, Mad!" said the latter in half-admiring indignation.

"What's up?" said the bewildered Madison.

"*You* ought to be, and scootin' out o' this," said Breckenridge grimly. "It's all very well to know nothin', but here Phil Larrabee's friends hev just picked him up drilled through with slugs and deader nor a crow, and now they're lettin' loose Larrabee's two half-brothers on you. And you must go like a durned fool and leave these yer things behind you in the bresh," he went on querulously, lifting Madison Clay's dust coat, hat and shotgun from his horse, which stood saddled at the door. "Luckily I picked them up in the woods comin' here. Ye ain't got more than time to get over the state line and among your folks thar afore they'll be down on you. Hustle, old man! What are you gawkin' and starin' at?"

Madison Clay had stared amazed and bewildered —horrorstricken. The incidents of the past night for the first time flashed upon him clearly—hopelessly! The shots, his finding Salomy Jane alone in the woods, her confusion and anxiety to rid herself of him, the disappearance of the shotgun, and now this new discovery of the taking of his hat and coat for a disguise! *She* had killed Phil

82

Larrabee in that disguise after provoking his first harmless shot! She, his own child, Salomy Jane, had disgraced herself by a man's crime, had disgraced him by usurping his right and taking a mean advantage, by deceit, of a foe!

"Gimme that gun," he said hoarsely.

Breckenridge handed him the gun in wonder and slowly gathering suspicion. Madison examined nipple and muzzle; one barrel had been discharged. It was true! The gun dropped from his hand.

"Look here, old man," said Breckenridge, with a darkening face, "there's bin no foul play here. Thar's bin no hiring of men, no deputy to do this job. *You* did it fair and square—yourself?"

"Yes, by God!" burst out Madison Clay in a hoarse voice. "Who says I didn't?"

Reassured, yet believing that Madison Clay had nerved himself for the act by an overdraught of whiskey which had affected his memory, Breckenridge said curtly, "Then wake up and lite out ef ye want me to stand by you."

"Go to the corral and pick me out a hoss," said Madison slowly yet not without a certain dignity of manner. "I've suthin' to say to Salomy Jane afore I go." He was holding her scribbled note, which he had just discovered, in his shaking hand.

Struck by his kinsman's manner and knowing the dependent relations of father and daughter, Breckenridge nodded and hurried away. Left to himself, Madison Clay ran his fingers through his hair and straightened out the paper on which Salomy Jane had scrawled her note, turned it over, and wrote on the back:

You might have told me you did it, and not leave your ole father to find it out how you disgraced yourself with him, too, by a low-down, underhanded woman's trick! I've said I done it and took the blame myself, and all the sneakiness of it that folks suspect. If I get away alive, and I don't care much which, you needn't foller. The house and stock are yours; but you ain't any longer the daughter of your disgraced father.

MADISON CLAY

He had scarcely finished the note, when with a clatter of hoofs and a led horse, Breckenridge reappeared at the door, elated and triumphant. "You're in luck, Mad! I found that stole hoss of Judge Boompointer's had got away and strayed among your stock in the corral. Take him and you're safe; he can't be outrun this side of the state line."

"I ain't no hoss thief," said Madison grimly.

"Nobody sez ye are, but you'd be wuss—a fool—ef you didn't take him. I'm testimony that you found him among your hosses; I'll tell Judge Boompointer you've got him, and ye kin send him back when you're safe. The judge will be mighty glad to get him back and call it quits. So ef you've writ to Salomy Jane, come."

Madison Clay no longer hesitated. Salomy Jane

84

might return at any moment—it would be part of her "fool womanishness"—and he was in no mood to see her before a third party. He laid the note on the table, gave a hurried glance around the house which he grimly believed he was leaving forever, and striding to the door, leaped on the stolen horse and swept away with his kinsman.

But that note lay for a week undisturbed on the table in full view of the open door. The house was invaded by leaves, pine cones, birds and squirrels during the hot, silent, empty days, and at night by shy, stealthy creatures, but never again, day or night, by any of the Clay family. It was known in the district that Clay had flown across the state line; his daughter was believed to have joined him the next day; and the house was supposed to be locked up. It lay off the main road and few passed that way. The starving cattle in the corral at last broke bounds and spread over the woods. And one night a stronger blast than usual swept through the house and carried the note from the table to the floor where, whirled into a crack in the flooring, it slowly rotted.

But though the sting of her father's reproach was spared her, Salomy Jane had no need of the letter to know what had happened. For as she entered the woods in the dim light of that morning she saw the figure of Dart gliding from the shadow of a pine toward her. The unaffected cry of joy that rose from her lips died there as she caught sight of his face in the open light.

"You are hurt," she said, clutching his arm passionately.

"No," he said. "But I wouldn't mind that if—"

"You're thinkin' I was afeard to come back last night when I heard the shootin', but I *did* come," she went on feverishly. "I ran back here when I heard the two shots, but you was gone. I went to the corral but your hoss wasn't there, and I thought you'd got away."

"I *did* get away," said Dart gloomily. "I killed the man, thinkin' he was huntin' *me* and forgettin' I was disguised. He thought I was your father."

"Yes," said the girl joyfully, "he was after dad and you—*you* killed him." She again caught his hand admiringly.

But he did not respond. Possibly there were points of honor which this horse thief felt vaguely with her father. "Listen," he said grimly. "Others think it was your father killed him. When *I* did it—for he fired at me first—I ran to the corral agin and took my hoss, thinkin' I might be follered. I made a clear circuit of the house, and when I found he was the only one and no one was follerin', I come back here and took off my disguise. Then I heard his friends find him in the woods and I know they suspected your father. And then another man come through the woods while I was hidin' and found the clothes and took 'em away." He stopped and stared at her gloomily.

But all this was unintelligible to the girl. "Dad would have got the better of him ef you hadn't," she said eagerly, "so what's the difference?"

"All the same," he said, "I must take his place."

She did not understand, but turned her head to her master. "Then you'll go back with me and tell him *all?*" she said obediently.

"Yes," he said.

She put her hand in his and they crept out of the wood together. She foresaw a thousand difficulties, but chiefest of all, that he did not love as she did. *She* would not have taken these risks against their happiness.

But alas for ethics and heroism. As they were issuing from the wood they heard the sound of galloping hoofs and had barely time to hide themselves before Madison Clay, on the stolen horse of Judge Boompointer, swept past them with his kinsman.

Salomy Jane turned to her lover.

And here I might, as a moral romancer, pause, leaving the guilty, passionate girl eloped with her disreputable lover, destined to lifelong shame and misery, misunderstood to the last by a criminal fastidious parent. But I am confronted by certain facts, on which this romance is based. A month later a handbill was posted on one of the sentinel pines announcing that the property would be sold by auction to the highest bidder by Mrs. John Dart, daughter of Madison Clay, Esq., and it was sold accordingly. Still later, by ten years, the chronicler of these pages visited a certain stock or breeding farm in the Blue Grass Country, famous for the popular racers it has produced. He was told that the owner was the "best judge of horse-flesh in the country." "Small wonder," added his informant, "for they say as a young man out in California he was a horse thief, and only saved himself by eloping with some rich farmer's daughter. But he's a straight-out and respectable man now, whose word about horses can't be bought; and as for his wife, *she's* a beauty! To see her at the Springs, rigged out in the latest fashion, you'd never think she had ever lived out of New York or wasn't the wife of a millionaire."

Marjorie Daw

Thomas Bailey Aldrich

I

DR. DILLON TO EDWARD DELANEY, ESQ., AT
THE PINES, NEAR RYE, N. H.

August 8, 187—.

MY DEAR SIR: I am happy to assure you that
your anxiety is without reason. Flemming will
be confined to the sofa for three or four
weeks, and will have to be careful at first how
he uses his leg. A fracture of this kind is always a tedious affair. Fortunately, the bone
was very skilfully set by the surgeon who
chanced to be in the drug-store where Flemming was brought after his fall, and I appre-
hend no permanent inconvenience from the
accident. *Flemming is doing perfectly well physically;* but I must confess that the irritable
and morbid state of mind into which he has
fallen causes me a great deal of uneasiness.
He is the last man in the world who ought to
break his leg. You know how impetuous our
friend is ordinarily, what a soul of restlessness
and energy, never content unless he is rushing at some object, like a sportive bull at a
red shawl; but amiable withal. He is no

longer amiable. His temper has become something frightful. Miss Fanny Flemming came up from Newport, where the family are staying for the summer, to nurse him; but he packed her off the next morning in tears. He has a complete set of Balzac's works, twenty-seven volumes, piled up near his sofa, to throw at Watkins whenever that exemplary serving-man appears with his meals. Yesterday I very innocently brought Flemming a small basket of lemons. You know it was a strip of lemon-peel on the curbstone that caused our friend's mischance. Well, he no sooner set his eyes upon these lemons than he fell into such a rage as I cannot adequately describe. This is only one of his moods, and the least distressing. At other times he sits with bowed head regarding his splintered limb, silent, sullen, despairing. When this fit is on him—and it sometimes lasts all day—nothing can distract his melancholy. He refuses to eat, does not even read the newspapers; books, except as projectiles for Watkins, have no charms for him. His state is truly pitiable.

Now, if he were a poor man, with a family depending on his daily labor, this irritability and despondency would be natural enough. But in a young fellow of twenty-four, with plenty of money and seemingly not a care in the world, the thing is monstrous. If he continues to give way to his vagaries in this manner, he will end by bringing on an inflammation of the fibula. It was the fibula he broke. I am at my wits' end to know what to prescribe for him. I have anæsthetics and lotions, to make people sleep and to soothe pain; but I've no medicine that will make a man have a little common sense. That is beyond my skill, but maybe it is not beyond yours. You are Flemming's intimate friend, his *fidus Achates*. Write to him, write to him frequently, distract his mind, cheer him up, and prevent him from becoming a confirmed case of melancholia. Perhaps he has some important plans disarranged by his present confinement. If he has you will know, and will know how to advise him judiciously. I trust your father finds the change beneficial? I am, my dear sir, with great respect, etc.

II

EDWARD DELANEY TO JOHN FLEMMING, WEST 38TH STREET, NEW YORK.

August 9,—.

MY DEAR JACK: I had a line from Dillon this morning, and was rejoiced to learn that your hurt is not so bad as reported. Like a certain personage, you are not so black and blue as you are painted. Dillon will put you on your pins again in two or three weeks, if you will only have patience and follow his counsels. Did you get my note of last Wednesday? I was greatly troubled when I heard of the accident.

I can imagine how tranquil and saintly you are with your leg in a trough! It is deuced awkward, to be sure, just as we had promised ourselves a glorious month together at the seaside; but we must make the best of it. It is unfortunate, too, that my father's health renders it impossible for me to leave him. I think he has much improved; the sea air is his native element; but he still needs my arm to lean upon in his walks, and requires someone more careful than a servant to look after him. I cannot come to you, dear Jack, but I have hours of unemployed time on hand, and I will write you a whole post-office full of letters if that will divert you. Heaven knows, I haven't anything to write about. It isn't as if we were living at one of the beach houses; then I could do you some character studies, and fill your imagination with groups of sea-goddesses, with their (or somebody else's) raven and blond manes hanging down their shoulders. You should have Aphrodite in morning wrapper, in evening costume, and in her prettiest bathing suit. But we are far from all that here. We have rooms in a farmhouse, on a crossroad, two miles from the hotels, and lead the quietest of lives.

I wish I were a novelist. This old house, with its sanded floors and high wainscots, and its narrow windows looking out upon a cluster of pines that turn themselves into Æolian-harps every time the wind blows, would be the place in which to write a summer romance. It should be a story with the odors of the forest and the breath of the sea in it. It should be a novel like one of that Russian fellow's,—what's his name?—Tourguénieff, Turguenef, Turgenif, Toorguniff, Turgénjew —nobody knows how to spell him. Yet I wonder if even a Liza or an Alexandra Paulovna could stir the heart of a man who has constant twinges in his leg. I wonder if one of our own Yankee girls of the best type, haughty and *spirituelle*, would be of any comfort to you in your present deplorable condition. If I thought so, I would hasten down to the Surf House and catch one for you; or, better still, I would find you one over the way.

Picture to yourself a large white house just across the road, nearly opposite our cottage. It is not a house, but a mansion, built, perhaps, in the colonial period, with rambling extensions, and gambrel roof, and a wide piazza on three sides—a self-possessed, high-bred piece of architecture, with its nose in the air. It stands back from the road, and has an obsequious retinue of fringed elms and oaks and weeping willows. Sometimes in the morning, and oftener in the afternoon, when the sun has withdrawn from that part of the mansion, a young woman appears on the piazza with some mysterious Penelope web of embroidery in her hand, or a book. There is a hammock over there—of pineapple fiber, it looks from here. A hammock is very becoming when one is eighteen, and has golden hair, and dark eyes, and an emerald-colored illusion dress looped up after the fashion of a Dresden china shepherdess, and is *chaussée* like a belle of the time of Louis Quatorze. All this splendor goes into that hammock, and sways there like a pond-lily in the golden afternoon. The window of my bedroom looks down on that piazza—and so do I.

But enough of this nonsense, which ill becomes a sedate young attorney taking his vacation with an invalid father. Drop me a line, dear Jack, and tell me how you really are. State your case. Write me a long, quiet letter. If you are violent or abusive, I'll take the law to you.

III

JOHN FLEMMING TO EDWARD DELANEY

August 11,—.

YOUR letter, dear Ned, was a godsend. Fancy what a fix I am in—I, who never had a day's sickness since I was born. My left leg weighs three tons. It is embalmed in spices and smothered in layers of fine linen, like a mummy. I can't move. I haven't moved for five thousand years. I'm of the time of Pharaoh.

I lie from morning till night on a lounge, staring into the hot street. Everybody is out of town enjoying himself. The brown-stone-front houses across the street resemble a row of particularly ugly coffins set up on end. A green mold is settling on the names of the deceased, carved on the silver door-plates. Sardonic spiders have sewed up the keyholes. All is silence and dust and desolation.—I interrupt this a moment, to take a shy at Watkins with the second volume of César Biroutteau. Missed him! I think I could bring him down with a copy of Sainte-Beuve or the Dictionnaire Universel, if I had it. These small Balzac books somehow don't quite fit my hand; but I shall fetch him yet. I've an idea Watkins is tapping the old gentleman's Château Yquem. Duplicate key of the wine-cellar. Hibernian soirées in the front basement. Young Cheops upstairs, snug in his cerements. Watkins glides into my chamber, with that colorless, hypocritical face of his drawn out long like an accordion; but I know he grins all the way downstairs, and is glad I have broken my leg. Was not my evil star in the very zenith when I ran up to town to attend that dinner at Delmonico's? I didn't come up altogether for that. It was partly to buy Frank Livingstone's roan mare Margot. And now I shall not be able to sit in the saddle these two months. I'll send the mare down to you at The Pines—is that the name of the place?

Old Dillon fancies that I have something on my mind. He drives me wild with lemons. Lemons for a mind diseased! Nonsense. I am only as restless as the devil under this confinement—a thing I'm not used to. Take a man who has never had so much as a head-ache or a toothache in his life, strap one of his legs in a section of water-spout, keep him in a room in the city for weeks, with the hot weather turned on, and then expect him to smile and purr and be happy! It is preposter-ous. I can't be cheerful or calm.

Your letter is the first consoling thing I have had since my disaster, ten days ago. It really cheered me up for half an hour. Send me a screed, Ned, as often as you can, if you love me. Anything will do. Write me more about that little girl in the hammock. That was very pretty, all that about the Dresden china shepherdess and the pond-lily; the im-agery a little mixed, perhaps, but very pretty. I didn't suppose you had so much sentimental furniture in your upper story. It shows how one may be familiar for years with the recep-tion-room of his neighbor, and never suspect what is directly under his mansard. I sup-posed your loft stuffed with dry legal parch-ments, mortgages and affidavits; you take down a package of manuscript, and lo! there are lyrics and sonnets and canzonettas. You really have a graphic descriptive touch, Edward Delaney, and I suspect you of anonymous love-tales in the magazines.

I shall be a bear until I hear from you again. Tell me all about your pretty *inconnue* across the road. What is her name? Who is she? Who's her father? Where's her mother? Who's her lover? You cannot imagine how this will occupy me. The more trifling the better. My imprisonment has weakened me intellectually to such a degree that I find your epistolary gifts quite considerable. I am passing into my second childhood. In a week or two I shall take to India-rubber rings and prongs of coral. A silver cup, with an appropriate inscription, would be a delicate attention on your part. In the meantime, write!

IV

EDWARD DELANEY TO JOHN FLEMMING
August 12,—.

THE sick pasha shall be amused. *Bismillah!* He wills it so. If the storyteller becomes prolix and tedious—the bow-string and the sack, and two Nubians to drop him into the Piscataqua! But, truly, Jack, I have a hard task. There is literally nothing here—except the little girl over the way. She is swinging in the hammock at this moment. It is to me compensation for many of the ills of life to see her now and then put out a small kid boot, which fits like a glove, and set herself going. Who is she, and what is her name? Her name is Daw. Only daughter of Mr. Richard W. Daw, ex-colonel and banker. Mother dead. One brother at Harvard, elder brother killed at the battle of Fair-Oaks, nine years ago. Old, rich family, the Daws. This is the homestead, where father and daughter pass eight months of the twelve; the rest of the year in Baltimore and Washington. The New England winter too many for the old gentleman. The daughter is called Marjorie—Marjorie Daw. Sounds odd at first, doesn't it? But after you say it over to yourself half a dozen times, you like it. There's a pleasing quaintness to it, something prim and violet-like. Must be a nice sort of girl to be called Marjorie Daw.

I had mine host of The Pines in the witness-box last night, and drew the foregoing testimony from him. He has charge of Mr. Daw's vegetable garden, and has known the family these thirty years. Of course I shall make the acquaintance of my neighbors before many days. It will be next to impossible for me not to meet Mr. Daw or Miss Daw in some of my walks. The young lady has a favorite path to the sea beach. I shall intercept her some morning, and touch my hat to her. Then the princess will bend her fair head to me with courteous surprise not unmixed with haughtiness. Will snub me, in fact. All this for thy sake, O Pasha of the Snapt Axletree! . . . How oddly things fall out! Ten minutes ago I was called down to the parlor—you know the kind of parlors in farmhouses on the coast, a sort of amphibious parlor, with seashells on the mantelpiece and spruce branches in the chimneyplace—where I found my father and Mr. Daw doing the antique polite to each other. He had come to pay his respects to his new neighbors. Mr. Daw is a tall, slim gentleman of about fifty-five, with a florid face and snow-white mustache and side-whiskers. Looks like Mr. Dombey, or as Mr. Dombey would have looked if he had served a few years in the British Army. Mr. Daw was a colonel in the late war, commanding the regiment in which his son was a lieutenant. Plucky old boy, backbone of New Hampshire granite. Before taking his leave, the colonel delivered himself of an invitation as if he were issuing a general order. Miss Daw has a few friends coming, at 4 P.M., to play croquet on the lawn (parade-ground) and have tea (cold rations) on the piazza. Will we honor them with our company? (or be sent to the guardhouse.) My father declines on the plea of ill-health. My father's son bows with as much suavity as he knows, and accepts.

In my next I shall have something to tell you. I shall have seen the little beauty face to face. I have a presentiment, Jack, that this Daw is a *rara avis!* Keep up your spirits, my boy, until I write you another letter—and send me along word how's your leg.

V

August 13,—.

THE party, my dear Jack, was as dreary as possible. A lieutenant of the navy, the rector of the Episcopal Church at Stillwater, and a society swell from Nahant. The lieutenant looked as if he had swallowed a couple of his buttons, and found the bullion rather indigestible; the rector was a pensive youth, of the daffydowndilly sort; and the swell from Nahant was a very weak tidal wave indeed. The women were much better, as they always are; the two Miss Kingsburys of Philadelphia, staying at the Sea-shell House, two bright and engaging girls. But Marjorie Daw!

The company broke up soon after tea, and I remained to smoke a cigar with the colonel on the piazza. It was like seeing a picture to see Miss Marjorie hovering around the old soldier, and doing a hundred gracious little things for him. She brought the cigars and lighted the tapers with her own delicate fingers, in the most enchanting fashion. As we sat there, she came and went in the summer twilight, and seemed, with her white dress and pale gold hair, like some lovely phantom that had sprung into existence out of the smoke-wreaths. If she had melted into air,

100

like the statue of Galatea in the play, I should have been more sorry than surprised.

It was easy to perceive that the old colonel worshipped her, and she him. I think the relation between an elderly father and a daughter just blooming into womanhood the most beautiful possible. There is in it a subtle sentiment that cannot exist in the case of mother and daughter, or that of son and mother. But this is getting into deep water.

I sat with the Daws until half past ten, and saw the moon rise on the sea. The ocean, that had stretched motionless and black against the horizon, was changed by magic into a broken field of glittering ice, interspersed with marvelous silvery fjords. In the far distance the Isles of Shoals loomed up like a group of huge bergs drifting down on us. The Polar regions in a June thaw! It was exceedingly fine. What did we talk about? We talked about the weather—and *you!* The weather has been disagreeable for several days past—and so have you. I glided from one topic to the other very naturally. I told my friends of your accident; how it had frustrated all our summer plans, and what our plans were. I played quite a spirited solo on the fibula. Then I described you; or, rather, I didn't. I spoke of your amiability, of your patience under this severe affliction; of your touching gratitude when Dillon brings you little presents of fruit; of your tenderness to your sister Fanny, whom you would not allow to stay in town to nurse you, and how you heroically sent her back to Newport, preferring to remain alone with Mary, the cook, and your man Watkins, to whom, by the way, you were devotedly attached. If you had been there, Jack, you wouldn't have known yourself. I should have excelled as a criminal lawyer, if I had not turned my attention to a different branch of jurisprudence.

Miss Marjorie asked all manner of leading questions concerning you. It did not occur to me then, but it struck me forcibly afterwards, that she evinced a singular interest in the conversation. When I got back to my room, I recalled how eagerly she leaned forward, with her full, snowy throat in strong moonlight, listening to what I said. Positively, I think I made her like you!

Miss Daw is a girl whom you would like immensely, I can tell you that. A beauty without affectation, a high and tender nature —if one can read the soul in the face. And the old colonel is a noble character, too.

I am glad the Daws are such pleasant people. The Pines in an isolated spot, and my resources are few. I fear I should have found life here somewhat monotonous before long, with no other society than that of my excellent sire. It is true, I might have made a target of the defenseless invalid; but I haven't a taste for artillery, *moi*.

VI

August 17,—.

FOR a man who hasn't a taste for artillery, it occurs to me, my friend, you are keeping up a pretty lively fire on my inner works. But go on. Cynicism is a small brass field-piece that eventually bursts and kills the artilleryman.

You may abuse me as much as you like, and I'll not complain; for I don't know what I should do without your letters. They are curing me. I haven't hurled anything at Watkins since last Sunday, partly because I have grown more amiable under your teaching, and partly because Watkins captured my ammunition one night, and carried it off to the library. He is rapidly losing the habit he had acquired of dodging whenever I rub my ear, or make any slight motion with my right arm. He is still suggestive of the wine-cellar, however. You may break, you may shatter Watkins, if you will, but the scent of the Roederer will hang round him still.

Ned, that Miss Daw must be a charming person. I should certainly like her. I like her already. When you spoke in your first letter of seeing a young girl swinging in a hammock under your chamber window, I was somehow strangely drawn to her. I cannot account for it in the least. What you have subsequently written of Miss Daw has strengthened the impression. You seem to be describing a woman I have known in some previous state of existence, or dreamed of in this. Upon my word, if you were to send me her photograph, I believe I should recognize her at a glance. Her manner, that listening attitude, her traits of character, as you indicate them, the light hair and the dark eyes—they are all familiar things to me. Asked a lot of questions, did she? Curious about me? That is strange.

You would laugh in your sleeve, you wretched old cynic, if you knew how I lie awake nights, with my gas turned down to a star, thinking of The Pines and the house across the road. How cool it must be down there! I long for the salt smell in the air. I picture the colonel smoking his cheroot on the piazza. I send you and Miss Daw off on afternoon rambles along the beach. Sometimes I let you stroll with her under the elms in the moonlight, for you are great friends by this time, I take it, and see each other every day. I know your ways and your manners! Then I fall into a truculent mood, and would like to destroy somebody. Have you noticed anything in the shape of a lover hanging around the colonial Lares and Penates? Does that lieutenant of the horse marines or that young Stillwater parson visit the house much? Not that I am pining for news of them, but any gossip of the kind would be in order. I wonder, Ned, you don't fall in love with Miss Daw. I am ripe to do it myself. Speaking of photographs, couldn't you manage to slip one of her *cartes-de-visite* from her album—she must have an album, you know—and send it to me? I will return it before it could be missed. That's a good fellow! Did the mare arrive safe and sound? It will be a capital animal this autumn for Central Park.

O—my leg? I forgot about my leg. It's better.

VII

EDWARD DELANEY TO JOHN FLEMMING
August 20,—.

YOU are correct in your surmises. I am on the most friendly terms with our neighbors. The colonel and my father smoke their afternoon cigar together in our sitting-room or on the piazza opposite, and I pass an hour or two of the day or the evening with the daughter. I am more and more struck by the beauty, modesty, and intelligence of Miss Daw.

You ask me why I do not fall in love with her. I will be frank, Jack: I have thought of that. She is young, rich, accomplished, uniting in herself more attractions, mental and personal, than I can recall in any girl of my acquaintance; but she lacks the something that would be necessary to inspire in me that kind of interest. Possessing this unknown quantity, a woman neither beautiful nor wealthy nor very young could bring me to her feet. But not Miss Daw. If we were ship-

wrecked together on an uninhabited island—
let me suggest a tropical island, for it costs no
more to be picturesque—I would build her a
bamboo hut, I would fetch her breadfruit and
cocoanuts, I would fry yams for her, I would
lure the ingenuous turtle and make her nour-
ishing soups, but I wouldn't make love to her
—not under eighteen months. I would like to
have her for a sister, that I might shield her
and counsel her, and spend half my income
on thread-laces and camel's-hair shawls. (We
are off the island now.) If such were not my
feeling, there would still be an obstacle to my
loving Miss Daw. A greater misfortune could
scarcely befall me than to love her. Flemming, I am about to make a revelation that
will astonish you. I may be all wrong in my
premises and consequently in my conclusions;
but you shall judge.

That night when I returned to my room after the croquet party at the Daws', and was
thinking over the trivial events of the evening. I was suddenly impressed by the air of
eager attention with which Miss Daw had followed my account of your accident. I think I
mentioned this to you. Well, the next morning, as I went to mail my letter, I overtook
Miss Daw on the road to Rye, where the
post-office is, and accompanied her thither
and back, an hour's walk. The conversation
again turned on you, and again I remarked
that inexplicable look of interest which had

106

lighted up her face the previous evening.
Since then, I have seen Miss Daw perhaps ten
times, perhaps oftener, and on each occasion
I found that when I was not speaking of you
or your sister, or some person or place associated with you, I was not holding her attention. She would be absent-minded, her eyes
would wander away from me to the sea, or to
some distant object in the landscape; her fingers would play with the leaves of a book in a
way that convinced me she was not listening.
At these moments if I abruptly changed the
theme—I did it several times as an
experiment—and dropped some remark about
my friend Flemming, then the somber blue
eyes would come back to me instantly.

Now, is not this the oddest thing in the
world? No, not the oddest. The effect which
you tell me was produced on you by my casual mention of an unknown girl swinging in a
hammock is certainly as strange. You can
conjecture how that passage in your letter of
Friday startled me. Is it possible, then, that
two people who have never met, and who are
hundreds of miles apart, can exert a magnetic
influence on each other? I have read of such
psychological phenomena, but never credited
them. I leave the solution of the problem to
you. As for myself, all other things being fa-
vorable, it would be impossible for me to fall
in love with a woman who listens to me only
when I am talking of my friend!

I am not aware that any one is paying marked attention to my fair neighbor. The lieutenant of the navy—he is stationed at Rivermouth—sometimes drops in of an evening, and sometimes the rector from Stillwater; the lieutenant the oftener. He was there last night. I would not be surprised if he had an eye to the heiress; but he is not formidable. Mistress Daw carries a neat little spear of irony, and the honest lieutenant seems to have a particular facility for impaling himself on the point of it. He is not dangerous, I should say; though I have known a woman to satirize a man for years, and marry him after all. Decidedly, the lowly rector is not dangerous; yet, again, who has not seen Cloth of Frieze victorious in the lists where Cloth of Gold went down?

As to the photograph. There is an exquisite ivorytype of Marjorie, in passe-partout, on the drawing-room mantelpiece. It would be missed at once, if taken. I would do anything reasonable for you, Jack; but I've no burning desire to be hauled up before the local justice of the peace, on a charge of petty larceny.

P.S.—Enclosed is a spray of mignonette, which I advise you to treat tenderly. Yes, we talked of you again last night, as usual. It is becoming a little dreary for me.

VIII

August 22,—.

YOUR letter in reply to my last has occupied my thoughts all the morning. I do not know what to think. Do you mean to say that you are seriously half in love with a woman whom you have never seen—with a shadow, a chimera? for what else can Miss Daw be to you? I do not understand it at all. I understand neither you nor her. You are a couple of ethereal beings moving in finer air than I can breathe with my commonplace lungs. Such delicacy of sentiment is something I admire without comprehending. I am bewildered. I am of the earth earthy, and I find myself in the incongruous position of having to do with mere souls, with natures so finely tempered that I run some risk of shattering them in my awkwardness. I am as Caliban among the spirits!

Reflecting on your letter, I am not sure it is wise in me to continue this correspondence. But no, Jack; I do wrong to doubt the good sense that forms the basis of your character. You are deeply interested in Miss Daw; you feel that she is a person whom you may perhaps greatly admire when you know her: at the same time you bear in mind that the chances are ten to five that, when you do come to know her, she will fall far short of your ideal, and you will not care for her in the least. Look at it in this sensible light, and I will hold back nothing from you.

Yesterday afternoon my father and myself rode over to Rivermouth with the Daws. A heavy rain in the morning had cooled the atmosphere and laid the dust. To Rivermouth is a drive of eight miles, along a winding road lined all the way with wild barberry-bushes. I never saw anything more brilliant than these bushes, the green of the foliage and the pink of the coral berries intensified by the rain. The colonel drove, with my father in front, Miss Daw and I on the back seat. I resolved that for the first five miles your name should not pass my lips. I was amused by the artful attempts she made, at the start, to break through my reticence. Then a silence fell upon her; and then she became suddenly gay. That keenness which I enjoyed so much when it was exercised on the lieutenant was not so satisfactory directed against myself. Miss Daw has great sweetness of disposition, but she can be disagreeable. She is like the young lady in the rhyme, with the curl on her forehead,

"When she is good,
She is very, very good,
And when she is bad, she is horrid!"

I kept to my resolution, however; but on the return home I relented, and talked of your mare! Miss Daw is going to try a side-saddle on Margot some morning. The animal is a trifle too light for my weight. By the by, I nearly forgot to say Miss Daw sat for a picture yesterday to a Rivermouth artist. If the negative turns out well, I am to have a copy. So our ends will be accomplished without crime. I wish, though, I could send you the ivorytype in the drawing-room; it is cleverly colored, and would give you an idea of her hair and eyes, which of course the other will not.

No, Jack, the spray of mignonette did not come from me. A man of twenty-eight doesn't enclose flowers in his letters—to another man. But don't attach too much significance to the circumstance. She gives sprays of mignonette to the rector, sprays to the lieutenant. She has even given a rose from her bosom to your slave. It is her jocund nature to scatter flowers, like Spring.

If my letters sometimes read disjointedly, you must understand that I never finish one at a sitting, but write at intervals, when the mood is on me.

The mood is not on me now.

IX

EDWARD DELANEY TO JOHN FLEMMING
August 23,—.

I HAVE just returned from the strangest interview with Marjorie. She has all but confessed to me her interest in you. But with what modesty and dignity! Her words elude my pen as I attempt to put them on paper; and, indeed, it was not so much what she said as her manner; and that I cannot reproduce. Perhaps it was of a piece with the strangeness of this whole business. That she should tacitly acknowledge to a third party the love she feels for a man she has never beheld! But I have lost, through your aid, the faculty of being surprised. I accept things as people do in dreams. Now that I am again in my room, it all appears like an illusion—the black masses of Rembrandtish shadow under the trees, the fireflies whirling in Pyrrhic dances among the shrubbery, the sea over there, Marjorie sitting on the hammock!

It is past midnight, and I am too sleepy to write more.

Thursday Morning.

My father has suddenly taken it into his head to spend a few days at the Shoals. In the meanwhile you will not hear from me. I see Marjorie walking in the garden with the colonel. I wish I could speak to her alone, but shall probably not have an opportunity before we leave.

X

EDWARD DELANEY TO JOHN FLEMMING

August 28,—.

YOU were passing into your second childhood, were you? Your intellect was so reduced that my epistolary gifts seemed quite considerable to you, did they? I rise superior to the sarcasm in your favor of the 11th instant, when I notice that five days' silence on my part is sufficient to throw you into the depths of despondency.

We returned only this morning from Appledore, that enchanted island—at four dollars per day. I find on my desk three letters from you! Evidently there is no lingering doubt in *your* mind as to the pleasure I derive from your correspondence. These letters are undated, but in what I take to be the latest are two passages that require my consideration. You will pardon my candor, dear Flemming, but the conviction forces itself upon me that as your leg grows stronger your head becomes weaker. You ask my advice on a certain point. I will give it. In my opinion you could do nothing more unwise than to address a note to Miss Daw, thanking her for the flower. It would, I am sure, offend her delicacy beyond pardon. She knows you only through me; you are to her an abstraction, a figure in a dream—a dream from which the faintest shock would awaken her. Of course, if you enclose a note to me and insist on its delivery, I shall deliver it; but I advise you not to do so.

You say you are able, with the aid of a cane, to walk about your chamber, and that you purpose to come to The Pines the instant

Dillon thinks you strong enough to stand the journey. Again I advise you not to. Do you not see that, every hour you remain away, Marjorie's glamor deepens, and your influence over her increases? You will ruin everything by precipitancy. Wait until you are entirely recovered; in any case, do not come without giving me warning. I fear the effect of your abrupt advent here—under the circumstances.

Miss Daw was evidently glad to see us back again, and gave me both hands in the frankest way. She stopped at the door a moment, this afternoon, in the carriage; she had been over to Rivermouth for her pictures. Unluckily the photographer had spilt some acid on the plate, and she was obliged to give him another sitting. I have an intuition that something is troubling Marjorie. She had an abstracted air not usual with her. However, it may be only my fancy. . . . I end this, leaving several things unsaid, to accompany my father on one of those long walks which are now his chief medicine—and mine!

XI

EDWARD DELANEY TO JOHN FLEMMING

August 29,—.

I WRITE in great haste to tell you what has taken place here since my letter of last night. I am in the utmost perplexity. Only one thing is plain—*you* must not dream of coming to

The Pines. Marjorie has told her father everything! I saw her for a few minutes, an hour ago, in the garden; and, as near as I could gather from her confused statement, the facts are these: Lieutenant Bradly—that's the naval officer stationed at Rivermouth—has been paying court to Miss Daw for some time past, but not so much to her liking as to that of the colonel, who it seems is an old friend of the young gentleman's father. Yesterday (I knew she was in some trouble when she drove up to our gate) the colonel spoke to Marjorie of Bradly—urged his suit, I infer. Marjorie expressed her dislike for the lieutenant with characteristic frankness, and finally confessed to her father—well, I really do not know what she confessed. It must have been the vaguest of confessions, and must have sufficiently puzzled the colonel. At any rate, it exasperated him. I suppose I am implicated in the matter, and that the colonel feels bitterly toward me. I do not see why: I have carried no messages between you and Miss Daw; I have behaved with the greatest discretion. I can find no flaw anywhere in my proceeding. I do not see that anybody has done anything —except the colonel himself.

It is probable, nevertheless, that the friendly relations between the two houses will be broken off. "A plague o' both your houses," say you. I will keep you informed, as well as I can, of what occurs over the way.

We shall remain here until the second week in September. Stay where you are, or, at all events, do not dream of joining me. . . . Colonel Daw is sitting on the piazza looking rather wicked. I have not seen Marjorie since I parted with her in the garden.

XII

EDWARD DELANEY TO THOMAS DILLION, M. D., MADISON SQUARE, NEW YORK.

August 30,—.

MY DEAR DOCTOR: If you have any influence over Flemming, I beg of you to exert it to prevent his coming to this place at present. There are circumstances, which I will explain to you before long, that make it of the first importance that he should not come into this neighborhood. His appearance here, I speak advisedly, would be disastrous to him. In urging him to remain in New York, or to go to some inland resort, you will be doing him and me a real service. Of course you will not mention my name in this connection. You know me well enough, my dear doctor, to be assured that, in begging your secret co-operation, I have reasons that will meet your entire approval when they are made plain to you. We shall return to town on the 15th of next month, and my first duty will be to present myself at your hospitable door and satisfy your curiosity, if I have excited it. My father, I am glad to state, has so greatly improved that he can no longer be regarded as an invalid. With great esteem, I am, etc., etc.

XIII

EDWARD DELANEY TO JOHN FLEMMING

August 31,—.

YOUR letter, announcing your mad determination to come here, has just reached me. I beseech you to reflect a moment. The step would be fatal to your interests and hers. You would furnish just cause for irritation to R. W. D.; and, though he loves Marjorie tenderly, he is capable of going to any lengths if opposed. You would not like, I am convinced, to be the means of causing him to treat *her* with severity. That would be the result of your presence at The Pines at this juncture. I am annoyed to be obliged to point out these things to you. We are on very delicate ground, Jack; the situation is critical, and the slightest mistake in a move would cost us the game. If you consider it worth the winning, be patient. Trust a little to my sagacity. Wait and see what happens. Moreover, I understand from Dillon that you are in no condition to take so long a journey. He thinks the air of the coast would be the worst thing possible for you; that you ought to go inland, if anywhere. Be advised by me. Be advised by Dillon.

XIV

September 1,—.

1.—TO EDWARD DELANEY
Letter received. Dillon be hanged. I think I ought to be on the ground.

J. F.

2.—TO JOHN FLEMMING
Stay where you are. You would only complicate matters. Do not move until you hear from me.

E. D.

3.—TO EDWARD DELANEY
My being at The Pines could be kept secret. I must see her.

J. F.

4.—TO JOHN FLEMMING
Do not think of it. It would be useless. R. W. D. has locked M. in her room. You would not be able to effect an interview.

E. D.

5.—TO EDWARD DELANEY
Locked her in her room. Good God. That settles the question. I shall leave by the twelve-fifteen express.

J. F.

XV

THE ARRIVAL

ON THE second of September, 187—, as the down express due at 3.40 left the station at Hampton, a young man, leaning on the shoulder of a servant, whom he addressed as Watkins, stepped from the platform into a hack, and requested to be driven to "The Pines." On arriving at the gate of a modest farmhouse, a few miles from the station, the young man descended with difficulty from the carriage, and, casting a hasty glance across the road, seemed much impressed by some peculiarity in the landscape. Again leaning on the shoulder of the person Watkins, he walked to the door of the farmhouse and inquired for Mr. Edward Delaney. He was informed by the aged man who answered his knock, that Mr. Edward Delaney had gone to Boston the day before, but that Mr. Jonas Delaney was within. This information did not appear satisfactory to the stranger, who inquired if Mr. Edward Delaney had left any message for Mr. John Flemming. There *was* a letter for Mr. Flemming, if he were that person. After a brief absence the aged man reappeared with a letter.

XVI

EDWARD DELANEY TO JOHN FLEMMING

September 1,—.

I AM horror-stricken at what I have done! When I began this correspondence I had no other purpose than to relieve the tedium of your sickchamber. Dillon told me to cheer you up. I tried to. I thought you entered into the spirit of the thing. I had no idea, until within a few days, that you were taking matters *au sérieux*.

What can I say? I am in sackcloth and ashes. I am a pariah, a dog of an outcast. I tried to make a little romance to interest you, something soothing and idyllic, and, by Jove! I have done it only too well! My father doesn't know a word of this, so don't jar the old gentleman any more than you can help. I fly from the wrath to come—when you arrive! For O, dear Jack, there isn't any colonial mansion on the other side of the road, there isn't any piazza, there isn't any hammock—there isn't any Marjorie Daw!

My Platonic Sweetheart

Mark Twain

I met her first when I was seventeen and she fifteen. It was in a dream. No, I did not meet her;
I overtook her. It was in a Missourian village
which I had never been in before, and was not in
at that time, except dreamwise; in the flesh I was
on the Atlantic seaboard ten or twelve hundred
miles away. The thing was sudden, and without
preparation—after the custom of dreams. There
I was, crossing a wooden bridge that had a wooden
rail and was untidy with scattered wisps of hay,
and there she was, five steps in front of me; half
a second previously neither of us was there. This
was the exit of the village, which lay immediately
behind us. Its last house was the blacksmith-shop;
and the peaceful clinking of the hammers—a
sound which nearly always seems remote, and is
always touched with a spirit of loneliness and a
feeling of soft regret for something, you don't
know what—was wafted to my ears over my shoulder; in front of us was the winding country road,
with woods on one side, and on the other a rail
fence, with blackberry vines and hazel bushes
crowding its angles; on an upper rail a bluebird,
and scurrying toward him along the same rail, a

fox-squirrel with his tail bent high like a shepherd's crook; beyond the fence a rich field of grain, and far away a farmer in shirtsleeves and straw hat wading knee-deep through it; no other representatives of life, and no noise at all; everywhere a Sabbath stillness.

I remember it all—and the girl, too, and just how she walked, and how she was dressed. In the first moment I was five steps behind her; in the next one I was at her side—without ever stepping or gliding; it merely happened; the transfer ignored space. I noticed that, but not with any surprise; it seemed a natural process.

I was at her side. I put my arm around her waist and drew her close to me, for I loved her; and although I did not know her, my behavior seemed to me quite natural and right, and I had no misgivings about it. She showed no surprise, no distress, no displeasure, but put an arm around my waist, and turned up her face to mine with a happy welcome in it, and when I bent down to kiss her she received the kiss as if she was expecting it, and as if it was quite natural for me to offer it and her to take it and have pleasure in it. The affection which I felt for her and which she manifestly felt for me was a quite simple fact; but the quality of it was another matter. It was not the affection of brother and sister—it was closer than that, more clinging, more endearing, more reverent; and it was not the love of sweethearts, for there was no fire in it. It was somewhere between the two, and was finer than either, and more exquisite, more profoundly contenting. We often experience this strange and gracious thing in our dream-loves; and we remember it as a feature of our childhood-loves, too.

We strolled along, across the bridge and down the road, chatting like the oldest friends. She called me George, and that seemed natural and right, though it was not my name; and I called her Alice, and she did not correct me, though without doubt it was not her name. Everything that happened seemed just natural and to be expected. Once I said, "What a dear little hand it is!" and without any words she laid it gracefully in mine for me to examine it. I did it, remarking upon its littleness, its delicate beauty, and its satin skin, then kissed it; she put it up to her lips without saying anything and kissed it in the same place.

Around a curve of the road, at the end of half a mile, we came to a log house, and entered it and found the table set and everything on it steaming hot—a roast turkey, corn in the ear, butterbeans, and the rest of the usual things—and a cat curled up asleep in a splint-bottomed chair by the fireplace; but no people; just emptiness and silence. She said she would look in the next room if I would wait for her. So I sat down, and she passed through the door, which closed behind her with a click of the latch. I waited and waited. Then I got up and followed, for I could not any longer bear to have her out of my sight. I passed through the door, and found myself in a strange sort of cemetery, a city of innumerable tombs and monuments stretching far and wide on every hand, and flushed with pink and gold lights flung from the sinking sun. I turned around, and the log house was gone. I ran here and there and yonder down the lanes between the rows of tombs, calling Alice; and presently the night closed down, and I could not find my way. Then I woke, in deep distress over my loss, and was in my bed in Philadelphia. And I was not seventeen, now, but nineteen.

Ten years afterward, in another dream, I found her. I was seventeen again, and she was still fifteen. I was in a grassy place in the twilight deeps of a magnolia forest some miles above Natchez, Mississippi; the trees were snowed over with great blossoms, and the air was loaded with their rich and strenuous fragrance; the ground was high, and through a rift in the wood a burnished patch of the river was visible in the distance. I was sitting on the grass, absorbed in thinking, when an arm was laid around my neck, and there was Alice sitting by my side and looking into my face. A deep and satisfied happiness and an unwordable gratitude rose in me, but with it there was no feeling of surprise; and there was no sense of a time-lapse; the ten years amounted to hardly even a yesterday; indeed, to hardly even a noticeable fraction of it. We dropped in the tranquilest way into affectionate caressings and pettings, and chatted along without a reference to the separation; which was natural, for I think we did not know there had been any that one might measure with either clock or almanac. She called me Jack and

I called her Helen, and those seemed the right and proper names, and perhaps neither of us suspected that we had ever borne others; or, if we did suspect it, it was probably not a matter of consequence.

She had been beautiful ten years before; she was just as beautiful still; girlishly young and sweet and innocent, and she was still that now. She had blue eyes, a hair of flossy gold before; she had black hair now, and dark-brown eyes. I noted these differences, but they did not suggest change; to me she was the same girl she was before, absolutely. It never occurred to me to ask what became of the log house; I doubt if I even thought of it. We were living in a simple and natural and beautiful world where everything that happened was natural and right, and was not perplexed with the unexpected or with any forms of surprise, and so there was no occasion for explanations and no interest attaching to such things.

We had a dear and pleasant time together, and were like a couple of ignorant and contented children. Helen had a summer hat on. She took it off presently and said, "It was in the way; now you can kiss me better." It seemed to me merely a bit of courteous and considerate wisdom, nothing more; and a natural thing for her to think of and do. We went wandering through the woods, and came to a limpid and shallow stream a matter of three yards wide. She said:

"I must not get my feet wet, dear; carry me over."

I took her in my arms and gave her my hat to

hold. This was to keep my own feet from getting wet. I did not know why this should have that effect; I merely knew it; and she knew it, too. I crossed the stream, and said I would go on carrying her, because it was so pleasant; and she said it was pleasant for her too, and wished we had thought of it sooner. It seemed to me a pity that we should have walked so far, both of us on foot, when we could have been having this higher enjoyment; and I spoke of it regretfully, as a something lost which could never be got back. She was troubled about it, too, and said there must be some way to get it back; and she would think. After musing deeply a little while she looked up radiant and proud, and said she had found it.

"Carry me back and start over again."

I can see, now, that that was no solution, but at the time it seemed luminous with intelligence, and I believed that there was not another little head in the world that could have worked out that difficult problem with such swiftness and success. I told her that, and it pleased her; and she said she was glad it all happened, so that I could see how capable she was. After thinking a moment she added that it was "quite atreous." The words seemed to mean something, I do not know why: in fact, it seemed to cover the whole ground and leave nothing more to say; I admired the nice aptness and the flashing felicity of the phrase, and was filled with respect for the marvelous mind that had been able to engender it. I think less of it now. It is a noticeable fact that the intellectual coinage of Dreamland often passes for more there than it would fetch here. Many a time in after years my dream-sweetheart threw off golden sayings which crumbled to ashes under my pencil when I was setting them down in my note-book after breakfast.

I carried her back and started over again; and all the long afternoon I bore her in my arms, miles upon miles, and it never occurred to either of us that there was anything remarkable in a youth like me being able to carry that sweet bundle around half a day without some sense of fatigue or need of rest. There are many dream-worlds, but none is so rightly and reasonably and pleasantly arranged as that one.

After dark we reached a great plantation-house, and it was her home. I carried her in, and the family knew me and I knew them, although we had not met before; and the mother asked me with ill disguised anxiety how much twelve times fourteen was, and I said a hundred and thirty-five, and she put it down on a piece of paper, saying it was her habit in the process of perfecting her education not to trust important particulars to her memory; and her husband was offering me a chair, but noticed that Helen was asleep, so he said it would be best not to disturb her; and he backed me softly against a wardrobe and said I could stand more easily now; then a negro came in, bowing humbly, with his slouch-hat in his hand, and asked me if I would have my measure taken. The question did not surprise me, but it confused me and worried me, and I said I should like to have advice about it. He started toward the door to call advisers; then he and the family and the lights began to grow dim, and in a few moments the place was pitch dark; but straightway there came a flood of moonlight and a gust of cold wind, and I found myself crossing a frozen lake, and my arms were empty. The wave of grief that swept through me woke me up, and I was sitting at my desk in the newspaper office in San Francisco, and I noticed by the clock that I had been asleep less than two minutes. And what was of more consequence, I was twenty-nine years old.

That was 1864. The next year and the year after I had momentary glimpses of my dream-sweetheart, but nothing more. These are set down in my note-books under their proper dates, but with no talks nor other particulars added; which is sufficient evidence to me that there were none to add. In both of these instances there was the sudden meeting and recognition, the eager approach, then the instant disappearance, leaving the world empty and of no worth. I remember the two images quite well; in fact, I remember all the images of that spirit, and can bring them before me without help of my note-book. The habit of writing down my dreams of all sorts while they were fresh in my mind, and then studying them and rehearsing them and trying to find out what the source of dreams is, and which of the two or three separate persons inhabiting us is their architect, has given me a good dream-memory—a thing which is not usual with people, for few drill the dream-memory—and no memory can be kept strong without that.

I spent a few months in the Hawaiian Islands in 1866, and in October of that year I delivered my maiden lecture; it was in San Francisco. In the following January I arrived in New York, and had just completed my thirty-first year. In that year I saw my platonic dream-sweetheart again. In this dream I was again standing on the stage of the Opera House in San Francisco, ready to lecture, and with the audience vividly individualized before me in the strong light. I began, spoke a few words, and stopped, cold with fright; for I discovered that I had no subject, no text, nothing to talk about. I choked for a while, then got out a few words, a lame, poor attempt at humor. The house made no response. There was a miserable pause, then another attempt, and another failure. There were a few scornful laughs; otherwise the house was silent, unsmilingly austere, deeply offended. I was consuming with shame. In my distress I tried to work upon its pity. I began to make servile apologies, mixed with gross and ill-timed flatteries, and to beg and plead for forgiveness; this was too much, and the people broke into insulting cries, whistlings, hootings, and cat-calls, and in the midst of this they rose and began to struggle in a confused mass toward the door. I stood dazed and helpless, looking out over this spectacle, and thinking how everybody would be talking about it next day, and I could not show myself in the streets. When the house was become wholly empty and still, I sat down on the only chair that was on the stage and bent my head down on the reading-desk to shut out the look of that place. Soon that familiar dream-voice spoke my name, and swept all my troubles away:

"Robert!"

I answered:

"Agnes!"

The next moment we two were lounging up the blossomy gorge called the Iao Valley, in the Hawaiian Islands. I recognized, without any explanations, that Robert was not my name, but only a pet name, a common noun, and meant "dear"; and both of us knew that Agnes was not a name, but only a pet name, a common noun, whose spirit was affectionate, but not conveyable with exactness in any but the dream-language. It was about the equivalent of "dear," but the dream-vocabulary shaves meanings finer and closer than do the world's daytime dictionaries. We did not know why those words should have those meanings; we had used words which had no existence in any known language, and had expected them to be understood, and they were understood. In my note-books there are several letters from this dream-sweetheart, in some unknown tongue—presumably dream-tongue—with translations added. I should like to be master of that tongue, then I could talk in shorthand. Here is one of those letters—the whole of it:

"Rax oha tal."

Translation.—"When you receive this it will remind you that I long to see your face and touch your hand, for the comfort of it and the peace."

It is swifter than waking thought; for thought is not thought at all, but only a vague and formless fog until it is articulated into words.

We wandered far up the fairy gorge, gathering the beautiful flowers of the ginger-plant and talking affectionate things, and tying and retying each other's ribbons and cravats, which didn't need it; and finally sat down in the shade of a tree and climbed the vine-hung precipices with our eyes, up and up and up toward the sky to where the drifting scarfs of white mist clove them across and left the green summits floating pale and remote, like spectral islands wandering in the deeps of space; and then we descended to earth and talked again.

"How still it is—and soft, and balmy, and reposeful! I could never tire of it. You like it, don't you, Robert?"

"Yes, and I like the whole region—all the islands. Maui. It is a darling island. I have been here before. Have you?"

"Once, but it wasn't an island then."

"What was it?"

"It was a sufa."

I understood. It was the dream-word for "part of a continent."

"What were the people like?"

"They hadn't come yet. There weren't any."

"Do you know, Agnes—that is Haleakala, the dead volcano, over there across the valley; was it here in your friend's time?"

"Yes, but it was burning."

"Do you travel much?"

"I think so. Not here much but in the stars a great deal."

"Is it pretty there?"

She used a couple of dream-words for "You will go with me some time and you will see." Noncommittal, as one perceives now, but I did not notice it then.

A man-of-war bird lit on her shoulder; I put out my hand and caught it. Its feathers began to fall out, and it turned into a kitten; then the kitten's body began to contract itself to a ball and put out hairy, long legs, and soon it was a tarantula; I was going to keep it, but it turned into a star-fish, and I threw it away. Agnes said it was not worth while to try to keep things; there was no stability about them. I suggested rocks; but she said a rock was like the rest; it wouldn't stay. She picked up a stone, and it turned into a bat and flew away. These curious matters interested me, but that was all; they did not stir my wonder.

While we were sitting there in the Iao gorge talking, a Kanaka came along who was wrinkled and bent and white-headed, and he stopped and talked to us in the native tongue, and we understood him without trouble and answered him in his own speech. He said he was a hundred and thirty years old, and he remembered Captain Cook well, and was present when he was murdered; saw it with his own eyes, and also helped. Then he showed us his gun, which was of strange make, and he said it was his own invention and was to shoot arrows with, though one loaded it with powder and it had a percussion lock. He said it would carry a hundred miles. It seemed a reasonable statement; I had no fault to find with it, and it did not in any way surprise me. He loaded it and fired an arrow aloft, and it darted into the sky and vanished. Then he went his way, saying that the arrow would fall near us in half an hour, and would go many yards into the earth, not minding the rocks.

I took the time, and we waited, reclining upon the mossy slant at the base of a tree, and gazing into the sky. By and by there was a hissing sound, followed by a dull impact, and Agnes uttered a groan. She said, in a series of fainting gasps:

"Take me in your arms—it passed through me—hold me to your heart—I am afraid to die —closer—closer. It is growing dark—I cannot see you. Don't leave me—where are you? You are not gone? You will not leave me? I would not leave you."

Then her spirit passed; she was clay in my arms.

The scene changed in an instant and I was awake and crossing Bond Street in New York with a friend, and it was snowing hard. We had been talking, and there had been no observable gaps in the conversation. I doubt if I had made any more than two steps while I was asleep. I am satisfied that even the most elaborate and incident-crowded dream is seldom more than a few seconds in length. It would not cost me very much of a strain to believe in Mohammed's seventy-year dream, which began when he knocked his glass over, and ended in time for him to catch it before the water was spilled.

Within a quarter of an hour I was in my quarters, undressed, ready for bed, and was jotting down my dream in my note-book. A striking thing happened now. I finished my notes, and was just going to turn out the gas when I was caught with a most strenuous gape, for it was very late and I was very drowsy. I fell asleep and dreamed again. What now follows occurred while I was asleep; and when I woke again the gape had completed itself, but not long before, I think, for I was still on my feet. I was in Athens—a city which I had not then seen, but I recognized the Parthenon from the pictures, although it had a fresh look and was in perfect repair. I passed by it and climbed a grassy hill toward a palatial sort of mansion which was built of red terra-cotta and had a spacious portico, whose roof was supported by a rank of fluted columns with Corinthian capitals. It was noonday, but I met no one. I passed into the house and entered the first room. It was very large and light, its walls were of polished and richly tinted and veined onyx, and its floor was a pictured pattern in soft colors laid in tiles. I noted the details of the furniture and the ornaments—a thing which I should not have been likely to do when awake

—and they took sharp hold and remained in my memory; they are not really dim yet, and this was more than thirty years ago.

There was a person present—Agnes. I was not surprised to see her, but only glad. She was in the simple Greek costume, and her hair and eyes were different as to color from those she had had when she died in the Hawaiian Islands half an hour before, but to me she was exactly her own beautiful little self as I had always known her, and she was still fifteen, and I was seventeen once more. She was sitting on an ivory settee, crocheting something or other, and had her crewels in a shallow willow work-basket in her lap. I sat down by her and we began to chat in the usual way. I remembered her death, but the pain and the grief and the bitterness which had been so sharp and so desolating to me at the moment that it happened had wholly passed from me now, and had left not a scar. I was grateful to have her back, but there was no realizable sense that she had ever been gone, and so it did not occur to me to speak about it, and consequently nothing important enough in it to make conversation out of.

When I think of that house and its belongings, I recognize what a master in taste and drawing and color and arrangement is the dream-artist who resides in us. In my waking hours, when the inferior artist in me is in command, I cannot draw even the simplest picture with a pencil, nor do anything with a brush and colors; I cannot bring before my mind's eye the detail image of any building known to me except my own house at home; of St. Paul's, St. Peter's, the Eiffel Tower, the Taj, the Capitol at Washington, I can reproduce only portions, partial glimpses; the same with Niagara Falls, the Matterhorn, and other familiar things in nature; I cannot bring before my mind's eye the face or figure of any human being known to me; I have seen my family at breakfast within the past two hours; I cannot bring their images before me, I do not know how they look; before me, as I write, I see a little grove of young trees in the garden; high above them projects the slender lance of a young pine, beyond it is a glimpse of the upper half of a dull-white chimney covered by an A-shaped little roof shingled with brown-red tiles, and half a mile away is a hill-top densely wooded, and the red is cloven by a curved, wide vacancy, which is smooth and grass-clad; I cannot shut my eyes and reproduce that picture as a whole at all, nor any single detail of it except the grassy curve, and that but vaguely and fleetingly.

But my dream-artist can draw anything, and do it perfectly; he can paint with all the colors and all the shades, and do it with delicacy and truth; he can place before me vivid images of palaces, cities, hamlets, hovels, mountains, valleys, lakes, skies, glowing in sunlight or moonlight, or veiled in driving gusts of snow or rain, and he can set before me people who are intensely alive, and who feel, and express their feelings in their faces, and who also talk and laugh, sing and swear. And when

I wake I can shut my eyes and bring back those people, and the scenery and the buildings; and not only in general view, but often in nice detail. While Agnes and I sat talking in that grand Athens house, several stately Greeks entered from another part of it, disputing warmly about something or other, and passed us by with courteous recognition; and among them was Socrates. I recognized him by his nose. A moment later the house and Agnes and Athens vanished away, and I was in my quarters in New York again and reaching for my note-book.

In our dreams—I know it!—we do make the journeys we seem to make; we do see the things we seem to see; the people, the horses, the cats, the dogs, the birds, the whales, are real, not chimeras; they are living spirits, not shadows; and they are immortal and indestructible. They go whither they will; they visit all resorts, all points of interest, even the twinkling suns that wander in the wastes of space. That is where those strange mountains are which slide from under our feet while we walk, and where those vast caverns are whose bewildering avenues close behind us and in front when we are lost, and shut us in. We know this because there are no such things here, and they must be there, because there is no other place.

This tale is long enough, and I will close it now. In the forty-four years that I have known my Dreamland sweetheart, I have seen her once in two years on an average. Mainly these were glimpses, but she was always immediately recognizable, notwithstanding she was so given to repair herself and getting up doubtful improvements in her hair and eyes. She was always fifteen, and looked it and acted it; and I was always seventeen, and never felt a day older. To me she is a real person, not a fiction, and her sweet and innocent society has been one of the prettiest and pleasantest experiences of my life. I know that to you her talk will not seem of the first intellectual order; but you should hear her in Dreamland— then you would see!

I saw her a week ago, just for a moment. Fifteen, as usual, and I seventeen, instead of going on sixty-three, as I was when I went to sleep. We were in India, and Bombay was in sight; also Windsor Castle, its towers and battlements veiled in a delicate haze, and from it the Thames flowed, curving and winding between its swarded banks, to our feet. I said:

"There is no question about it, England is the most beautiful of all countries."

Her face lighted with approval, and she said, with that sweet and earnest irrelevance of hers:

"It is, because it is so marginal."

Then she disappeared. It was just as well; she could probably have added nothing to that rounded and perfect statement without damaging its symmetry.

This glimpse of her carries me back to Maui, and that time when I saw her gasp out her young life. That was a terrible thing to me at the time.

It was preternaturally vivid; and the pain and the grief and the misery of it to me transcended many sufferings that I have known in waking life. For everything in a dream is more deep and strong and sharp and real than is ever its pale imitation in the unreal life which is ours when we go about awake and clothed with our artificial selves in this vague and dull-tinted artificial world. When we die we shall slough off this cheap intellect, perhaps, and go abroad into Dreamland clothed in our real selves, and aggrandized and enriched by the command over the mysterious mental magician who is here not our slave, but only our guest.

The Treasure of Far Island

Willa Cather

Dark brown is the river,
Golden is the sand;
It flows along forever,
With trees on either hand.
—*Robert Louis Stevenson.*

I

Far Island is an oval sand bar, half a mile in length and perhaps a hundred yards wide, which lies about two miles up from Empire City in a turbid little Nebraska river. The island is known chiefly to the children who dwell in that region, and generation after generation of them have claimed it; fished there, and pitched their tents under the great arched tree, and built camp fires on its level, sandy outskirts. In the middle of the island, which is always above water except in flood time, grow thousands of yellow-green creek willows and cottonwood seedlings, brilliantly green, even when the hottest winds blow, by reason of the surrounding moisture. In the summer months, when the capricious stream is low, the children's empire is extended by many rods, and a long irregular beach of white sand is exposed along the east coast of the island, never out of the water long enough to acquire any vegetation, but dazzling white, ripple marked, and full of possibilities for the imagination. The island is No-Man's-Land; every summer a new chief claims it and it has been called by many names; but it seemed particularly to belong to the two children who christened it Far Island, partially because they were the original discoverers and claimants, but more especially because they were of that favored race whom a New England sage called the true land-lords and sea-lords of the world.

One afternoon, early in June, the Silvery Beaches of Far Island were glistening in the sun like pounded glass, and the same slanting yellow rays that scorched the sand beat upon the windows of the passenger train from the East as it swung into the Republican Valley from the uplands. Then a young man dressed in a suit of gray tweed changed his seat in order to be on the side of the car next the river. When he crossed the car several women looked up and smiled, for it was with a movement of boyish abandon and an audible chuckle of delight that he threw himself into the seat to watch for the shining curves of the river as they unwound through the trees. He was sufficiently distinguished in appearance to interest even tired women at the end of a long, sultry day's travel. As the train rumbled over a trestle built above a hollow grown up with sunflowers and ironweed, he sniffed with delight the rank odor, familiar to the prairie-bred man, that is exhaled by such places as evening approaches. "Ha," he murmured under his breath, "there's the white chalk cliff where the Indians used to run the buffalo over Bison Leap—we kids called it—the remote sea wall of the boy world. I'm getting home sure enough. And heavens! there's the island, Far Island, the Ultima Thule; and the arched tree, and Spy Glass Hill, and the Silvery Beaches; my heart's going like a boy's. 'Once on a day he sailed away, over the sea to Skye.'"

He sat bolt upright with his lips tightly closed and his chest swelling, for he was none other than the original discoverer of the island, Douglass Burnham, the playwright—our only playwright, certain critics contend—and, for the first time since he left it a boy, he was coming home. It was only twelve years ago that he had gone away, when Pagie and Temp and Birkner and Shorty Thompson had stood on the station siding and waved him goodbye, while he shut his teeth to keep the tears back; and now the train bore him up the old river valley, through the meadows where he used to hunt for cattails, along the streams where he had paddled his canvas boat, and past the willow-grown island where he had buried the pirate's treasure—a man with a man's work done and the world well in hand. Success had never tasted quite so sweet as it tasted then. The whistle sounded, the brakeman called Empire City, and Douglass crossed to the other side of the car and looked out toward the town, which lay half a mile up from the station on a low range of hills, half hidden by the tall cottonwood trees that still shaded its streets. Down the curve of the track he could see the old railroad "eating house," painted the red Burlington color; on the hill above the town the standpipe towered up from the treetops. Douglass felt the years dropping away from him. The train stopped. Waiting on the platform stood his father and a tall spare man, with a straggling colorless beard, whose dejected stoop and shapeless hat and ill-fitting clothes were in themselves both introduction and biography. The narrow chest, long arms, and skinny neck were not to be mistaken. It was Rhinehold Birkner, old Rhine who had not been energetic enough to keep up his father's undertaking business, and who now sold sewing machines and parlor organs in a feeble attempt to support an invalid wife and ten children, all colorless and narrow chested like himself. Douglass sprang from the platform and grasped his father's hand.

"Hello, father, hello, Rhine, where are the other fellows? Why, that's so, you must be the only one left. Heavens! how we *have* scattered. What a lot of talking we two have got before us."

Probably no event had transpired since Rhine's first baby was born that had meant so much to him as Douglass's return, but he only chuckled, putting his limp, rough hand into the young man's smooth, warm one, and ventured,

"Jest the same old coon, Doug."

"How's mother, father?" Douglass asked as he hunted for his checks.

"She's well, son, but she thought she couldn't leave supper to come down to meet you. She has been cooking pretty much all day and worrying for fear the train would be late and your supper would spoil."

"Of course she has. When I am elected to the Academy mother will worry about my supper." Douglass felt a trifle nervous and made a dash for the shabby little street car which ever since he could remember had been drawn by mules that wore jingling bells on their collars.

A silence settled down over the occupants of the car as the mules trotted off. Douglass felt that his father stood somewhat in awe of him, or at least in awe of that dread Providence which ordered such dark things as that a hard-headed, money-saving real-estate man should be the father of a white-fingered playwright who spent more on his fads in a year than his father had saved by the thrift of a lifetime. All the hundred things Douglass had had to say seemed congested upon his tongue, and though he had a good measure of that cheerful assurance common to young people whom the world has made much of, he felt a strange embarrassment in the presence of this angular gray-whiskered man who used to warm his jacket for him in the hayloft.

His mother was waiting for him under the bittersweet vines on the porch, just where she had always stood to greet him when he came home for his college vacations, and, as Douglass had lived in a world where the emotions are cultivated and not despised, he was not ashamed of the lump that rose in his throat when he took her in his arms. She hurried him out of the dark into the parlor lamplight and looked him over from head to foot to assure herself that he was still the handsomest of men, and then she told him to go into her bedroom to wash his face for supper. She followed him, unable to take her eyes from this splendid creature whom all the world claimed but who was only hers after all. She watched him take off his coat and collar, rejoicing in the freshness of his linen and the whiteness of his skin; even the color of his silk suspenders seemed a matter of importance to her.

"Douglass," she said impressively, "Mrs. Governor gives a reception for you tomorrow night, and I have promised her that you will read some selections from your plays."

This was a matter which was very near Mrs. Burnham's heart. Those dazzling first nights and receptions and author's dinners which happened out in the great world were merely hearsay, but it was a proud day when her son was held in honor by the women of her own town, of her own church; women she had shopped and marketed and gone to sewing circle with, women whose cakes and watermelon pickles won premiums over hers at the county fair.

"Read?" ejaculated Douglass, looking out over the towel and pausing in his brisk rubbing, "why, mother, dear, I can't read, not any more than a John rabbit. Besides, plays aren't meant to be read. Let me give them one of my old stunts; 'The Polish Boy' or 'Regulus to the Carthaginians.'"

"But you must do it, my son; it won't do to disappoint Mrs. Governor. Margie was over this morning to see about it. She has grown into a very pretty girl." When his mother spoke in that tone Douglass acquiesced, just as naturally as he helped himself to her violet water, the same kind, he noticed, that he used to covertly sprinkle on his handkerchief when he was primping for Sunday school after she had gone to church.

"Mrs. Governor still leads the pack, then? What a civilizing influence she has been in this community. Taught most of us all the manners we ever knew. Little Margie has grown up pretty, you say? Well, I should never have thought it. How many boys have I slugged for yelling 'Reddy, go dye your hair green' at her. She was not an indifferent slugger herself and never exactly stood in need of masculine protection. What a wild Indian she was! Game, clear through, though! I never found such a mind in a girl. But *is* she a girl? I somehow always fancied she would grow up a man—and a ripping fine one. Oh, I see you are looking at me hard! No, mother, the girls don't trouble me much." His eyes met hers laughingly in the glass as he parted his hair. "You spoiled me so outrageously that women tell me frankly I'm a selfish cad and they will have none of me."

His mother handed him his coat with a troubled

glance. "I was afraid, my son, that some of those actresses—"

The young man laughed outright. "Oh, never worry about them, mother. Wait till you've seen them at rehearsals in soiled shirtwaists wearing out their antiques and doing what they call 'resting' their hair. Poor things! They have to work too hard to bother about being attractive."

He went out into the dining room where the table was set for him just as it had always been when he came home on that same eight o'clock train from college. There were all his favorite viands and the old family silver spread on the white cloth with the maidenhair fern pattern, under the soft lamplight. It had been years since he had eaten by the mild light of a kerosene lamp. By his plate stood his own glass that his grandmother had given him with "For a Good Boy" ground on the surface which was dewy from the ice within. The other glasses were unclouded and held only fresh water from the pump, for his mother was very economical about ice and held the most exaggerated views as to the pernicious effects of ice water on the human stomach. Douglass only got it because he was the first dramatist of the country and a great man. When he decided that he would like a cocktail and asked for whiskey, his mother dealt him out a niggardly tablespoonful, saying, "That's as much as you ought to have at your age, Douglass." When he went out into the kitchen to greet the old servant and get some ice for his drink, his mother hurried after him crying with solicitude,

"I'll get the ice for you, Douglass. Don't you go into the refrigerator; you always leave the ice uncovered and it wastes."

Douglass threw up his hands, "Mother, whatever I may do in the world I shall never be clever enough to be trusted with that refrigerator. 'Into all the chambers of the palace mayest thou go, save into this thou shalt not go.'" And now he knew he was at home, indeed, for his father stood chuckling in the doorway, washing his hands from the milking, and the old servant threw her apron over her head to stifle her laughter at this strange reception of a celebrity. The memory of his luxurious rooms in New York, where he lived when he was an artist, faded dim; he was but a boy again in his father's house and must not keep supper waiting.

The next evening Douglass with resignation accompanied his father and mother to the reception given in his honor. The town had advanced somewhat since his day; and he was amused to see his father appear in an apology for a frock coat and a black tie, such as Kentucky politicians wear. Although people wore frock coats nowadays they still walked to receptions, and as Douglass climbed the hill the whole situation struck him as farcical. He dropped his mother's arm and ran up to the porch with his hat in his hand, laughing. "Margie!" he called, intending to dash through the house until he found her. But in the vestibule he bumped up against something large and splendid, then stopped and caught his breath. A woman stood in the dark by the hall lamp with a lighted match in her hand. She was in white and very tall. The match burned but a moment; a moment the light played on her hair, red as Etruscan gold and piled high above the curve of the neck and head; a moment upon the oval chin, the lips curving upward and red as a crimson cactus flower; the deep, gray, fearless eyes; the white shoulders framed about with darkness. Then the match went out, leaving Douglass to wonder whether, like Anchises, he had seen the vision that should forever blind him to the beauty of mortal women.

"I beg your pardon," he stammered, backing toward the door, "I was looking for Miss Van Dyck. Is she—" Perhaps it was a mere breath of stifled laughter, perhaps it was a recognition by some sense more trustworthy than sight and subtler than mind; but there seemed a certain familiarity in the darkness about him, a certain sense of the security and peace which one experiences among dear and intimate things, and with widening eyes he said softly,

"Tell me, is this Margie?"

There was just a murmur of laughter from the tall, white figure. "I was going to be presented to you in the most proper form, and now you've spoiled it all. How are you, Douglass, and did you get a whipping this time? You've played hooky longer than usual. Ten years, isn't it?" She put out her hand in the dark and he took it and drew it through his arm.

"No, I didn't get a whipping, but I may get worse. I wish I'd come back five years ago. I would if I had known," he said promptly.

The reading was just as stupid as he had said it would be, but his audience enjoyed it and he enjoyed his audience. There was the old deacon who had once caught him in his watermelon patch and set the dog on him; the president of the W.C.T.U., with her memorable black lace shawl and cane, who still continued to send him temperance tracts, mindful of the hundredth sheep in the parable; his old Sunday school teacher, a good man of limited information who never read anything but his Bible and *Teachers' Quarterly*, and who had once hung a cheap edition of *Camille* on the church Christmas tree for Douglass, with an inscription on the inside to the effect that the fear of the Lord is the beginning of Wisdom. There was the village criminal lawyer, one of those brilliant wrecks sometimes found in small towns, who, when he was so drunk he could not walk, used to lie back in his office chair and read Shakespeare by the hour to a little barefoot boy. Next him sat the rich banker who used to offer the boys a quarter to hitch up his horse for him, and then drive off, forgetting all about the quarter. Then there were fathers and mothers of Douglass's old clansmen and vassals who were scattered all over the world now. After the reading Douglass spent half an hour chatting with nice tiresome old ladies who reminded him of how much he used to like their teacakes and cookies, and answering labored compliments with genuine feeling. Then he went with a clear conscience and light heart whither his eyes had been wandering ever since he had entered the house.

"Margie, I needn't apologize for not recognizing you, since it was such an involuntary compliment. However did you manage to grow up like this? Was it boarding school that did it? I might have recognized you with your hair down, and oh, I'd know you anywhere when you smile! The teeth are just the same. Do you still crack nuts with them?"

"I haven't tried it for a long time. How remarkably little the years change you, Douglass. I haven't seen you since the night you brought out *The Clover Leaf*, and I heard your curtain speech. Oh, I was very proud of our Pirate Chief!"

Douglass sat down on the piano stool and looked searchingly into her eyes, which met his with laughing frankness.

"What! you were in New York then and didn't let me know? There was a day when you wouldn't have treated me so badly. Didn't you want to see me just a little bit—out of curiosity?"

"Oh, I was visiting some school friends who said it would be atrocious to bother you, and the newspapers were full of interesting details about your being so busy that you ate and got shaved at the theatre. Then one's time isn't one's own when one is visiting, you know." She saw the hurt

151

expression on his face and repented, adding gayly, "But I may as well confess that I kept a sharp lookout for you on the street, and when I did meet you you didn't know me."

"And you didn't stop me? That's worse yet. How in Heaven's name was I to know you? Accost a goddess and say, 'Oh yes, you used to be a Pirate Chief and wear a butcher knife in your belt.' But I hadn't grown into an Apollo, save the mark! and you knew me well enough. I couldn't have passed you like that in a strange land."

"No, you do your duty by your countrymen, Douglass. You haven't grown haughty. One by one our old townspeople go out to see the world and bring us back tales of your glory. What un-promising specimens have you not dined and wined in New York! Why even old Skin Jackson, when he went to New York to have his eyes treated, you took to the Waldorf and to the Play-ers' Club, where he drank with the Immortals. How do you have the courage to do it? *Did* he wear those dreadful gold nugget shirt studs that he dug up in Colorado when we were young?"

"Even the same, Margie, and he scored a hit with them. But you are dodging the point. When and where did you see me in New York?"

"Oh, it was one evening when you were crossing Madison Square. You were probably going to the theatre for Flashingham and Miss Grew were with you and you seemed in a hurry." Margie wished now that she had not mentioned the incident. "I remember that was the time I so deeply offended

152

your mother on my return by telling her that Miss Grew had announced her engagement to you. How did it come out? She certainly did announce it."

"Doubtless, but it was entirely a misunderstanding on the lady's part. We never were anything of the sort," said Douglass impatiently. "That is a disgusting habit of Edith's; she announces a new engagement every fortnight as mechanically as the butler announces dinner. About once a month she calls the dear Twelfth Night girls together to a solemn high tea and gently breaks the news of a new engagement, and they kiss and cry over her and say the things they have said a dozen times before and go away tittering. Why she has been engaged to every society chap in New York and to the whole Milton family, with the possible exception of Sir Henry, and her papa has cabled his blessing all over the known world to her. But it is a waste of time to talk about such nonsense; don't let's," he urged.

"I think it is very interesting; I don't indulge in weekly engagements myself. But there is one thing I do want to know, Douglass; I want to know how you did it."

"Did what?"

Margie threw out her hands with an impetuous gesture. "Oh, all of it, all the wonderful things you have done. You remember that night when we lay on the sand bar—"

"The Uttermost Desert," interrupted Douglass softly.

"Yes, the Uttermost Desert, and in the light of

the driftwood fire we planned the conquest of the world? Well, other people plan, too, and fight and suffer and fail the world over, and a very few succeed at the bitter end when they are old and it is no longer worth while. But you have done it as they used to do it in the fairy tales, without soiling your golden armor, and I can't find one line in your face to tell me that you have suffered or found life bitter to your tongue. How have you cheated fate?"

Douglass looked about him and saw that the guests had thronged about the punchbowl, and his mother, beaming in her new black satin, was relating touching incidents of his infancy to a group of old ladies. He leaned forward, clasped his hands between his knees, and launched into an animated description of how his first play, written at college, had taken the fancy of an old school friend of his father's who had turned manager. The second, a political farce, had put him fairly on his feet. Then followed his historical drama, *Lord Fairfax*, in which he had at first failed completely. He told her of those desperate days in New York when he would draw his blinds and work by lamplight until he was utterly exhausted, of how he fell ill and lost the thread of his play and used to wander about the streets trying to beat it out of the paving stones when the very policemen who jostled him on the crossings knew more about *Lord Fairfax* than he.

As he talked he felt the old sense of power, lost for many years; the power of conveying himself wholly to her in speech, of awakening in her mind every tint and shadow and vague association that was in his at the moment. He quite forgot the beauty of the woman beside him in the exultant realization of comradeship, the egoistic satisfaction of being wholly understood. Suddenly he stopped short.

"Come, Margie, you're not playing fair, you're telling me nothing about yourself. What plays have you been playing? Pirate or enchanted princess or sleeping beauty or Helen of Troy, to the disaster of men?"

Margie sighed as she awoke out of the fairyland. Doug's tales were as wonderful as ever.

"Oh, I stopped playing long ago. I have grown up and you have not. Some one has said that is wherein geniuses are different; they go on playing and never grow up. So you see you're only a case of arrested development, after all."

"I don't believe it, you play still, I can see it in your eyes. And don't say genius to me. People say that to me only when they want to be disagreeable or tell me how they would have written my plays. The word is my bogie. But tell me, are the cattails ripe in the Salt Marshes, and will your mother let you wade if the sun is warm, and do the winds still smell sharp with salt when they blow through the mists at night?"

"Why, Douglass, did the wind always smell salty to you there too? It does to me yet, and you know there isn't a particle of salt there. Why did we ever name them the Salt Marshes?"

"Because they *were* the Salt Marshes and couldn't have had any other name any more than the Far Island could. I went down to those pestiferous Maremma marshes in Italy to see whether they would be as real as our marshes, but they were not real at all; only miles and miles of bog. And do the nightingales still sing in the grove?"

"Yes. Other people call them ring doves—but they still sing there."

"And you still call them nightingales to yourself and laugh at the density of big people?"

"Yes, sometimes."

Later in the evening Douglass found another opportunity, and this time he was fortunate enough to encounter Margie alone as she was crossing the veranda.

"Do you know why I have come home in June, instead of July as I had intended, Margie? Well, sit down and let me tell you. They don't need you in there just now. About a month ago I changed my apartment in New York, and as I was sorting over my traps I came across a box of childish souvenirs. Among them was a faded bit of paper on which a map was drawn with elaborate care. It was the map of an island with curly blue lines all around it to represent water, such as we used always to draw around the continents in our geography class. On the west coast of the island a red sword was sticking upright in the earth. Beneath this scientific drawing was an inscription to the effect that '*whoso should dig twelve paces west of the huge fallen tree, in direct line with the path made by the setting sun on the water on the tenth day of June, should find the great treasure and his heart's desire!'"*

Margie laughed and applauded gently with her hands. "And so you have come to dig for it; come two thousand miles almost. There's a dramatic situation for you. I have my map still, and I've often contemplated going down to Far Island and digging, but it wouldn't have been fair, for the treasure was really yours, after all."

"Well, you are going now, and on the tenth day of June, that's next Friday, for that's what I came home for, and I had to spoil the plans and temper of a manager and all his company to do it."

"Nonsense, there are too many mosquitoes on Far Island and I mind them more than I used to. Besides there are no good boats like the *Jolly Roger* nowadays."

"We'll go if I have to build another *Jolly Roger*. You can't make me believe you are afraid of mosquitoes. I know too well the mettle of your pasture. Please do, Margie, please." He used his old insidious coaxing tone.

"Douglass, you have made me do dreadful things enough by using that tone of voice to me. I believe you used to hypnotize me. Will you never, never grow up?"

"Never so long as there are pirate's treasures to dig for and you will play with me, Margie. Oh, I wish I had some of the cake that Alice ate in Wonderland and could make you a little girl again."

157

That night, after the household was asleep, Douglass went out for a walk about the old town, treading the ways he had trod when he was a founder of cities and a leader of hosts. But he saw few of the old landmarks, for the blaze of Etruscan gold was in his eyes, and he felt as a man might feel who in some sleepy humdrum Italian village had unearthed a new marble goddess, as beautiful as she of Milo; and he felt as a boy might feel who had lost all his favorite marbles and his best pea shooter and the dog that slept with him, and had found them all again. He tried to follow, step by step, the wonderful friendship of his childhood.

A child's normal attitude toward the world is that of the artist, pure and simple. The rest of us have to do with the solids of this world, whereas only their form and color exist for the painter. So, in every wood and street and building there are things, not seen of older people at all, which make up their whole desirableness or objectionableness to children. There are maps and pictures formed by cracks in the walls of bare and unsightly sleeping chambers which make them beautiful; smooth places on the lawn where the grass is greener than anywhere else and which are good to sit upon; trees which are valuable by reason of the peculiar way in which the branches grow, and certain spots under the scrub willows along the creek which are in a manner sacred, like the sacrificial groves of the Druids, so that a boy is almost afraid to walk there. Then there are certain carpets which are more beautiful than others, because with a very little help from the imagination they become the rose garden of the Thousand and One Nights; and certain couches which are peculiarly adapted for playing Sindbad in his days of ease, after the toilsome voyages were over. A child's standard of value is so entirely his own, and his peculiar part and possessions in the material objects around him are so different from those of his elders, that it may be said his rights are granted by a different lease. To these two children the entire external world, like the people who dwelt in it, had been valued solely for what they suggested to the imagination, and people and places alike were merely stage properties, contributing more or less to the intensity of their inner life.

II

"Green leaves a-floating
Castles of the foam,
Boats of mine a-boating
When will all come home?"

sang Douglass as they pulled from the mill wharf out into the rapid current of the river, which that morning seemed the most beautiful and noble of rivers, an enchanted river flowing peacefully out of Arcady with the Happy Isles somewhere in the distance. The ripples were touched with silver and the sky was as blue as though it had just been made today; the cow bells sounded faintly from the meadows along the shore like the bells of fairy cities ringing on the day the prince errant brought home his bride; the meadows that sloped to the water's edge were the greenest in all the world because they were the meadows of the long ago; and the flowers that grew there were the freshest and sweetest of growing things because once, long ago in the golden age, two children had gathered other flowers like them, and the beauties of vanished summers were everywhere. Douglass sat in the end of the boat, his back to the sun and his straw hat tilted back on his head, pulling slowly and feeling that the day was fine rather than seeing it; for his eyes were fixed upon his helmsman in the other end of the boat, who sat with her hat in her lap, shading her face with a white parasol, and her wonderful hair piled high on her head like a helmet of gleaming bronze.

Of all the possessions of their childhood's Wonderland, Far Island had been dearest; it was graven on their hearts as Calais was upon Mary Tudor's. Long before they had set foot upon it the island was the goal of their loftiest ambitions and most delightful imaginings. They had wondered what trees grew there and what delightful spots were hidden away under the matted grapevines. They had even decided that a race of kindly dwarfs must inhabit it and had built up a civilization and historic annals for these imaginary inhabitants, surrounding the sand bar with all the mystery and enchantment which was attributed to certain islands of the sea by the mariners of

Greece. Douglass and Margie had sometimes found it expedient to admit other children into their world, but for the most part these were but hewers of wood and drawers of water, who helped to shift the scenery and construct the balcony and place the king's throne, and were no more in the atmosphere of the play than were the supers who watched Mr. Keane's famous duel with Richmond. Indeed Douglass frequently selected the younger and more passive boys for his vassals on the principle that they did as they were bid and made no trouble. But there is something of the explorer in the least imaginative of boys, and when Douglass came to the building of his famous boat, the *Jolly Roger*, he found willing hands to help him. Indeed the sawing and hammering, the shavings and cut fingers and blood blisters fell chiefly to the lot of dazzled lads who claimed no part in the craft, and who gladly trotted and sweated for their board and keep in this fascinating play world which was so much more exhilarating than any they could make for themselves.

"Think of it, Margie, we are really going back to the island after so many years, just you and I, the captain and his mate. Where are the other gallant lads that sailed with us then?"

"Where are the snows of yester' year?" sighed Margie softly. "It is very sad to grow up."

"Sad for them, yes. But we have never grown up, you know, we have only grown more considerate of our complexions," nodding at the parasol. "What a little mass of freckles you used to be, but

I liked you freckled, too. Let me see: old Temp is commanding a regiment in the Philippines, and Bake has a cattle ranch in Wyoming, Mac is a government clerk in Washington, Jim keeps his father's hardware store, poor Ned and Shorty went down in a catboat on the Hudson while they were at college (I went out to hunt for the bodies, you know), and old Rhine is selling sewing machines; he never did get away at all, did he?

"No, not for any length of time. You know it used to frighten Rhine to go to the next town to see a circus. He went to Arizona once for his lungs, but his family never could tell where he was for he headed all his letters 'Empire City, Nebraska,' from habit."

"Oh, that's delightful, Margie, you must let me use that. Rhine would carry Empire City through Europe with him and never know he was out of it. Have I told you about Pagie? Well, you know Pagie is travelling for a New York tailoring house and I let his people make some clothes for me that I had to give to Flashingham's valet. When he first came to town he tried to be gay, with his fond mother's prayers still about him, a visible nimbus, and the Sunday school boy written all over his open countenance and downy lip and large, white butter teeth. But I know, at heart, he still detested naughty words and whiskey made him sick. One day I was standing at the Hoffman House bar with some fellows, when a slender youth, who looked like a nice girl masquerading as a rake, stepped up and ordered a claret and seltzer. The whine was unmistakable. I turned and said, even before I had looked at him squarely, 'Oh, Pagie! if your mother saw you here!' "

"Poor Pagie! I'll warrant he would rather have had bread and sugar. Do you remember how, at the Sunday school concerts on Children's Day, you and Pagie and Shorty and Temp used to stand in a row behind the flower-wreathed pulpit rail, all in your new round-about suits with large silk bows tied under your collars, your hands behind you, and assure us with sonorous voices that you would come rejoicing bringing in the sheaves? Somehow, even then, I never doubted that you would do it."

The keel grated on the sand and Douglass sprang ashore and gave her his hand.

"Descend, O Miranda, upon your island! Do you know, Margie, it makes me seem fifteen again to feel this sand crunching under my feet. I wonder if I ever again shall feel such a thrill of triumph as I felt when I first leaped upon this sand bar? None of my first nights have given me anything like it. Do you remember *really*, and did you feel the same?"

"Of course I remember, and I knew that you were playing a double rôle that day, and that you were really the trail-breaker and world-finder inside of the pirate all the while. Here are the same ripple marks on the Silvery Beaches, and here is the great arched tree, let's run for it." She started fleetly across the glittering sand and Douglass fell behind to watch with immoderate joy that splendid, generous body that governed itself so well in the open air. There was a wholesomeness of the sun and soil in her that was utterly lacking in the women among whom he had lived for so long. She had preserved that strength of arm and freedom of limb that had made her so fine a playfellow, and which modern modes of life have nigh robbed the world of altogether. Surely, he thought, it was like that that Diana's women sped after the stag down the slopes of Ida, with shouting and bright spear. She caught an overhanging branch and swung herself upon the embankment and, leaning against the trunk of a tree, awaited him flushed and panting, her bosom rising and falling with her quick drawn breaths.

"Why did you close the tree behind you, Margie? I have always wanted to see just how Dryads keep house," he exclaimed, brushing away a dried leaf that had fallen on her shoulder.

"Don't strain your inventive powers to make compliments, Douglass; this is your vacation and you are to rest your imagination. See, the willows have scarcely grown at all. I'm sure we shall hear Pagie whimpering over there on the Uttermost Desert where we marooned him, or singing hymns to keep up his courage. Now for the Huge Fallen Tree. Do you suppose the floods have moved it?"

They struck through the dense willow thicket, matted with fragrant wild grapevines which Douglass beat down with his spade, and came upon the great white log, the bleached skeleton of a tree, and found the cross hacked upon it, the rough gashes of the hatchet now worn smooth by the wind and rain and the seething of spring freshets. Near the cross were cut the initials of the entire pirate crew; some of them were cut on gravestones now. The scrub willows had grown over the spot where they had decided the treasure must lie, and together they set to work to break them away. Douglass paused more than once to watch the strong young creature beside him, outlined against the tender green foliage, reaching high and low and snapping the withes where they were weakest. He was still wondering whether it was not all a dream picture, and was half afraid that his man would call him to tell him that some piqued and faded woman was awaiting him at the theatre to quarrel about her part.

"Still averse to manual labor, Douglass?" she laughed as she turned to bend a tall sapling. "The most remarkable thing about your enthusiasm was that you had only to sing of the glories of toil to make other people do all the work for you."

"No, Margie, I was thinking very hard indeed —about the Thracian women when they broke the boughs wherewith they flayed unhappy Orpheus."

"Now, Douglass, you'll spoil the play. A sentimental pirate is impossible. Pagie was a sentimental pirate and that was what spoiled him. A little more of this and I will maroon you upon the Uttermost Desert."

Douglass laughed and settled himself back among the green boughs and gazed at her with the abandoned admiration of an artist contemplating a masterpiece.

When they came to the digging of the treasure a little exertion was enough to unearth what had seemed hidden so fabulously deep in olden time. The chest was rotten and fell apart as the spade struck it, but the glass jar was intact, covered with sand and slime. Douglass spread his handkerchief upon the sand and weighted the corners down with pebbles and upon it poured the treasure of Far Island. There was the manuscript written in blood, a confession of fantastic crimes, and the Spaniard's heart in a bottle of alcohol, and Temp's Confederate bank notes, damp and grewsome to the touch, and Pagie's rare tobacco tags, their brilliant colors faded entirely away, and poor Shorty's bars of tinfoil, dull and eaten with rust.

"And, Douglass," cried Margie, "there is your father's silver ring that was made from a nugget; he whipped you for burying it. You remember it was given to a Christian knight by an English queen, and when he was slain before Jerusalem a Saracen took it and we killed the Saracen in the desert and cut off his finger to get the ring. It is strange how those wild imaginings of ours seem, in retrospect, realities, things that I actually lived through. I suppose that in cold fact my life was a good deal like that of other little girls who grow up in a village; but whenever I look back on it, it is all exultation and romance—sea fights and splendid galleys and Roman triumphs and brilliant caravans winding through the desert."

"To people who live by imagination at all, that is the only life that goes deep enough to leave memories. We were artists in those days, creating for the day only; making epics sung once and then forgotten, building empires that set with the sun. Nobody worked for money then, and nobody worked for fame, but only for the joy of the doing. Keats said the same thing more elegantly in his May Day Ode, and we were not so unlike those Hellenic poets who were content to sing to the shepherds and forget and be forgotten, 'rich in the simple worship of a day.'"

"Why, Douglass," she cried as she bent her face down to the little glass jar, "it was really our childhood that we buried here, never guessing what a precious thing we were putting under the ground. That was the real treasure of Far Island, and we might dig up the whole island for it but all the king's horses and all the king's men could not bring it back to us. That voyage we made to bury our trinkets, just before you went away to school, seems like unconscious symbolism, and somehow it stands out from all the other good times we knew then as the happiest of all." She looked off where the setting sun hung low above the water.

"Shall I tell you why, Margie? That was the end of our childhood, and there the golden days died in a blaze of glory, passed in music out of sight. That night, after our boat had drifted away from us, when we had to wade down the river hand in hand, we two, and the noises and the coldness of the water frightened us, and there were quicksands and sharp rocks and deep holes to shun, and terrible things lurking in the woods on the shore, you cried in a different way from the way you sometimes cried when you hurt yourself, and I found that I loved you afraid better than I had ever loved you fearless, and in that moment we grew up, and shut the gates of Eden behind us, and our empire was at an end."

"And now we are only kings in exile," sighed Margie, softly, "who wander back to look down from the mountain tops upon the happy land we used to rule."

Douglass took her hand gently; "If there is to be any Eden on earth again for us, dear, we must make it with our two hearts."

There was a sudden brightness of tears in her eyes, and she drew away from him. "Ah, Douglass, you are determined to spoil it all. It is you who have grown up and taken on the ways of the world. The play is at an end for me." She tried to rise, but he held her firmly.

"From the moment I looked into your eyes in the vestibule that night we have been parts of the same dream again. Why, Margie, we have more romance behind us than most men and women ever live."

Margie's face grew whiter, but she pushed his hand away and the look in her eyes grew harder. "This is only a new play, Douglass, and you will weary of it tomorrow. I am not so good at playing as I used to be. I am no longer content with the simple worship of a day."

In her touch, in her white face, he divined the greatness of what she had to give. He bit his lip and answered, "I think you owe me more confidence than that, if only for the sake of those days when we trusted each other entirely."

She turned with a quick flash of remorseful tenderness, as she used to do when she hurt him at play. "I only want to keep you from hurting us both, Douglass. We neither of us could go on feeling like this. It's only the dregs of the old enchantment. Things have always come easily to you, I know, for at your birth nature and fortune joined to make you great. But they do not come so to me; I should wake and weep."

"Then weep, my princess, for I will wake you now!"

The fire and fancy that had so bewitched her girlhood that no other man had been able to dim the memory of it came furiously back upon her, with arms that were new and strange and strong, and with tenderness stranger still in this wild fellow of dreams and jests; and all her vows never to grace another of his Roman triumphs were forgotten.

"You are right, Margie; the pirate play is ended and the time has come to divide the prizes, and I choose what I chose fifteen years ago. Out of the spoils of a lifetime of crime and bloodshed I claimed only the captive princess, and I claim her still. I have sought the world over for her,

only to find her at last in the land of lost content."

Margie lifted her face from his shoulder, and, after the manner of women of her kind, she played her last card rhapsodically. "And she, O Douglass! the years she has waited have been longer than the waiting of Penelope, and she has woven a thousand webs of dreams by night and torn them asunder by day, and looked out across the Salt Marshes for the night train, and still you did not come. I was only your pensioner like Shorty and Temp and the rest, and I could not play anything alone. You took my world with you when you went and left me only a village of mud huts and my loneliness."

As her eyes and then her lips met his in the dying light, he knew that she had caught the spirit of the play, and that she would ford the river by night with him again and never be afraid.

The locust chirped in the thicket; the setting sun threw a track of flame across the water; the willows burned with fire and were not consumed; a glory was upon the sand and the river and upon the Silvery Beaches; and these two looked about over God's world and saw that it was good. In the western sky the palaces of crystal and gold were quenched in night, like the cities of old empires; and out of the east rose the same moon that has glorified all the romances of the world—that lighted Paris over the blue Ægean and the feet of young Montague to the Capulets' orchard. The dinner hour in Empire City was long past, but the two upon the island wist naught of these things, for they had become as the gods, who dwell in their golden houses, recking little of the woes and labors of mortals, neither heeding any fall of rain or snow.

The Brushwood Boy

Rudyard Kipling

Girls and boys, come out to play:
The moon is shining as bright as day!
Leave your supper and leave your sleep,
And come with your playfellows out in
    the street!
Up the ladder and down the wall—

A child of three sat up in his crib and screamed at the top of his voice, his fists clinched and his eyes full of terror. At first no one heard, for his nursery lay in the west wing, and the nurse was talking to a gardener among the laurels. Then the housekeeper passed that way, and hurried to soothe him. He was her special pet, and she disapproved of the nurse.

'What was it, then? What was it, then? There's nothing to frighten him, Georgie dear.'

'It was—it was a policeman! He was on the Down—I saw him! He came in. Jane *said* he would.'

'Policemen don't come into houses, dearie. Turn over, and take my hand.'

'I saw him—on the Down. He came here. Where is your hand, Harper?'

The housekeeper waited till the sobs changed

to the regular breathing of sleep before she stole out.

'Jane, what nonsense have you been telling Master Georgie about policemen?'

'I haven't told him anything.'

'You have. He's been dreaming about them.'

'We met Tisdall on Dowhead when we were in the donkey-cart this morning. P'raps that's what put it into his head.'

'Oh! Now you aren't going to frighten the child into fits with your silly tales, and the master know nothing about it. If ever I catch you again,' etc.

A child of six was telling himself stories as he lay in bed. It was a new power, and he kept it a secret. A month before it had occurred to him to carry on a nursery tale left unfinished by his mother, and he was delighted to find the tale as it came out of his own head just as surprising as though he were listening to it 'all new from the beginning.' There was a prince in that tale, and he killed dragons, but only for one night. Ever afterwards Georgie dubbed himself prince, pasha, giant-killer, and all the rest (you see, he could not tell any one, for fear of being laughed at), and his tales faded gradually into dreamland, where adventures were so many that he could not recall the half of them. They all began in the same way, or, as Georgie explained to the shadows of the night-light, there was 'the same starting-off place'—a pile of brushwood stacked somewhere near a beach; and round this pile Georgie found himself running races with little boys and girls. These ended, ships ran high up the dry land and opened into cardboard boxes; or gilt-and-green iron railings that surrounded beautiful gardens turned all soft, and could be walked through and overthrown so long as he remembered it was only a dream. He could never hold that knowledge more than a few seconds 'ere things became real, and instead of pushing down houses full of grown-up people (a just revenge) he sat miserably upon gigantic door-steps trying to sing the multiplication-table up to four times six.

The princess of his tales was a person of wonderful beauty (she came from the old illustrated edition of Grimm, now out of print), and as she always applauded Georgie's valour among the dragons and buffaloes, he gave her the two finest names he had ever heard in his life—Annie and Louise, pronounced 'Annie*an*louise.' When the dreams swamped the stories, she would change into one of the little girls round the brushwood-pile, still keeping her title and crown. She saw Georgie drown once in a dream-sea by the beach (it was the day after he had been taken to bathe in a real sea by his nurse); and he said as he sank 'Poor Annie*an*louise! She'll be sorry for me now!' But 'Annie*an*louise,' walking slowly on the beach, called, ' "Ha! ha!" said the duck, laughing,' which to a waking mind might not seem to bear on the situation. It consoled Georgie at once, and must have been some kind of spell, for it raised the bottom of the deep, and he waded out with a twelve-inch flower-pot on each foot. As he was strictly forbidden to meddle with flower-pots in real life, he felt triumphantly wicked.

The movement of the grown-ups, whom Georgie tolerated, but did not pretend to understand, removed his world, when he was seven years old, to a place called 'Oxford-on-a-visit.' Here were huge buildings surrounded by vast prairies, with streets of infinite length, and, above all, something called the 'buttery,' which Georgie was dying to see, because he knew it must be greasy, and therefore delightful. He perceived how correct were his judgments when his nurse led him through a stone arch into the presence of an enormously fat man, who asked him if he would like some bread and cheese. Georgie was used to eating all round the clock, so he took what 'buttery' gave him, and would have taken some brown liquid called 'auditale,' but that his nurse led him away to an afternoon performance of a thing called 'Pepper's Ghost.' This was intensely thrilling. People's heads came off and flew all over the stage, and skeletons danced bone by bone, while Mr. Pepper himself, beyond question a man of the worst, waved his arms and flapped a long gown, and in a deep bass voice (Georgie had never heard a man sing before) told of his sorrows unspeakable. Some grown-up or other tried to explain that the illusion was made with mirrors, and that there was no need to be frightened. Georgie did not know what illusions were, but he did know that a mirror was the looking-glass with the ivory handle on his mother's dressing-table. Therefore the 'grown-ups,' and Georgie cast about for amusement between scenes. Next to him sat a little girl dressed all in black, her hair combed off her forehead exactly like the girl in the book called 'Alice in Wonderland,' which had been given him on his last birthday. The little girl looked at Georgie and Georgie looked at her. There seemed to be no need of any further introduction.

'I've got a cut on my thumb,' said he. It was the first work of his first real knife, a savage triangular hack, and he esteemed it a most valuable possession.

'I'm tho thorry!' she lisped. 'Let me look—pleathe.'

'There's a di-ack-lum plaster on, but it's all raw under,' Georgie answered, complying.

'Dothent it hurt?'—her grey eyes were full of pity and interest.

'Awf'ly. Perhaps it will give me lockjaw.'

'It lookth very horrid. I'm *tho* thorry!' She put a forefinger to his hand, and held her head side-wise for a better view.

Here the nurse turned and shook him severely. 'You mustn't talk to strange little girls, Master Georgie.'

'She isn't strange. She's very nice. I like her, an' I've showed her my new cut.'

'The idea! You change places with me.'

She moved him over, and shut out the little girl from his view, while the grown-up behind renewed the futile explanations.

'I am *not* afraid, truly,' said the boy, wriggling in despair; 'but why don't you go to sleep in the afternoons, same as Provostoforiel?'

Georgie had been introduced to a grown-up of that name, who slept in his presence without apology. Georgie understood that he was the most important grown-up in Oxford; hence he strove to gild his rebuke with flatteries. This grown-up did not seem to like it, but he collapsed, and Georgie lay back in his seat, silent and enraptured. Mr. Pepper was singing again, and the deep, ringing voice, the red fire, and the misty, waving gown all seemed to be mixed up with the little girl who had been so kind about his cut. When the performance was ended she nodded to Georgie and Georgie nodded in return. He spoke no more than was necessary till bedtime, but meditated on new colours, and sounds, and lights, and music, and things as far as he understood them; the deep-mouthed agony of Mr. Pepper mingling with the little girl's lisp. That night he made a new tale, from which he shamelessly removed the Rapunzel-Rapunzel-let-down-your-hair princess, gold crown, Grimm edition, and all, and put a new Annie*an*-louise in her place. So it was perfectly right and natural that when he came to the brushwood-pile he should find her waiting for him, her hair combed off her forehead, more like Alice in Wonderland than ever, and the races and adventures began.

Ten years at an English public school do not encourage dreaming. Georgie won his growth and chest measurement, and a few other things which did not appear in the bills, under a system of cricket, football, and paper-chases, from four to five days a week, which provided for three lawful cuts of a ground-ash if any boy absented himself from these entertainments. He became a rumple-collared, dusty-hatted fag of the Lower Third, and a light half-back at Little Side football; was pushed and prodded through the slack backwaters of the Lower Fourth, where the raffle of a school generally accumulates; won his Second Fifteen cap at football, enjoyed the dignity of a study with two companions in it, and began to look forward to office as a sub-prefect. At last he blossomed into full glory as head of the school, ex-officio captain of the games; head of his house, where he and his lieutenants preserved discipline and decency among seventy boys from twelve to seventeen; general arbiter in the quarrels that spring up among the touchy Sixth—and intimate friend and ally of the Head himself. When he stepped forth in the black jersey, white knickers, and black stockings of the First Fifteen, the new match-ball under his arm, and his old and frayed cap at the back of his head, the small fry of the lower forms stood apart and worshipped, and the 'new caps' of the team talked to him ostentatiously, that the world might see. And so, in summer, when he came back to the pavilion after a slow but eminently safe game, it mattered not whether he had made nothing, or, as once happened, a hundred

178

and three, the school shouted just the same, and womenfolk who had come to look at the match looked at Cottar—Cottar *major;* 'that's Cottar!' Above all, he was responsible for that thing called the tone of the school, and few realise with what passionate devotion a certain type of boy throws himself into his work. Home was a far-away country, full of ponies and fishing, and shooting, and men-visitors who interfered with one's plans; but school was his real world, where things of vital importance happened and crises arose that must be dealt with promptly and quietly. Not for nothing was it written, 'Let the Consuls look to it that the Republic takes no harm,' and Georgie was glad to be back in authority when the holidays ended. Behind him, but not too near, was the wise and temperate Head, now suggesting the wisdom of the serpent, now counselling the mildness of the dove; leading him on to see, more by half-hints than by any direct word, how boys and men are all of a piece, and how he who can handle the one will assuredly in time control the other.

For the rest, the school was not encouraged to dwell on its emotions, but rather to keep in hard condition, to avoid false quantities, and to enter the army direct, without the help of the expensive London crammer, under whose roof young blood learns too much. Cottar *major* went the way of hundreds before him. The Head gave him six months' final polish, taught him what kind of answers best please a certain kind of examiners, and handed him over to the properly constituted authorities, who passed him into Sandhurst. Here he had sense enough to see that he was in the Lower Third once more, and behaved with respect towards his seniors, till they in turn respected him, and he was promoted to the rank of corporal, and sat in authority over mixed people with all the vices of men and boys combined. His reward was another string of athletic cups, a good-conduct sword, and, at last, Her Majesty's Commission as a subaltern in a first-class line regiment. He did not know that he bore with him from school and college a character worth much fine gold, but was pleased to find his mess so kindly. He had plenty of money of his own; his training had set the public-school mask upon his face, and had taught him how many were the 'things no fellow can do.' By virtue of the same training he kept his pores open and his mouth shut.

The regular working of the Empire shifted his world to India, where he tasted utter loneliness in subaltern's quarters—one room and one bullock-trunk—and, with his mess, learned the new life from the beginning. But there were horses in the land—ponies at reasonable price; there was polo for such as could afford it; there were the disreputable remnants of a pack of hounds, and Cottar worried his way along without too much despair. It dawned on him that a regiment in India was nearer the chance of active service than he had conceived, and that a man might as well study his profession. A Major of the new school backed this idea with enthusiasm, and he and Cottar accumulated a library of military works, and read and argued and disputed far into the nights. But the Adjutant said the old thing: 'Get to know your men, young 'un, and they'll follow you anywhere. That's all you want—know your men.' Cottar thought he knew them fairly well at cricket and the regimental sports, but he never realised the true inwardness of them till he was sent off with a detachment of twenty to sit down in a mud fort near a rushing river which was spanned by a bridge of boats. When the floods came they went forth and hunted strayed pontoons along the banks. Otherwise there was nothing to do, and the men got drunk, gambled and quarrelled. They were a sickly crew, for a junior subaltern is by custom saddled with the worst men. Cottar endured their rioting as long as he could, and then sent down-country for a dozen pairs of boxing-gloves.

'I wouldn't blame you for fightin',' said he, 'if you only knew how to use your hands; but you don't. Take these things and I'll show you.' The men appreciated his efforts. Now, instead of blaspheming and swearing at a comrade, and threatening to shoot him, they could take him apart and soothe themselves to exhaustion. As one explained whom Cottar found with a shut eye and a diamond-shaped mouth spitting blood through an embrasure: 'We tried it with the gloves, sir, for another twenty minutes, and *that* done us no good, sir. Then we took off the gloves and tried it that way for another twenty minutes, same as you showed us, sir, an' that done us a world o' good. 'Twasn't fightin', sir; there was a bet on.'

Cottar dared not laugh, but he invited his men to other sports, such as racing across country in shirt and trousers after a trail of torn paper, and to single-stick in the evenings, till the native population, who had a lust for sport in every form, wished to know whether the white men understood wrestling. They sent in an ambassador, who took the soldiers by the neck and threw them about the dust; and the entire command were all for this new game. They spent money on learning new falls and holds, which was better than buying other doubtful commodities; and the peasantry grinned five deep round the tournaments.

That detachment, who had gone up in bullock-carts, returned to headquarters at an average rate of thirty miles a day, fair heel-and-toe; no sick, no prisoners, and no court-martials pending. They scattered themselves among their friends, singing the praises of their Lieutenant and looking for causes of offence.

'How did you do it, young 'un?' the Adjutant asked.

'Oh, I sweated the beef off 'em, and then I sweated some muscle on to 'em. It was rather a lark.'

'If that's your way of lookin' at it, we can give you all the larks you want. Young Davies isn't feelin' quite fit, and he's next for detachment duty. Care to go for him?'

182

'Sure he wouldn't mind? I don't want to shove myself forward, you know.'

'You needn't bother on Davies's account. We'll give you the sweepin's of the corps, and you can see what you can make of 'em.'

'All right,' said Cottar. 'It's better fun than loafin' about cantonments.'

'Rummy thing,' said the Adjutant, after Cottar had returned to his wilderness with twenty other devils worse than the first. 'If Cottar only knew it, half the women in the station would give their eyes—confound 'em!—to have the young 'un in tow.'

'That accounts for Mrs. Elery sayin' I was workin' my nice new boy too hard,' said a Wing-Commander.

'Oh, yes; and "Why doesn't he come to the band-stand in the evenings?" and "Can't I get him to make up a four at tennis with the Hammon girls?"' the Adjutant snorted. 'Look at young Davies makin' an ass of himself over mutton-dressed-as-lamb old enough to be his mother!'

'No one can accuse young Cottar of runnin' after women, white or black,' the Major replied thoughtfully. 'But, then, that's the kind that generally goes the worst mucker in the end.'

'Not Cottar. I've only run across one of his muster before—a fellow called Ingles, in South Africa. He was just the same hard-trained, athletic-sports build of animal. Always kept himself in the pink of condition. Didn't do him much good, though. Shot at Wesselstroom the week before Majuba. Wonder how the young 'un will lick his detachment into shape.'

Cottar turned up six weeks later, on foot, with his pupils. He never told his experiences, but the men spoke enthusiastically, and fragments of it leaked back to the Colonel through sergeants, batmen, and the like.

There was great jealousy between the first and second detachments, but the men united in adoring Cottar, and their way of showing it was by sparing him all the trouble that men know how to make for an unloved officer. He sought popularity as little as he had sought it at school, and therefore it came to him. He favoured no one— not even when the company sloven pulled the company cricket-match out of the fire with an unexpected forty-three at the last moment. There was very little getting round him, for he seemed to know by instinct exactly when and where to head off a malingerer; but he did not forget that the difference between a dazed and sulky junior of the upper school and a bewildered, brow-beaten lump of a private fresh from the depôt was very small indeed. The sergeants, seeing these things, told him secrets generally hid from young officers. His words were quoted as barrack authority on bets in canteen and at tea; and the veriest shrew of the corps, bursting with charges against other women who had used the cooking-ranges out of turn, forbore to speak when Cottar, as the regulations ordained, asked of a morning if there were 'any complaints.'

'I'm full o' complaints,' said Mrs. Corporal Morrison, 'an' I'd kill O'Halloran's fat cow of a wife any day, but ye know how it is. 'E puts 'is head just inside the door, an' looks down 'is blessed nose so bashful, an' he whispers, "Any complaints?" Ye can't complain after that. *I* want to kiss him. Some day I think I will. Heigh-ho! She'll be a lucky woman that gets Young Innocence. See 'im now, girls. Do yer blame him?'

Cottar was cantering across to polo, and he looked a very satisfactory figure of a man as he gave easily to the first excited bucks of his pony, and slipped over a low mud wall to the practice-ground. There were more than Mrs. Corporal Morrison who felt as she did. But Cottar was busy for eleven hours of the day. He did not care to have his tennis spoiled by petticoats in the court; and after one long afternoon at a garden-party, he explained to his Major that this sort of thing was 'futile piffle,' and the Major laughed. Theirs was not a married mess, except for the Colonel's wife, and Cottar stood in awe of the good lady. She said 'my regiment,' and the world knows what that means. None the less, when they wanted her to give away the prizes after a shooting-match, and she refused because one of the prize-winners was married to a girl who had made a jest of her behind her broad back, the mess ordered Cottar to 'tackle her,' in his best calling-kit. This he did, simply and laboriously, and she gave way altogether.

'She only wanted to know the facts of the case,' he explained. 'I just told her, and she saw at once.'

'Ye-es,' said the Adjutant. 'I expect that's what she did. 'Comin' to the Fusiliers' dance to-night, Galahad?'

'No, thanks. I've got a fight on with the Major.' The virtuous apprentice sat up till midnight in the Major's quarters, with a stop-watch and a pair of compasses, shifting little painted lead blocks about a four-inch map.

Then he turned in and slept the sleep of innocence, which is full of healthy dreams. One peculiarity of his dreams he noticed at the beginning of his second hot weather. Two or three times a month they duplicated or ran in series. He would find himself sliding into dreamland by the same road—a road that ran along a beach near a pile of brushwood. To the right lay the sea, sometimes at full tide, sometimes withdrawn to the very horizon; but he knew it for the same sea. By that road he would travel over a swell of rising ground covered with short, withered grass, into valleys of wonder and unreason. Beyond the ridge, which was crowned with some sort of street-lamp, anything was possible; but up to the lamp it seemed to him that he knew the road as well as he knew the parade-ground. He learned to look forward to the place; for, once there, he was sure of a good night's rest, and Indian hot weather can be rather trying. First, shadowy under closing eyelids, would come the outline of the brushwood-pile; next the white sand of the beach road, almost overhanging the black, changeful sea; then the turn inland and uphill to the single light. When he was unrestful for any reason, he would tell himself how he was sure to get there—sure to get there—if he shut his eyes and surrendered to the drift of things. But one night after a foolishly hard hour's polo (the thermometer was 94 ° in his quarters at ten o'clock), sleep stood away from him altogether, though he did his best to find the well-known road, the point where true sleep began. At last he saw the brushwood-pile, and hurried along to the ridge, for behind him he felt was the wide-awake, sultry world. He reached the lamp in safety, tingling with drowsiness, when a policeman—a common country policeman— sprang up before him and touched him on the shoulder ere he could dive into the dim valley below. He was filled with terror,—the hopeless terror of dreams,—for the policeman said, in the awful, distinct voice of the dream-people, 'I am Policeman Day coming back from the City of Sleep. You come with me.' Georgie knew it was true—that just beyond him in the valley lay the lights of the City of Sleep, where he would have been sheltered, and that this Policeman Thing had full power and authority to head him back to miserable wakefulness. He found himself looking at the moonlight on the wall, dripping with fright; and he never overcame that horror, though he met the policeman several times that hot weather, and his coming was the forerunner of a bad night.

But other dreams—perfectly absurd ones— filled him with an incommunicable delight. All those that he remembered began by the brushwood-pile. For instance, he found a small clock-work steamer (he had noticed it many nights before) lying by the sea-road, and stepped into it, whereupon it moved with surpassing swiftness over an absolutely level sea. This was glorious, for he felt he was exploring great matters; and it stopped by a lily carved in stone, which, most naturally, floated on the water. Seeing the lily was labelled 'Hong-Kong,' Georgie said: 'Of course. This is precisely what I expected Hong-Kong would be like. How magnificent!' Thousands of miles farther on it halted at yet another stone lily, labelled 'Java'; and this again delighted him hugely, because he knew that now he was at the world's end. But the little boat ran on and on till it stopped in a deep fresh-water dock, the sides of which were carven marble, green with moss. Lily-pads lay on the water, and reeds arched above. Some one moved among the reeds—some one whom Georgie knew he had travelled to this world's end to reach. Therefore everything was entirely well with him. He was unspeakably happy, and vaulted over the ship's side to find this person. When his feet touched that still water, it changed, with the rustle of unrolling maps, to nothing less than a sixth quarter of the globe, beyond the most remote imaginings of man—a place where islands were coloured yellow and blue, their lettering strung across their faces. They gave on unknown seas, and Georgie's urgent desire was to return swiftly across this floating atlas to known bearings. He told himself repeatedly that it was no good to hurry; but still he hurried desperately, and the islands slipped and slid under his feet, the straits yawned and widened, till he found himself utterly lost in the world's fourth dimension, with no hope of return. Yet only a little distance away he could see the old world with the rivers and mountain-chains marked according to the Sandhurst rules of map-making. Then that person for whom he had come to the Lily Lock (that was its name) ran up across unexplored territories, and showed him a way. They fled hand in hand till they reached a road that spanned ravines, and ran along the edge of precipices, and was tunnelled through mountains. 'This goes to our brushwood-pile,' said his companion; and all his trouble was at an end. He took a pony, because he understood that this was the Thirty-Mile-Ride, and he must ride swiftly; and raced through the clattering tunnels and round the curves, always downhill, till he heard the sea to his left, and saw it raging under a full moon against sandy cliffs. It was heavy going, but he recognised the nature of the country, the dark purple downs inland, and the bents that whistled in the wind. The road was eaten away in places, and the sea lashed at him— black, foamless tongues of smooth and glossy rollers; but he was sure that there was less danger from the sea than from 'Them,' whoever 'They' were, inland to his right. He knew, too, that he would be safe if he could reach the down with the lamp on it. This came as he expected: he saw the one light a mile ahead along the beach, dismounted, turned to the right, walked quietly over to the brushwood-pile, found the little steamer had returned to the beach whence he had un-moored it, and—must have fallen asleep, for he could remember no more. 'I'm gettin' the hang of the geography of that place,' he said to himself, as he shaved next morning. 'I must have made some sort of circle. Let's see. The Thirty-Mile-Ride (now how the deuce did I know it was called the Thirty-Mile-Ride?) joins the sea-road beyond the first down where the lamp is. And that atlas-country lies at the back of the Thirty-Mile-Ride, somewhere out to the right beyond the hills and tunnels. Rummy thing, dreams. 'Wonder what makes mine fit into each other so?'

He continued on his solid way through the re-curring duties of the seasons. The regiment was shifted to another station, and he enjoyed road-marching for two months, with a good deal of mixed shooting thrown in; and when they reached their new cantonments he became a member of the local Tent Club, and chased the mighty boar on horseback with a short stabbing-spear. There he met the *mahseer* of the Poonch, beside whom the tarpon is as a herring, and he who lands him can say that he is a fisherman. This was as new and as fascinating as the big game shooting that fell to his portion, when he had himself photo-graphed for the mother's benefit, sitting on the flank of his first tiger.

Then the Adjutant was promoted, and Cottar rejoiced with him, for he admired the Adjutant greatly, and marvelled who might be big enough to fill his place; so that he nearly collapsed when the mantle fell on his own shoulders, and the Colonel said a few sweet things that made him blush. An Adjutant's position does not differ materially from that of head of the school, and Cottar stood in the same relation to the Colonel as he had to his old Head in England. Only, tempers wear out in hot weather, and things were said and done that tried him sorely, and he made glorious blunders, from which the regimental sergeant-major pulled him with a loyal soul and a shut mouth. Slovens and incompetents raged against him; the weak-minded strove to lure him from the ways of justice; the small-minded—yea, men who Cottar believed would never do 'things no fellow can do'—imputed motives mean and circuitous to actions that he had not spent a thought upon; and he tasted injustice, and it made him very sick. But his consolation came on parade, when he looked down the full companies, and reflected how few were in hospital or cells, and wondered when the time would come to try the machine of his love and labour. But they needed and expected the whole of a man's working day, and maybe three or four hours of the night. Curiously enough, he never dreamed about the regiment as he was popularly supposed to. The mind, set free from the day's doings, generally ceased working altogether, or, if it moved at all, carried him along the old beach road to the downs, the lamp-post, and, once in a while, to terrible Policeman Day. The second time

191

that he returned to the world's lost continent (this was a dream that repeated itself again and again, with variations, on the same ground) he knew that if he only sat still the person from the Lily Lock would help him; and he was not disappointed. Sometimes he was trapped in mines of vast depth hollowed out of the heart of the world, where men in torment chanted echoing songs; and he heard this person coming along through the galleries, and everything was made safe and delightful. They met again in low-roofed Indian railway carriages that halted in a garden surrounded by gilt-and-green railings, where a mob of stony white people, all unfriendly, sat at breakfast-tables covered with roses, and separated Georgie from his companion, while underground voices sang deep-voiced songs. Georgie was filled with enormous despair till they two met again. They foregathered in the middle of an endless hot tropic night and crept into a huge house that stood, he knew, somewhere north of the railway station where the people ate among the roses. It was surrounded with gardens, all moist and dripping; and in one room, reached through leagues of whitewashed passages, a Sick Thing lay in bed. Now the least noise, Georgie knew, would unchain some waiting horror, and his companion knew it too; but when their eyes met across the bed, Georgie was disgusted to see that she was a child—a little girl in strapped shoes, with her black hair combed back from her forehead.

'What disgraceful folly!' he thought. 'Now she could do nothing whatever if Its head came off.'

Then the thing coughed, and the ceiling shattered down in plaster on the mosquito-netting, and 'They' rushed in from all quarters. He dragged the child through the stifling garden, voices chanting behind them, and they rode the Thirty-Mile-Ride under whip and spur along the sandy beach by the booming sea, till they came to the downs, the lamp-post, the brushwood-pile, which was safety. Very often dreams would break up about them in this fashion, and they would be separated, to endure awful adventures alone. But the most amusing times were when he and she had a clear understanding that it was all make-believe, and walked through mile-wide roaring rivers without even taking off their shoes, or set light to populous cities to see how they would burn, and were rude as any children to the vague shadows met in their rambles. Later in the night they were sure to suffer for this, either at the hands of the Railway People eating among the roses, or in the tropic uplands at the far end of the Thirty-Mile-Ride. Together, this did not much affright them; but often Georgie would hear her shrill cry of 'Boy! Boy!' half a world away, and hurry to her rescue before 'They' maltreated her.

He and she explored the dark purple downs as far inland from the brushwood-pile as they dared, but that was always a dangerous matter. The interior was filled with 'Them' and 'They' went about singing in the hollows, and Georgie and she felt safer on or near the seaboard. So thoroughly had he come to know the place of his dreams that even waking he accepted it as a real country, and made a rough sketch of it. He kept his own counsel, of course; but the permanence of the land puzzled him. His ordinary dreams were as formless and as fleeting as any healthy dreams could be, but once at the brushwood-pile he moved within known limits and could see where he was going. There were months at a time when nothing notable crossed his sleep. Then the dreams would come in a batch of five or six, and next morning the map that he kept in his writing-case would be written up to date, for Georgie was a most methodical person. There was, indeed, a danger—his seniors said so—of his developing into a regular 'Auntie Fuss' of an Adjutant, and when an officer once takes to old-maidism there is more hope for the virgin of seventy than for him.

But fate sent the change that was needed, in the shape of a little winter campaign on the border, which, after the manner of little campaigns, flashed out into a very ugly war; and Cottar's regiment was chosen among the first.

'Now,' said a Major, 'this'll shake the cobwebs out of us all—especially you, Galahad; and we can see what your hen-with-one-chick attitude has done for the regiment.'

Cottar nearly wept with joy as the campaign went forward. They were fit—physically fit beyond the other troops; they were good children in camp, wet or dry, fed or unfed; and they followed their officers with the quick suppleness and trained obedience of a first-class football fifteen. They were cut off from their apology for a base, and cheerfully cut their way back to it again; they crowned and cleaned out hills full of the enemy with the precision of well-broken dogs of chase; and in the hour of retreat, when, hampered with the sick and wounded of the column, they were persecuted down eleven miles of waterless valley, they, serving as rearguard, covered themselves with a great glory in the eyes of fellow-professionals. Any regiment can advance, but few know how to retreat with a sting in the tail. Then they turned to and made roads, most often under fire, and dismantled some inconvenient mud redoubts. They were the last corps to be withdrawn when the rubbish of the campaign was all swept up; and after a month in standing camp, which tries morals severely, they departed to their own place singing—

'E's goin' to do without 'em—
Don't want 'em any more;
'E's goin' to do without 'em,
As 'e's often done before,
'E's goin' to be a martyr
On a 'ighly novel plan,
An' all the boys and girls will say,
'Ow! what a nice young man—man—man!
Ow! what a nice young man!'

There came out a *Gazette*, in which Cottar found

that he had been behaving with 'courage and cool-ness and discretion' in all his capacities; that he had assisted the wounded under fire, and blown in a gate, also under fire. Net results, his captaincy and a brevet majority, coupled with the Distin-guished Service Order.

As to his wounded, he explained that they were both heavy men, whom he could lift more easily than any one else. 'Otherwise, of course, I should have sent out one of my chaps; and, of course, about that gate business, we were safe the minute we were well under the walls.' But this did not prevent his men from cheering him furiously whenever they saw him, or the mess from giving him a dinner on the eve of his departure to En-gland. (A year's leave was among the things he had 'snaffled out of the campaign,' to use his own words.) The doctor, who had taken quite as much as was good for him, quoted poetry about 'a good blade carving the casques of men,' and so on, and everybody told Cottar that he was an excellent person; but when he rose to make his maiden speech they shouted so that he was understood to say, 'It isn't any use tryin' to speak with you chaps rottin' me like this. Let's have some pool.'

It is not unpleasant to spend eight-and-twenty days in an easy-going steamer on warm waters, in the company of a woman who lets you see that you are head and shoulders superior to the rest of the world, even though that woman may be, and most often is, ten counted years your senior. P.

196

& O. boats are not lighted with the disgustful particularity of Atlantic liners. There is more phosphorescence at the bows, and greater silence and darkness by the hand-steering gear aft.

Awful things might have happened to Georgie, but for the little fact that he had never studied the first principles of the game he was expected to play. So when Mrs. Zuleika, at Aden, told him how motherly an interest she felt in his welfare, medals, brevet, and all, Georgie took her at the foot of the letter, and promptly talked of his own mother, three hundred miles nearer each day, of his home, and so forth, all the way up the Red Sea. It was much easier than he had supposed to converse with a woman for an hour at a time. Then Mrs. Zuleika, turning from parental affection, spoke of love in the abstract as a thing not unworthy of study, and in discreet twilights after dinner demanded confidences. Georgie would have been delighted to supply them, but he had none, and did not know it was his duty to manufacture them. Mrs. Zuleika expressed surprise and unbelief, and asked those questions which deep asks of deep. She learned all that was necessary to conviction, and, being very much a woman, resumed (Georgie never knew that she had abandoned) the motherly attitude.

'Do you know,' she said, somewhere in the Mediterranean, 'I think you're the very dearest boy I have ever met in my life, and I'd like you to remember me a little. You will when you are older, but I want you to remember me now. You'll make some girl very happy.'

'Oh! 'Hope so,' said Georgie, gravely; 'but there's heaps of time for marryin', an' all that sort of thing, ain't there?'

'That depends. Here are your bean-bags for the Ladies' Competition. I think I'm growing too old to care for these *tamashas*.'

They were getting up sports, and Georgie was on the committee. He never noticed how perfectly the bags were sewn, but another woman did, and smiled—once. He liked Mrs. Zuleika greatly. She was a bit old, of course, but uncommonly nice. There was no nonsense about her.

A few nights after they passed Gibraltar his dream returned to him. She who waited by the brushwood-pile was no longer a little girl, but a woman with black hair that grew into a 'widow's peak,' combed back from her forehead. He knew her for the child in black, the companion of the last six years, and, as it had been in the time of the meetings on the Lost Continent, he was filled with delight unspeakable. 'They,' for some dreamland reason, were friendly or had gone away that night, and the two flitted together over all their country, from the brushwood-pile up the Thirty-Mile-Ride, till they saw the House of the Sick Thing, a pin-point in the distance to the left; stamped through the Railway Waiting-room where the roses lay on the spread breakfast-tables; and returned, by the ford and the city they had once burned for sport, to the great swells of the downs under the lamp-post. Wherever they moved a strong singing followed them underground, but this night there was no panic. All the land was empty except for themselves, and at the last (they were sitting by the lamp-post hand in hand) she turned and kissed him. He woke with a start, staring at the waving curtain of the cabin door; he could almost have sworn that the kiss was real.

Next morning the ship was rolling in a Biscay sea, and people were not happy; but as Georgie came to breakfast, shaven, tubbed, and smelling of soap, several turned to look at him because of the light in his eyes and the splendour of his countenance.

'Well, you look beastly fit,' snapped a neighbour. 'Any one left you a legacy in the middle of the Bay?'

Georgie reached for the curry, with a seraphic grin. 'I suppose it's the gettin' so near home, and all that. I do feel rather festive this mornin'. 'Rolls a bit, doesn't she?'

Mrs. Zuleika stayed in her cabin till the end of the voyage, when she left without bidding him farewell, and wept passionately on the dockhead for pure joy of meeting her children, who, she had often said, were so like their father.

Georgie headed for his own county, wild with delight of first long furlough after the lean seasons. Nothing was changed in that orderly life, from the coachman who met him at the station to the white peacock that stormed at the carriage from the stone wall above the shaven lawns. The house took toll of him with due regard to precedence—first the mother; then the father; then the house-keeper, who wept and praised God; then the butler; and so on down to the under-keeper, who had been dog-boy in Georgie's youth, and called him 'Master Georgie,' and was reproved by the groom who had taught Georgie to ride.

'Not a thing changed,' he sighed contentedly, when the three of them sat down to dinner in the late sunlight, while the rabbits crept out upon the lawn below the cedars, and the big trout in the ponds by the home paddock rose for their evening meal.

'*Our* changes are all over, dear,' cooed the mother; 'and now I am getting used to your size and your tan (you're very brown, Georgie), I see you haven't changed in the least. You're exactly like the pater.'

The father beamed on this man after his own heart,—'Youngest Major in the army, and should have had the V. C., sir,'—and the butler listened with his professional mask off when Master Georgie spoke of war as it is waged to-day, and his father cross-questioned.

They went out on the terrace to smoke among the roses, and the shadow of the old house lay long across the wonderful English foliage, which is the only living green in the world.

'Perfect! By Jove, it's perfect!' Georgie was looking at the round-bosomed woods beyond the home paddock, where the white pheasant-boxes were ranged; and the golden air was full of a hundred sacred scents and sounds. Georgie felt his father's arm tighten in his.

'It's not half bad—but *hodie mihi, cras tibi*, isn't it? I suppose you'll be turning up some fine day with a girl under your arm, if you haven't one now, eh?'

'You can make your mind easy, sir. I haven't one.'

'Not in all these years?' said the mother.

'I hadn't time, mummy. They keep a man pretty busy, these days, in the service, and most of our mess are unmarried, too.'

'But you must have met hundreds in society—at balls, and so on?'

'I'm like the Tenth, mummy: I don't dance.'

'Don't dance! What have you been doing with yourself, then—backing other men's bills?' said the father.

'Oh yes; I've done a little of that too; but you see, as things are now, a man has all his work cut out for him to keep abreast of his profession, and my days were always too full to let me lark about half the night.'

'Hmm!'—suspiciously.

'It's never too late to learn. We ought to give some kind of housewarming for the people about, now you've come back. Unless you want to go straight up to town, dear?'

'No. I don't want anything better than this. Let's sit still and enjoy ourselves. I suppose there will be something for me to ride if I look for it?'

'Seeing I've been kept down to the old brown pair for the last six weeks because all the others were being got ready for Master Georgie, I should say there might be,' the father chuckled. 'They're reminding me in a hundred ways that I must take the second place now.'

'Brutes!'

'The pater doesn't mean it, dear; but every one has been trying to make your home-coming a success; and you *do* like it, don't you?'

'Perfect! Perfect! There's no place like England —when you've done your work.'

'That's the proper way to look at it, my son.'

And so up and down the flagged walk till their shadows grew long in the moonlight, and the mother went indoors and played such songs as a small boy once clamoured for, and the squat silver candlesticks were brought in, and Georgie climbed to the two rooms in the west wing that had been his nursery and his play-room in the beginning. Then who should come to tuck him up for the night but the mother? And she sat down on the bed, and they talked for a long hour, as mother and son should, if there is to be any future for our empire. With a simple woman's deep guile she asked questions and suggested answers that should have waked some sign in the face on the pillow, but there was neither quiver of eyelid nor quickening of breath, neither evasion nor delay in reply. So she blessed him and kissed him on the mouth, which is not always a mother's property, and said something to her husband later, at which he laughed profane and incredulous laughs.

All the establishment waited on Georgie next morning, from the tallest six-year-old, 'with a mouth like a kid glove, Master Georgie,' to the under-keeper strolling carelessly along the horizon, Georgie's pet rod in his hand, and 'There's a four-pounder risin' below the lasher. You don't 'ave 'em in Injia, Mast—Major Georgie.' It was all beautiful beyond telling, even though the mother insisted on taking him out in the landau (the leather had the hot Sunday smell of his youth), and showing him off to her friends at all the houses for six miles round; and the pater bore him up to town and a lunch at the club, where he introduced him, quite carelessly, to not less than thirty ancient warriors whose sons were not the youngest Majors in the army, and had not the D.S.O. After that it was Georgie's turn; and remembering his friends, he filled up the house with that kind of officer who lived in cheap lodgings at Southsea or Montpelier Square, Brompton— good men all, but not well off. The mother perceived that they needed girls to play with; and as there was no scarcity of girls, the house hummed like a dovecote in spring. They tore up the place for amateur theatricals; they disappeared in the gardens when they ought to have been rehearsing; they swept off every available horse and vehicle, especially the governess-cart and the fat pony; they fell into the trout-pond; they picnicked and they tennised; and they sat on gates in the twilight, two by two, and Georgie found that he was not in the least necessary to their entertainment.

'My word!' said he, when he saw the last of their dear backs. 'They told me they'd enjoyed 'emselves, but they haven't done half the things they said they would.'

'I know they've enjoyed themselves—immensely,' said the mother. 'You're a public benefactor, dear.'

'Now we can be quiet again, can't we?'

'Oh, quite. I've a very dear friend of mine that I want you to know. She couldn't come with the house so full, because she's an invalid, and she was away when you first came. She's a Mrs. Lacy.'

'Lacy! I don't remember the name about here.'

'No; they came after you went to India—from Oxford. Her husband died there, and she lost some money, I believe. They bought The Firs on the Bassett Road. She's a very sweet woman, and we're very fond of them both.'

'She's a widow, didn't you say?'

'She has a daughter. Surely I said so, dear?'

'Does she fall into trout-ponds, and gas and giggle, and "Oh, Major Cottah!" and all that sort of thing?'

'No, indeed. She's a very quiet girl, and very musical. She always came over here with her music-books—composing, you know; and she generally works all day, so you won't——'

''Talking about Miriam?' said the pater, coming up. The mother edged toward him within elbow reach. There was no finesse about Georgie's

father. 'Oh, Miriam's a dear girl. Plays beautifully. Rides beautifully, too. She's a regular pet
of the household. 'Used to call me——' The elbow
went home, and ignorant, but obedient always,
the pater shut himself off.

'What used she to call you, sir?'

'All sorts of pet names. I'm very fond of Miriam.'

'Sounds Jewish—Miriam.'

'Jew! You'll be calling yourself a Jew next. She's
one of the Herefordshire Lacys. When her aunt
dies——' Again the elbow.

'Oh, you won't see anything of her, Georgie.
She's busy with her music or her mother all day.
Besides, you're going up to town to-morrow,
aren't you? I thought you said something about
an Institute meeting?' The mother spoke.

'Going up to town *now?* What nonsense!' Once
more the pater was silenced.

'I had some idea of it, but I'm not quite sure,'
said the son of the house. Why did the mother try
to get him away because a musical girl and her
invalid parent were expected? He did not approve
of unknown females calling his father pet names.
He would observe these pushing persons who had
been only seven years in the county.

All of which the delighted mother read in his
countenance, herself keeping an air of sweet disinterestedness.

'They'll be here this evening for dinner. I'm
sending the carriage over for them, and they won't
stay more than a week.'

'Perhaps I shall go up to town. I don't quite know yet.' Georgie moved away irresolutely. There was a lecture at the United Services Institute on the supply of ammunition in the field, and the one man whose theories most irritated Major Cottar would deliver it. A heated discussion was sure to follow, and perhaps he might find himself moved to speak. He took his rod that afternoon and went down to thrash it out among the trout.

'Good sport, dear!' said the mother, from the terrace.

''Fraid it won't be, mummy. All those men from town, and the girls particularly, have put every trout off his feed for weeks. There isn't one of 'em that cares for fishin'—really. Fancy stampin' and shoutin' on the bank, and tellin' every fish for half a mile exactly what you're goin' to do, and then chuckin' a brute of a fly at him! By Jove, it would scare *me* if I was a trout!'

But things were not as bad as he had expected. The black gnat was on the water, and the water was strictly preserved. A three-quarter-pounder at the second cast set him for the campaign, and he worked down-stream, crouching behind the reed and meadow-sweet; creeping between a hornbeam hedge and a foot-wide strip of bank, where he could see the trout, but where they could not distinguish him from the background; lying on his stomach to switch the blue-upright sidewise through the checkered shadows of a gravelly ripple under overarching trees. But he had known every inch of the water since he was four feet high. The aged and astute between sunk roots, with the large and fat that lay in the frothy scum below some strong rush of water, sucking lazily as carp, came to trouble in their turn, at the hand that imitated so delicately the flicker and wimple of an egg-dropping fly. Consequently, Georgie found himself five miles from home when he ought to have been dressing for dinner. The housekeeper had taken good care that her boy should not go empty; and before he changed to the white moth he sat down to excellent claret with sandwiches of potted egg and things that adoring women make and men never notice. Then back, to surprise the otter grubbing for fresh-water mussels, the rabbits on the edge of the beechwoods foraging in the clover, and the policeman-like white owl stooping to the little field-mice, till the moon was strong, and he took his rod apart, and went home through well-remembered gaps in the hedges. He fetched a compass round the house, for, though he might have broken every law of the establishment every hour, the law of his boyhood was unbreakable: after fishing you went in by the south garden back-door, cleaned up in the outer scullery, and did not present yourself to your elders and your betters till you had washed and changed.

'Half-past ten, by Jove! Well, we'll make the sport an excuse. They wouldn't want to see me the first evening, at any rate. Gone to bed, probably.' He skirted by the open French windows of the drawing-room. 'No, they haven't. They look very comfy in there.'

He could see his father in his own particular chair, the mother in hers, and the back of a girl at the piano by the big potpourri-jar. The garden showed half divine in the moonlight, and he turned down through the roses to finish his pipe.

A prelude ended, and there floated out a voice of the kind that in his childhood he used to call 'creamy'—a full, true contralto; and this is the song that he heard, every syllable of it:

Over the edge of the purple down,
Where the single lamplight gleams,
Know ye the road to the Merciful Town
That is hard by the Sea of Dreams—
Where the poor may lay their wrongs away,
And the sick may forget to weep?
But we—pity us! Oh, pity us!—
We wakeful; ah, pity us!—
We must go back with Policeman Day—
Back from the City of Sleep!

Weary they turn from the scroll and crown,
Fetter and prayer and plough—
They that go up to the Merciful Town,
For her gates are closing now.
It is their right in the Baths of Night
Body and soul to steep;
But we—pity us! ah, pity us!—
We wakeful; oh, pity us!—
We must go back with Policeman Day—
Back from the City of Sleep!

Over the edge of the purple down,
Ere the tender dreams begin,
Look—we may look—at the Merciful Town,
But we may not enter in!
Outcasts all, from her guarded wall
Back to our watch we creep:
We—pity us! ah, pity us!—
We wakeful; oh, pity us!—
We that go back with Policeman Day—
Back from the City of Sleep!

At the last echo he was aware that his mouth was dry and unknown pulses were beating in the roof of it. The housekeeper, who would have it that he must have fallen in and caught a chill, was waiting to advise him on the stairs, and, since he neither saw nor answered her, carried a wild tale abroad that brought his mother knocking at the door.

'Anything happened, dear? Harper said she thought you weren't——'

'No; it's nothing. I'm all right, mummy. *Please* don't bother.'

He did not recognise his own voice, but that was a small matter beside what he was considering. Obviously, most obviously, the whole coincidence was crazy lunacy. He proved it to the satisfaction of Major George Cottar, who was going up to town to-morrow to hear a lecture on the supply of ammunition in the field; and having so proved it, the soul and brain and heart and body of Georgie cried joyously: 'That's the Lily Lock girl—the Lost

Continent girl—the Thirty-Mile-Ride girl—the Brushwood girl! *I* know her!'

He waked, stiff and cramped in his chair, to reconsider the situation by sunlight, when it did not appear normal. But a man must eat, and he went to breakfast, his heart between his teeth, holding himself severely in hand.

'Late, as usual,' said the mother. 'My boy, Miriam.'

A tall girl in black raised her eyes to his, and Georgie's life training deserted him—just as soon as he realised that she did not know. He stared coolly and critically. There was the abundant black hair, growing in a widow's peak, turned back from the forehead, with that peculiar ripple over the right ear; there were the grey eyes set a little close together; the short upper lip, resolute chin, and the known poise of the head. There was also the small, well-cut mouth that had kissed him.

'Georgie—*dear!*' said the mother, amazedly, for Miriam was flushing under the stare.

'I—I beg your pardon!' he gulped. 'I don't know whether the mother has told you, but I'm rather an idiot at times, specially before I've had my breakfast. It's—it's a family failing.' He turned to explore among the hot-water dishes on the sideboard, rejoicing that she did not know—she did not know.

His conversation for the rest of the meal was mildly insane, though the mother thought she had never seen her boy look half so handsome. How could any girl, least of all one of Miriam's discernment, forbear to fall down and worship? But deeply Miriam was displeased. She had never been stared at in that fashion before, and promptly retired into her shell when Georgie announced that he had changed his mind about going to town, and would stay to play with Miss Lacy if she had nothing better to do.

'Oh, but don't let me throw you out. I'm at work. I've things to do all the morning.'

'What possessed Georgie to behave so oddly?' the mother sighed to herself. 'Miriam's a bundle of feelings—like her mother.'

'You compose, don't you? Must be a fine thing to be able to do that. ('Pig—oh, pig!' thought Miriam.) I think I heard you singin' when I came in last night after fishin'. All about a Sea of Dreams, wasn't it? (Miriam shuddered to the core of the soul that afflicted her.) Awfully pretty song. How d'you think of such things?'

'You only composed the music, dear, didn't you?'

'The words too, mummy. I'm sure of it,' said Georgie, with a sparkling eye. No; she did not know.

'Yeth; I wrote the words too.' Miriam spoke slowly, for she knew she lisped when she was nervous.

'Now how *could* you tell, Georgie?' said the mother, as delighted as though the youngest Major in the army were ten years old, showing off before company.

'I was sure of it, somehow. Oh, there are heaps

211

of things about me, mummy, that you don't understand. Looks as if it were goin' to be a hot day—for England. Would you care for a ride this afternoon, Miss Lacy? We can start out after tea, if you'd like it.'

Miriam could not in decency refuse, but any woman might see she was not filled with delight.

'That will be very nice, if you take the Bassett Road. It will save me sending Martin down to the village,' said the mother, filling in gaps.

Like all good managers, the mother had her one weakness—a mania for little strategies that should economise horses and vehicles. Her menfolk complained that she turned them into common carriers, and there was a legend in the family that she had once said to the pater on the morning of a meet: 'If you *should* kill near Bassett, dear, and if it isn't too late, would you mind just popping over and matching me this?'

'I knew that was coming. You'd never miss a chance, mother. If it's fish or a trunk, I won't.' Georgie laughed.

'It's only a duck. They can do it up very neatly at Mallett's,' said the mother simply. 'You won't mind, will you? We'll have a scratch dinner at nine, because it's so hot.'

The long summer day dragged itself out for centuries; but at last there was tea on the lawn, and Miriam appeared.

She was in the saddle before he could offer to help, with the clean spring of the child who mounted the pony for the Thirty-Mile-Ride. The

212

day held mercilessly, though Georgie got down thrice to look for imaginary stones in Rufus's foot. One cannot say even simple things in broad light, and this that Georgie meditated was not simple. So he spoke seldom, and Miriam was divided between relief and scorn. It annoyed her that the great hulking thing should know she had written the words of the over-night song; for though a maiden may sing her most secret fancies aloud, she does not care to have them trampled over by the male Philistine. They rode into the little red-brick street of Bassett, and Georgie made untold fuss over the disposition of that duck. It must go in just such a package, and be fastened to the saddle in just such a manner, though eight o'clock had passed and they were miles from dinner.

'We must be quick!' said Miriam, bored and angry.

'There's no great hurry; but we can cut over Dowhead Down, and let 'em out on the grass. That will save us half an hour.'

The horses capered on the short, sweet-smelling turf, and the delaying shadows gathered in the valley as they cantered over the great dun down that overhangs Bassett and the Western coaching-road. Insensibly the pace quickened without thought of molehills; Rufus, gentleman that he was, waiting on Miriam's Dandy till they should have cleared the rise. Then down the two-mile slope they raced together, the wind whistling in their ears, to the steady throb of eight hoofs and the light click-click of the shifting bits.

'Oh, that was glorious!' Miriam cried, reining in. 'Dandy and I are old friends, but I don't think we've ever gone better together.'

'No; but you've gone quicker, once or twice.'

'Really? When?'

Georgie moistened his lips. 'Don't you remember the Thirty-Mile-Ride—with me—when "They" were after us—on the beach road, with the sea to the left—going toward the Lamp-post on the Downs?'

The girl gasped. 'What—what do you mean?' she said hysterically.

'The Thirty-Mile-Ride, and—and all the rest of it.'

'You mean——? I didn't sing anything about the Thirty-Mile-Ride. I know I didn't. I have never told a living soul.'

'You told about Policeman Day, and the lamp at the top of the downs, and the City of Sleep. It all joins on, you know—it's the same country— and it was easy enough to see where you had been.'

'Good God!—It joins on—of course it does; but—I have been—you have been——Oh, let's walk, please, or I shall fall off!'

Georgie ranged alongside, and laid a hand that shook below her bridle-hand, pulling Dandy into a walk. Miriam was sobbing as he had seen a man sob under the touch of the bullet.

'It's all right—it's all right,' he whispered feebly. 'Only—only it's true, you know.'

'True! Am I mad?'

'Not unless I'm mad as well. *Do* try to think a

214

minute quietly. How could any one conceivably know anything about the Thirty-Mile-Ride having anything to do with you, unless he had been there?'

'But where? But *where?* Tell me!'

'There—wherever it may be—in our country, I suppose. Do you remember the first time you rode it—the Thirty-Mile-Ride, I mean? You must.'

'It was all dreams—all dreams!'

'Yes, but tell, please; because I know.'

'Let me think. I—we were on no account to make any noise—on no account to make any noise.' She was staring between Dandy's ears with eyes that did not see, and suffocating heart.

'Because "It" was dying in the big house?' Georgie went on, reining in again.

'There was a garden with green-and-gilt railings—all hot. Do *you* remember?'

'I ought to. I was sitting on the other side of the bed before. "It" coughed and "They" came in.'

'You!'—the deep voice was unnaturally full and strong and the girl's wide-opened eyes burned in the dusk as she stared him through and through. 'Then you're the Boy—my Brushwood Boy, and I've known you all my life!'

She fell forward on Dandy's neck. Georgie forced himself out of the weakness that was overmastering his limbs, and slid an arm round her waist. The head dropped on his shoulder, and he found himself with parched lips saying things that

215

up till then he believed existed only in printed works of fiction. Mercifully the horses were quiet. She made no attempt to draw herself away when she recovered, but lay still, whispering, 'Of course you're the Boy, and I didn't know—I didn't know.'

'I knew last night; and when I saw you at breakfast——'

'Oh, *that* was why! I wondered at the time. You would, of course.'

'I couldn't speak before this. Keep your head where it is, dear. It's all right now—all right now, isn't it?'

'But how was it *I* didn't know—after all these years and years? I remember—oh, what lots of things I remember!'

'Tell me some. I'll look after the horses.'

'I remember waiting for you when the steamer came in. Do you?'

'At the Lily Lock, beyond Hong-Kong and Java?'

'Do *you* call it that, too?'

'You told me it was when I was lost in the continent. That was you that showed me the way through the mountains?'

'When the islands slid? It must have been, because you're the only one I remember. All the others were "Them."'

'Awful brutes they were, too.'

'Yes, I remember showing you the Thirty-Mile-Ride the first time. You ride just as you used to —then. You *are* you!'

'That's odd. I thought that of you this afternoon. Isn't it wonderful?'

'What does it all mean? Why should you and I of the millions of people in the world have this—this thing between us? What does it mean? I'm frightened.'

'This!' said Georgie. The horses quickened their pace. They thought they had heard an order. 'Perhaps when we die we may find out more, but it means this now.'

There was no answer. What could she say? As the world went, they had known each other rather less than eight and a half hours, but the matter was one that did not concern the world. There was a very long silence, while the breath in their nostrils drew cold and sharp as it might have been fumes of ether.

'That's the second,' Georgie whispered. 'You remember, don't you?'

'It's not!'—furiously. 'It's not!'

'On the downs the other night—months ago. You were just as you are now, and we went over the country for miles and miles.'

'It was all empty, too. "They" had gone away. Nobody frightened us. I wonder why, Boy?'

'Oh, if you remember *that*, you must remember the rest. Confess!'

'I remember lots of things, but I *know* I didn't. I never have—till just now.'

'You *did*, dear.'

'I know I didn't, because—oh, it's no use keeping anything back!—because I truthfully meant to.'

'And truthfully did.'

'No; meant to; but some one else came by.'

'There wasn't any one else. There never has been.'

'There was—there always is. It was another woman—out there on the sea. I saw her. It was the 26th of May. I've got it written down somewhere.'

'Oh, *you've* kept a record of your dreams, too? That's odd about the other woman, because I happened to be on the sea just then.'

'I was right. How do I know what you've done—when you were awake? And I thought it was only *you!*'

'You never were more wrong in your life. What a little temper you've got! Listen to me a minute, dear.' And Georgie, though he knew it not, committed black perjury. 'It—it isn't the kind of thing one says to any one, because they'd laugh; but on my word and honour, darling, I've never been kissed by a living soul outside of my own people in all my life. Don't laugh, dear. I wouldn't tell any one but you, but it's the solemn truth.'

'I knew! You are you. Oh, I *knew* you'd come some day; but I didn't know you were you in the least till you spoke.'

'Then give me another.'

'And you never cared or looked anywhere?

Why, all the round world must have loved you from the very minute they saw you, Boy.'

'They kept it to themselves if they did. No; I never cared.'

'And we shall be late for dinner—horribly late. Oh, how can I look at you in the light before your mother—and mine!'

'We'll play you're Miss Lacy till the proper time comes. What's the shortest limit for people to get engaged? S'pose we have got to go through all the fuss of an engagement, haven't we?'

'Oh, I don't want to talk about that. It's so commonplace. I've thought of something that you don't know. I'm sure of it. What's my name?'

'Miri—no, it isn't, by Jove! Wait half a second, and it'll come back to me. You aren't—you can't? Why, *those* old tales—before I went to school! I've never thought of 'em from that day to this. Are you the original, only Annie*an*louise?'

'It was what you always called me ever since the beginning. Oh! We've turned into the avenue, and we must be an hour late.'

'What does it matter? The chain goes as far back as those days? It must, of course—of course it must. I've got to ride round with this pestilent old bird—confound him!'

'"Ha! ha!" said the duck, laughing. Do you remember *that?*'

'Yes, I do—flower-pots on my feet, and all. We've been together all this while; and I've got to say good-bye to you till dinner. *Sure* I'll see you at dinner-time? *Sure* you won't sneak up to your room, darling, and leave me all the evening? Good-bye, dear—good-bye.'

'Good-bye, Boy, good-bye. Mind the arch! Don't let Rufus bolt into his stable. Good-bye. Yes, I'll come down to dinner; but—what shall I do when I see you in the light!'

The Idyll of Miss Sarah Brown

Damon Runyon

Of all the high players this country ever sees, there is no doubt but that the guy they call The Sky is the highest. In fact, the reason he is called The Sky is because he goes so high when it comes to betting on any proposition whatever. He will bet all he has, and nobody can bet any more than this.

His right name is Obadiah Masterson, and he is originally out of a little town in southern Colorado where he learns to shoot craps, and play cards, and one thing and another, and where his old man is a very well-known citizen, and something of a sport himself. In fact, The Sky tells me that when he finally cleans up all the loose scratch around his home town and decides he needs more room, his old man has a little private talk with him and says to him like this:

"Son," the old guy says, "you are now going out into the wide, wide world to make your own way, and it is a very good thing to do, as there are no more opportunities for you in this burg. I am only sorry," he says, "that I am not able to bank-roll you to a very large start, but," he says, "not having any potatoes to give you, I am now going to stake you to some very valuable advice,

221

which I personally collect in my years of experience around and about, and I hope and trust you will always bear this advice in mind.

"Son," the old guy says, "no matter how far you travel, or how smart you get, always remember this: Some day, somewhere," he says, "a guy is going to come to you and show you a nice brand-new deck of cards on which the seal is never broken, and this guy is going to offer to bet you that the jack of spades will jump out of this deck and squirt cider in your ear. But, son," the old guy says, "do not bet him, for as sure as you do you are going to get an ear full of cider."

Well, The Sky remembers what his old man says, and he is always very cautious about betting on such propositions as the jack of spades jumping out of a sealed deck of cards and squirting cider in his ear, and so he makes few mistakes as he goes along. In fact, the only real mistake The Sky makes is when he hits St. Louis after leaving his old home town, and loses all his potatoes betting a guy St. Louis is the biggest town in the world.

Now of course this is before The Sky ever sees any bigger towns, and he is never much of a hand for reading up on matters such as this. In fact, the only reading The Sky ever does as he goes along through life is in these Gideon Bibles such as he finds in the hotel rooms where he lives, for The Sky never lives anywhere else but in hotel rooms for years.

He tells me that he reads many items of great interest in these Gideon Bibles, and furthermore

The Sky says that several times these Gideon Bibles keep him from getting out of line, such as the time he finds himself pretty much frozen-in over in Cincinnati, what with owing everybody in town except maybe the mayor from playing games of chance of one kind and another.

Well, The Sky says he sees no way of meeting these obligations and he is figuring the only thing he can do is to take a run-out powder, when he happens to read in one of these Gideon Bibles where it says like this:

"Better is it," the Gideon Bible says, "that thou shouldest not vow, than that thou shouldest vow and not pay."

Well, The Sky says he can see that there is no doubt whatever but that this means a guy shall not welsh, so he remains in Cincinnati until he manages to wiggle himself out of the situation, and from that day to this, The Sky never thinks of welshing.

He is maybe thirty years old, and is a tall guy with a round kisser, and big blue eyes, and he always looks as innocent as a little baby. But The Sky is by no means as innocent as he looks. In fact, The Sky is smarter than three Philadelphia lawyers, which makes him very smart, indeed, and he is well established as a high player in New Orleans, and Chicago, and Los Angeles, and wherever else there is any action in the way of card-playing, or crap-shooting, or horse-racing, or betting on the baseball games, for The Sky is always moving around the country following the action.

But while The Sky will bet on anything whatever, he is more of a short-card player and a crap shooter than anything else, and furthermore he is a great hand for propositions, such as are always coming up among citizens who follow games of chance for a living. Many citizens prefer betting on propositions to anything you can think of, because they figure a proposition gives them a chance to out-smart somebody, and in fact I know citizens who will sit up all night making up propositions to offer other citizens the next day.

A proposition may be only a problem in cards, such as what is the price against a guy getting aces back-to-back, or how often a pair of deuces will win a hand in stud, and then again it may be some very daffy proposition, indeed, although the daffier any proposition seems to be, the more some citizens like it. And no one ever sees The Sky when he does not have some proposition of his own.

The first time he ever shows up around this town, he goes to a baseball game at the Polo Grounds with several prominent citizens, and while he is at the ball game, he buys himself a sack of Harry Stevens' peanuts, which he dumps in a side pocket of his coat. He is eating these peanuts all through the game, and after the game is over and he is walking across the field with the citizens, he says to them like this:

"What price," The Sky says, "I cannot throw a peanut from second base to the home plate?"

Well, everybody knows that a peanut is too light for anybody to throw it this far, so Big Nig, the crap shooter, who always likes to have a little the best of it running for him, speaks as follows:

"You can have 3 to 1 from me, stranger," Big Nig says.

"Two C's against six," The Sky says, and then he stands on second base, and takes a peanut out of his pocket, and not only whips it to the home plate, but on into the lap of a fat guy who is still sitting in the grand stand putting the zing on Bill Terry for not taking Walker out of the box when Walker is getting a pasting from the other club.

Well, naturally, this is a most astonishing throw, indeed, but afterwards it comes out that The Sky throws a peanut loaded with lead, and of course it is not one of Harry Stevens' peanuts, either, as Harry is not selling peanuts full of lead at a dime a bag, with the price of lead what it is.

It is only a few nights after this that The Sky states another most unusual proposition to a group of citizens sitting in Mindy's restaurant when he offers to bet a C note that he can go down into Mindy's cellar and catch a live rat with his bare hands and everybody is greatly astonished when Mindy himself steps up and takes the bet, for ordinarily Mindy will not bet you a nickel he is alive.

But it seems that Mindy knows that The Sky plants a tame rat in the cellar, and this rat knows

225

The Sky and loves him dearly, and will let him catch it any time he wishes, and it also seems that Mindy knows that one of his dish washers happens upon this rat, and not knowing it is tame, knocks it flatter than a pancake. So when The Sky goes down into the cellar and starts trying to catch a rat with his bare hands, he is greatly surprised how inhospitable the rat turns out to be, because it is one of Mindy's personal rats, and Mindy is around afterwards saying he will lay plenty of 7 to 5 against even Strangler Lewis being able to catch one of his rats with his bare hands, or with boxing gloves on.

I am only telling you all this to show you what a smart guy The Sky is, and I am only sorry I do not have time to tell you about many other very remarkable propositions that he thinks up outside of his regular business.

It is well-known to one and all that he is very honest in every respect, and that he hates and despises cheaters at cards, or dice, and furthermore The Sky never wishes to play with any the best of it himself, or anyway not much. He will never take the inside of any situation, as many gamblers love to do, such as owning a gambling house, and having the percentage run for him instead of against him, for always The Sky is strictly a player, because he says he will never care to settle down in one spot long enough to become the owner of anything.

In fact, in all the years The Sky is drifting around the country, nobody ever knows him to own anything except maybe a bank roll, and when he comes to Broadway the last time, which is the time I am now speaking of, he has a hundred G's in cash money, and an extra suit of clothes, and this is all he has in the world. He never owns such a thing as a house, or an automobile, or a piece of jewelry. He never owns a watch, because The Sky says time means nothing to him.

Of course some guys will figure a hundred G's comes under the head of owning something, but as far as The Sky is concerned, money is nothing but just something for him to play with and the dollars may as well be doughnuts as far as value goes with him. The only time The Sky ever thinks of money as money is when he is broke, and the only way he can tell he is broke is when he reaches into his pocket and finds nothing there but his fingers.

Then it is necessary for The Sky to go out and dig up some fresh scratch somewhere, and when it comes to digging up scratch, The Sky is practically supernatural. He can get more potatoes on the strength of a telegram to some place or other than John D. Rockefeller can get on collateral, for everybody knows The Sky's word is as good as wheat in the bin.

Now one Sunday evening The Sky is walking along Broadway, and at the corner of Forty-ninth Street he comes upon a little bunch of mission workers who are holding a religious meeting, such as mission workers love to do of a Sunday evening, the idea being that they may round up a few sinners here and there, although personally I always claim the mission workers come out too early to catch any sinners on this part of Broadway. At such an hour the sinners are still in bed resting up from their sinning of the night before, so they will be in good shape for more sinning a little later on.

There are only four of these mission workers, and two of them are old guys, and one is an old doll, while the other is a young doll who is tootling on a cornet. And after a couple of ganders at this young doll, The Sky is a goner, for this is one of the most beautiful young dolls anybody ever sees on Broadway, and especially as a mission worker. Her name is Miss Sarah Brown.

She is tall, and thin, and has a first-class shape, and her hair is a light brown, going on blond, and her eyes are like I do not know what, except that they are one-hundred-per-cent eyes in every respect. Furthermore, she is not a bad cornet player, if you like cornet players, although at this spot on Broadway she has to play against a scat band in a chop-suey joint near by, and this is tough competition, although at that many citizens believe Miss Sarah Brown will win by a large score if she only gets a little more support from one of the old guys with her who has a big bass drum, but does not pound it hearty enough.

Well, The Sky stands there listening to Miss Sarah Brown tootling on the cornet for quite a spell, and then he hears her make a speech in which she puts the blast on sin very good, and boosts religion quite some, and says if there are any souls around that need saving the owners of same may step forward at once. But no one steps forward, so The Sky comes over to Mindy's restaurant where many citizens are congregated, and starts telling us about Miss Sarah Brown. But of course we already know about Miss Sarah Brown, because she is so beautiful, and so good.

Furthermore, everybody feels somewhat sorry for Miss Sarah Brown, for while she is always tootling the cornet, and making speeches, and looking to save any souls that need saving, she never seems to find any souls to save, or at least her bunch of mission workers never gets any bigger. In fact, it gets smaller, as she started out with a guy who plays a very fair sort of trombone, but this guy takes it on the lam one night with the trombone, which one and all consider a dirty trick.

Now from this time on, The Sky does not take any interest in anything but Miss Sarah Brown, and any night she is out on the corner with the other mission workers, you will see The Sky standing around looking at her, and naturally after a few weeks of this, Miss Sarah Brown must know The Sky is looking at her, or she is dumber than seems possible. And nobody ever figures Miss Sarah Brown dumb, as she is always on her toes, and seems plenty able to take care of herself, even on Broadway.

Sometimes after the street meeting is over, The Sky follows the mission workers to their headquarters in an old storeroom around in Forty-eighth Street where they generally hold an indoor session, and I hear The Sky drops many a large coarse note in the collection box while looking at Miss Sarah Brown, and there is no doubt these notes come in handy around the mission, as I hear business is by no means so good there.

It is called the Save-a-Soul Mission, and it is run mainly by Miss Sarah Brown's grandfather, an old guy with whiskers, by the name of Arvide Abernathy, but Miss Sarah Brown seems to do most of the work, including tootling the cornet, and visiting the poor people around and about, and all this and that, and many citizens claim it is a great shame that such a beautiful doll is wasting her time being good.

How The Sky ever becomes acquainted with Miss Sarah Brown is a very great mystery, but the next thing anybody knows, he is saying hello to her, and she is smiling at him out of her one-hundred-per-cent eyes, and one evening when I happen to be with The Sky we run into her walking along Forty-ninth Street, and The Sky hauls off and stops her, and says it is a nice evening, which it is, at that. Then The Sky says to Miss Sarah Brown like this:

"Well," The Sky says, "how is the mission dodge going these days? Are you saving any souls?" he says.

Well, it seems from what Miss Sarah Brown says the soul-saving is very slow, indeed, these days.

"In fact," Miss Sarah Brown says, "I worry

230

greatly about how few souls we seem to save. Sometimes I wonder if we are lacking in grace."

She goes on up the street, and The Sky stands looking after her, and he says to me like this:

"I wish I can think of some way to help this little doll," he says, "especially," he says, "in saving a few souls to build up her mob at the mission. I must speak to her again, and see if I can figure something out."

But The Sky does not get to speak to Miss Sarah Brown again, because somebody weighs in the sacks on him by telling her he is nothing but a professional gambler, and that he is a very undesirable character, and that his only interest in hanging around the mission is because she is a good-looking doll. So all of a sudden Miss Sarah Brown plays plenty of chill for The Sky. Furthermore, she sends him word that she does not care to accept any more of his potatoes in the collection box, because his potatoes are nothing but ill-gotten gains.

Well, naturally, this hurts The Sky's feelings no little, so he quits standing around looking at Miss Sarah Brown, and going to the mission, and takes to mingling again with the citizens in Mindy's, and showing some interest in the affairs of the community, especially the crap games.

Of course the crap games that are going on at this time are nothing much, because practically everybody in the world is broke, but there is a head-and-head game run by Nathan Detroit over a garage in Fifty-second Street where there is occasionally some action, and who shows up at this crap game early one evening but The Sky, although it seems he shows up there more to find company than anything else.

In fact, he only stands around watching the play, and talking with other guys who are also standing around and watching, and many of these guys are very high shots during the gold rush, although most of them are now as clean as a jaybird, and maybe cleaner. One of these guys is a guy by the name of Brandy Bottle Bates, who is known from coast to coast as a high player when he has anything to play with, and who is called Brandy Bottle Bates because it seems that years ago he is a great hand for belting a brandy bottle around.

This Brandy Bottle Bates is a big, black-looking guy, with a large beezer, and a head shaped like a pear, and he is considered a very immoral and wicked character, but he is a pretty slick gambler, and a fast man with a dollar when he is in the money.

Well, finally The Sky asks Brandy Bottle why he is not playing and Brandy laughs, and states as follows:

"Why," he says, "in the first place I have no potatoes, and in the second place I doubt if it will do me much good if I do have any potatoes the way I am going the past year. Why," Brandy Bottle says, "I cannot win a bet to save my soul."

Now this crack seems to give The Sky an idea, as he stands looking at Brandy Bottle very strangely, and while he is looking, Big Nig, the crap shooter, picks up the dice and hits three times hand-running, bing, bing, bing. Then Bit Nig comes out on a six and Brandy Bottle Bates speaks as follows:

"You see how my luck is," he says. "Here is Big Nig hotter than a stove, and here I am without a bob to follow him with, especially," Brandy says, "when he is looking for nothing but a six. Why," he says, "Nig can make sixes all night when he is hot. If he does not make this six, the way he is, I will be willing to turn square and quit gambling forever."

"Well, Brandy," The Sky says, "I will make you a proposition. I will lay you a G note Big Nig does not get his six. I will lay you a G note against nothing but your soul," he says. "I mean if Big Nig does not get his six, you are to turn square and join Miss Sarah Brown's mission for six months."

"Bet!" Brandy Bottle Bates says right away, meaning the proposition is on, although the chances are he does not quite understand the proposition. All Brandy understands is The Sky wishes to wager that Big Nig does not make his six, and Brandy Bottle Bates will be willing to bet his soul a couple of times over on Big Nig making his six, and figure he is getting the best of it, at that, as Brandy has great confidence in Nig.

Well, sure enough, Big Nig makes the six, so The Sky weeds Brandy Bottle Bates a G note, although everybody around is saying The Sky

233

makes a terrible overlay of the natural price in giving Brandy Bottle a G against his soul. Furthermore, everybody around figures the chances are The Sky only wishes to give Brandy an opportunity to get in action, and nobody figures The Sky is on the level about trying to win Brandy Bottle Bates' soul, especially as The Sky does not seem to wish to go any further after paying the bet.

He only stands there looking on and seeming somewhat depressed as Brandy Bottle goes into action on his own account with the G note, fading other guys around the table with cash money. But Brandy Bottle Bates seems to figure what is in The Sky's mind pretty well, because Brandy Bottle is a crafty old guy.

It finally comes his turn to handle the dice, and he hits a couple of times, and then he comes out on a four, and anybody will tell you that a four is a very tough point to make, even with a lead pencil. Then Brandy Bottle turns to The Sky and speaks to him as follows:

"Well, Sky," he says, "I will take the odds off you on this one. I know you do not want my dough," he says. "I know you only want my soul for Miss Sarah Brown, and," he says, "without wishing to be fresh about it, I know why you want it for her. I am young once myself," Brandy Bottle says. "And you know if I lose to you, I will be over there in Forty-eighth Street in an hour pounding on the door, for Brandy always settles.

"But, Sky," he says, "now I am in the money,

and my price goes up. Will you lay me ten G's against my soul I do not make this four?"

"Bet!" The Sky says, and right away Brandy Bottle hits with a four.

Well, when word goes around that The Sky is up at Nathan Detroit's crap game trying to win Brandy Bottle Bates' soul for Miss Sarah Brown, the excitement is practically intense. Somebody telephones Mindy's, where a large number of citizens are sitting around arguing about this and that, and telling one another how much they will bet in support of their arguments, if only they have something to bet, and Mindy himself is almost killed in the rush for the door.

One of the first guys out of Mindy's and up to the crap game is Regret, the horse player, and as he comes in Brandy Bottle is looking for a nine, and The Sky is laying him twelve G's against his soul that he does not make this nine, for it seems Brandy Bottle's soul keeps getting more and more expensive.

Well, Regret wishes to bet his soul against a G that Brandy Bottle gets his nine, and is greatly insulted when The Sky cannot figure his price any better than a double saw, but finally Regret accepts this price, and Brandy Bottle hits again.

Now many other citizens request a little action from The Sky, and if there is one thing The Sky cannot deny a citizen it is action, so he says he will lay them according to how he figures their word to join Miss Sarah Brown's mission if Brandy Bottle misses out, but about this time The Sky finds he has no more potatoes on him, being now around thirty-five G's loser, and he wishes to give markers.

But Brandy Bottle says that while ordinarily he will be pleased to extend The Sky this accommodation, he does not care to accept markers against his soul, so then The Sky has to leave the joint and go over to his hotel two or three blocks away, and get the night clerk to open his damper so The Sky can get the rest of his bank roll. In the meantime the crap game continues at Nathan Detroit's among the small operators, while the other citizens stand around and say that while they hear of many a daffy proposition in their time, this is the daffiest that ever comes to their attention, although Big Nig claims he hears of a daffier one, but cannot think what it is.

Big Nig claims that all gamblers are daffy anyway, and in fact he says if they are not daffy they will not be gamblers, and while he is arguing this matter back comes The Sky with fresh scratch, and Brandy Bottle Bates takes up where he leaves off, although Brandy says he is accepting the worst of it, as the dice have a chance to cool off.

Now the upshot of the whole business is that Brandy Bottle hits thirteen licks in a row, and the last lick he makes is on a ten, and it is for twenty G's against his soul, with about a dozen other citizens getting anywhere from one to five C's against their souls, and complaining bitterly of the price.

And as Brandy Bottle makes his ten, I happen

to look at The Sky and I see him watching Brandy with a very peculiar expression on his face, and furthermore I see The Sky's right hand creeping inside his coat where I know he always packs a Betsy in a shoulder holster, so I can see something is wrong somewhere.

But before I can figure out what it is, there is quite a fuss at the door, and loud talking, and a doll's voice, and all of a sudden in bobs nobody else but Miss Sarah Brown. It is plain to be seen that she is all steamed up about something.

She marches right up to the crap table where Brandy Bottle Bates and The Sky and the other citizens are standing, and one and all are feeling sorry for Dobber, the doorman, thinking of what Nathan Detroit is bound to say to him for letting her in. The dice are still lying on the table showing Brandy Bottle Bates' last throw, which cleans The Sky and gives many citizens the first means they enjoy in several months.

Well, Miss Sarah Brown looks at The Sky, and The Sky looks at Miss Sarah Brown, and Miss Sarah Brown looks at the citizens around and about, and one and all are somewhat dumbfounded, and nobody seems to be able to think of much to say, although The Sky finally speaks up as follows:

"Good evening," The Sky says. "It is a nice evening," he says. "I am trying to win a few souls for you around here, but," he says, "I seem to be about half out of luck."

"Well," Miss Sarah Brown says, looking at The

Sky most severely out of her hundred-per-cent eyes, "you are taking too much upon yourself. I can win any souls I need myself. You better be thinking of your own soul. By the way," she says, "are you risking your own soul, or just your money?"

Well, of course up to this time The Sky is not risking anything but his potatoes, so he only shakes his head to Miss Sarah Brown's question, and looks somewhat disorganized.

"I know something about gambling," Miss Sarah Brown says, "especially about crap games. I ought to," she says. "It ruins my poor papa and my brother Joe. If you wish to gamble for souls, Mister Sky, gamble for your own soul."

Now Miss Sarah Brown opens a small black leather pocketbook she is carrying in one hand, and pulls out a two-dollar bill, and it is such a two-dollar bill as seems to have seen much service in its time, and holding up this deuce, Miss Sarah Brown speaks as follows:

"I will gamble with you, Mister Sky," she says. "I will gamble with you," she says, "on the same terms you gamble with these parties here. This two dollars against your soul, Mister Sky. It is all I have, but," she says, "it is more than your soul is worth."

Well, of course anybody can see that Miss Sarah Brown is doing this because she is very angry, and wishes to make The Sky look small, but right away The Sky's duke comes from inside his coat, and he picks up the dice and hands them to her and speaks as follows:

"Roll them," The Sky says, and Miss Sarah Brown snatches the dice out of his hand and gives them a quick sling on the table in such a way that anybody can see she is not a professional crap shooter, and not even an amateur crap shooter, for all amateur crap shooters first breathe on the dice, and rattle them good, and make remarks to them, such as "Come on, baby!"

In fact, there is some criticism of Miss Sarah Brown afterwards on account of her haste, as many citizens are eager to string with her to hit, while others are just as anxious to bet she misses, and she does not give them a chance to get down.

Well, Scranton Slim is the stick guy, and he takes a gander at the dice as they hit up against the side of the table and bounce back, and then Slim hollers, "Winner, winner, winner," as stick guys love to do, and what is showing on the dice as big as life, but a six and a five, which makes eleven, no matter how you figure, so The Sky's soul belongs to Miss Sarah Brown.

She turns at once and pushes through the citizens around the table without even waiting to pick up the deuce she lays down when she grabs the dice. Afterwards a most obnoxious character by the name of Red Nose Regan tries to claim the deuce as a sleeper and gets the heave-o from Nathan Detroit, who becomes very indignant about this, stating that Red Nose is trying to give his joint a wrong rap.

Naturally, The Sky follows Miss Brown, and Dobber, the doorman, tells me that as they are waiting for him to unlock the door and let them out, Miss Sarah Brown turns on The Sky and speaks to him as follows:

"You are a fool," Miss Sarah Brown says.

Well, at this Dobber figures The Sky is bound to let one go, as this seems to be most insulting language, but instead of letting one go, The Sky only smiles at Miss Sarah Brown and says to her like this:

"Why," The Sky says, "Paul says 'If any man among you seemeth to be wise in this world, let him become a fool, that he may be wise.' I love you, Miss Sarah Brown," The Sky says.

Well, now, Dobber has a pretty fair sort of memory, and he says that Miss Sarah Brown tells The Sky that since he seems to know so much about the Bible, maybe he remembers the second verse of the Song of Solomon, but the chances are Dobber muffs the number of the verse, because I look the matter up in one of these Gideon Bibles, and the verse seems a little too much for Miss Sarah Brown, although of course you never can tell.

Anyway, this is about all there is to the story, except that Brandy Bottle Bates slides out during the confusion so quietly even Dobber scarcely remembers letting him out, and he takes most of The Sky's potatoes with him, but he soon gets batted in against the faro bank out in Chicago, and the last anybody hears of him he gets religion all over again, and is preaching out in San Jose, so The Sky always claims he beats Brandy for his soul, at that.

I see The Sky the other night at Forty-ninth Street and Broadway, and he is with quite a raft of mission workers, including Mrs. Sky, for it seems that the soul-saving business picks up wonderfully, and The Sky is giving a big bass drum such a first-class whacking that the scat band in the chop-suey joint can scarcely be heard. Furthermore, The Sky is hollering between whacks, and I never see a guy look happier, especially when Mrs. Sky smiles at him out of her hundred-percent eyes. But I do not linger long, because The Sky gets a gander at me, and right away he begins hollering:

"I see before me a sinner of deepest dye," he hollers. "Oh, sinner, repent before it is too late. Join with us, sinner," he hollers, "and let us save your soul."

Naturally, this crack about me being a sinner embarrasses me no little, as it is by no means true, and it is a good thing for The Sky there is no copper in me, or I will go to Mrs. Sky, who is always bragging about how she wins The Sky's soul by outplaying him at his own game, and tell her the truth.

And the truth is that the dice with which she wins The Sky's soul, and which are the same dice with which Brandy Bottle Bates wins all his po-

241

tatoes, are strictly phony, and that she gets into Nathan Detroit's just in time to keep The Sky from killing old Brandy Bottle.

The Gift of the Magi

O. Henry

One dollar and eighty-seven cents. That was all. And sixty cents of it was in pennies. Pennies saved one and two at a time by bulldozing the grocer and the vegetable man and the butcher until one's cheeks burned with the silent imputation of parsimony that such close dealing implied. Three times Della counted it. One dollar and eighty-seven cents. And the next day would be Christmas.

There was clearly nothing to do but flop down on the shabby little couch and howl. So Della did it. Which instigates the moral reflection that life is made up of sobs, sniffles, and smiles, with sniffles predominating.

While the mistress of the home is gradually subsiding from the first stage to the second, take a look at the home. A furnished flat at $8 per week. It did not exactly beggar description, but it certainly had that word on the lookout for the mendicancy squad.

In the vestibule below was a letter-box into which no letter would go, and an electric button from which no mortal finger could coax a ring.

Also appertaining thereunto was a card bearing the name "Mr. James Dillingham Young."

The "Dillingham" had been flung to the breeze during a former period of prosperity when its possessor was being paid $30 per week. Now, when the income was shrunk to $20, the letters of "Dillingham" looked blurred, as though they were thinking seriously of contracting to a modest and unassuming D. But whenever Mr. James Dillingham Young came home and reached his flat above he was called "Jim" and greatly hugged by Mrs. James Dillingham Young, already introduced to you as Della. Which is all very good.

Della finished her cry and attended to her cheeks with the powder rag. She stood by the window and looked out dully at a gray cat walking a gray fence in a gray backyard. Tomorrow would be Christmas Day, and she had only $1.87 with which to buy Jim a present. She had been saving every penny she could for months, with this result. Twenty dollars a week doesn't go far. Expenses had been greater than she had calculated. They always are. Only $1.87 to buy a present for Jim. Her Jim. Many a happy hour she had spent planning for something nice for him. Something fine and rare and sterling—something just a little bit near to being worthy of the honor of being owned by Jim.

There was a pier-glass between the windows of the room. Perhaps you have seen a pier-glass in an $8 flat. A very thin and very agile person may, by observing his reflection in a rapid sequence of longitudinal strips, obtain a fairly accurate conception of his looks. Della, being slender, had mastered the art.

Suddenly she whirled from the window and stood before the glass. Her eyes were shining brilliantly, but her face had lost its color within twenty seconds. Rapidly she pulled down her hair and let it fall to its full length.

Now, there were two possessions of the James Dillingham Youngs in which they both took a mighty pride. One was Jim's gold watch that had been his father's and his grandfather's. The other was Della's hair. Had the Queen of Sheba lived in the flat across the airshaft, Della would have let her hair hang out the window some day to dry just to depreciate Her Majesty's jewels and gifts. Had King Solomon been the janitor, with all his treasures piled up in the basement, Jim would have pulled out his watch every time he passed, just to see him pluck at his beard from envy.

So now Della's beautiful hair fell about her rippling and shining like a cascade of brown waters. It reached below her knee and made itself almost a garment for her. And then she did it up again nervously and quickly. Once she faltered for a minute and stood still while a tear or two splashed on the worn red carpet.

On went her old brown jacket; on went her old brown hat. With a whirl of skirts and with the brilliant sparkle still in her eyes, she fluttered out the door and down the stairs to the street.

Where she stopped the sign read: "Mme. Sofronie. Hair Goods of All Kinds." One flight up Della ran, and collected herself, panting. Madame, large, too white, chilly, hardly looked the "Sofronie."

"Will you buy my hair?" asked Della.

"I buy hair," said Madame. "Take yer hat off and let's have a sight at the looks of it."

Down rippled the brown cascade.

"Twenty dollars," said Madame, lifting the mass with a practised hand.

"Give it to me quick," said Della.

Oh, and the next two hours tripped by on rosy wings. Forget the hashed metaphor. She was ransacking the stores for Jim's present.

She found it at last. It surely had been made for Jim and no one else. There was no other like it in any of the stores, and she had turned all of them inside out. It was a platinum fob chain simple and chaste in design, properly proclaiming its value by substance alone and not by meretricious ornamentation—as all good things should do. It was even worthy of The Watch. As soon as she saw it she knew that it must be Jim's. It was like him. Quietness and value—the description applied to both. Twenty-one dollars they took from her for it, and she hurried home with the 87 cents. With that chain on his watch Jim might be properly anxious about the time in any company. Grand as the watch was, he sometimes looked at it on the sly on account of the old leather strap that he used in place of a chain.

When Della reached home her intoxication gave

way a little to prudence and reason. She got out her curling irons and lighted the gas and went to work repairing the ravages made by generosity added to love. Which is always a tremendous task, dear friends—a mammoth task.

Within forty minutes her head was covered with tiny, close-lying curls that made her look wonderfully like a truant schoolboy. She looked at her reflection in the mirror long, carefully, and critically.

"If Jim doesn't kill me," she said to herself, "before he takes a second look at me, he'll say I look like a Coney Island chorus girl. But what could I do—oh! what could I do with a dollar and eighty-seven cents?"

At 7 o'clock the coffee was made and the frying-pan was on the back of the stove hot and ready to cook the chops.

Jim was never late. Della doubled the fob chain in her hand and sat on the corner of the table near the door that he always entered. Then she heard his step on the stair away down on the first flight, and she turned white for just a moment. She had a habit of saying little silent prayers about the simplest everyday things, and now she whispered: "Please God, make him think I am still pretty."

The door opened and Jim stepped in and closed it. He looked thin and very serious. Poor fellow, he was only twenty-two—and to be burdened with a family! He needed a new overcoat and he was without gloves.

Jim stopped inside the door, as immovable as

a setter at the scent of quail. His eyes were fixed upon Della, and there was an expression in them that she could not read, and it terrified her. It was not anger, nor surprise, nor disapproval, nor horror, nor any of the sentiments that she had been prepared for. He simply stared at her fixedly with that peculiar expression on his face.

Della wriggled off the table and went for him.

"Jim, darling," she cried, "don't look at me that way. I had my hair cut off and sold it because I couldn't have lived through Christmas without giving you a present. It'll grow out again—you won't mind, will you? I just had to do it. My hair grows awfully fast. Say 'Merry Christmas!' Jim, and let's be happy. You don't know what a nice —what a beautiful, nice gift I've got for you."

"You've cut off your hair?" asked Jim, laboriously, as if he had not arrived at that patent fact yet even after the hardest mental labor.

"Cut it off and sold it," said Della. "Don't you like me just as well, anyhow? I'm me without my hair, ain't I?"

Jim looked about the room curiously.

"You say your hair is gone?" he said, with an air almost of idiocy.

"You needn't look for it," said Della. "It's sold, I tell you—sold and gone, too. It's Christmas Eve, boy. Be good to me, for it went for you. Maybe the hairs of my head were numbered," she went on with a sudden serious sweetness, "but nobody could ever count my love for you. Shall I put the chops on, Jim?"

Out of his trance Jim seemed quickly to wake. He enfolded his Della. For ten seconds let us regard with discreet scrutiny some inconsequential object in the other direction. Eight dollars a week or a million a year—what is the difference? A mathematician or a wit would give you the wrong answer. The magi brought valuable gifts, but that was not among them. This dark assertion will be illuminated later on.

Jim drew a package from his overcoat pocket and threw it upon the table.

"Don't make any mistake, Dell," he said, "about me. I don't think there's anything in the way of a haircut or a shave or a shampoo that could make me like my girl any less. But if you'll unwrap that package you may see why you had me going a while at first."

White fingers and nimble tore at the string and paper. And then an ecstatic scream of joy; and then, alas! a quick feminine change to hysterical tears and wails, necessitating the immediate employment of all the comforting powers of the lord of the flat.

For there lay The Combs—the set of combs, side and back, that Della had worshipped for long in a Broadway window. Beautiful combs, pure tortoise shell, with jewelled rims—just the shade to wear in the beautiful vanished hair. They were expensive combs, she knew, and her heart had simply craved and yearned over them without the least hope of possession. And now, they were hers, but the tresses that should have adorned the coveted adornments were gone.

But she hugged them to her bosom, and at length she was able to look up with dim eyes and a smile and say: "My hair grows so fast, Jim!"

And then Della leaped up like a little singed cat and cried, "Oh, oh!"

Jim had not yet seen his beautiful present. She held it out to him eagerly upon her open palm. The dull precious metal seemed to flash with a reflection of her bright and ardent spirit.

"Isn't it a dandy, Jim? I hunted all over town to find it. You'll have to look at the time a hundred times a day now. Give me your watch. I want to see how it looks on it."

Instead of obeying, Jim tumbled down on the couch and put his hands under the back of his head and smiled.

"Dell," said he, "let's put our Christmas presents away and keep 'em a while. They're too nice to use just at present. I sold the watch to get the money to buy your combs. And now suppose you put the chops on."

The magi, as you know, were wise men—wonderfully wise men—who brought gifts to the Babe in the manger. They invented the art of giving Christmas presents. Being wise, their gifts were no doubt wise ones, possibly bearing the privilege of exchange in case of duplication. And here I have lamely related to you the uneventful chronicle of two foolish children in a flat who most unwisely sacrificed for each other the greatest treasures of their house. But in a last word to the wise of these days let it be said that of all who give gifts these two were the wisest. Of all who give and receive gifts, such as they are wisest. Everywhere they are wisest. They are the magi.

The Furnished Room

O. Henry

Restless, shifting, fugacious as time itself is a certain vast bulk of the population of the red brick district of the lower West Side. Homeless, they have a hundred homes. They flit from furnished room to furnished room, transients forever—transients in abode, transients in heart and mind. They sing "Home, Sweet Home" in ragtime; they carry their *lares et penates* in a bandbox; their vine is entwined about a picture hat; a rubber plant is their fig tree.

Hence the houses of this district, having had a thousand dwellers, should have a thousand tales to tell, mostly dull ones, no doubt; but it would be strange if there could not be found a ghost or two in the wake of all these vagrant guests.

One evening after dark a young man prowled among these crumbling red mansions, ringing their bells. At the twelfth he rested his lean hand-baggage upon the step and wiped the dust from his hatband and forehead. The bell sounded faint and far away in some remote, hollow depths.

To the door of this, the twelfth house whose bell he had rung, came a housekeeper who made him think of an unwholesome, surfeited worm that had eaten its nut to a hollow shell and now sought to fill the vacancy with edible lodgers.

He asked if there was a room to let.

"Come in," said the housekeeper. Her voice came from her throat; her throat seemed lined with fur. "I have the third-floor-back, vacant since a week back. Should you wish to look at it?"

The young man followed her up the stairs. A faint light from no particular source mitigated the shadows of the halls. They trod noiselessly upon a stair carpet that its own loom would have forsworn. It seemed to have become vegetable; to have degenerated in that rank, sunless air to lush lichen or spreading moss that grew in patches to the staircase and was viscid under the foot like organic matter. At each turn of the stairs were vacant niches in the wall. Perhaps plants had once been set within them. If so they had died in that foul and tainted air. It may be that statues of the saints had stood there, but it was not difficult to conceive that imps and devils had dragged them forth in the darkness and down to the unholy depths of some furnished pit below.

"This is the room," said the housekeeper, from her furry throat. "It's a nice room. It ain't often vacant. I had some most elegant people in it last summer—no trouble at all, and paid in advance to the minute. The water's at the end of the hall. Sprowls and Mooney kept it three months. They done a vaudeville sketch. Miss B'retta Sprowls— you may have heard of her—oh, that was just the stage names—right there over the dresser is where the marriage certificate hung, framed. The gas is here, and you see there is plenty of closet room. It's a room everybody likes. It never stays idle long."

"Do you have many theatrical people rooming here?" asked the young man.

"They comes and goes. A good proportion of my lodgers is connected with the theaters. Yes, sir, this is the theatrical district. Actor people never stays long anywhere. I get my share. Yes, they comes and they goes."

He engaged the room, paying for a week in advance. He was tired, he said, and would take possession at once. He counted out the money. The room had been made ready, she said, even to towels and water. As the housekeeper moved away he put, for the thousandth time, the question that he carried at the end of his tongue.

"A young girl—Miss Vashner—Miss Eloise Vashner—do you remember such a one among your lodgers? She would be singing on the stage, most likely. A fair girl, of medium height and slender, with reddish, gold hair and dark mole near her left eyebrow."

"No, I don't remember the name. Them stage people has names they change as often as their rooms. They comes and they goes. No, I don't call that one to mind."

No. Always no. Five months of ceaseless interrogation and the inevitable negative. So much time spent by days in questioning managers, agents, schools and choruses; by night among the audiences of theaters from all-star casts down to music halls so low that he dreaded to find what he most hoped for. He who had loved her best had tried to find her. He was sure that since her disappearance from home this great, water-grit city held her somewhere, but it was like a monstrous quicksand, shifting its particles constantly, with no foundation, its upper granules of today buried tomorrow in ooze and slime.

The furnished room received its latest guest with a first glow of pseudo-hospitality, a hectic, haggard, perfunctory welcome like the specious smile of a demirep. The sophistical comfort came in reflected gleams from the decayed furniture, the ragged brocade upholstery of a couch and two chairs, a foot-wide cheap pier glass between the two windows, from one or two gilt picture frames and a brass bedstead in a corner.

The guest reclined, inert, upon a chair, while the room, confused in speech as though it were an apartment in Babel, tried to discourse to him of its divers tenantry.

A polychromatic rug like some brilliant-flowered rectangular, tropical islet lay surrounded by a billowy sea of soiled matting. Upon the gay-papered wall were those pictures that pursue the homeless one from house to house—The Huguenot Lovers, The First Quarrel, The Wedding Breakfast, Psyche at the Fountain. The mantel's chastely severe outline was ingloriously veiled behind some pert drapery drawn rakishly askew like the sashes of the Amazonian ballet. Upon it was some desolate flotsam cast aside by the room's marooned when a lucky sail had borne them to a fresh port—a trifling vase or two, pictures of actresses, a medicine bottle, some stray cards out of a deck.

One by one, as the characters of a cryptograph became explicit, the little signs left by the furnished room's procession of guests developed a significance. The threadbare space in the rug in front of the dresser told that lovely woman had marched in the throng. The tiny fingerprints on the wall spoke of little prisoners trying to feel their way to sun and air. A splattered stain, raying like the shadow of a bursting bomb, witnessed where a hurled glass or bottle had splintered with its contents against the wall. Across the pier glass had been scrawled with a diamond in staggering letters the name "Marie." It seemed that the succession of dwellers in the furnished room had turned in fury—perhaps tempted beyond forebearance by its garish coldness—and wreaked upon it their passions. The furniture was chipped and bruised; the couch, distorted by bursting springs, seemed a horrible monster that had been slain during the stress of some grotesque convulsion. Some more potent upheaval had cloven a great slice from the marble mantel. Each plank in the floor owned its particular cant and shriek as from a separate and individual agony. It seemed incredible that all this malice and injury had been wrought upon the room by those who had called it for a time their home; and yet it may have been the cheated home instinct surviving blindly, the resentful rage at false household gods that had kindled their wrath. A hut that is our own we can sweep and adorn and cherish.

The young tenant in the chair allowed these thoughts to file, soft-shod, through his mind, while there drifted into the room furnished sounds and furnished scents. He heard in one room a tittering and incontinent, slack laughter; in others the monologue of a scold, the rattling of dice, a lullaby, and one crying dully; above him a banjo tinkled with spirit. Doors banged somewhere; the elevated trains roared intermittently; a cat yowled miserably upon a back fence. And he breathed the breath of the house—a dank savor rather than a smell—a cold, musty effluvium as from underground vaults mingled with the reeking exhalations of linoleum and mildewed and rotten woodwork.

Then suddenly, as he rested there, the room was filled with the strong, sweet odor of mignonette. It came as upon a single buffet of wind with such sureness and fragrance and emphasis that it almost seemed a living visitant. And the man cried aloud: "What, dear?" as if he had been called, and sprang up and faced about. The rich odor clung to him and wrapped him around. He reached out his arms for it, all his senses for the time confused and commingled. How could one be peremptorily called by an odor? Surely it must have been a sound. But, was it not the sound that had touched, that had caressed him?

"She has been in this room," he cried, and he sprang to wrest from it a token, for he knew he would recognize the smallest thing that had belonged to her or that she had touched. This enveloping scent of mignonette, the odor that she had loved and made her own—whence came it?

The room had been but carelessly set in order. Scattered upon the flimsy dresser scarf were half a dozen hairpins—those discreet, indistinguishable friends of womankind, feminine of gender, infinite mood and uncommunicative of tense. These he ignored, conscious of their triumphant lack of identity. Ransacking the drawers of the dresser he came upon a discarded, tiny, ragged handkerchief. He pressed it to his face. It was racy and insolent with heliotrope; he hurled it to the floor. In another drawer he found odd buttons, a theater program, a pawn-broker's card, two lost marshmallows, a book on the divination of dreams. In the last was a woman's black satin hair bow, which halted him, poised between ice and fire. But the black satin hair bow also is femininity's demure, impersonal common ornament and tells no tales.

And then he traversed the room like a hound on the scent, skimming the walls, considering the corners of the bulging matting on his hands and knees, rummaging mantel and tables, the curtains and hangings, the drunken cabinet in the corner, for a visible sign, unable to perceive that she was there beside, around, against, within, above him, clinging to him, wooing him, calling him so poign-

258

antly through the finer senses that even his grosser ones became cognizant of the call. Once again he answered loudly: "Yes, dear!" and turned, wild-eyed, to gaze on vacancy, for he could not yet discern form and color and love and outstretched arms in the odor of mignonette. Oh, God! whence that odor, and since when have odors had a voice to call? Thus he groped.

He burrowed in crevices and corners, and found corks and cigarettes. These he passed in passive contempt. But once he found in a fold of the matting a half-smoked cigar, and this he ground beneath his heel with a green and trenchant oath. He sifted the room from end to end. He found dreary and ignoble small records of many a peripatetic tenant; but of her whom he sought, and who may have lodged there, and whose spirit seemed to hover there, he found no trace.

And then he thought of the housekeeper.

He ran from the haunted room downstairs and to a door that showed a crack of light. She came out to his knock. He smothered his excitement as best he could.

"Will you tell me, madam," he besought her, "who occupied the room I have before I came?"

"Yes, sir. I can tell you again. 'Twas Sprowls and Mooney, as I said. Miss B'retta Sprowls it was in the theaters, but Missis Mooney she was. My house is well known for respectability. The marriage certificate hung, framed, on a nail over—"

"What kind of a lady was Miss Sprowls—in looks, I mean?"

"Why, black-haired, sir, short, and stout, with a comical face. They left a week ago Tuesday."

"And before they occupied it?"

"Why, there was a single gentleman connected with the draying business. He left owing me a week. Before him was Missis Crowder and her two children, that stayed four months; and back of them was old Mr. Doyle, whose sons paid for him. He kept the room six months. That goes back a year, sir, and further I do not remember."

He thanked her and crept back to his room. The room was dead. The essence that had vivified it was gone. The perfume of mignonette had departed. In its place was the old, stale odor of moldy house furniture, of atmosphere in storage.

The ebbing of his hope drained his faith. He sat staring at the yellow, singing gaslight. Soon he walked to the bed and began to tear the sheets into strips. With the blade of his knife he drove them tightly into every crevice around windows and door. When all was snug and taut he turned out the light, turned the gas full on again and laid himself gratefully upon the bed.

It was Mrs. McCool's night to go with the can for beer. So she fetched it and sat with Mrs. Purdy in one of those subterranean retreats where housekeepers foregather and the worm dieth seldom.

"I rented out my third-floor-back this evening," said Mrs. Purdy, across a fine circle of foam. "A young man took it. He went up to bed two hours ago."

"Now, did ye, Mrs. Purdy, ma'am?" said Mrs. McCool, with intense admiration. "You do be a wonder for rentin' rooms of that kind. And did ye tell him, then?" she concluded in a husky whisper laden with mystery.

"Rooms," said Mrs. Purdy, in her furriest tones, "are furnished for to rent. I did not tell him, Mrs. McCool."

" 'Tis right ye are, ma'am; 'tis by renting rooms we kape alive. Ye have the rale sense for business, ma'am. There be many people will rayjict the rentin' of a room if they be tould a suicide has been after dyin' in the bed of it."

"As you say, we has our living to be making," remarked Mrs. Purdy.

"Yis, ma'am; 'tis true. 'Tis just one wake ago this day I helped ye lay out the third-floor-back. A pretty slip of a colleen she was to be killin' herself wid the gas—a swate little face she had, Mrs. Purdy, ma'am."

"She'd a-been called handsome, as you say," said Mrs. Purdy, assenting but critical, "but for that mole she had a-growin' by her left eyebrow. Do fill up your glass again, Mrs. McCool."

The Introducers

Edith Wharton

At nine o'clock on an August morning Mr. Frederick Tilney descended the terrace steps of Sea Lodge and strolled across the lawn to the cliffs.

The upper windows of the long white façade above the terrace were all close shuttered, for at nine o'clock Newport still sleeps, and he who is stirring enough to venture forth at that unwanted hour may enjoy what no wealth could buy a little later—the privilege of being alone.

Though Mr. Tilney's habits of life, combined with the elegance of his appearance, declared him to be socially disposed, he was not insensible to the rarer pleasures of self-communion, and on this occasion he found peculiar gratification in the thought of having to himself the whole opulent extent of turf and flower border between Ochre Point and Bailey's Beach. The morning was brilliant, with a blue horizon line pure of fog, and such a sparkle on every leaf and grass blade, and on every restless facet of the ever-moving sea, as would have tempted a less sophisticated fancy to visions of wet bows and a leaping stern, or of woodland climbs up the course of a mountain stream.

But it was so long since Mr. Tilney had found a savor in such innocent diversion, that the unblemished fairness of the morning suggested to him only a lazy well-being associated with escape from social duties, and the chance to finish the French novel over which he had fallen asleep at three o'clock that morning.

It was odd how he was growing to value his rare opportunities of being alone. He, who in his earlier years had depended on the stimulus of companionship as the fagged diner-out depends on the fillip of his first glass of champagne, was not beginning to watch for and cherish every momentary escape from the crowd. It had grown to such a passion with him, this craving to have the world to himself, that he had overcome the habit of late rising, and learned to curtail the complications of his toilet, in order to secure a half hour of solitude before he was caught back into the whizzing social machinery.

"And talk of the solitude of the desert, it's nothing to the Newport cliffs at this hour," he mused, as he threw himself down on a shaded seat invitingly placed near the path which follows the shore. "Sometimes I feel as if the sea, and the cliffs, and the skyline out there, were all a part of the stupid show—the expensive stage setting of a rottenly cheap play—to be folded up and packed away with the rest of the rubbish when the performance is over; it's good to come out and find it here at this hour, all by itself, and not giving a hang for the ridiculous goings-on of which it happens to be made the temporary background. Well—there's one comfort: none of the other fools really *see* it —it's here only for those who seek it out at such an hour—and as I'm the only human being who does, it's here only for me, and belongs only to me, and not to the impenetrable asses who think they own it because they've paid for it as so many thousand dollars a foot!"

And Mr. Tilney, throwing out his chest with the irrepressible pride of possessorship, cast an eye of approval along the windings of the deserted path which skirted the lawn of Sea Lodge and lost itself in the trim shrubberies of the adjoining estate.

"Yes—it's mine—all mine—and this is the only real possessorship, after all! No fear of intruders at this hour—no need of warning signposts, and polite requests to keep to the path. I don't suppose anybody ever walked along this path at my hour, and I don't care who walks here for the rest of the day!" But at this point his meditations were interrupted by the sight of a white gleam through the adjacent foliage; and a moment later all his theories as to the habits of his neighbors had been rudely shattered by the appearance of a lady who, under the sheltering arch of a wide lace sunshade, was advancing indolently toward his seat.

"Why, you've got my bench!" she exclaimed, pausing before him, with merriment and indignation mingling in her eyes as sun and wind contended on the ripples behind her.

"*Your* bench?" echoed Tilney, rising at her approach, and dissembling his annoyance under a fair pretense of hospitality. "If ever I thought anything on earth was mine, it's this bench."

The lady, who was young, tall and critical looking, drew her straight brows together and smilingly pondered his assertion.

"I suppose you thought that because it happens to stand in the grounds of Sea Lodge instead of Cliffwood—*we* haven't any benches, by the way; but my theory is a little different, as it happens. I think things belong only to the people who know how to appreciate them."

"Why, so do I—if the bench isn't mine, at least the theory is!" Tilney protested.

"Well, it's mine too, and it makes the bench mine, you see," the young lady argued with earnestness, "because hitherto I've been the only person who appreciated sitting on it at this hour."

"Ah, hitherto, perhaps—but not since I arrived here last week. I haven't missed a morning," Tilney declared.

She smiled. "That explains the misunderstanding. I've been away for a week, and before that no one ever, ever sat on my bench at this hour."

"And since then no one has ever, ever sat on *my* bench at this hour; but, my dear Miss Grantham," Tilney gallantly concluded, "I shall be only too honored if you will make the first exception to the rule by sitting on it in my company this morning."

Miss Grantham was evidently a young lady of judicial temper, for she weighed this assertion as carefully as the other, before answering, with a slight tinge of condescension: "I don't know that you have any more right to ask me to sit on *my* bench, than I have to ask you to sit on *yours*, but for my part I am magnanimous enough to assume just for once that it's ours."

Tilney bowed his thanks and seated himself at her side. "I realize how magnanimous it is of you," he returned, "for, just as you came round the corner, I was saying to myself that this bench was really the only thing in the world I could call my own—"

"And now I've taken half of it away from you! But then," she rejoined, "you've taken the other half from *me;* and as I was under the same delusion as yourself, we are both in the same situation, and had better accommodate ourselves, as best we can to the diminished glory of joint ownership."

"It would be ungrateful of me to reject so reasonable a proposal; but in return for my consent, would you mind telling me how you happen to attach such excessive importance to the ownership of this bench?"

"It isn't the bench alone—it's the bench and the hour. They are the only things I have to myself."

Tilney met her lovely eyes with a look of intelligence. "Ah, that's surprising—very surprising."

"Why so?" she exclaimed, a little resentfully.

"Because it's so exactly my own feeling."

Miss Grantham smiled and caressed the folds

of her lace gown. "And is it so surprising that we should happen to have the same feelings?"

"Not in all respects, I trust; but I never suspected you of an inclination for solitude."

She returned his scrutiny with a glance as penetrating. "Well, you don't look like a recluse yourself; yet I think I should have guessed that you sometimes have a longing to be alone."

"A longing? Good heavens, it's a passion, it's becoming a mania!"

"Ah, how well I understand that. It's the only thing that can tear me from my bed!"

"I confess one doesn't associate you with the sunrise," he said, letting his glance rest with amusement on the intricate simplicity of her apparel.

"And you!" she smiled back at him. "If our friends were to be told that Fred Tilney and Belle Grantham were to be found sitting on the cliffs at nine o'clock in the morning, the day after the Summerton ball—"

"And that they had come there, not to meet each other, but to escape from everyone else—"

"Oh, there's the point; that's what makes it interesting. If we're in the same box, why shouldn't we be on the same bench?"

"It requires no argument to convince me that we should. But *are* we in the same box? You see I've just come, and when I saw you last night I supposed you were stopping with the Summertons."

She shook her head. "No, I'm next door, at Cliffwood, for the summer."

"At Cliffwood? With the Bixbys?" He glanced at the fantastic chimneys and profusely carved gables which made the neighboring villa rise from its shrubberies like a *pièce montée* from a flower-decked dish.

"Well, why not, if *you're* at Sea Lodge with Mr. Magraw?"

"Oh, I'm only a poor itinerate devil—"

"And what am I but a circulating beauty? Didn't you know I'd gone into the business, too? I hope you won't let professional jealousy interfere with our friendship."

"I'm not sure that I can help it, if you've really gone into the business. But when I last saw you —where was it?—oh, in Athens—"

"Things were different, were they not?" she interposed. "I was sketching and you were archaeologizing—do you remember that divine day at Delphi? Not that you took much notice of me, by the way—"

"Wasn't one warned off the premises by the report that you were engaged to Lord Pytchley?"

She colored, and negligently dropped her sunshade between her eyes and his. "Well, I wasn't, you see—and my sketches were not good enough to sell. So I've taken to this kind of thing instead. But I thought you meant to stick to your digging."

He hesitated. "I was very keen about it for a time but I had a touch of the sun out in Greece that summer and a rich fellow picked me up on his steam yacht and carried me off to the Black Sea and then to a salmon river in Norway. I meant to go back, but I dawdled, and the first thing I knew they put another chap in my place. And now I'm Hutchins Magraw's secretary."

He sat staring absently at the distant skyline and, perceiving that he was no longer conscious of her presence, she quietly shifted her sunshade and let her eyes rest for a moment on his moody profile.

"Yes—that's what I call it, too. I'm Mrs. Bixby's secretary—or Sadie's, I forget which. But how much writing do you do?"

"Well, not much. The butler attends to the invitations."

"I merely keep an eye on Sadie's spelling, and see that she doesn't sign herself 'lovingly' to young men. Mrs. Bixby has no correspondents, and the dinner invitations are engraved."

"And what are your other duties?"

"Oh, the usual things—reminding Mrs. Bixby not to speak of her husband as *Mr. Bixby,* not to send in her cards when people are at home, not to let the butler say 'fine claret' in a sticky whisper in people's ears, not to speak of town as 'the city,' and not to let Mr. Bixby tell what things cost. Mrs. Bixby takes the bit in her teeth at times, but Sadie is such a dear adaptable creature that, when I've broken her of trying to relieve her callers of their hats, I shall really have nothing left to do. That habit is hard to eradicate, because she is such a good girl, and it was so carefully inculcated at her finishing school."

Tilney reflected. "Magraw is a good fellow too. There's really nothing to do except to tone him down a little—as you say, one feels as if one didn't earn one's keep."

She flashed round upon him instantly. "Ah, but I didn't say that. I said the ostensible duties were easy—but how about the others?"

He looked at her a little consciously. "What do you mean by the others?"

"I don't know how far you live up to your duties, but I'm horribly conscientious about mine. And of course what we're both paid for is to be introducers," she said.

"Introducers?" He colored slightly and, flinging his arm over the back of the bench, turned to command a fuller view of her face. "Yes, that is what we're paid for, I suppose."

"And that's what I hate about it, don't you?"

"Uncommonly," he assented with emphasis.

"It isn't that the Bixbys are not nice people—they are, deep down, you know—or at least they would be, if they were leading a real life among their real friends. But the very fact that one is abetting them to lead a false life, and renounce and deny their past, and impose themselves on people who wouldn't look at them if it were not for their money, and who rather resent their intrusion as it is—well, if one oughtn't to be paid well for doing such a job as that, I don't know what it is to work for my living!"

Tilney continued to observe with appreciation the dramatic play of feature by means of which she expressed her rising disgust at her task; but when she ended he merely said in a detached tone: "It's charming, how you've preserved your illusions."

"My illusions? Why, I haven't enough left for decency!"

"Oh, yes you have. About the Bixbys, and what they would be if one hadn't egged them on. Why not say to yourself that, if they were not vulgar at heart, they would never have to let themselves be taken in by this kind of humbug?"

"Is that what you say about Mr. Magraw?"

"I've told you that Magraw is a good fellow. But when I ran across him he was simply aching to see the show, and all I've done is to get him a seat in the front row."

"Yes—but are you not expected to do something more for him?"

"Something more—in what line?"

"Well, I think the Bixbys expect me to make a match for Sadie."

"The deuce they do! Well, we'll marry her to my man."

Miss Grantham uttered a cry of dismay. "Don't suggest it even in joke! Don't you see what a catastrophe it would be?"

"Why should it be a catastrophe?"

"Don't you really see? In the first place we should both be out of a job, and in the second, I should earn the everlasting enmity of the Bixbys.

What they want for Sadie is not money but position. Mrs. Bixby tells me that every day."

Tilney received this in mediative silence; then he said with a slight laugh: "Well, if position is all they want, why don't you choose *me* as your candidate?"

Miss Grantham did not echo his laugh; she simply concentrated her gaze on his with a slowly deepening interest before answering: "It's a funny idea—but I believe they might do worse."

Tilney's hilarity increased.

"At any rate," she continued, without noticing it, "there's one thing that you and no one else can do for them and I really believe that Mrs. Bixby, in her present mood, would be capable of rewarding you with her daughter's hand."

"Good heavens! Then I should have to take a look at Miss Bixby before doing it."

"Oh, Sadie's charming. Didn't you notice her last night at the ball? I managed to smuggle her in, though I couldn't get the others invited. What Mrs. Bixby wants," Miss Grantham earnestly continued, "what she's absolutely sickening for at this moment, is to have Sadie invited to Aline Leicester's little Louis XV dance tomorrow night. And you are the only person in Newport who can do it. I didn't even have a chance to try—for the very day my invitation came I happened to meet Aline, and she said at once: 'Belle, I see the Bixbys in your eye; but I don't see them in my ballroom.' After that, I tried a little wire-pulling, but it simply made her more obstinate—you know her latest pose is to snub the new millionaires; and you are the only person who can persuade her to make an exception for the Bixbys. Aline's family feeling is tremendously strong, and everyone knows you are her favorite cousin."

Tilney listened attentively to this plea; but when it had ended he said, with discouraging gesture: "I was just going to try to get an invitation for Magraw!"

"Lump them together then—it will be just as easy; and if you *should* want Mr. Bixby to do anything for you—such as putting you on to a good tip—"

"Thanks, but I've been put on to too many good tips. If it weren't for the good tips I've had, I should be living like a gentleman on my income."

"Well, you'll make Mrs. Bixby think you the most eligible young man in Newport. And if you could persuade Aline to ask Sadie to the dinner before the dance—"

"*Comme vous y allez!* What would be my return for that?"

She rose with a charming gesture. "Who knows, after all? Perhaps only the pleasure of doing me a very great favor."

"That settles it. I'll do what I can. But how about getting your costumes at such short notice?"

"Oh, we cabled out to Worth on the chance." She held out her hand for good-bye. "If only there were something I could do for *you!*"

"Well, there is, as it happens," he rejoined with

a smile. "If I succeed in my attempt, let Magraw dance the cotillon with you at Aline's."

She hesitated, visibly embarrassed. "I should be delighted, of course. I'm engaged already, but that's nothing. Only—I'm going to be horribly frank—the Bixbys are rather a heavy load, and I'm not sure I can carry your friend too!"

"Oh, yes, you can. That's my reason for asking you. You see, I really can't help Magraw much. It takes a woman to give a man a start. Aline will say, 'Oh, bring him, if you choose—' but when he comes she won't take any notice of him, or introduce him to any of the nice women. He was too shy to go to the Summertons' last night—he's really very shy under his loudness—so Aline's dance will be his first appearance in Newport; and if he's seen dancing the cotillon with you, at a little *sauterie* like that, with only a handful of people in the room, why, he's made, and my hard work is over for the season."

She smiled. "If you take a fancy to Sadie, perhaps it's over for life."

"And if *you*—by George! No, I don't think I want you to dance the cotillon with Magraw."

"Why not? Do you grudge me a comfortable home for my old age?"

He stood gazing at her as though for the first time his eyes took in the full measure of her grace.

"No—but I grudge *him* even a cotillon with you."

"Ah, you and I were not made to dance cotillons with one another; or do anything together, except

274

conspire at sunrise for each other's material advancement. And that reminds me—I shan't see you again today, for we are going to Narragansett on Mr. Bixby's yacht, and tonight we have a dinner at home. But if you succeed with Aline, will you send me a line in the evening?"

He shook his head as they clasped hands once more. "No; but I'll tell you about it here tomorrow morning."

"Very well—I'll be punctual!" she called out to him, as she sped away through the shrubbery.

II

It was, in fact, Miss Grantham who was first on the scene the next morning; and, so eager was she to learn the result of the mission with which she had charged her friend, that, instead of profiting by her few moments of solitude, she sat watching the path and chafing at Mr. Tilney's delay.

When he arrived, politeness restrained the question on her lips; but his first word was to assure her of his success. "You are to bring Miss Bixby to the dinner," he announced.

"Oh, thank you, thank you—you're wonderful!" she exclaimed; "and if there's anything in the world I can do—" She paused suddenly, remembering her side of the compact, and added with nobility: "If it is of any possible advantage to Mr. Magraw to make my acquaintance, I shall be very glad—"

She had already observed in Tilney a marked depression of manner, which even this handsome reaffirmation of her purpose did not dispel.

"Oh," he merely said, "I did not mean to hold you so closely to your bargain—" and with that he seated himself at her side, and lapsed into a state of dumb preoccupation.

Miss Grantham suffered this as long as it was possible for a young lady of spirit to endure; then she determined to make Mr. Tilney aware of her presence by withdrawing it.

"I am afraid," she said, rising with a smile, "that, though you welcomed me so handsomely yesterday, my being here seriously interferes with your enjoyment of the hour, and I am going to propose a compromise. Since it is agreed that we are joint proprietors of this bench, and entitled to an equal share of its advantages, and since our sitting on it together practically negates those advantages, I suggest that we occupy it on alternate mornings—and to show my gratitude for the favor you have done me, I will set the example by withdrawing today."

Tilney met her smile with a look of unrelieved melancholy. "I don't wonder," he said, "that you find solitude less oppressive than my company; but, since our purpose in seeking this bench is to snatch an hour's quiet enjoyment, and since enjoyment of any sort is impossible to me today, it is obviously you who are entitled to remain here, and I who ought to take myself away." And he held out his hand in farewell.

Miss Grantham detained it in hers. "To have you surrender your rights because you are too miserable to enjoy them, leaves me with no heart to profit by my own; and if you wish me to remain you must stay also, and tell me what it is that troubles you."

She reseated herself as she spoke, and Tilney, with a deprecating gesture, resumed his place at her side.

"My dear Miss Grantham, the subject is too trifling to mention; I was only trying to calculate how long one could live in Venice on a hundred dollars."

"Why in Venice—and why a hundred dollars?"

"Because, when my passage is paid, it will be all the ready money I possess, and I have always heard that one could live very moderately in Venice."

Miss Grantham flushed and threw a quick glance at him. "You're not thinking of deserting?" she cried, reproachfully.

The young man returned her look. "Deserting—whom?" he inquired.

"Well, me, if you choose! You can't think the comfort it's been to me, since yesterday, to know that there were two of us. I understand now how humane it is to chain convicts together!"

Tilney considered this with a faint smile. "How long have you been at it?" he asked.

"At the Bixbys? I joined them last April in Paris."

"Ah, well—I've been six months with Magraw.

It wasn't so bad when we were yachting and knocking about the world—but since we've taken to society it has become unendurable."

"Yes. I didn't mind ordering the Bixbys' dresses as much as I mind providing opportunities for their wearing them."

"I don't so much mind trotting Magraw about—though you know it's nonsense about your having to dance with him this evening—"

"No matter about that. What *is* it that bothers you?"

"The whole preposterous situation. Magraw's the best fellow in the world—but there are moments when he takes me for the butler."

"Oh, I know," she sympathized. "Mrs. Bixby—"

"That isn't the worst, though; it's the reaction. He took me for the butler yesterday afternoon—and in the evening I found a ruby scarfpin on my dressing table."

But her sympathy was ready for any demand on it. "I know, I know—" she reiterated; and then, breaking off, she added with a mounting color, "You know I couldn't go to the dance tonight if Mrs. Bixby didn't pay for my dress."

"Oh, the cases are not the same; and it's different for a woman."

"Why are the cases not the same? And why should I not be humiliated by what humiliates you?"

He shrugged his shoulders ironically. "I'm not

humiliated by anything that poor Magraw does to me; I'm humiliated by what I do to *him!*"

"What you do?"

"Yes. What right have I to behave like a gentlemen, and return his scarfpins?"

"At least you do return them! And I can't return the dresses. Oh, it's detestable either way!" she exclaimed.

"Yes, especially when one succumbs to the weakness of hating *them* instead of one's self. I hate Magraw this morning," he confessed.

She rose with an impatient glance at her watch. "Dear me, I must go. I promised Sadie to see the dressmaker at half-past nine; she's coming to alter our fancy dresses. You see I felt sure you would get Sadie's invitation. I want you to know her," she continued. "She's really a very nice girl. I should like her immensely if I didn't have to accept so many favors from her."

"Ah, you've just expressed my feeling about Magraw. I really should like your opinion of him," he added.

"Well, you shall have it—tomorrow morning."

"Here?" he rejoined with sudden interest.

"Why not? You know I mean to dance with him this evening."

The morning after the dance it was Miss Grantham's turn to arrive late at the tryst; and when she did so, it was with the air of having a duty to discharge rather than a pleasure to enjoy.

"Mr. Tilney," she said, advancing resolutely to

the bench on which he sat awaiting her, "my only object in coming this morning is—"

He rose with extended hand. "To let me thank you, I hope, for the generous way in which you fulfilled your share of the compact? It was awfully good of you to be so nice to Magraw."

She colored vividly, but held his gaze. "As it happens, I *liked* Mr. Magraw. But if I had known the means you had used to obtain his invitation—"

Tilney colored in turn, but they continued to face each other boldly.

"Did Aline betray me? How like a woman!" he exclaimed.

"I can quite understand," Miss Grantham witheringly continued, "the importance you attached to having Mr. Magraw invited to your cousin's dance. *You had to make some return for the scarf pin*. But to use my name as a pretext—to tell Aline Leicester that I was trying to marry Mr. Magraw!"

"Oh, I didn't say *trying*—I said you meant to," Tilney corrected.

"As if that made it any better! To let that man think—"

"He'll never hear of it; and you don't seem to realize that it's not easy to extract an invitation from Aline."

"I don't know that it was absolutely necessary that Mr. Magraw should receive one!"

Tilney, at this, raised his head with a challenging air. "You appeared to think it absolutely necessary that Miss Bixby should."

"Well—I don't see—"

"You don't see how I got *hers?* I dare say you'll think the same method is even more objectionable when the situation is reversed—"

She stared at him with growing disapproval. "You don't mean to say that you let Aline think you wanted to marry Sadie Bixby?"

"I told you there was nothing I wouldn't stoop to. I suppose you think that horribly low."

Her stare resolved itself into a faint sound of laughter. "Good heavens, how enchanted Mrs. Bixby will be!"

"The deuce she will—but of course the joke can easily be explained."

"To whom? To Mrs. Bixby? I'm glad you think so. I should have said it would be difficult."

"Oh, Mrs. Bixby will never hear of it. I told Aline in the strictest confidence—"

"Everyone at the dance was congratulating me on my conquest of Mr. Magraw. I don't see why Aline should keep one secret and not the other."

Tilney's brow darkened ominously. "Well, at any rate, I'll soon undeceive Magraw!"

"A thousand thanks. And I suppose you leave it to me to undeceive Sadie? She talked of you all the way home. Of course, you're almost the only decent man she's met."

"Ah, then the remedy is simple enough. You've only to introduce a few others."

"Yes, I've thought of that." Miss Grantham examined him with a cold smile. "But are you quite sure you want me to?"

Tilney met her question with another. "What on earth do you mean?"

"I'm not stupid in such cases, and I could see that Sadie was interested. Did you find her so perfectly impossible?"

"Impossible? I thought her very pretty."

"That's going to the other extreme—but she certainly looked her best last night. Still, before deciding, I should want you to see her by daylight—and without the paint—"

"Oh, she had on very little paint. One could see her own color through it."

"Yes—she has an unfortunate way of getting red—"

"At my age I should call it blushing."

Miss Grantham's face grew suddenly stern. "Of course," she said, "I should never forgive myself if you were only trifling with Sadie—"

Tilney paused. "But if I were in earnest—?" he suggested.

She gazed at him intently for a moment. "After all, I might be saving her from something worse!"

III

For two mornings after that Tilney, to his secret regret, had the bench on the cliffs to himself. On the third morning he was detained indoors somewhat later than usual on pressing business of his employer's; and when he emerged from the house he was surprised, and considerably dismayed, to find his seat tenanted by the incongruous figure of Mr. Hutchins Magraw.

Given his patron's unmatutinal habits, and rooted indifference to the beauties of nature, it was impossible to conceive what whim had drawn him to so unlikely a spot at so improbable an hour; and Tilney's first impulse was to approach the seat, and allay his curiosity by direct inquiry. Hardly, however, had he begun to advance when the flutter of a white skirt through the Cliffwood shrubberies caused him to retreat abruptly into the convert of lilac bushes edging the lawn. It was by a mere accident, of course, that an unknown female, wearing a white gown, happened to be walking along the path from that particular direction. The path was open to the public, and there was no reason to assume any coincidence between—

Tilney drew a sharp breath. Mr. Magraw had risen and was advancing in the direction of the approaching petticoat; and as it was impossible for him to recognize its wearer from where he sat, it was obvious that he expected someone, and that the invisible female was no casual stroller drawn forth by the beauty of the morning. The next moment this conjecture was unpleasantly confirmed; for Miss Grantham emerged from the shrubbery, and placed her hand in Mr. Magraw's without perceptible surprise. He, then, had also been expected; and she had actually had the effrontery to select, as the scene of their tryst, the seat which, by every right of friendship, should have been kept sacred to her conversations with Fred Tilney!

"The idea of telling him about my bench!" Resentment of her perfidy was for the moment uppermost in Tilney's breast, or was, at any rate, the only sentiment to which he chose to give explicit expression. But other considerations surged indignantly beneath it—wonder at woman's unaccountableness, disgust at her facility, disappointment, above all, that this one little episode, saved from the wreckage of many shattered illusions, should have had so premature and unpoetic an ending.

"Magraw—if only it hadn't been Magraw!"

He had meant to turn away and re-enter the house; but a feeling of mingled curiosity and wretchedness kept him rooted in his hiding place, while he followed with his eyes the broad swaggering back of Mr. Hutchins Magraw, as it attended Miss Grantham's slender silhouette across the lawn.

"I hadn't realized how disgustingly fat the man has grown. One would think a fellow with that outline would know better than to rig himself out in a check a foot square, and impale his double chin on the points of that preposterous collar! It's odd how little the most fastidious women notice such details. If they did, fewer men would make themselves ridiculous. Why are they standing there, looking up at the house? Perhaps, after all, it *was* an accident, their meeting. No—they're making straight for the bench—by George, I believe they were looking at the house to make sure *I* wasn't coming! Don't be alarmed, my dear Miss Grantham, I've no desire to interfere with your amusements. I see now, though, why Magraw was in such a hurry to have me balance his bankbook this morning. Just a dodge to keep me indoors, of course. It's beastly bad taste, anyhow, to make a poor devil like me go over a bankbook with such an indecently big balance. That's the kind of thing that makes a man turn socialist. Why the devil should Magraw have all those millions while I— well, to be sure, poor devil, he needs them all to make up for his other deficiencies. I'd like to see how long Belle Grantham would share that bench with him if it weren't for his bank account! It must be hard work to talk to Magraw at nine o'clock in the morning. I wonder what the deuce she's saying to him?"

The two objects of Tilney's contemplation had by this time settled themselves on the seat which their observer still chose to call his own, and something in their attitudes seemed to announce that theirs was no transient alighting, but the deliberate installation which precedes an earnest talk.

"Well, she could talk to anybody, at any hour of the day or night! That's her trade, poor girl, as much as it is mine. Only I can't see why she should give Magraw *my* particular hours. Now that I've given him such a good start they've plenty of other chances of meeting. But perhaps she's afraid of competition, and wants to clinch the business by this morning's interview. Poor girl! How she must hate it at heart! It'll do her the justice to say that if she had enough to keep body and soul together she'd never look at a Magraw. But if this hand-to-mouth life is hard on a man it's ten times worse for a woman—and her day is over sooner, too. Poor girl! No wonder she shrinks at the idea of growing old in such a trade. To see people cooling off, and the newcomers crowding her out—how can I blame her for being afraid to face such a future? Why, I ought to do what I can to help her—but to help her to Magraw! Bah—there's something rotten in our social system; but it isn't her fault, and only a primitive ass of a man would be fool enough to blame her, instead of pitying her as a fellow victim."

At this point Miss Grantham started up with an apprehensive gesture with which Tilney was painfully familiar. "She's had to look at her watch to realize how time was flying! She doesn't seem to find it goes on slowly with Magraw. Perhaps my pity's wasted, after all. That's the way she always lingers on after she had said she couldn't possibly stay another minute. Poor Magraw! She's playing him for all she's worth, and I don't suppose he even knows he's on the hook. Oh, I don't blame her—not in the least!—only I think she might have chosen another place for their meetings. Hardened wretch as I am, I was beginning to have a sentiment for the bench—it would never have occurred to me to sit there with Miss Bixby, for instance. It's queer how a woman's taste deteriorates when she associates with common men—

but I mean to let Miss Grantham know that, though she's welcome to Magraw, she can't have my bench into the bargain!"

By this time the couple under observation had completed their lingering adieux, the gentleman returned across the lawn to his house, while the lady retraced her way toward Cliffwood. Tilney remained in concealment while Mr. Magraw strode by within a few feet, the fatuous smile of self-complacency upon his lips; then the young man, emerging behind his patron's back, struck across the lawn and overtook Miss Grantham as she turned into the adjoining grounds.

She paused as she became aware of Tilney's approach, and cast a rapid glance in the direction from which he had come; but he had taken care not to show himself till Magraw had vanished in the shrubberies, and he was quick to note the look of reassurance in Miss Grantham's eyes. She held out her hand, blushing slightly, but self-possessed.

"*J'ai failli attendre!*" she quoted with an indulgent smile; and the smile had well-nigh stung her companion to immediate retaliation. But he meditated a subtler revenge, and dissembling his resentment, asked innocently: "Have you been here long?"

"It has certainly seemed so," she replied in the same tone.

"Well, at any rate, my involuntary delay has enabled you to enjoy what you originally came out to see" and, in reply to her puzzled glance, he added pointedly: "The pleasures of solitude."

Unmoved by the thrust, she turned a smiling look on him. "But what if you have made them lose their flavor?"

"Then it was almost worth my while to have stayed away!"

She held out her hand. "The experiment was so successful that you need not try it again," she said sweetly. "But time flies, and I must hasten back into captivity."

He detained her hand to ask sentimentally: "I hope you are not losing your taste for freedom?" and she replied, as she hastened away: "Come and see—come and see tomorrow!"

He stood in the path where she had left him, and slowly drew from his pocket Mr. Magraw's latest gift—a jeweled cigarette case. He took out the cigarettes, transferred them to his pocket, and then, with a free swing of the arm, flung their receptacle into the sea.

"Do *you* come and see tomorrow!" he muttered, addressing himself to Miss Grantham's retreating figure; then he lit a cigarette, and walked rapidly back to Sea Lodge.

"I shouldn't have thought it of her!" he said as he entered the house.

IV

Two mornings later Tilney, with a beating heart, descended the terrace of Sea Lodge, and once more directed himself toward the bench on the cliff.

He was not only on time, but a few minutes before the hour; yet it was something of a surprise to him to find the bench still untenanted. He seated himself, lit a cigarette with deliberation, and drew from his pocket a note stamped Cliffwood and bearing the date of the previous evening.

"Dear Mr. Tilney," it ran, "Much as I dislike to intrude upon the solitude which I know you value so highly, I must ask you to spare me a few moments tomorrow morning, and I send this line in advance in order that my coming may not interfere with *any other arrangements*.

> Yours sincerely,
> Belle Grantham."

Tilney reread this note with an air of considerable complacency; then he laid it carefully back in his notecase, and rose to meet Miss Grantham as she made her appearance around the curve of the path.

The morning was chilly and veiled in a slight haze, too translucent to be called a fog, but per-

289

ceptible enough to cast a faint grayness over sea and sky. Seen in this tempered light, Miss Grantham's face seemed to lose its usual vivacity and be subdued to the influence of the atmosphere; and her manner of greeting Tilney had the same tinge of soberness.

"I must excuse myself," she began, "for again intruding on your privacy—"

"*My* privacy?" Tilney gallantly interposed. "Was it not long since understood between us that the privacy of this spot belongs as much to you as to me?"

"Long since—yes," she replied, "but so much has happened in the interval." She paused, and added in a significant tone, "Since I came here yesterday morning and found you sitting on this bench with Sadie Bixby."

Tilney feigned a successful show of embarrassment. "You came here yesterday morning—?"

"By appointment, as you evidently do *not* remember," she continued coldly. "It is a mistake one does not make twice, and my only object in asking to see you this morning—"

"One moment," Tilney interposed, "Before you go on, I must stay in my own defense that I assumed our compact about the use of this seat had been abrogated when I came out the day before yesterday and found *you* sharing it with Magraw."

There was no mistaking the effect of this thrust. Her color rose painfully, and she forced a laugh as she replied: "The day before yesterday? Ah, yes—that was the morning you were so late. Mr. Magraw saw me from the house and took pity on my deserted state."

Tilney colored also at this fresh evidence of her duplicity.

"I beg your pardon—but does not your memory deceive you? It seemed to me that Magraw was waiting on the bench, and that it was *you* who took pity—if I am not mistaken."

She drew herself up and flashed an outraged glance at him. "You were watching us then?" she exclaimed.

"Oh—*watching!* I was merely repairing to our seat at my usual hour."

"At your usual hour? But Mr. Magraw told me you were not coming—that you would be busy all the morning with some writing—" She broke off, seeing herself more deeply involved with each word.

"Some writing he had given me to do? Precisely," Tilney answered with scorn. "Only, he had underrated either my impatience to see you, or my head for figures—or both."

She received this in an embarrassed silence and, softened by her embarrassment, he added: "It is not for me to discuss your arrangements, but I confess I wondered a little that you chose our bench as a meeting place."

She hesitated a moment and then said in a deprecating tone, "It is the only place where I can see anyone alone!"

"And you wished to see Magraw alone?"

Their eyes met defiantly but hers fell first as she answered, "Yes—I did wish to."

Tilney bowed ceremoniously. "In that case, of course, nothing remains to be said."

They had both remained standing during this short colloquy; but she now seated herself and signed to him to do the same.

"Yes—something remains for me to say, and it was for the purpose of saying it that I asked you to meet me this morning."

Tilney, without replying, placed himself at the opposite end of the bench.

"What I wish to ask," she continued in a decisive tone, "is your object in meeting Miss Bixby here yesterday."

The temerity of the question was so surprising to her companion that for a moment he gazed at her without speaking; then he replied with a faint smile, "If there is any right of priority in such inquiries, perhaps I am entitled to ask first what was your object in meeting Magraw here the day before that."

She repressed her impatience and returned gently, "The cases are surely not quite alike but I thought I had already given you my answer."

"That you wished to see him alone? Well, I had the same object in asking Miss Bixby to meet me."

"But you must see that in the case of a young girl—especially a girl as inexperienced as Sadie—"

Tilney raised his hand with a deprecating gesture. "Are you not falling into the conventional mistake of assuming that a man cannot seek to be alone with a young girl except for the purpose of making love to her?"

"Well, what other purpose—?"

He looked at her calmly. "Then it was to promote that purpose that you asked Magraw to meet you here the day before I met Miss Bixby?"

It was Miss Grantham's turn to color and she fulfilled the obligation handsomely. "I see no object in such cross-questioning—"

"Ah, pardon me, but it was you who began it."

"It was my duty to question you about Sadie. You can't imagine I do it for my pleasure—but her parents are too inexperienced to protect her."

"To protect her? Then you consider me hopelessly detrimental—?"

Miss Grantham drew a quick breath. "Why not have told me at once that you wished to marry her? Everyone is saying so, of course, but I could not help remembering that your intentions have not always been so—"

"Specific?" he suggested ironically.

"Well, you are still unmarried," she observed.

"Yes," he said, musingly. "It takes a pretty varied experience of life to find out that there are worse states than marriage."

Miss Grantham rose with a smile. "Since you *have* found it out," she said generously, "I can congratulate you with perfect sincerity. Sadie is a dear little creature—"

"But too good for me? Is that what you meant to add?"

"No, for when you find out how good she is you'll want to be worthy of her."

He received this in silence but when she held out her hand for goodbye he said: "I wonder if it's not my duty to protect Magraw? He hasn't even an inexperienced parent."

She met his smile steadily but he felt the sudden resistance of her hand. "Mr. Magraw," she returned, withdrawing it, "would be quite safe if Sadie were."

"If Sadie—?"

She broke into a laugh. "If you're planning to take the bread out of my mouth, I must do something in the way of self-preservation." And as he remained silent, feeling a rather tragic import under her pleasantry, she added wearily, "I can't begin this kind of thing over again—I simply can't!"

Tilney's discouraged gesture showed his comprehension of her words. "To whom do you say it?" he exclaimed.

"Well, then, let us drop phrases and admit frankly that we're trying to marry each other's wards—or whatever you choose to call them!"

He did not answer and she continued, with a kind of nervous animation, "And that we'll do all we can—that we *honorably* can—to help each other's plans and see each other through."

The young man still remained silent, his eyes absently fixed on the line of sea from which the veil of mist was gradually receding, and before he had found a reply a footman, hastening across the lawn from the house, broke in upon his meditations.

"Beg pardon, sir, but Mr. Magraw wishes you to come in immediately, sir, to answer the telephone for him."

Tilney turned abruptly toward his companion. "By heaven, yes, we'll see each other through!" he exclaimed.

Though Tilney and Miss Grantham had parted without any reference to future meetings at the same spot, each was now drawn to the bench on the cliffs by a new motive—the not unpardonable desire to see if the other had again extended its hospitality to a third party.

Their mutual reconnoitering did not, for several mornings, carry them farther than the most distant point from which the bench was visible when, perceiving it to be untenanted, they respectively retreated, without having discovered each other's maneuver.

The fifth day, however, was so foggy that distant espionage was impossible; and Tilney's suspicions having been aroused by the unusual amount of correspondence with which his patron had burdened him overnight, he determined to ascertain by direct inspection if the sanctity of the bench had again been violated. It would have been hard to say why, in his own thoughts, he still applied such terms to the possibility of Miss Grantham's resorting to the spot in company with her suitor. Tilney fully acquiesced in the inevitableness of the course they had agreed upon; but if his reason accepted the consequences, his sensibilities made the process unpleasant to contemplate. He would have been prepared to append his signature to a matrimonial contract drawn up between Miss Grantham and his employer; but it irritated him that an arrangement so purely utilitarian should be disguised under the charming futilities of courtship.

"The real grossness is not in viewing marriage as a business partnership, but in pretending that one doesn't," he summed up, as he crossed the damp lawn with the waves of gray fog coiling around him like a phantom sea.

Through their pale surges he could just discern, as he approached the bench, an indeterminate outline hovering near it and the outline proclaiming itself, on nearer inspection, as of his own sex. Tilney was about to turn aside when another figure appeared from the direction of Cliffwood.

"It's odd," he mused, trying to philosophize upon his own discomfiture "—it's odd how the fog distorts a silhouette. I could have sworn I should have known hers anywhere and yet this deceptive vapor—or my nerves, or the two together—make her look so much shorter—and I'll swear I never saw her swing her arm as she walked. I suppose it comes from associating with a bounder like—"

He drew back with a suppressed exclamation as the small feminine outline showed more clearly through a partial break in the fog.

"Why, it looks—no, it can't be! Hanged if I know, she's so bundled up. Well, it's not *she* at any rate and if Magraw, at this stage of the proceedings, has the indecency to be meeting other women here, it's almost my duty to the poor girl to let her know before it's too late to break with him."

He was surprised at the immediate sense of lightness which this conclusion produced in him. He was sorry for Miss Grantham, of course, when she'd so nearly landed her man; but, hang it, there were as good fish in the sea and meanwhile she must, at all costs, be saved from the humiliation of committing herself further. His first impulse had been the somewhat cruel one of putting the unvarnished facts before her but further reflection made him shrink from this course and cast about for some more humane expedient.

"If she could only be made to think that she can do better than Magraw; and she ought to, with half a chance, poor child! I can't be wholly sorry that she should not be sacrificed to this particular monster—not that Magraw's not a good fellow in himself; I dare say the Minotaur was locked in his own set—but he should have stayed there, that's all."

While engaged in these considerations, Tilney had prudently withdrawn into the Cliffwood shrubberies and he was just deciding to effect his escape through the Bixbys' grounds, rather than run the chance of being discovered by the tenants of the bench, when, on issuing from his retreat, he beheld the indistinct gleam of a white dress halfway down the Cliffwood lawn. This time, even though the fog had thickened, there was no mistaking the form and movement of the shrouded figure. Or was it some subtler sense than that of sight that so positively assured him of Miss Grantham's nearness? At any rate, he advanced to meet her without a moment's hesitation, determined to protect her, by whatever expedient, from the embarrassment of interrupting the colloquy on the bench. He had but a moment in which to consider how this should be effected; but it was not the first time he had trusted to his gift of improvisation in delicate situations and he was now sustained by the unwonted sense of his complete disinterestedness. The progress of his own affairs had in fact made it impossible for him to interfere from personal motives and he thus had the support of knowing that his intervention was quite unaffected by selfish considerations.

"I'm almost glad," he reflected, "that I *am* committed, if one of the first consequences is to enable me to act as her friend without any afterthought or any possibility of her suspecting me of not playing fair. One of my reasons for wanting to settle my own future has always been the desire to help her, and little Sadie is far too good a girl not to understand—"

At this point he found himself face to face with Miss Grantham, who, suddenly discerning him through the fog, drew back with a slight start of surprise.

"I had a feeling that I might meet you this morning," he said in a tone of undisguised pleasure, and, even as he spoke, his half-formed plan for her rescue began to dissolve in the glow of happiness which her nearness always produced. He was annoyed to find that his self-control was so completely at the mercy of her presence; but he could no more resist the sudden reaction of his pulses from reason to feeling than he could dispel the softly enveloping fog which seemed to act as the accomplice of his wishes.

"If I can only make her think she can do better than Magraw," he kept mechanically repeating to himself; but the only expedient that occurred to him was one which both prudence and honor rejected.

Miss Grantham's first words threw his ideas into still deeper confusion.

"Mr. Tilney," she said, without heeding his greeting, "are you, or are you not, engaged to Sadie Bixby?"

The abruptness of the inquiry, and the sternness of her tone, had a not wholly unpleasing effect on the young man; but their only perceptible results was to reduce him to an embarrassed silence.

Miss Grantham gave a faint laugh. "I suppose I may consider myself answered? And in that case, I have only to apologize for asking so indiscreet a question—"

Tilney cleared his throat nervously. "I am not aware that I have either answered your question or shown that I regarded it as indiscreet—"

"Your silence did both," she returned with some impatience. He made no reply and after a moment's pause she added, with a sudden assumption of playfulness, "Well, if this is really to be our last meeting, as I suppose it is, shall we not celebrate it by sitting together for a few moments on our poor dear old bench?"

As she spoke she began to move in the direction of the seat, apparently assuming that her companion would offer no opposition to her proposal. But Tilney, with a vague exclamation, laid his hand on her arm, "Don't you think it's rather too damp to sit out of doors?"

He reddened under the laugh with which she met this incongruous objection.

"My poor friend—would she really mind so much? I was foolish enough to think you might give me this last morning—"

"The whole day is at your service," he interposed nervously, "but—"

"Ah, yes, there will always be a *but* between us now. No wonder men get on so much better than women; they are so much more prudent! Now, even if I were engaged to Mr. Magraw—" She broke off, and he fancied he could see her flush through the fog.

He turned on her abruptly. "*Are* you? There's the point!" he exclaimed.

She drew back slightly disconcerted but, recovering herself at once, added in the same playful tone: "I was about to say that, even if I *were*, I should not feel there was any disloyalty to my future in giving this last hour to *our* past."

Her light emphasis on the pronoun threw him into a glow of pleasure through which discretion and foresight loomed as remote as objects in the fog; but when she added, with a half-sad laugh, "I should not hesitate to go back to our bench for the last time—" he broke out, with a fresh leap of apprehension, "Ah, but you couldn't, if it meant to you what it does to me!"

He had spoken the words haphazardly, snatching at them as the readiest means of diverting her purpose; but once uttered they seemed to fill the whole air and to create a silence which neither speaker had, for a moment, the courage to fill.

Womanlike, Miss Grantham was the first to recover her self-possession. "I am sure," she said sweetly, "that we shall both look back often on our quiet morning talks; and I can't think that the persons with whom our futures may be associated will be defrauded by our treasuring such memories."

She spoke with a sadness so poignant to Tilney that for a moment he stood without replying, and during the pause she again advanced a few steps nearer to the bench.

The young man broke into a scornful laugh, "*Defrauded?* Good heavens—one can't defraud people of treasures they are utterly incapable of valuing!"

She caught this up with a vehemence that surprised him. "Oh, do you feel that too? It's just what I mean," she exclaimed.

"Feel it—?" He stopped before her, blocking her way. "Do you suppose I've felt anything else, night or day, since the accursed day when we agreed—?"

He interrupted himself with a last effort at self-control, and she replied in a low tone of exquisite pleading: "Well, then, if you *do* feel it, why not go back for a moment to our bench?"

Tilney groaned. "Can't we talk as well here? Let us walk a little way—we shall be alone anywhere in this fog." ("Anywhere but on that confounded bench," he mentally added.)

Miss Grantham uttered an ironical exclamation. "Ah, you've promised her, I see. Was it one of the conditions? In that case, of course—"

"There were no conditions—and if there had been—"

"Oh, be careful! I want to talk of our past, and not of our future."

Tilney groaned again. "If only it *could* be our future—Belle, what a beastly bad turn we've done each other, after all!"

"Don't let us talk of the present either please." She laid a restraining touch on his arm. "Why should we give each other this pain when it's too late?"

"Too late?" He paused, remembering that, for him at least, it *was* too late, but an irresistible impulse prompted him to add, "If it hadn't been, tell me at least—*would you have dared to*, Belle?"

They stood looking at each other, mysteriously isolated in the magic circle of the fog.

"Dared? I am daring more now—more than I have courage for!" she murmured, half to herself.

The admission had well-nigh broken down the last barriers of Tilney's self-restraint, but at the moment of surrender he suddenly recalled his own state of bondage. He had but to lead Miss Grantham to the bench and she would find herself free; but when she turned to reward him as liberators expect to be rewarded, with what a sorry countenance must he refuse her gift!

He dropped the hand he had caught in his, and said in a low voice, "You were right just now, and I was wrong. We must not even talk of our past, lest we should be tempted to think of our present or our future. I happen to know that I am not doing anyone a serious wrong in speaking to you as I have; but my own case is different."

"Your own case is different?" Miss Grantham interposed, with a sudden change of voice and expression. "If you think you can make love to me without doing Mr. Magraw a serious wrong, I should like to know why I may not listen to you without—"

Tilney received her attack with a disarming humility. "I said the cases were different because, in a moment of incredible folly, I have tried to attract the interest of a trustful, affectionate girl—"

Miss Grantham interrupted him with a laugh. "Do you mean that," she asked ironically, "for a description of Sadie Bixby?"

Her tone aroused an incongruous flash of resentment in Tilney. "I see no difficulty," he returned, "in identifying the young lady from my words."

"If you really believe them to apply to her, I cannot see how you can excuse yourself for being here with me at this moment!" She laughed again and then, to Tilney's surprise, drew nearer and once more laid her hand on his arm.

"My poor friend, it is I who am the real offender and not you. Believe me, I would not have let you speak to me as you have today if I had not known—if I had not almost felt it my duty to be kind to you—to do what I could to atone—"

"To be kind to me? To atone? What on earth are you talking about?" exclaimed Tilney, startled by this unexpected echo of his inmost thoughts.

"Alas, it was a foolish impulse and one which only our old friendship could justify. I forgot for a moment that I was not free, in my desire to prepare you—to console you in advance—for a blow—"

"A blow? You're not *married?*" burst from Tilney.

She paused, and gazed at him wonderingly but not unkindly.

"I was speaking of yourself—yourself and Sadie. I feel myself so deeply to blame—"

Tilney interrupted her with an air of inexpressible relief. "We're both to blame for abetting each other in such suicidal folly. As if either of us was made to give up life and liberty for a bank balance!

But I don't reproach you, Belle—it was more my fault than yours—and I deserve that I should be the one to pay the penalty!"

"The penalty? The penalty of marrying Sadie?" she breathlessly interposed.

"Of marrying anyone but you!" he returned recklessly, and at the retort a veil of sadness fell suddenly upon her eager face.

"It's too late to think of that now, but if you really feel as you say—"

Tilney again cut her short. "It's too late for me, I know, but if *you* really feel as you say, thank heaven, Belle, it's not too late for you!"

She drew back a step and both paused, as though dazed by the shock of their flying words. But as Tilney again approached her, she raised her hand and said gravely: "I don't know what you mean, but I can explain what *I* mean if you'll only—"

"One moment, please. I can explain, too, if you'll only—"

He caught her hand and began to lead her hurriedly across the lawn to the bench.

"Only what?" she panted, trying to keep pace with his flying strides, and he called back across his shoulder, "Only come to the bench—and be quick!"

"To the bench? Why, haven't I been trying all this time to take you there?" she cried after him, between tears and laughter.

"Yes, but I didn't know, at least *you* didn't know—"

"Didn't know what?"

"Whom you'd find there!"

She pulled back at this, detaining him forcibly. "Good heavens," she gasped, "do you mean to say that *you've* known all this time?"

"Do you think I should have dared to say what I have if I hadn't—?"

"Hadn't known about Sadie—?"

"*Sadie?* I suppose you mean Magraw?"

"Mr. Magraw?" She stopped short, and snatched her hand away with an indignant gesture.

"Mr. Tilney, who do you think is sitting on that bench?"

He faced around on her with equal indignation. "I don't *think*, I know. Magraw is sitting there with a woman."

"You're utterly mistaken! I happen to know that it's Sadie Bixby who is sitting there with a man."

There was a long pause between them, charged with a gradual rush of inner enlightenment; then Tilney suddenly burst into a huge, world-defying laugh.

"Well, then, don't you see—?"

"I don't see anything more than if the fog were inside me!" she wailed.

"Don't you see that Magraw and Miss Bixby must be sitting there together, and that, in that case, nothing remains for you and me but to find a new seat for ourselves?"

The Horse Dealer's Daughter

D. H. Lawrence

Well, Mabel, and what are you going to do with yourself?" asked Joe, with foolish flippancy. He felt quite safe himself. Without listening for an answer, he turned aside, worked a grain of tobacco to the tip of his tongue, and spat it out. He did not care about anything, since he felt safe himself.

The three brothers and the sister sat round the desolate breakfast-table, attempting some sort of desultory consultation. The morning's post had given the final tap to the family fortunes, and all was over. The dreary dining-room itself, with its heavy mahogany furniture, looked as if it were waiting to be done away with.

But the consultation amounted to nothing. There was a strange air of ineffectuality about the three men, as they sprawled at table, smoking and reflecting vaguely on their own condition. The girl was alone, a rather short, sullen-looking young woman of twenty-seven. She did not share the same life as her brothers. She would have been good-looking, save for the impressive fixity of her face, 'bull-dog', as her brothers called it.

There was a confused tramping of horses' feet outside. The three men all sprawled round in their chairs to watch. Beyond the dark holly bushes that separated the strip of lawn from the high-road, they could see a cavalcade of shire horses swinging out of their own yard, being taken for exercise. This was the last time. These were the last horses that would go through their hands. The young men watched with critical, callous look. They were all frightened at the collapse of their lives, and the sense of disaster in which they were involved left them no inner freedom.

Yet they were three fine, well-set fellows enough. Joe, the eldest, was a man of thirty-three, broad and handsome in a hot, flushed way. His face was red, he twisted his black moustache over a thick finger, his eyes were shallow and restless. He had a sensual way of uncovering his teeth when he laughed, and his bearing was stupid. Now he watched the horses with a glazed look of helplessness in his eyes, a certain stupor of downfall.

The great draught-horses swung past. They were tied head to tail, four of them, and they heaved along to where a lane branched off from the high-road, planting their great hoofs floutingly in the fine black mud, swinging their great rounded haunches sumptuously, and trotting a few sudden steps as they were led into the lane, round the corner. Every movement showed a massive, slumbrous strength, and a stupidity which held them in subjection. The groom at the head looked back, jerking the leading rope. And the cavalcade moved out of sight up the lane, the tail of the last horse, bobbed up tight and stiff, held out taut from the swinging great haunches as they rocked behind the hedges in a motion-like sleep.

Joe watched with glazed hopeless eyes. The horses were almost like his own body to him. He felt he was done for now. Luckily he was engaged to a woman as old as himself, and therefore her father, who was steward of a neighbouring estate, would provide him with a job. He would marry and go into harness. His life was over, he would be a subject animal now.

He turned uneasily aside, the retreating steps of the horses echoing in his ears. Then, with foolish restlessness, he reached for the scraps of bacon-rind from the plates, and making a faint whistling sound, flung them to the terrier that lay against the fender. He watched the dog swallow them, and waited till the creature looked into his eyes. Then a faint grin came on his face, and in a high, foolish voice he said:

"You won't get much more bacon, shall you, you little b——?"

The dog faintly and dismally wagged its tail, then lowered its haunches, circled round, and lay down again.

There was another helpless silence at the table. Joe sprawled uneasily in his seat, not willing to go till the family conclave was dissolved. Fred Henry, the second brother, was erect, clean-limbed, alert. He had watched the passing of the horses with more *sang-froid*. If he was an animal, like Joe, he was an animal which controls, not one which is controlled. He was master of any horse, and he carried himself with a well-tempered air of mastery. But he was not master of the situations of life. He pushed his coarse brown moustache upwards, off his lip, and glanced irritably at his sister, who sat impassive and inscrutable.

"You'll go and stop with Lucy for a bit, shan't you?" he asked. The girl did not answer.

"I don't see what else you can do," persisted Fred Henry.

"Go as a skivvy," Joe interpolated laconically.

The girl did not move a muscle.

"If I was her, I should go in for training for a nurse," said Malcolm, the youngest of them all. He was the baby of the family, a young man of twenty-two, with a fresh, jaunty *museau*.

But Mabel did not take any notice of him. They had talked at her and round her for so many years, that she hardly heard them at all.

The marble clock on the mantelpiece softly chimed the half-hour, the dog rose uneasily from the hearth-rug and looked at the party at the breakfast-table. But still they sat on in ineffectual conclave.

"Oh, all right," said Joe suddenly, apropos of nothing. "I'll get a move on."

He pushed back his chair, straddled his knees with a downward jerk, to get them free, in horsey fashion, and went to the fire. Still he did not go out of the room; he was curious to know what the others would do or say. He began to charge his pipe, looking down at the dog and saying in a high, affected voice:

"Going wi' me? Going wi' me are ter? Tha'rt goin' further than tha counts on just now, dost hear?"

The dog faintly wagged its tail, the man stuck out his jaw and covered his pipe with his hands, and puffed intently, losing himself in the tobacco, looking down all the while at the dog with an absent brown eye. The dog looked up at him in mournful distrust. Joe stood with his knees stuck out, in real horsey fashion.

"Have you had a letter from Lucy?" Fred Henry asked of his sister.

"Last week," came the neutral reply.

"And what does she say?"

There was no answer.

"Does she *ask* you to go and stop there?" persisted Fred Henry.

"She says I can if I like."

"Well, then, you'd better. Tell her you'll come on Monday."

This was received in silence.

"That's what you'll do then, is it?" said Fred Henry, in some exasperation.

But she made no answer. There was a silence of futility and irritation in the room. Malcolm grinned fatuously.

"You'll have to make up your mind between now and next Wednesday," said Joe loudly, "or else find yourself lodgings on the kerbstone."

The face of the young woman darkened, but she sat on immutable.

"Here's Jack Fergusson!" exclaimed Malcolm, who was looking aimlessly out of the window.

"Where?" exclaimed Joe loudly.

"Just gone past."

"Coming in?"

Malcolm craned his neck to see the gate.

"Yes," he said.

There was a silence. Mabel sat on like one condemned, at the head of the table. Then a whistle was heard from the kitchen. The dog got up and barked sharply. Joe opened the door and shouted:

"Come on."

After a moment a young man entered. He was muffled up in overcoat and a purple woollen scarf, and his tweed cap, which he did not remove, was pulled down on his head. He was of medium height, his face was rather long and pale, his eyes looked tired.

"Hello, Jack! Well, Jack!" exclaimed Malcolm and Joe. Fred Henry merely said: "Jack."

"What's doing?" asked the newcomer, evidently addressing Fred Henry.

"Same. We've got to be out by Wednesday. Got a cold?"

"I have—got it bad, too."

"Why don't you stop in?"

"*Me* stop in? When I can't stand on my legs, perhaps I shall have a chance." The young man spoke huskily. He had a slight Scotch accent.

"It's a knock-out, isn't it," said Joe, boisterously, "if a doctor goes round croaking with a cold. Looks bad for the patients, doesn't it?"

The young doctor looked at him slowly.

"Anything the matter with *you*, then?" he asked sarcastically.

"Not as I know of. Damn your eyes, I hope not. Why?"

"I thought you were very concerned about the patients, wondered if you might be one yourself."

"Damn it, no, I've never been patient to no flaming doctor, and hope I never shall be," returned Joe.

At this point Mabel rose from the table, and they all seemed to become aware of her existence. She began putting the dishes together. The young doctor looked at her, but did not address her. He had not greeted her. She went out of the room with the tray, her face impassive and unchanged.

"When are you off then, all of you?" asked the doctor.

"I'm catching the eleven-forty," replied Malcolm. "Are you goin' down wi' th' trap, Joe?"

"Yes, I've told you I'm going down wi' th' trap, haven't I?"

"We'd better be getting her in then. So long, Jack, if I don't see you before I go," said Malcolm, shaking hands.

He went out, followed by Joe, who seemed to have his tail between his legs.

"Well, this is the devil's own," exclaimed the doctor, when he was left alone with Fred Henry. "Going before Wednesday, are you?"

"That's the orders," replied the other.

"Where, to Northampton?"

313

"That's it."

"The devil!" exclaimed Fergusson, with quiet chagrin.

And there was silence between the two.

"All settled up, are you?" asked Fergusson.

"About."

There was another pause.

"Well, I shall miss yer, Freddy, boy," said the young doctor.

"And I shall miss thee, Jack," returned the other.

"Miss you like hell," mused the doctor.

Fred Henry turned aside. There was nothing to say. Mabel came in again, to finish clearing the table.

"What are *you* going to do, then, Miss Pervin?" asked Fergusson. "Going to your sister's, are you?"

Mabel looked at him with her steady, dangerous eyes, that always made him uncomfortable, unsettling his superficial ease.

"No," she said.

"Well, what in the name of fortune *are* you going to do? Say what you mean to do," cried Fred Henry, with futile intensity.

But she only averted her head, and continued her work. She folded the white table-cloth, and put on the chenille cloth.

"The sulkiest bitch that ever trod!" muttered her brother.

But she finished her task with perfectly impassive face, the young doctor watching her inter-estedly all the while. Then she went out.

Fred Henry stared after her, clenching his lips, his blue eyes fixing in sharp antagonism, as he made a grimace of sour exasperation.

"You could bray her into bits, and that's all you'd get out of her," he said, in a small, narrowed tone.

The doctor smiled faintly.

"What's she *going* to do, then?" he asked.

"Strike me if *I* know!" returned the other.

There was a pause. Then the doctor stirred.

"I'll be seeing you to-night, shall I?" he said to his friend.

"Ay—where's it to be? Are we going over to Jessdale?"

"I don't know. I've got such a cold on me. I'll come round to the 'Moon and Stars', anyway."

"Let Lizzie and May miss their night for once, eh?"

"That's it—if I feel as I do now."

"All's one——"

The two young men went through the passage and down to the back door together. The house was large, but it was servantless now, and desolate. At the back was a small bricked houseyard and beyond that a big square, gravelled fine and red, and having stables on two sides. Sloping, dank, winter-dark fields stretched away on the open sides.

But the stables were empty. Joseph Pervin, the father of the family, had been a man of no education, who had become a fairly large horse dealer. The stables had been full of horses, there was a great turmoil and come-and-go of horses and of dealers and grooms. Then the kitchen was full of servants. But of late things had declined. The old man had married a second time, to retrieve his fortunes. Now he was dead and everything was gone to the dogs, there was nothing but debt and threatening.

For months, Mabel had been servantless in the big house, keeping the home together in penury for her ineffectual brothers. She had kept house for ten years. But previously it was with unstinted means. Then, however brutal and coarse everything was, the sense of money had kept her proud, confident. The men might be foul-mouthed, the women in the kitchen might have bad reputations, her brothers might have illegitimate children. But so long as there was money, the girl felt herself established, and brutally proud, reserved.

No company came to the house, save dealers and coarse men. Mabel had no associates of her own sex, after her sister went away. But she did not mind. She went regularly to church, she attended to her father. And she lived in the memory of her mother, who had died when she was fourteen, and whom she had loved. She had loved her father, too, in a different way, depending upon him, and feeling secure in him, until at the age of fifty-four he married again. And then she had set hard against him. Now he had died and left them all hopelessly in debt.

She had suffered badly during the period of poverty. Nothing, however, could shake the curious, sullen, animal pride that dominated each member of the family. Now, for Mabel, the end had come. Still she would not cast about her. She would follow her own way just the same. She would always hold the keys of her own situation. Mindless and persistent, she endured from day to day. Why should she think? Why should she answer anybody? It was enough that this was the end, and there was no way out. She need not pass any more darkly along the main street of the small town, avoiding every eye. She need not demean herself any more, going into the shops and buying the cheapest food. This was at an end. She thought of nobody, not even of herself. Mindless and persistent, she seemed in a sort of ecstasy to be coming nearer to her fulfilment, her own glorification, approaching her dead mother, who was glorified.

In the afternoon she took a little bag, with shears and sponge and a small scrubbing-brush, and went out. It was a grey, wintry day, with saddened, dark green fields and an atmosphere blackened by the smoke of foundries not far off. She went quickly, darkly along the causeway, heeding nobody, through the town to the churchyard.

There she always felt secure, as if no one could see her, although as a matter of fact she was exposed to the stare of everyone who passed along under the churchyard wall. Nevertheless, once under the shadow of the great looming church, among the graves, she felt immune from the world, reserved within the thick churchyard wall as in another country.

Carefully she clipped the grass from the grave, and arranged the pinky white, small chrysanthemums in the tin cross. When this was done, she took an empty jar from a neighbouring grave, brought water, and carefully, most scrupulously sponged the marble headstone and the coping-stone.

It gave her sincere satisfaction to do this. She felt in immediate contact with the world of her mother. She took minute pains, went through the park in a state bordering on pure happiness, as if in performing this task she came into a subtle, intimate connection with her mother. For the life she followed here in the world was far less real than the world of death she inherited from her mother.

The doctor's house was just by the church. Fergusson, being a mere hired assistant, was slave to the country-side. As he hurried now to attend to the out-patients in the surgery, glancing across the graveyard with his quick eye, he saw the girl at her task at the grave. She seemed so intent and remote, it was like looking into another world. Some mystical element was touched in him. He slowed down as he walked, watching her as if spellbound.

She lifted her eyes, feeling him looking. Their eyes met. And each looked again at once, each feeling, in some way, found out by the other. He lifted his cap and passed on down the road. There remained distinct in his consciousness, like a vision, the memory of her face, lifted from the tombstone in the churchyard, and looking at him with slow, large, portentous eyes. It *was* portentous, her face. It seemed to mesmerise him. There was a heavy power in her eyes which laid hold of his whole being, as if he had drunk some powerful drug. He had been feeling weak and done before. Now the life came back into him, he felt delivered from his own fretted, daily self.

He finished his duties at the surgery as quickly as might be, hastily filling up the bottles of the waiting people with cheap drugs. Then, in perpetual haste, he set off again to visit several cases in another part of his round, before tea-time. At all times he preferred to walk if he could, but particularly when he was not well. He fancied the motion restored him.

The afternoon was falling. It was grey, deadened, and wintry, with a slow, moist, heavy coldness sinking in and deadening all the faculties. But why should he think or notice? He hastily climbed the hill and turned across the dark green fields, following the black cinder-track. In the distance, across a shallow dip in the country, the small town was clustered like smouldering ash, a tower, a spire, a heap of low, raw, extinct houses. And on the nearest fringe of the town, sloping into the dip, was Oldmeadow, the Pervins' house. He could see the stables and the outbuildings distinctly, as they lay towards him on the slope. Well, he would not go there many more times! Another resource would be lost to him, another place gone: the only company he cared for in the alien, ugly little town he was losing. Nothing but work, drudgery, constant hastening from dwelling to dwelling among the colliers and the iron-workers. It wore him out, but at the same time he had a craving for it. It was a stimulant to him to be in the homes of the working people, moving, as it were, through the innermost body of their life. His nerves were excited and gratified. He could come so near, into the very lives of the rough, inarticulate, powerfully emotional men and women. He grumbled, he said he hated the hellish hole. But as a matter of fact it excited him, the contact with the rough, strongly-feeling people was a stimulant applied direct to his nerves.

Below Oldmeadow, in the green, shallow, soddened hollow of fields, lay a square, deep pond. Roving across the landscape, the doctor's quick eye detected a figure in black passing through the gate of the field, down towards the pond. He looked again. It would be Mabel Pervin. His mind suddenly became alive and attentive.

Why was she going down there? He pulled up on the path on the slope above, and stood staring. He could just make sure of the small black figure moving in the hollow of the failing day. He seemed to see her in the midst of such obscurity, that he was like a clairvoyant, seeing rather with the mind's eye than with ordinary sight. Yet he could see her positively enough, whilst he kept his eye attentive. He felt, if he looked away from her, in the thick, ugly falling dusk, he would lose her altogether.

He followed her minutely as she moved, direct and intent, like something transmitted rather than stirring in voluntary activity, straight down the field towards the pond. There she stood on the bank for a moment. She never raised her head. Then she waded slowly into the water.

He stood motionless as the small black figure walked slowly and deliberately towards the centre of the pond, very slowly, gradually moving deeper into the motionless water, and still moving forward as the water got up to her breast. Then he could see her no more in the dusk of the dead afternoon.

"There!" he exclaimed. "Would you believe it?"

And he hastened straight down, running over the wet, soddened fields, pushing through the hedges, down into the depression of callous wintry obscurity. It took him several minutes to come to the pond. He stood on the bank, breathing heavily. He could see nothing. His eyes seemed to penetrate the dead water. Yes, perhaps that was the dark shadow of her black clothing beneath the surface of the water.

He slowly ventured into the pond. The bottom was deep, soft clay, he sank in, and the water clasped dead cold round his legs. As he stirred he could smell the cold, rotten clay that fouled up into the water. It was objectionable in his lungs. Still, repelled and yet not heeding, he moved deeper into the pond. The cold water rose over his thighs, over his loins, upon his abdomen. The lower part of his body was all sunk in the hideous cold element. And the bottom was so deeply soft and uncertain, he was afraid of pitching with his mouth underneath. He could not swim, and was afraid.

He crouched a little, spreading his hands under the water and moving them round, trying to feel for her. The dead cold pond swayed upon his chest. He moved again, a little deeper, and again, with his hands underneath, he felt all around under the water. And he touched her clothing. But it evaded his fingers. He made a desperate effort to grasp it.

And so doing he lost his balance and went under, horribly, suffocating in the foul earthy water, struggling madly for a few moments. At last, after what seemed an eternity, he got his footing, rose again into the air and looked around. He gasped, and knew he was in the world. Then he looked at the water. She had risen near him. He grasped her clothing, and drawing her nearer, turned to take his way to land again.

He went very slowly, carefully, absorbed in the slow progress. He rose higher, climbing out of the pond. The water was now only about his legs; he was thankful, full of relief to be out of the clutches of the pond. He lifted her and staggered on to the bank, out of the horror of wet, grey clay.

He laid her down on the bank. She was quite unconscious and running with water. He made the water come from her mouth, he worked to restore her. He did not have to work very long before he could feel the breathing begin again in her; she was breathing naturally. He worked a little longer. He could feel her live beneath his hands; she was coming back. He wiped her face, wrapped her in his overcoat, looked round into the dim, dark grey world, then lifted her and staggered down the bank and across the fields.

It seemed an unthinkably long way, and his burden so heavy he felt he would never get to the house. But at last he was in the stable-yard, and then in the house-yard. He opened the door and went into the house. In the kitchen he laid her down on the hearth-rug and called. The house was empty. But the fire was burning in the grate.

Then again he kneeled to attend to her. She was breathing regularly, her eyes were wide open and as if conscious, but there seemed something missing in her look. She was conscious in herself, but unconscious of her surroundings.

He ran upstairs, took blankets from a bed, and put them before the fire to warm. Then he removed her saturated, earthy-smelling clothing, rubbed her dry with a towel, and wrapped her naked in the blankets. Then he went into the dining-room, to look for spirits. There was a little whisky. He drank a gulp himself, and put some into her mouth.

The effect was instantaneous. She looked full into his face, as if she had been seeing him for some time, and yet had only just become conscious of him.

"Dr. Fergusson?" she said.

"What?" he answered.

He was divesting himself of his coat, intending to find some dry clothing upstairs. He could not bear the smell of the dead, clayey water, and he was mortally afraid for his own health.

"What did I do?" she asked.

"Walked into the pond," he replied. He had begun to shudder like one sick, and could hardly attend to her. Her eyes remained full on him, he seemed to be going dark in his mind, looking back at her helplessly. The shuddering became quieter in him, his life came back to him, dark and unknowing, but strong again.

"Was I out of my mind?" she asked, while her eyes were fixed on him all the time.

"Maybe, for a moment," he replied. He felt quiet, because his strength had come back. The strange fretful strain had left him.

"Am I out of my mind now?" she asked.

"Are you?" he reflected a moment. "No," he answered truthfully, "I don't see that you are." He turned his face aside. He was afraid now, because he felt dazed, and felt dimly that her power was stronger than his, in this issue. And she continued to look at him fixedly all the time. "Can you tell me where I shall find some dry things to put on?" he asked.

"Did you dive into the pond for me?" she asked.

"No," he answered. "I walked in. But I went in overhead as well."

There was silence for a moment. He hesitated. He very much wanted to go upstairs to get into dry clothing. But there was another desire in him. And she seemed to hold him. His will seemed to have gone to sleep, and left him, standing there slack before her. But he felt warm inside himself. He did not shudder at all, though his clothes were sodden on him.

"Why did you?" she asked.

"Because I didn't want you to do such a foolish thing," he said.

"It wasn't foolish," she said, still gazing at him as she lay on the floor, with a sofa cushion under her head. "It was the right thing to do. *I* knew best, then."

"I'll go and shift these wet things," he said. But still he had not the power to move out of her presence, until she sent him. It was as if she had the life of his body in her hands, and he could not extricate himself. Or perhaps he did not want to.

Suddenly she sat up. Then she became aware of her own immediate condition. She felt the blankets about her, she knew her own limbs. For a moment it seemed as if her reason were going. She looked round, with wild eye, as if seeking something. He stood still with fear. She saw her clothing lying scattered.

"Who undressed me?" she asked, her eyes resting full and inevitably on his face.

"I did," he replied, "to bring you round."

For some moments she sat and gazed at him awfully, her lips parted.

"Do you love me, then?" she asked.

He only stood and stared at her, fascinated. His soul seemed to melt.

She shuffled forward on her knees, and put her arms round him, round his legs, as he stood there, pressing her breasts against his knees and thighs, clutching him with strange, convulsive certainty, pressing his thighs against her, drawing him to her face, her throat, as she looked up at him with flaring, humble eyes of transfiguration, triumphant in first possession.

"You love me," she murmured, in strange transport, yearning and triumphant and confident. "You love me. I know you love me, I know."

And she was passionately kissing his knees, through the wet clothing, passionately and indiscriminately kissing his knees, his legs, as if unaware of everything.

He looked down at the tangled wet hair, the wild, bare, animal shoulders. He was amazed, bewildered, and afraid. He had never thought of loving her. He had never wanted to love her. When he rescued her and restored her, he was a doctor, and she was a patient. He had had no single personal thought of her. Nay, this introduction of the personal element was very distasteful to him, a violation of his professional honour. It was horrible to have her there embracing his knees. It was horrible. He revolted from it, violently. And yet—and yet—he had not the power to break away.

She looked at him again, with the same supplication of powerful love, and that same transcendent, frightening light of triumph. In view of the delicate flame which seemed to come from her face like a light, he was powerless. And yet he had never intended to love her. He had never intended. And something stubborn in him could not give way.

"You love me," she repeated, in a murmur of deep, rhapsodic assurance. "You love me."

Her hands were drawing him, drawing him down to her. He was afraid, even a little horrified. For he had, really, no intention of loving her. Yet her hands were drawing him towards her. He put out his hand quickly to steady himself, and grasped her bare shoulder. A flame seemed to burn the hand that grasped her soft shoulder. He had no intention of loving her: his whole will was against his yielding. It was horrible. And yet wonderful was the touch of her shoulders, beautiful the shining of her face. Was she perhaps mad? He had a horror of yielding to her. Yet something in him ached also.

He had been staring away at the door, away from her. But his hand remained on her shoulder. She had gone suddenly very still. He looked down at her. Her eyes were now wide with fear, with doubt, the light was dying from her face, a shadow of terrible greyness was returning. He could not bear the touch of her eyes' question upon him, and the look of death behind the question.

With an inward groan he gave way, and let his heart yield towards her. A sudden gentle smile came on his face. And her eyes, which never left his face, slowly, slowly filled with tears. He watched the strange water rise in her eyes, like some slow fountain coming up. And his heart seemed to burn and melt away in his breast.

He could not bear to look at her any more. He dropped on his knees and caught her head with his arms and pressed her face against his throat. She was very still. His heart, which seemed to have broken, was burning with a kind of agony in his breast. And he felt her slow, hot tears wetting his throat. But he could not move.

He felt the hot tears wet his neck and the hollows of his neck, and he remained motionless, suspended through one of man's eternities. Only now it had become indispensable to him to have her face pressed close to him; he could never let her go again. He could never let her head go away from the close clutch of his arm. He wanted to remain like that for ever, with his heart hurting him in a pain that was also life to him. Without knowing, he was looking down on her damp, soft brown hair.

Then, as it were suddenly, he smelt the horrid stagnant smell of that water. And at the same moment she drew away from him and looked at him. Her eyes were wistful and unfathomable. He was afraid of them, and he fell to kissing her, not knowing what he was doing. He wanted her eyes not to have that terrible, wistful, unfathomable look.

When she turned her face to him again, a faint delicate flush was glowing, and there was again dawning that terrible shining of joy in her eyes, which really terrified him, and yet which he now wanted to see, because he feared the look of doubt still more.

"You love me?" she said, rather faltering.

"Yes." The word cost him a painful effort. Not because it wasn't true. But because it was too newly true, the *saying* seemed to tear open again his newly-torn heart. And he hardly wanted it to be true, even now.

She lifted her face to him, and he bent forward and kissed her on the mouth, gently, with the one kiss that is an eternal pledge. And as he kissed her his heart strained again in his breast. He never intended to love her. But now it was over. He had crossed over the gulf to her, and all that he had left behind had shrivelled and become void.

After the kiss, her eyes again slowly filled with tears. She sat still, away from him, with her face drooped aside, and her hands folded in her lap. The tears fell very slowly. There was complete silence. He too sat there motionless and silent on the hearth-rug. The strange pain of his heart that was broken seemed to consume him. That he should love her? That this was love! That he should be ripped open in this way! Him, a doctor!

How they would all jeer if they knew! It was agony to him to think they might know.

In the curious naked pain of the thought he looked again to her. She was sitting there drooped into a muse. He saw a tear fall, and his heart flared hot. He saw for the first time that one of her shoulders was quite uncovered, one arm bare, he could see one of her small breasts; dimly, because it had become almost dark in the room.

"Why are you crying?" he asked, in an altered voice.

She looked up at him, and behind her tears the consciousness of her situation for the first time brought a dark look of shame to her eyes.

"I'm not crying, really," she said, watching him, half frightened.

He reached his hand, and softly closed it on her bare arm.

"I love you! I love you!" he said in a soft, low vibrating voice, unlike himself.

She shrank, and dropped her head. The soft, penetrating grip of his hand on her arm distressed her. She looked up at him.

"I want to go," she said. "I want to go and get you some dry things."

"Why?" he said. "I'm all right."

"But I want to go," she said. "And I want you to change your things."

He released her arm, and she wrapped herself in the blanket, looking at him rather frightened. And still she did not rise.

"Kiss me," she said wistfully.

He kissed her, but briefly, half in anger.

Then, after a second, she rose nervously, all mixed up in the blanket. He watched her in her confusion as she tried to extricate herself and wrap herself up so that she could walk. He watched her relentlessly, as she knew. And as she went, the blanket trailing, and as he saw a glimpse of her feet and her white leg, he tried to remember her as she was when he had wrapped her in the blanket. But then he didn't want to remember, because she had been nothing to him then, and his nature revolted from remembering her as she was when she was nothing to him.

A tumbling, muffled noise from within the dark house startled him. Then he heard her voice: "There are clothes." He rose and went to the foot of the stairs, and gathered up the garments she had thrown down. Then he came back to the fire, to rub himself down and dress. He grinned at his own appearance when he had finished.

The fire was sinking, so he put on coal. The house was now quite dark, save for the light of a street-lamp that shone in faintly from beyond the holly trees. He lit the gas with matches he found on the mantelpiece. Then he emptied the pockets of his own clothes, and threw all his wet things in a heap into the scullery. After which he gathered up her sodden clothes, gently, and put them in a separate heap on the copper-top in the scullery.

It was six o'clock on the clock. His own watch

had stopped. He ought to go back to the surgery. He waited, and still she did not come down. So he went to the foot of the stairs and called:

"I shall have to go."

Almost immediately he heard her coming down. She had on her best dress of black voile, and her hair was tidy, but still damp. She looked at him —and in spite of herself, smiled.

"I don't like you in those clothes," she said.

"Do I look a sight?" he answered.

They were shy of one another.

"I'll make you some tea," she said.

"No, I must go."

"Must you?" And she looked at him again with the wide, strained, doubtful eyes. And again, from the pain of his breast, he knew how he loved her. He went and bent to kiss her, gently, passionately, with his heart's painful kiss.

"And my hair smells so horrible," she murmured in distraction. "And I'm so awful, I'm so awful! Oh no, I'm too awful!" And she broke into bitter, heart-broken sobbing. "You can't want to love me, I'm horrible."

"Don't be silly, don't be silly," he said, trying to comfort her, kissing her, holding her in his arms. "I want you, I want to marry you, we're going to be married, quickly, quickly—to-morrow if I can."

But she only sobbed terribly, and cried:

"I feel awful. I feel awful. I feel I'm horrible to you."

"No, I want you, I want you," was all he answered, blindly, with that terrible intonation which frightened her almost more than her horror lest he should *not* want her.

About Two Nice People

Shirley Jackson

A problem of some importance, certainly, these days, is that of anger. When one half of the world is angry at the other half, or one half of a nation is angry at the rest, or one side of town feuds with the other side, it is hardly surprising, when you stop to think about it, that so many people lose their tempers with so many other people. Even if, as in this case, they are two people not usually angry, two people whose lives are obscure and whose emotions are gentle, whose smiles are amiable and whose voices are more apt to be cheerful than raised in fury. Two people, in other words, who would much rather be friends than not and who yet, for some reason, perhaps chemical or sociological or environmental, enter upon a mutual feeling of dislike so intense that only a very drastic means can bring them out of it.

Take two such people:

Ellen Webster was what is referred to among her friends as a "sweet" girl. She had pretty, soft hair and dark, soft eyes, and she dressed in soft colors and wore frequently a lovely old-fashioned brooch which had belonged to her grandmother. Ellen thought of herself as a very happy and very lucky person, because she had a good job, was able to buy herself a fair number of soft-colored dresses and skirts and sweaters and coats and hats; she had, by working hard at it evenings, transformed her one-room apartment from a bare, neat place into a charming little refuge with her sewing basket on the table and a canary at the window; she had a reasonable conviction that someday, perhaps soon, she would fall in love with a nice young man and they would be married and Ellen would devote herself wholeheartedly to children and baking cakes and mending socks. This not-very-unusual situation, with its perfectly ordinary state of mind, was a source of great happiness to Ellen. She was, in a word, not one of those who rail against their fate, who live in sullen hatred of the world. She was—her friends were right—a sweet girl.

On the other hand, even if you would not have called Walter Nesmith sweet, you would very readily have thought of him as a "nice" fellow, or an "agreeable" person, or even—if you happened to be a little old white-haired lady—a "dear boy." There was a subtle resemblance between Ellen Webster and Walter Nesmith. Both of them were the first resort of their friends in trouble, for instance. Walter's ambitions, which included the rest of his life, were refreshingly similar to Ellen's: Walter thought that someday he might meet some sweet girl, and would then devote himself wholeheartedly to coming home of an evening to read his paper and perhaps work in the garden on Sundays.

Walter thought that he would like to have two children, a boy and a girl. Ellen thought that she would like to have three children, a boy and two girls. Walter was very fond of cherry pie, Ellen preferred Boston cream. Ellen enjoyed romantic movies, Walter preferred Westerns. They read almost exactly the same books.

In the ordinary course of events, the friction between Ellen and Walter would have been very slight. But—and what could cause a thing like this?—the ordinary course of events was shattered by a trifle like a telephone call.

Ellen's telephone number was 3—4126. Walter's telephone number was 3—4216. Ellen lived in apartment 3-A and Walter lived in apartment 3-B; these apartments were across the hall from each other and very often Ellen, opening her door at precisely quarter of nine in the morning and going toward the elevator, met Walter, who opened *his* door at precisely quarter of nine in the morning and went toward the elevator. On these occasions Ellen customarily said "Good morning" and looked steadfastly the other way, Walter usually answered "Good morning," and avoided looking in her direction. Ellen thought that a girl who allowed herself to be informal with strangers created a bad impression, and Walter thought that a man who took advantage of living in the same building to strike up an acquaintance with a girl was a man of little principle. One particularly fine morning, he said to Ellen in the elevator, "Lovely day," and she replied, "Yes, isn't it?" and both of them felt scarcely that they had been bold. How this mutual respect for each other's dignity could have degenerated into fury is a mystery not easily understood.

It happened that one evening—and, to do her strict justice, Ellen had had a hard day, she was coming down with a cold, it had rained steadily for a week, her stockings were unwashed, and she had broken a fingernail—the phone which had the number 3—4126 rang. Ellen had been opening a can of chicken soup in the kitchenette, and she had her hands full; she said "Darn," and managed to drop and break a cup in her hurry to answer the phone.

"Hello?" she said, thinking, *This is going to be something cheerful.*

"Hello, is Walter there?"

"Walter?"

"Walter Nesmith. I want to speak to Walter, please."

"This is the wrong number," Ellen said thinking with the self-pity that comes with the first stages of a head cold that no one ever called *her.*

"Is this three—four two one six?"

"This is three four one two six," Ellen said, and hung up.

At that time, although she knew that the person in the apartment across the hall was named Walter Nesmith, she could not have told the color of his hair or even of the outside of his apartment door.

She went back to her soup and had a match in her hand to light the stove when the phone rang again.

"Hello?" Ellen said without enthusiasm; this *could* be someone cheerful, she was thinking.

"Hello, is Walter there?"

"This is the wrong number again," Ellen said; if she had not been such a very sweet girl she might have let more irritation show in her voice.

"I *want to speak* to Walter Nesmith, *please.*"

"This is three—four one two six again," Ellen said patiently. "You want three—four two one six."

"What?" said the voice.

"This," said Ellen, "is number three—four one two six. The number you want is three—four two one six." Like anyone who has tried to say a series of numbers several times, she found her anger growing. Surely anyone of *normal* intelligence, she was thinking, surely anyone *ought* to be able to dial a phone, anyone who can't dial a phone shouldn't be allowed to have a nickel.

She got all the way back into the kitchenette and was reaching out for the can of soup before the phone rang again. This time when she answered she said "Hello?" rather sharply for Ellen, and with no illusions about who it was going to be.

"Hello, may I please speak to Walter?"

At that point it started. Ellen had a headache and it was raining and she was tired and she was

338

apparently not going to get any chicken soup until this annoyance was stopped.

"Just a minute," she said into the phone.

She put the phone down with an understandable bang on the table, and marched, without taking time to think, out of her apartment and up to the door across the hall. "Walter Nesmith" said a small card at the doorbell. Ellen rang the doorbell with what was, for her, a vicious poke. When the door opened she said immediately, without looking at him:

"Are you Walter Nesmith?"

Now Walter had had a hard day, too, and *he* was coming down with a cold, and *he* had been trying ineffectually to make himself a cup of hot tea in which he intended to put a spoonful of honey to ease his throat, that being a remedy his aunt had always recommended for the first onslaught of a cold. If there had been one fraction less irritation in Ellen's voice, or if Walter had not taken off his shoes when he came home that night, it might very probably have turned out to be a pleasant introduction, with Walter and Ellen dining together on chicken soup and hot tea, and perhaps even sharing a bottle of cough medicine. But when Walter opened the door and heard Ellen's voice, he was unable to answer her cordially, and so he said briefly:

"I am. Why?"

"Will you please come and answer my phone?" said Ellen, too annoyed to realize that this request might perhaps bewilder Walter.

339

"Answer your phone?" said Walter stupidly.

"Answer my phone," said Ellen firmly. She turned and went back across the hall, and Walter stood in his doorway in his stocking feet and watched her numbly. "Come on," she said sharply, as she went into her own apartment, and Walter, wondering briefly if they allowed harmless lunatics to live alone as though they were just like other people, hesitated for an instant and then followed her, on the theory that it would be wiser to do what she said when she seemed so cross, and reassuring himself that he could leave the door open and yell for help if necessary. Ellen stamped into her apartment and pointed at the phone where it lay on the table. "There. Answer it."

Eying her sideways, Walter edged over to the phone and picked it up. "Hello," he said nervously. Then, "Hello? Hello?" Looking at her over the top of the phone, he said, "What do you want me to do now?"

"Do you mean to say," said Ellen ominously, "that that terrible terrible person has hung up?"

"I guess so," said Walter, and fled back to his apartment.

The door had only just closed behind him when the phone rang again, and Ellen, answering it, heard, "May I speak to Walter, please?"

Not a very serious mischance, surely. But the next morning Walter pointedly avoided going down in the elevator with Ellen, and sometime during that day the deliveryman left a package addressed to Ellen at Walter's door.

When Walter found the package he took it manfully under his arm and went boldly across the hall, and rang Ellen's doorbell. When Ellen opened her door she thought at first—and she may have been justified—that Walter had come to apologize for the phone call the evening before, and she even thought that the package under his arm might contain something delightfully unexpected, like a box of candy. They lost another chance then; if Walter had not held out the package and said "Here," Ellen would not have gone on thinking that he was trying to apologize in his own shy way, and she would certainly not have smiled warmly, and said, "You *shouldn't* have bothered."

Walter, who regarded transporting a misdelivered parcel across the hall as relatively little bother, said blankly, "No bother at all," and Ellen, still deceived, said, "But it really wasn't *that* important."

Walter went back into his own apartment convinced that this was a very odd girl indeed, and Ellen, finding that the package had been mailed to her and contained a wool scarf knitted by a cousin, was as much angry as embarrassed because, once having imagined that an apology is forthcoming, it is very annoying not to have one after all, and particularly to have a wool scarf instead of a box of candy.

How this situation disintegrated into the white-hot fury which rose between these two is a puzzle, except for the basic fact that when once a series

341

of misadventures has begun between two people, everything tends to contribute further to a state of misunderstanding. Thus, Ellen opened a letter of Walter's by mistake, and Walter dropped a bottle of milk—he was still trying to cure his cold, and thought that perhaps mild toast was the thing—directly outside Ellen's door, so that even after his nervous attempts to clear it up, the floor was still littered with fragments of glass, and puddled with milk.

Then Ellen—who believed by now that Walter had thrown the bottle of milk against her door—allowed herself to become so far confused by this succession of small annoyances that she actually wrote and mailed a letter to Walter, asking politely that he try to turn down his radio a little in the evenings. Walter replied with a frigid letter to the effect that certainly if he had known that she was bothered by his radio, he should surely never have dreamed—

That evening, perhaps by accident, his radio was so loud that Ellen's canary woke up and chirped hysterically, and Ellen, pacing her floor in incoherent fury, might have been heard—if there had been anyone to hear her, and if Walter's radio had not been so loud—to say, "I'll get even with him!" A phrase, it must be said, which Ellen had never used before in her life.

Ellen made her preparations with a sort of loving care that might well have been lavished on some more worthy object. When the alarm went off she turned in her sleep and smiled before quite waking up, and, once awake and the alarm turned off, she almost laughed out loud. In her slippers and gown, the clock in her hand, she went across her small apartment to the phone; the number was one she was not soon apt to forget. The dial tone sounded amazingly loud, and for a minute she was almost frightened out of her resolution. Then, setting her teeth, she dialed the number, her hand steady. After a second's interminable wait, the ringing began. The phone at the other end rang three times, four times, with what seemed interminable waits between, as though even the mechanical phone system hesitated at this act. Then, at last, there was an irritable crash at the other end of the line, and a voice said, "Wah?"

"Good morning," said Ellen brightly. "I'm so terribly sorry to disturb you at this hour."

"Wah?"

"This is Ellen Webster," said Ellen still brightly. "I called to tell you that my clock has stopped—"

"Wah?"

"—and I wonder if you could tell me what time it is?"

There was a short pause at the other end of the line. Then after a minute, his voice came back: "Tenny minna fah."

"I beg your pardon?"

There was another short pause at the other end of the line, as of someone opening his eyes with a shock. "Twenty minutes after four," he said. *"Twenty minutes after four."*

"The reason I thought of asking you," Ellen said sweetly, "was that you were so *very* obliging before. About the radio, I mean."

"—calling a person at—"

"Thanks so much," said Ellen. "Good-by."

She felt fairly certain that he would not call her back, but she sat on her bed and giggled a little before she went back to sleep.

Walter's response to this was miserably weak: he contacted a neighboring delicatessen a day or so later, and had an assortment of evil-smelling cheese left in Ellen's apartment while she was out. This, which required persuading the superintendent to open Ellen's apartment so that the package might be left inside, was a poor revenge but a monstrous exercise of imagination upon Walter's part, so that, in one sense, Ellen was already bringing out in him qualities he never knew he had. The cheese, it turned out, more than evened the score: the apartment was small, the day was warm, and Ellen did not get home until late, and long after most of the other tenants on the floor had gone to the superintendent with their complaints about something dead in the woodwork.

Since breaking and entering had thus become one of the rules of their game, Ellen felt privileged to retaliate in kind upon Walter. It was with great joy, some evenings later, that Ellen, sitting in her odorous apartment, heard Walter's scream of pure terror when he put his feet into his slippers and found a raw egg in each.

Walter had another weapon, however, which he

had been so far reluctant to use; it was a howitzer of such proportions that Walter felt its use would end warfare utterly. After the raw eggs he felt no compunction whatever in bringing out his heavy artillery.

It seemed to Ellen, at first, as though peace had been declared. For almost a week things went along smoothly; Walter kept his radio turned down almost to inaudibility, so that Ellen got plenty of sleep. She was over her cold, the sun had come out, and on Saturday morning she spent three hours shopping, and found exactly the dress she wanted at less than she expected to pay.

About Saturday noon she stepped out of the elevator, her packages under her arm, and walked briskly down the hall to her apartment, making, as usual, a wide half-circle to avoid coming into contact with the area around Walter's door.

Her apartment door, to her surprise, was open, but before she had time to phrase a question in her own mind, she had stepped inside and come face to face with a lady who—not to make any more mysteries—was Walter Nesmith's aunt, and a wicked old lady in her own way, possessing none of Walter's timidity and none of his tact.

"Who?" said Ellen weakly, standing in the doorway.

"Come in and close the door," said the old lady darkly. "I don't think you'll want your neighbors to hear what I have to say. I," she continued as Ellen obeyed mechanically, "am Mrs. Harold

Vongarten Nesmith. Walter Nesmith, young woman, is my nephew."

"Then you are in the wrong apartment," said Ellen, quite politely considering the reaction which Walter Nesmith's name was beginning by now to arouse in her. "You want Apartment Three-B, across the hall."

"I do *not*," said the old lady firmly. "I came here to see the designing young woman who has been shamelessly pursuing my nephew, and to warn her"—the old lady shook her gloves menacingly—"to warn her that *not one cent* shall she have from me if she marries Walter Nesmith."

"Marries?" said Ellen, thoughts too great for words in her heart.

"It has long been my opinion that some young woman would be after Walter Nesmith for his money," said Walter's aunt with satisfaction.

"Believe me," said Ellen wholeheartedly, "there is not that much money in the world."

"You deny it?" The old lady leaned back and smiled triumphantly. "I expected something of the sort. Walter," she called suddenly, and then, putting her head back and howling. "Wal-l-l-l-l-ter."

"Sh-h-h," said Ellen fearfully. "They'll hear you all over."

"I expect them to," said the old lady. "Wal-l-l-l-l——Oh, there you are."

Ellen turned, and saw Walter Nesmith, with triumph in his eyes, peering around the edge of the door. "Did it work?" he asked.

"She denies everything," said his aunt.

"About the eggs?" Walter said, confused. "You mean, she denies about the eggs and the phone call and——"

"Look," Ellen said to Walter, stamping across the floor to look him straight in the eye, "of all the insufferable, conceited, rude, self-satisfied——"

"What?" said Walter.

"I wouldn't want to marry you," said Ellen, "if—if—" She stopped for a word, helpless.

"If he were the last man on earth," Walter's aunt supplied obligingly. "I think she's really after your *money*, Walter."

Walter stared at his aunt. "I didn't tell you to tell her—" he began. He gasped, and tried again. "I mean," he said, "I never thought—" He appealed to Ellen. "I don't want to marry you, either," he said, and the gasped again, and said, "I mean, I told my aunt to come and tell you—"

"If this is a proposal," Ellen said coldly, "I decline."

"All I wanted her to do was scare you," Walter said finally.

"It's a good way," his aunt said complacently. "Turned out to be the only way with your Uncle Charles and a Hungarian adventuress."

"I mean," Walter said desperately to Ellen, "she owns this building. I mean, I wanted her to tell you that if you didn't stop—I mean, I wanted her to scare you—"

"Apartments are too hard to get these days," his aunt said. "That would have been *too* unkind."

"That's how I got my apartment at all, you see," Walter said to Ellen, still under the impression he was explaining something Ellen wanted to understand.

"Since you have an apartment," Ellen said with restraint, "may I suggest that you take your aunt and the both of you—"

The phone rang.

"Excuse me," said Ellen mechanically, moving to answer it. "Hello?" she said.

"Hello, may I speak to Walter, please?"

Ellen smiled rather in the manner that Lady Macbeth might have smiled if she found a run in her stocking.

"It's for you," she said, holding the phone out to Walter.

"For me?" he said, surprised. "Who is it?"

"I really could not say," said Ellen sweetly. "Since you have so many friends that one phone is not adequate to answer all their calls—"

Since Walter made no move to take the phone, she put it gently back on the hook.

"They'll call again," she assured him, still smiling in that terrible fashion.

"I ought to turn you both out," said Walter's aunt. She turned to Ellen. "Young woman," she said, "do you deny that all this nonsense with eggs and telephone calls is an attempt to entangle my nephew into matrimony?"

"Certainly not," Ellen said. "I mean, I *do* deny it."

"Walter Nesmith," said his aunt, "do you admit that all your finagling with cheeses and radios is an attempt to strike up an acquaintance with this young woman?"

"Certainly," said Walter. "I mean, I do *not* admit it."

"Good," said Walter's aunt. "You are precisely the pair of silly fools I would have picked out for each other." She rose with great dignity, motioned Walter away from her, and started for the door. "Remember," she said, shaking her gloves again at Ellen, "not one cent."

She opened the door and started down the hall, her handkerchief over her eyes, and—a sorry thing in such an old lady—laughing until she had to stop and lean against the wall near the elevator.

"I'm sorry," Walter was saying to Ellen, almost babbling, "I'm *really* sorry this time—please believe me, I had *no* idea—I wouldn't for the world—nothing but the most profound respect— a joke, you know—hope you didn't really think —"

"I understand perfectly," Ellen said icily. "It is all perfectly clear. It only goes to show what I have always believed about young men who think that all they have to do is—"

The phone rang.

Ellen waited a minute before she spoke. Then she said, "You might as well answer it."

"I'm *terribly* sorry," Walter said, not moving toward the phone. "I mean, I'm *terribly* sorry." He waved his hands in the air. "About what she said about what she thought about what you

349

wanted me to do—" His voice trailed off miserably.

Suddenly Ellen began to giggle.

Anger is certainly a problem that will bear much analysis. It is hardly surprising that one person may be angry at another, particularly if these are two people who are gentle, usually, and rarely angry, whose emotions tend to be mild and who would rather be friends with everyone then be enemies with anyone. Such an anger argues a situation so acute that only the most drastic readjustment can remedy it.

Either Walter Nesmith or Ellen Webster could have moved, of course. But, as Walter's aunt had pointed out, apartments are not that easy to come by, and their motives and their telephone numbers were by now so inextricably mixed that on the whole it seemed more reasonable not to bother.

Moreover, Walter's aunt, who still snickers when her nephew's name is mentioned, did not keep them long in suspense, after all. She was not lavish, certainly, but she wrote them a letter which both of them found completely confusing and which enclosed a check adequate for a down payment on the extremely modest house in the country they decided upon without disagreement. They even compromised and had four children— two boys and two girls.

How Beautiful with Shoes

Wilbur Daniel Steele

By the time the milking was finished, the sow, which had farrowed the past week, was making such a row that the girl spilled a pint of warm milk down the trough lead to quiet the animal before taking the pail to the well house. Then in the quiet she heard a sound of hoofs on the bridge, where the road crossed the creek a hundred yards below the house, and she set the pail down on the ground beside her bare, barn-soiled feet. She picked it up again. She set it down. It was as if she calculated its weight.

That was what she was doing, as a matter of fact, setting off against its pull toward the well house the pull of that wagon team in the road, with little more of personal will or wish in the matter than has a wooden weathervane between two currents in the wind. And as with the vane, so with the wooden girl—the added behest of a whiplash cracking in the distance was enough; leaving the pail at the barn door, she set off in a deliberate, docile beeline through the cowyard, over the fence, and down in a diagonal across the farm's one tilled field toward the willow brake that walled the road at the dip. And once under way,

351

though her mother came to the kitchen door and called in her high, flat voice, "Amarantha, where you goin', Amarantha?" the girl went on apparently unmoved, as though she had been as deaf as the woman in the doorway; indeed, if there was emotion in her it was the purely sensuous one of feeling the clods of the furrows breaking softly between her toes. It was springtime in the mountains.

"Amarantha, why don't you answer me, Amarantha?"

For moments after the girl had disappeared beyond the willows the widow continued to call, unaware through long habit of how absurd it sounded, the name which that strange man her husband had put upon their daughter in one of his moods. Mrs. Doggett had been deaf so long she did not realize that nobody else ever thought of it for the broad-fleshed, slow-minded girl, but called her Mary, or even more simply, Mare.

Ruby Herter had stopped his team this side of the bridge, the mules' heads turned into the lane to his father's farm beyond the road. A big-barreled, heavy-limbed fellow with a square, sallow, not unhandsome face, he took out youth in ponderous gestures of masterfulness; it was like him to have cracked his whip above his animals' ears the moment before he pulled them to a halt. When he saw the girl getting over the fence under the willows he tongued the wad of tobacco out of his mouth into his palm, threw it away beyond the

352

road, and drew a sleeve of his jumper across his lips.

"Don't run yourself out o' breath, Mare; I got all night."

"I was comin'." It sounded sullen only because it was matter of fact.

"Well, keep a-comin' and give us a smack." Hunched on the wagon seat, he remained motionless for some time after she had arrived at the hub, and when he stirred it was but to cut a fresh bit of tobacco, as if already he had forgotten why he threw the old one away. Having satisfied his humor, he unbent, climbed down, kissed her passive mouth, and hugged her up to him, roughly and loosely, his hands careless of contours. It was not out of the way; they were used to handling animals both of them; and it was spring. A slow warmth pervaded the girl, formless, nameless, almost impersonal.

Her betrothed pulled her head back by the braid of her yellow hair. He studied her face, his brows gathered and his chin out.

"Listen, Mare, you wouldn't leave nobody else hug and kiss you, dang you!"

She shook her head, without vehemence or anxiety.

"Who's that?" She harkened up the road. "Pull your team out," she added, as a Ford came in sight around the bend above the house, driven at speed. "Geddap!" she said to the mules herself.

But the car came to a halt near them, and one of the five men crowded in it called, "Come on,

353

Ruby, climb in. They's a loony loose out o' Dayville Asylum, and they got him trailed over somewheres on Split Ridge, and Judge North phoned up to Slosson's store for ever'body come help circle him—come on, hop the runnin'-board!"

Ruby hesitated, an eye on his team.

"Scared, Ruby?" The driver raced his engine. "They say this boy's a killer."

"Mare, take the team in and tell Pa." The car was already moving when Ruby jumped it. A moment after it had sounded on the bridge it was out of sight.

"Amarantha, Amarantha, why don't you come, Amarantha?"

Returning from her errand, fifteen minutes later, Mare heard the plaint lifted in the twilight. The sun had dipped behind the back ridge, though the sky was still bright with day, the dusk began to smoke up out of the plowed field like a ground fog. The girl had returned through it, got the milk, and started toward the well house before the widow saw her.

"Daughter, seems to me you might!" she expostulated without change of key. "Here's some young man friend o' yourn stopped to say howdy, and I been rackin' my lungs out after you. . . . Put that milk in the cool and come!"

Some young man friend? But there was no good to be got from puzzling. Mare poured the milk in the pan in the dark of the low house over the well, and as she came out, stooping, she saw a figure waiting for her, black in silhouette against the yellowing sky.

"Who are you?" she asked, a native timidity making her sound sulky.

"'Amarantha!'" the fellow mused. "That's poetry." And she knew then that she did not know him.

She walked past, her arms straight down and her eyes front. Strangers always affected her with a kind of muscular terror simply by being strangers. So she gained the kitchen steps, aware by his tread that he followed. There, taking courage at the sight of her mother in the doorway, she turned on him, her eyes down at the level of his knees.

"Who are you and what d' y' want?"

He still mused. "Amarantha! Amarantha in Carolina! That makes me happy!"

Mare hazarded one upward look. She saw that he had red hair, brown eyes, and hollows under his cheekbones, and though the green sweater he wore on top of a gray overall was plainly not meant for him, sizes too large as far as girth went, yet he was built so long of limb that his wrists came inches out of the sleeves and made his big hands look even bigger.

Mrs. Doggett complained. "Why don't you introduce us, daughter?"

The girl opened her mouth and closed it again. Her mother, unaware that no sound had come out of it, smiled and nodded, evidently taking to the tall, homely fellow and tickled by the way he could not seem to get his eyes off her daughter. But the daughter saw none of it, all her attention centered upon the stranger's hands.

Restless, hard-fleshed, and chap-bitten, they were like a countryman's hands; but the fingers were longer than the ordinary, and slightly spatulate at their ends, and these ends were slowly and continuously at play among themselves.

The girl could not have explained how it came to her to be frightened and at the same time to be calm, for she was inept with words. It was simply that in an animal way she knew animals, knew them in health and ailing, and when they were ailing she knew by instinct, as her father had known, how to move so as not to fret them.

Her mother had gone in to light up; from beside the lampshelf she called back, "If he's aimin' to stay to supper you should've told me, Amarantha, though I guess there's plenty of the side-meat to go 'round, if you'll bring me in a few more turnips and potatoes, though it is late."

At the words the man's cheeks moved in and out. "I'm very hungry," he said.

Mare nodded deliberately. Deliberately, as if her mother could hear her, she said over her shoulder, "I'll go get the potatoes and turnips, Ma." While she spoke she was moving, slowly, softly, at first, toward the right of the yard, where the fence gave over into the field. Unluckily her mother spied her through the window.

"Amarantha, where *are* you goin'?"

"I'm goin' to get the potatoes and turnips." She

356

neither raised her voice nor glanced back, but lengthened her stride. He won't hurt her, she said to herself. He won't hurt her; it's me, not her, she kept repeating, while she got over the fence and down into the shadow that lay more than ever like a fog on the field.

The desire to believe that it actually did hide her, the temptation to break from her rapid but orderly walk grew till she could no longer fight it. She saw the road willows only a dash ahead of her. She ran, her feet floundering among the furrows.

She neither heard nor saw him, but when she realized he was with her she knew he had been with her all the while. She stopped, and he stopped, and so they stood, with the dark open of the field all around. Glancing sidewise presently, she saw he was no longer looking at her with those strangely importunate brown eyes of his, but had raised them to the crest of the wooded ridge behind her.

By and by, "What does it make you think of?" he asked. And when she made no move to see, "Turn around and look!" he said, and though it was low and almost tender in its tone, she knew enough to turn.

A ray of the sunset hidden in the west struck through the tops of the topmost trees, far and small up there, a thin, bright hem.

"What does it make you think of, Amarantha? . . . Answer!"

"Fire," she made herself say.

"Or blood."

"Or blood, yeh. That's right, or blood." She had heard a Ford going up the road beyond the willows, and her attention was not on what she said.

The man soliloquized. "Fire and blood, both; spare one or the other, and where is beauty, the way the world is? It's an awful thing to have to carry, but Christ had it. Christ came with a sword. I love beauty, Amarantha. . . . I say, I love beauty!"

"Yeh, that's right, I hear." What she heard was the car stopping at the house.

"Not prettiness. Prettiness'll have to go with ugliness, because it's only ugliness trigged up. But beauty!" Now again he was looking at her. "Do you know how beautiful you are, Amarantha, Amarantha sweet and fair?" Of a sudden, reaching behind her, he began to unravel the meshes of her hair braid, the long, flat-tipped fingers at once impatient and infinitely gentle. "Braid no more that shining hair!"

Flat-faced Mare Doggett tried to see around those glowing eyes so near to hers, but wise in her instinct, did not try too hard. "Yeh," she temporized. "I mean, no, I mean."

"Amarantha, I've come a long, long way for you. Will you come away with me now?"

"Yeh—that is—in a minute I will, mister— yeh . . ."

"Because you want to, Amarantha? Because you love me as I love you? Answer!"

"Yeh—sure—us . . . *Ruby!*"

The man tried to run, but there were six against him, coming up out of the dark that lay in the plowed ground. Mare stood where she was while they knocked him down and got a rope around him; after that she walked back toward the house with Ruby and Older Haskins, her father's cousin.

Ruby wiped his brow and felt of his muscles. "Gees, you're lucky we come, Mare. We're no more'n past the town, when they come hollerin' he'd broke over this way."

When they came to the fence the girl sat on the rail for a moment and rebraided her hair before she went into the house, where they were making her mother smell ammonia.

Lots of cars were coming. Judge North was coming, somebody said. When Mare heard this she went into her bedroom off the kitchen and got her shoes and put them on. They were brand-new two-dollar shoes with cloth tops, and she had only begun to break them in last Sunday; she wished afterwards she had put her stockings on too, for they would have eased the seams. Or else that she had put on the old button pair, even though the soles were worn through.

Judge North arrived. He thought first of taking the loony straight through to Dayville that night, but then decided to keep him in the lockup at the courthouse till morning and make the drive by day. Older Haskins stayed in, gentling Mrs. Doggett, while Ruby went out to help get the man into the Judge's sedan. Now that she had them on, Mare didn't like to take the shoes off till Older went; it might make him feel small, she thought.

Older Haskins had a lot of facts about the loony.

"His name's Humble Jewett," he told them. "They belong back in Breed County, all them Jewetts, and I don't reckon there's none of 'em that's not a mite unbalanced. He went to college though, worked his way, and he taught somethin' 'rother in some academy-school a spell, till he went off his head all of a sudden and took after folks with an axe. I remember it in the paper at the time. They give out one while how the Principal wasn't goin' to live, and there was others—there was a girl he tried to strangle. That was four-five year back."

Ruby came in guffawing. "Know the only thing they can get 'im to say, Mare? Only God thing he'll say is 'Amarantha, she's goin' with me.' . . . Mare!"

"Yeh, I know."

The cover of the kettle the girl was handling slid off the stove with a clatter. A sudden sick wave passed over her. She went out to the back, out into the air. It was not till now she knew how frightened she had been.

Ruby went home, but Older Haskins stayed to supper with them, and helped Mare do the dishes afterward; it was nearly nine when he left. The mother was already in bed, and Mare was about to sit down to get those shoes off her wretched feet at last, when she heard the cow carrying on up at the barn, lowing and kicking, and next minute the sow was in it with a horning note. It might be a fox passing by to get at the henhouse, or a weasel. Mare forgot her feet, took a broom handle they used in boiling clothes, opened the back door, and stepped out. Blinking the lamplight from her eyes, she peered up toward the outbuildings, and saw the gable end of the barn standing like a red arrow in the dark, and the top of a butternut tree beyond it drawn in skeleton traceries, and just then a cock crowed.

She went to the right corner of the house and saw where the light came from, ruddy above the woods down the valley. Returning into the house, she bent close to her mother's ear and shouted, "Somethin's a-fire down to the town, looks like," then went out again and up to the barn. "Soh! Soh!" she called in to the animals. She climbed up and stood on the top rail of the cow-pen fence, only to find she could not locate the flame even there.

Ten rods behind the buildings a mass of rock mounted higher than their ridgepoles, a chopped off buttress of the back ridge, covered with oak scrub and wild grapes and blackberries, whose thorny ropes the girl beat away from her skirt with the broom handle as she scrambled up in the wine-colored dark. Once at the top, and the brush held aside, she could see the tongue-tip of the conflagration half a mile away at the town. And she knew by the bearing of the two church steeples that it was the building where the lockup was that was burning.

There is a horror in knowing animals trapped in a fire, no matter what the animals.

"Oh, my God!" Mare said.

A car went down the road. Then there was a horse galloping. That would be Older Haskins probably. People were out at Ruby's father's farm; she could hear their voices raised. There must have been another car up from the other way, for lights wheeled and shouts were exchanged in the neighborhood of the bridge. Next thing she knew, Ruby was at the house below, looking for her probably.

He was telling her mother, Mrs. Doggett was not used to him, so he had to shout even louder than Mare had to.

"What y' reckon he done, the hellion! he broke the door and killed Lew Fyke and set the courthouse afire! . . . Where's Mare?"

Her mother would not know. Mare called. "Here, up the rock here."

She had better go down. Ruby would likely break his bones if he tried to climb the rock in the dark, not knowing the way. But the sight of the fire fascinated her simple spirit, the fearful element, more fearful than ever now, with the news. "Yes, I'm comin'," she called sulkily, hearing feet in the brush. "You wait; I'm comin'."

When she turned and saw it was Humble Jewett, right behind her among the branches, she opened her mouth to screech. She was not quick enough. Before a sound came out he got one hand over her face and the other around her body.

Mare had always thought she was strong, and the loony looked gangling, yet she was so easy for him that he need not hurt her. He made no haste and little noise as he carried her deeper into the undergrowth. Where the hill began to mount it was harder though. Presently he set her on her feet. He let the hand that had been over her mouth slip down to her throat, where the broad-tipped fingers wound, tender as yearning, weightless as caress.

"I was afraid you'd scream before you knew who 'twas, Amarantha. But I didn't want to hurt your lips, dear heart, your lovely, quiet lips."

It was so dark under the trees she could hardly see him, but she felt his breath on her mouth, near to. But then, instead of kissing her, he said, "No! No!" took from her throat for an instant the hand that had held her mouth, kissed its palm, and put it back softly against her skin.

"Now, my love, let's go before they come."

She stood stock-still. Her mother's voice was to be heard in the distance, strident and meaningless. More cars were on the road. Nearer, around the rock, there were sounds of tramping and thrashing. Ruby fussed and cursed. He shouted, "Mare, dang you, where are you, Mare?" his voice harsh with uneasy anger. Now, if she aimed to do anything, was the time to do it. But there was neither breath nor power in her windpipe. It was as if those yearning fingers had paralyzed the muscles.

"Come!" The arm he put around her shivered against her shoulder blades. It was anger. "I hate

killing. It's a dirty, ugly thing. It makes me sick."
He gagged, judging by the sound. But then he
ground his teeth. "Come away, my love!"

She found herself moving. Once when she
broke a branch underfoot with an instinctive awkwardness he chided her. "Quiet, my heart, else
they'll hear!" She made herself heavy. He thought
she grew tired and bore more of her weight till he
was breathing hard.

Men came up the hill. There must have been a
dozen spread out, by the angle of their voices as
they kept touch. Always Humble Jewett kept caressing Mare's throat with one hand; all she could
do was hang back.

"You're tired and you're frightened," he said
at last. "Get down here."

There were twigs in the dark, the overhang of
a thicket of some sort. He thrust her in under this,
and lay beside her on the bed of groundpine. The
hand that was not in love with her throat reached
across her; she felt the weight of its forearm on
her shoulder and its fingers among the strands of
her hair, eagerly, but tenderly, busy. Not once
did he stop speaking, no louder than breathing,
his lips to her ear.

"Amarantha sweet and fair—Ah, braid no more
that shining hair . . ."

Mare had never heard of Lovelace, the poet;
she thought the loony was just going on, hardly
listened, got little sense. But the cadence of it
added to the lethargy of all her flesh.

"*Like a dew of golden thread—Most excellently ravelled . . .*"

Voices loudened; feet came tramping; a pair went past not two rods away.

"*. . . Do not then wind up the light—In ribbands, and o'ercloud in night . . .*"

The search went on up the woods, men shouting to one another and beating the brush.

"*. . . But shake your head and scatter day.* I've never loved, Amarantha. They've tried me with prettiness, but prettiness is too cheap, yes, it's too cheap."

Mare was cold, and the coldness made her lazy. All she knew was that he talked on.

"But dogwood blowing in the spring isn't cheap. The earth of a field isn't cheap. Lots of times I've lain down and kissed the earth of a field, Amarantha. That's beauty, and a kiss for beauty." His breath moved up her cheek. He trembled violently. "No, no, not yet!" He got to his knees and pulled her by an arm. "We can go now."

They went back down the slope, but at an angle, so that when they came to the level they passed two hundred yards to the north of the house, and crossed the road there. More and more her walking was like sleepwalking, the feet numb in their shoes. Even where he had to let go of her, crossing the creek on stones, she stepped where he stepped with an obtuse docility. The voices of the searchers on the back ridge were small in distance when they began to climb the fence of Coward Hill, on the opposite side of the valley.

There is an old farm on top of Coward Hill, big hayfields as flat as tables. It had been half-past nine when Mare stood on the rock above the barn; it was toward midnight when Humble Jewett put aside the last branches of the woods and let her out on the height, and a half a moon had risen. And a wind blew there, tossing the withered tops of last year's grasses, and mists ran with the wind, and ragged shadows with the mists, and mares'-tails of clear moonlight among the shadows, so that now the boles of birches on the forest's edge beyond the fences were but opal blurs and now cut alabaster. It struck so cold against the girl's cold flesh, this wind, that another wind of shivers blew through her, and she put her hands over her face and eyes. But the madman stood with his eyes open and his mouth open, drinking the moonlight and the wet wind.

His voice, when he spoke at last, was thick in his throat.

"Get down on your knees." He got down on his and pulled her after. "And pray!"

Once in England a poet sang four lines. Four hundred years have forgotten his name, but they have remembered his lines. The daft man knelt upright, his face raised to the wild scud, his long wrists hanging to the dead grass. He began simply:

> *O western wind, when wilt thou blow*
> *That the small rain down can rain?*

The Adam's apple was big in his bent throat. As simply he finished.

>*Christ, that my love were in my arms*
>*And I in my bed again!*

Mare got up and ran. She ran without aim or feeling in the power of the wind. She told herself again that the mists would hide her from him, as she had done at dusk. And again, seeing that he ran at her shoulder, she knew he had been there all the while, making a race of it, flailing the air with his long arms for joy of play in the cloud of spring, throwing his knees high, leaping the moon-blue waves of the brown grass, shaking his bright hair; and her own hair was a weight behind her, lying level on the wind. Once a shape went bounding ahead of them for instants; she did not realize it was a fox till it was gone.

She never thought of stopping; she never thought of anything, except once, Oh, my God, I wish I had my shoes off! And what would have been the good in stopping or in turning another way, when it was only play? The man's ecstasy magnified his strength. When a snake fence came at them he took the top rail in flight, like a college hurdler, and seeing the girl hesitate and half turn as if to flee, he would have releaped it without touching a hand. But then she got a loom of buildings, climbed over quickly, before he should jump, and ran along the lane that ran with the fence.

Mare had never been up there, but she knew

that the farm and the house belonged to a man named Wyker, a kind of cousin of Ruby Herter's, a violent, bearded old fellow who lived by himself. She could not believe her luck. When she had run half the distance and Jewett had not grabbed her, doubt grabbed her instead. "Oh, my God, go careful!" she told herself. "Go slow!" she implored herself, and stopped running, to walk.

Here was a misgiving the deeper in that it touched her special knowledge. She had never known an animal so far gone that its instincts failed it; a starving rat will scent the trap sooner than a fed one. Yet, after one glance at the house they approached, Jewett paid it no further attention, but walked with his eyes to the right, where the cloud had blown away, and wooded ridges, like black waves rimed with silver, ran down away toward the Valley of Virginia.

"I've never lived!" In his single cry there were two things, beatitude and pain.

Between the bigness of the falling world and his eyes the flag of her hair blew. He reached out and let it whip between his fingers. Mare was afraid it would break the spell then, and he would stop looking away and look at the house again. So she did something incredible; she spoke.

"It's a pretty—I mean—a beautiful view down that-a-way."

"God Almighty beautiful, to take your breath away. I knew I'd never loved, Beloved—" He caught a foot under the long end of one of the boards that covered the well and went down heavily on his hands and knees. It seemed to make no difference. "But I never knew I'd never lived," he finished in the same tone of strong rapture, quadruped in the grass, while Mare ran for the door and grabbed the latch.

When the latch would not give, she lost what little sense she had. She pounded with her fists. She cried with all her might: "Oh—hey—in there—hey—in there!" Then Jewett came and took her gently between his hands and drew her away, and then, though she was free, she stood in something like an awful embarrassment while he tried shouting.

"Hey! Friend! whoever you are, wake up and let my love and me come in!"

"No!" wailed the girl.

He grew peremptory. "Hey, wake up!" He tried the latch. He passed to full fury in a wink's time; he cursed, he kicked, he beat the door till Mare thought he would break his hands. Withdrawing, he ran at it with his shoulder; it burst at the latch, went slamming in, and left a black emptiness. His anger dissolved in a big laugh. Turning in time to catch her by a wrist, he cried joyously, "Come, my Sweet One!"

"No! No! Please—aw—listen. There ain't nobody there. He ain't to home. It wouldn't be right to go in anybody's house if they wasn't to home, you know that."

His laugh was blither than ever. He caught her high in his arms.

"I'd do the same by his love and him if 'twas

369

my house, I would." At the threshold he paused and thought. "That is, if she was the true love of his heart forever."

The room was the parlor. Moonlight slanted in at the door, and another shaft came through a window and fell across a sofa, its covering dilapidated, showing its wadding in places. The air was sour, but both of them were farm-bred.

"Don't, Amarantha!" His words were pleading in her ear. "Don't be so frightened."

He set her down on the sofa. As his hands let go of her they were shaking.

"But look, I'm frightened too." He knelt on the floor before her, reached out his hands, withdrew them. "See, I'm afraid to touch you." He mused, his eyes rounded. "Of all the ugly things there are, fear is the ugliest. And yet, see, it can be the very beautifulest. That's a strange queer thing."

The wind blew in and out of the room, bringing the thin, little bitter sweetness of new April at night. The moonlight that came across Mare's shoulders fell full upon his face, but hers it left dark, ringed by the aureole of her disordered hair.

"Why do you wear a halo, Love?" He thought about it. "Because you're an angel, is that why?" The swift, untempered logic of the mad led him to dismay. His hands came flying to hers, to make sure they were of earth; and he touched her breast, her shoulders, and her hair. Peace returned to his eyes as his fingers twined among the strands.

"Thy hair is as a flock of goats that appear from

370

Gilead . . ." He spoke like a man dreaming. *"Thy temples are like a piece of pomegranate within thy locks."*

Mare never knew that he could not see her for the moonlight.

"Do you remember, Love?"

She dared not shake her head under his hand. "Yeh, I reckon," she temporized.

"You remember how I sat at your feet, long ago, like this, and made up a song? And all the poets in all the world have never made one to touch it, have they, Love?"

"Ugh-ugh—never."

"How beautiful are thy feet with shoes . . . Remember?"

"Oh, my God, what's he sayin' now?" she wailed to herself.

"How beautiful are thy feet with shoes. O prince's daughter! the joints of thy thighs are like jewels, the work of the hands of a cunning workman.

Thy navel is like a round goblet, which wanteth not liquor; thy belly is like an heap of wheat set about with lilies.

Thy two breasts are like two young roes that are twins."

Mare had not been to church since she was a little girl, when her mother's black dress wore out. "No, no!" she wailed under her breath. "You're awful to say such awful things." She might have shouted it; nothing could have shaken the man

371

now, rapt in the immortal, passionate periods of Solomon's Song.

". . . now also thy breasts shall be as clusters of the vine, and the smell of thy nose like apples."

Hotness touched Mare's face for the first time. "Aw, no, don't talk so!"

"And the roof of thy mouth like the best wine for my beloved . . . causing the lips of them that are asleep to speak."

He had ended. His expression changed. Ecstasy gave place to anger, love to hate. And Mare felt the change in the weight of the fingers in her hair.

"What do you mean, I mustn't say it like that?" But it was not to her his fury spoke, for he answered himself straightaway. "Like poetry, Mr. Jewett; I won't have blasphemy around my school."

"Poetry. My God! If that isn't poetry—if that isn't music—" . . . "It's Bible, Jewett. What you're paid to teach here is *literature*."

"Doctor Ryeworth, you're the blasphemer and you're an ignorant man." . . . "And you're principal. And I won't have you going around reading sacred allegory like earthly love."

"Ryeworth, you're an old man, a dull man, a dirty man, and you'd be better dead."

Jewett's hands had slid down from Mare's head. "Then I went to put my fingers around his throat, so. But my stomach turned, and I didn't do it. I went to my room. I laughed all the way to my room. I sat in my room at my table and laughed. I laughed all afternoon and long after dark came. And then, about ten, somebody came and stood beside me in my room."

" 'Wherefore dost thou laugh, son?'

"Then I knew who He was, He was Christ.

" 'I was laughing about that dirty, ignorant, crazy old fool, Lord.'

" 'Wherefore dost thou laugh?'

"I didn't laugh any more. He didn't say any more. I kneeled down, bowed my head.

" 'Thy will be done! Where is he, Lord?'

" 'Over at the girls' dormitory, waiting for Blossom Sinckley.'

"Brassy Blossom, dirty Blossom . . ."

It had come so suddenly it was nearly too late. Mare tore at his hands with hers, tried with all her strength to pull her neck away.

"Filthy Blossom! and him an old filthy man, Blossom! and you'll find him in Hell when you reach there, Blossom. . . ."

It was more the nearness of his face than the hurt of his hands that gave her power of fright to choke out three words.

"I—ain't—Blossom!"

Light ran in crooked veins. Through the veins she saw his face bewildered. His hands loosened. One fell down and hung; the other he lifted and put over his eyes, took it away again and looked at her.

"Amarantha!" His remorse was fearful to see. "What have I done!" His hands returned to hover over the hurts, ravening with pity, grief and tenderness. Tears fell down his cheeks. And with that, dammed desire broke its dam.

"Amarantha, my love, my dove, my beautiful love—"

"*And I ain't Amarantha neither, I'm Mary! Mary, that's my name!*"

She had no notion what she had done. He was like a crystal crucible that a chemist watches, changing hue in a wink with one adeptly added drop; but hers was not the chemist's eye. All she knew was that she felt light and free of him; all she could see of his face as he stood away above the moonlight were the whites of his eyes.

"Mary!" he muttered. A slight paroxysm shook his frame. So in the transparent crucible desire changed its hue. He retreated farther, stood in the dark by some tall piece of furniture. And still she could see the whites of his eyes.

"Mary! Mary Adorable!" A wonder was in him. "Mother of God."

Mare held her breath. She eyed the door, but it was too far. And already he came back to go on his knees before her, his shoulders so bowed and his face so lifted that it must have cracked his neck, she thought; all she could see on the face was pain.

"Mary Mother, I'm sick to my death. I'm so tired."

She had seen a dog like that, one she had loosed

from a trap after it had been there three days, its caught leg half gnawed free. Something about the eyes.

"Mary Mother, take me in your arms . . ."

Once again her muscles tightened. But he made no move.

". . . and give me sleep."

No, they were worse than the dog's eyes.

"Sleep, sleep! why won't they let me sleep? Haven't I done it all yet, Mother? Haven't I washed them yet of all their sins? I've drunk the cup that was given me; is there another? They've mocked me and reviled me, broken my brow with thorns and my hands with nails, and I've forgiven them, for they knew not what they did. Can't I go to sleep now, Mother?"

Mare could not have said why, but now she was more frightened than she had ever been. Her hands lay heavy on her knees, side by side, and she could not take them away when he bowed his head and rested his face upon them.

After a moment he said one thing more. "Take me down gently when you take me from the Tree."

Gradually the weight of his body came against her shins, and he slept.

The moon streak that entered by the eastern window crept north across the floor, thinner and thinner; the one that fell through the southern doorway traveled east and grew fat. For a while Mare's feet pained her terribly and her legs too.

She dared not move them, though, and by and by they did not hurt so much.

A dozen times, moving her head slowly on her neck, she canvassed the shadows of the room for a weapon. Each time her eyes came back to a heavy earthenware pitcher on a stand some feet to the left of the sofa. It would have had flowers in it when Wyker's wife was alive; probably it had not been moved from its dust ring since she died. It would be a long grab, perhaps too long; still, it might be done if she had her hands.

To get her hands from under the sleeper's head was the task she set herself. She pulled first one, then the other, infinitesimally. She waited. Again she tugged a very, very little. The order of his breathing was not disturbed. But at the third trial he stirred.

"Gently! gently!" His own muttering waked him more. With some drowsy instinct of possession he threw one hand across her wrists, pinning them together between thumb and fingers. She kept dead quiet, shut her eyes, lengthened her breathing, as if she too slept.

There came a time when what was pretense grew a peril; strange as it was, she had to fight to keep her eyes open. She never knew whether or not she really napped. But something changed in the air, and she was wide awake again. The moonlight was fading on the doorsill, and the light that runs before dawn waxed in the window behind her head.

And then she heard a voice in the distance, lifted

in maundering song. It was old man Wyker coming home after a night, and it was plain he had had some whiskey.

Now a new terror laid hold of Mare.

"Shut up, you fool you!" she wanted to shout. "Come quiet, quiet!" She might have chanced it now to throw the sleeper away from her and scramble and run, had his powers of strength and quickness not taken her simple imagination utterly in thrall.

Happily the singing stopped. What had occurred was that the farmer had espied the open door and, even befuddled as he was, wanted to know more about it quietly. He was so quiet that Mare had begun to fear he had gone away. He had the squirrel-hunter's foot, and the first she knew of him was when she looked and saw his head in the doorway, his hard, soiled, whiskery face half upside-down with craning.

He had been to the town. Between drinks he had wandered in and out of the night's excitement; had even gone a short distance with one search party himself. Now he took in the situation in the room. He used his forefinger. First he held it to his lips. Next he pointed it with a jabbing motion at the sleeper. Then he tapped his own forehead and described wheels. Lastly, with his whole hand, he made pushing gestures, for Mare to wait. Then he vanished as silently as he had appeared.

The minutes dragged. The light in the east strengthened and turned rosy. Once she thought she heard a board creaking in another part of the house, and looked down sharply to see if the loony stirred. All she could see of his face was a temple with freckles on it and the sharp ridge of a cheekbone, but even from so little she knew how deeply and peacefully he slept. The door darkened. Wyker was there again. In one hand he carried something heavy; with the other he beckoned.

"Come jumpin'!" he said out loud.

Mare went jumping, but her cramped legs threw her down halfway to the sill; the rest of the distance she rolled and crawled. Just as she tumbled through the door it seemed as if the world had come to an end above her; two barrels of a shotgun discharged into a room make a noise. Afterwards all she could hear in there was something twisting and bumping on the floor boards. She got up and ran.

Mare's mother had gone to pieces; neighbor women put her to bed when Mare came home. They wanted to put Mare to bed, but she would not let them. She sat on the edge of her bed in her lean-to bedroom off the kitchen, just as she was, her hair down all over her shoulders and her shoes on, and stared away from them, at a place in the wallpaper.

"Yeh, I'll go myself. Lea' me be!"

The women exchanged quick glances, thinned their lips, and left her be. "God knows," was all they would answer to the questionings of those that had not gone in, "but she's gettin' herself to bed."

When the doctor came through he found her

sitting just as she had been, still dressed, her hair down on her shoulders and her shoes on.

"What d' y' want?" she muttered and stared at the place in the wallpaper.

How could Doc Paradise say, when he did not know himself?

"I didn't know if you might be—might be feeling very smart, Mary."

"I'm all right. Lea' me be."

It was a heavy responsibility. Doc shouldered it. "No, it's all right," he said to the men in the road. Ruby Herter stood a little apart, chewing sullenly and looking another way. Doc raised his voice to make certain it carried. "Nope, nothing."

Ruby's ears got red, and he clamped his jaws. He knew he ought to go in and see Mare, but he was not going to do it while everybody hung around waiting to see if he would. A mule tied near him reached out and mouthed his sleeve in idle innocence; he wheeled and banged a fist against the side of the animal's head.

"Well, what d' y' aim to do 'bout it?" he challenged its owner.

He looked at the sun then. It was ten in the morning. "Hell, I got work!" he flared, and set off down the road for home. Doc looked at Judge North, and the Judge started off after Ruby. But Ruby shook his head angrily. "Lea' me be!" He went on, and the Judge came back.

It got to be eleven and then noon. People began to say, "Like enough she'd be as thankful if the

379

whole neighborhood wasn't camped here." But none went away.

As a matter of fact they were no bother to the girl. She never saw them. The only move she made was to bend her ankles over and rest her feet on the edge; her shoes hurt terribly and her feet knew it, though she did not. She sat all the while staring at that one figure in the wallpaper, and she never saw the figure.

Strange as the night had been, this day was stranger. Fright and physical pain are perishable things once they are gone. But while pain merely dulls and telescopes in memory and remains diluted pain, terror looked back upon has nothing of terror left. A gambling chance taken, at no matter what odds, and won was a sure thing since the world's beginning; perils come through safely were never perilous. But what fright does do in retrospect is this—it heightens each sensuous recollection, like a hare, clear lacquer laid on wood, bringing out the color and grain of it vividly.

Last night Mare had lain stupid with fear on groundpine beneath a bush, loud footfalls and light whispers confused in her ear. Only now, in her room, did she smell the groundpine.

Only now did the conscious part of her brain begin to make words of the whispering.

Amarantha, she remembered, *Amarantha sweet and fair.* That was as far as she could go for the moment, except that the rhyme with "fair" was "hair." But then a puzzle, held in abeyance, brought other words. She wondered what "ravel

Ed" could mean. *Most excellently ravell-ed.* It was left to her mother to bring the end.

They gave up trying to keep her mother out at last. The poor woman's prostration took the form of fussiness.

"Good gracious, daughter, you look a sight. Them new shoes, half ruined; ain't your feet *dead?* And look at your hair, all tangled like a wild one!"

She got a comb.

"Be quiet, daughter; what's ailin' you. Don't shake your head!"

"But shake your head and scatter day."

"What you say, Amarantha?" Mrs. Doggett held an ear down.

"Go 'way! Lea' me be!"

Her mother was hurt and left. And Mare ran, as she stared at the wallpaper.

Christ, that my love were in my arms . . .

Mare ran. She ran through a wind white with moonlight and wet with "the small rain." And the wind she ran through, it ran through her, and made her shiver as she ran. And the man beside her leaped high over the waves of the dead grasses and gathered the wind in his arms, and her hair was heavy and his was tossing, and a little fox ran before them across the top of the world. And the world spread down around in waves of black and silver, more immense than she had ever known the world could be, and more beautiful.

God Almighty beautiful, to take your breath away!

Mare wondered, and she was not used to wondering. "Is it only crazy folks ever run like that and talk that way?"

She no longer ran; she walked; for her breath was gone. And there was some other reason, some other reason. Oh, yes, it was because her feet were hurting her. So, at last, and roundabout, her shoes had made contact with her brain.

Bending over the side of the bed, she loosened one of them mechanically. She pulled it half off. But then she looked down at it sharply, and she pulled it on again.

How beautiful . . .

Color overspread her face in a slow wave.

How beautiful are thy feet with shoes . . .

"Is it only crazy folks ever say such things?"

O prince's daughter!

"Or call you that?"

By and by there was a knock at the door. It opened, and Ruby Herter came in.

"Hello, Mare old girl!" His face was red. He scowled and kicked at the floor. "I'd 'a' been over sooner, except we got a mule down sick." He looked at his dumb betrothed. "Come on, cheer up, forget it! He won't scare you no more, not that boy, not what's left o' him. What you lookin' at, sourface? Ain't you glad to see me?"

Mare quit looking at the wallpaper and looked at the floor.

"Yeh," she said.

"That's more like it, babe." He came and sat beside her, reached down behind her and gave her a spank. "Come on, give us a kiss, babe!" He wiped his mouth on his jumper sleeve, a good farmer's sleeve, spotted with milking. He put his hands on her; he was used to handling animals. "Hey, you, warm up a little; reckon I'm goin' to do all the lovin'?"

"Ruby, lea' me be!"

"What!"

She was up, twisting. He was up, purple.

"What's ailin' of you, Mare? What you bawlin' about?"

"Nothin'—only go 'way!"

She pushed him to the door and through it with all her strength, and closed it in his face, and stood with her weight against it, crying, "Go 'way! Go 'way! Lea' me be!"

Two Gentle People

Graham Greene

They sat on a bench in the Parc Monceau for a
long time without speaking to one another. It was
a hopeful day of early summer with a spray of
white clouds lapping across the sky in front of a
small breeze: at any moment the wind might drop
and the sky become empty and entirely blue, but
it was too late now—the sun would have set first.

In younger people it might have been a day for
a chance encounter—secret behind the long bar-
rier of perambulators with only babies and nurses
in sight. But they were both of them middle-aged,
and neither was inclined to cherish an illusion of
possessing a lost youth, though he was better looking than he believed, with his silky old-world
moustache like a badge of good behaviour, and
she was prettier than the looking-glass ever told
her. Modesty and disillusion gave them something
in common; though they were separated by five
feet of green metal they could have been a married
couple who had grown to resemble each other.
Pigeons like old grey tennis balls rolled unnoticed
around their feet. They each occasionally looked
at a watch, though never at one another. For both

384

of them this period of solitude and peace was limited.

The man was tall and thin. He had what are called sensitive features, and the cliché fitted him; his face was comfortably, though handsomely, banal—there would be no ugly surprises when he spoke, for a man may be sensitive without imagination. He had carried with him an umbrella which suggested caution. In her case one noticed first the long and lovely legs as unsensual as those in a society portrait. From her expression she found the summer day sad, yet she was reluctant to obey the command of her watch and go—somewhere—inside.

They would never have spoken to each other if two teen-aged louts had not passed by, one with a blaring radio slung over his shoulder, the other kicking out at the preoccupied pigeons. One of his kicks found a random mark, and on they went in a din of pop, leaving the pigeon lurching on the path.

The man rose, grasping his umbrella like a riding-whip. 'Infernal young scoundrels,' he exclaimed, and the phrase sounded more Edwardian because of the faint American intonation—Henry James might surely have employed it.

'The poor bird,' the woman said. The bird struggled upon the gravel, scattering little stones. One wing hung slack and a leg must have been broken too, for the pigeon swivelled round in circles unable to rise. The other pigeons moved away, with disinterest, searching the gravel for crumbs.

'If you would look away for just a minute,' the man said. He laid his umbrella down again and walked rapidly to the bird where it thrashed around; then he picked it up, and quickly and expertly he wrung its neck—it was a kind of skill anyone of breeding ought to possess. He looked round for a refuse bin in which he tidily deposited the body.

'There was nothing else to do,' he remarked apologetically when he returned.

'I could not myself have done it,' the woman said, carefully grammatical in a foreign tongue.

'Taking life is *our* privilege,' he replied with irony rather than pride.

When he sat down the distance between them had narrowed; they were able to speak freely about the weather and the first real day of summer. The last week had been unseasonably cold, and even today. . . . He admired the way in which she spoke English and apologized for his own lack of French, but she reassured him: it was no ingrained talent. She had been 'finished' at an English school at Margate.

'That's a seaside resort, isn't it?'

'The sea always seemed very grey,' she told him, and for a while they lapsed into separate silences. Then perhaps thinking of the dead pigeon she asked him if he had been in the army. 'No, I was over forty when the war came,' he said. 'I served on a government mission, in India. I became very fond of India.' He began to describe to her Agra, Lucknow, the old city of Delhi, his eyes alight with memories. The new Delhi he did not like, built by a Britisher—Lut-Lut-Lut? No matter. It reminded him of Washington.

'Then you do not like Washington?'

'To tell you the truth,' he said, 'I am not very happy in my own country. You see, I like old things. I found myself more at home—can you believe it?—in India, even with the British. And now in France I find it's the same. My grandfather was British Consul in Nice.'

'The Promenade des Anglais was very new then,' she said.

'Yes, but it aged. What we Americans build never ages beautifully. The Chrysler Building, Hilton hotels . . .'

'Are you married?' she asked. He hesitated a moment before replying, 'Yes,' as though he wished to be quite, quite accurate. He put out his hand and felt for his umbrella—it gave him confidence in this surprising situation of talking so openly to a stranger.

'I ought not to have asked you,' she said, still careful with her grammar.

'Why not?' He excused her awkwardly.

'I was interested in what you said.' She gave him a little smile. 'The question came. It was *imprévu.*'

'Are *you* married?' he asked, but only to put her at her ease, for he could see her ring.

'Yes.'

By this time they seemed to know a great deal about each other, and he felt it was churlish not to surrender his identity. He said, 'My name is Greaves. Henry C. Greaves.'

'Mine is Marie-Claire. Marie-Claire Duval.'

'What a lovely afternoon it has been,' the man called Greaves said.

'But it gets a little cold when the sun sinks.' They escaped from each other again with regret.

'A beautiful umbrella you have,' she said, and it was quite true—the gold band was distinguished, and even from a few feet away one could see there was a monogram engraved there—an H certainly, entwined perhaps with a C or a G.

'A present,' he said without pleasure.

'I admired so much the way you acted with the pigeon. As for me I am *lâche*.'

'That I am quite sure is not true,' he said kindly.

'Oh, it is. It is.'

'Only in the sense that we are all cowards about something.'

'You are not,' she said, remembering the pigeon with gratitude.

'Oh yes, I am,' he replied, 'in one whole area of life.' He seemed on the brink of a personal revelation, and she clung to his coat-tail to pull him back; she literally clung to it, for lifting the edge of his jacket she exclaimed, 'You have been touching some wet paint.' The ruse succeeded; he became solicitous about her dress, but examining the bench they both agreed the source was not there. 'They have been painting on my staircase,' he said.

'You have a house here?'

388

'No, an apartment on the fourth floor.'

'With an *ascenseur?*'

'Unfortunately not,' he said sadly. 'It's a very old house in the *dix-septième.*'

The door of his unknown life had opened a crack, and she wanted to give something of her own life in return, but not too much. A 'brink' would give her vertigo. She said, 'My apartment is only too depressingly new. In the *huitième*. The door opens electrically without being touched. Like in an airport.'

A strong current of revelation carried them along. He learned how she always bought her cheeses in the Place de la Madeleine—it was quite an expedition from her side of the *huitième*, near the Avenue George V, and once she had been rewarded by finding Tante Yvonne, the General's wife, at her elbow choosing a Brie. He on the other hand bought his cheeses in the Rue de Tocqueville, only round the corner from his apartment.

'You yourself?'

'Yes, I do the marketing,' he said in a voice suddenly abrupt.

She said, 'It is a little cold now. I think we should go.'

'Do you come to the Parc often?'

'It is the first time.'

'What a strange coincidence,' he said. 'It's the first time for me too. Even though I live close by.'

'And I live quite far away.'

They looked at one another with a certain awe, aware of the mysteries of providence. He said, 'I don't suppose you would be free to have a little dinner with me.'

Excitement made her lapse into French. '*Je suis libre, mais vous . . . votre femme. . . ?*'

'She is dining elsewhere,' he said. 'And your husband?'

'He will not be back before eleven.'

He suggested the Brasserie Lorraine, which was only a few minutes' walk away, and she was glad that he had not chosen something more chic or more flamboyant. The heavy bourgeois atmosphere of the *brasserie* gave her confidence, and, though she had small appetite herself, she was glad to watch the comfortable military progress down the ranks of the sauerkraut trolley. The menu too was long enough to give them time to readjust to the startling intimacy of dining together. When the order had been given, they both began to speak at once. 'I never expected . . .'

'It's funny the way things happen,' he added, laying unintentionally a heavy inscribed monument over that conversation.

'Tell me about your grandfather, the consul.'

'I never knew him,' he said. It was much more difficult to talk on a restaurant sofa than on a park bench.

'Why did your father go to America?'

'The spirit of adventure perhaps,' he said. 'And I suppose it was the spirit of adventure which brought me back to live in Europe. America didn't mean Coca-Cola and *Time-Life* when my father was young.'

'And have you found adventure? How stupid of me to ask. Of course you married here?'

'I brought my wife with me,' he said. 'Poor Patience.'

'Poor?'

'She is fond of Coca-Cola.'

'You can get it here,' she said, this time with intentional stupidity.

'Yes.'

The wine-waiter came and he ordered a Sancerre. 'If that will suit you?'

'I know so little about wine,' she said.

'I thought all French people . . .'

'We leave it to our husbands,' she said, and in his turn he felt an obscure hurt. The sofa was shared by a husband now as well as a wife, and for a while the *sole meunière* gave them an excuse not to talk. And yet silence was not a genuine escape. In the silence the two ghosts would have become more firmly planted, if the woman had not found the courage to speak.

'Have you any children?' she asked.

'No. Have you?'

'No.'

'Are you sorry?'

She said, 'I suppose one is always sorry to have missed something.'

'I'm glad at least I did not miss the Parc Monceau today.'

'Yes, I am glad too.'

The silence after that was a comfortable silence: the two ghosts went away and left them alone.

Once their fingers touched over the sugar-castor (they had chosen strawberries). Neither of them had any desire for further questions; they seemed to know each other more completely than they knew anyone else. It was like a happy marriage; the stage of discovery was over—they had passed the test of jealousy, and now they were tranquil in their middle age. Time and death remained the only enemies, and coffee was like the warning of old age. After that it was necessary to hold sadness at bay with a brandy, though not successfully. It was as though they had experienced a lifetime, which was measured as with butterflies in hours.

He remarked of the passing head waiter, 'He looks like an undertaker.'

'Yes,' she said. So he paid the bill and they went outside. It was a death-agony they were too gentle to resist for long. He asked, 'Can I see you home?'

'I would rather not. Really not. You live so close.'

'We could have another drink on the *terrasse?*' he suggested with half a sad heart.

'It would do nothing more for us,' she said. 'The evening was perfect. *Tu es vraiment gentil.*' She noticed too late that she had used '*tu*' and she hoped his French was bad enough for him not to have noticed. They did not exchange addresses or telephone numbers, for neither of them dared to suggest it: the hour had come too late in both their lives. He found her a taxi and she drove away towards the great illuminated Arc, and he walked home by the Rue Jouffroy, slowly. What is cowardice in the young is wisdom in the old, but all the same one can be ashamed of wisdom.

Marie-Claire walked through the self-opening doors and thought, as she always did, of airports and escapes. On the sixth floor she let herself into the flat. An abstract painting in cruel tones of scarlet and yellow faced the door and treated her like a stranger.

She went straight to her room, as softly as possible, locked the door and sat down on her single bed. Through the wall she could hear her husband's voice and laugh. She wondered who was with him tonight—Toni or François. François had painted the abstract picture, and Toni, who danced in ballet, always claimed, especially before strangers, to have modelled for the little stone phallus with painted eyes that had a place of honour in the living-room. She began to undress. While the voice next door spun its web, images of the bench in the Parc Monceau returned and of the sauerkraut trolley in the Brasserie Lorraine. If he had heard her come in, her husband would soon proceed to action: it excited him to know that she was a witness. The voice said, 'Pierre, Pierre,' reproachfully. Pierre was a new name to her. She spread her fingers on the dressing-table to take off her rings and she thought of the sugar-castor for the strawberries, but at the sound of the little yelps and giggles from next door the sugar-castor turned into the phallus with painted eyes.

393

She lay down and screwed beads of wax into her ears, and she shut her eyes and thought how different things might have been if fifteen years ago she had sat on a bench in the Parc Monceau, watching a man with pity killing a pigeon.

'I can smell a woman on you,' Patience Greaves said with pleasure, sitting up against two pillows. The top pillow was punctured with brown cigarette burns.

'Oh no, you can't. It's your imagination, dear.'

'You said you would be home by ten.'

'It's only twenty past now.'

'You've been up in the Rue de Douai, haven't you, in one of those bars, looking for a *fille*.'

'I sat in the Parc Monceau and then I had dinner at the Brasserie Lorraine. Can I give you your drops?'

'You want me to sleep so that I won't expect anything. That's it, isn't it, you're too old now to do it twice.'

He mixed the drops from the carafe of water on the table between the twin beds. Anything he might say would be wrong when Patience was in a mood like this. Poor Patience, he thought, holding out the drops towards the face crowned with red curls, how she misses America—she will never believe that the Coca-Cola tastes the same here. Luckily this would not be one of their worst nights, for she drank from the glass without further argument, while he sat beside her and remembered the street outside the *brasserie* and how—by accident he was sure—he had been called '*tu*'.

'What are you thinking?' Patience asked. 'Are you still in the Rue de Douai?'

'I was only thinking that things might have been different,' he said.

It was the biggest protest he had ever allowed himself to make against the condition of life.

Courtship

Edna O'Brien

A favorite school poem was "The Mother" by Patrick Pearce. It was a wrenching poem condoling the plight of a mother who had seen her two strong sons go out and die, "in bloody protest for a glorious thing." Mrs. Flynn had also known tragedy, her husband having died from pleurisy and her youngest son, Frank, having drowned while away on holiday. For a time she wept and gnashed, her fate being similar to the poor distraught mother's in the poem. I did not know her then but there were stories of how she balked at hearing the tragic news. When the guards came to tell her that Frank was drowned, she simply pressed her hands to her ears and ran out of the house, into the garden, saying to leave her alone, to stop pestering people. When at last they made her listen, her screaming was such that the curate heard it two miles away. Her son was eighteen and very brainy.

By the time I met her she seemed calm and reconciled, a busy woman who owned a shop and a mill and who had three other sons, all of whom were over six feet and who seemed gigantic beside her, because she was a diminutive woman with gray permed hair. Her pride in them was obvious and transmitted itself to all who knew her. It was not anything she said, it was just the way she would look up at them as if they were a breed of gods, and sometimes she would take a clothes brush and brush one of their lapels, just to confirm that closeness. They all had dark eyes and thick curly hair, and there was not a girl in the parish who did not dream of being courted by one of them. Of the three, Michael was the most sought after. It was his lovely manner, as the women said; even the old women melted when they described how he put them at their ease when they went to sell eggs or buy groceries. He was a famous hurley player, and the wizard way that he scored a goal was renowned and immortalized in verses that the men carried in their pockets. If his team was ever in danger of losing and he had been put out for a foul—as he often was—the crowd would clamor for him and the referee had no choice but to let him back. His specialty was to score a goal in the very last minute of the game, when the opposing team thought themselves certain of victory; and this goal and the eerie way in which it was scored would be a talking point for weeks. Then after the match the fans would carry him on their shoulders, and the crowd would mill around, trying to touch his feet or his hands, just as in the Gospels the crowd milled about trying to touch Our Lord. That night in a dance hall, girls would vie to dance with him. He had a steady girl called Moira, but when he traveled to hurling matches he met other girls at dances, and for weeks some new girl, some Ellen, or some Dolly, or some Kate, would plague him with love letters. I learned this from Peggy, their maid, when I went there on my first ever holiday. I had yearned to go for many years and at last the chance came, because my sister, who used to go, had set her sights on the city and went instead to cousins in Limerick who had a sweet shop that adjoined a chip shop. As in many other things I had taken her place; I was her substitute, and the realization of this was not without its undercurrent of jealousy and pique.

On my first day in their house I felt very gawky, and kept avoiding the brothers and crying in the passage. I wanted to go home but was too ashamed to mention it. It was Michael who rescued me.

"Will you do me a favor?" he said.

The favor was very simple—it was to make him apple fritters. If there was anything in the world he craved, it was apple fritters. I was to make them surreptitiously, when his mother was not looking.

"Can't," I said.

His mother and Peggy were constantly about and the thought of defying them quite impossible.

"Suppose they went off for a day, would you make them then?"

"Of course."

That "of course," so quick, so yielding, already making it clear that I was eager to serve him.

In a matter of days I had settled in and thought no place on earth so thrilling and so bustling as their house and their shop. They stocked everything—groceries, animal feed, serge for suits, winceyette, cotton, paraffin, cakes, confectionery, boots, Wellingtons, and cable-knit sweaters that were made by spinsters and lonely women up in the mountains. They even sold underwear for ladies and gents, and these were the subject of much innuendo and mirth. The ladies' corsets were of pink broderie Anglaise, and sometimes one of the brothers would take one out of its cellophane and put it on over his trousers, as a joke. Of course, that was when the shop was empty and his mother had gone to confession, or to see a sick neighbor. They respected their mother and in her presence never resorted to shady language.

What I liked about staying there was the jokes, the levity, and the constant activity—cakes being delivered, meal being weighed, eggs being brought in and having to be counted as well as washed, orders having to be got ready, and at any moment a compliment or a pinch in the arm from one of the brothers. It was all so exhilarating. At night more diversion, when the men convened in the back bar, drank porter, and talked in monosyllables until they got drunk, and then ranted and raved and got obstreperous when it came to politics. If they were too unruly Michael would roll up his sleeves, take off his wristwatch, and tell them that unless they "cut out the bull" they would be rudely ejected to the yard outside.

In the morning the brothers joked and made references to the dramas of the night before, while their mother always said it was inviting disaster to have men in after hours. The guards rarely raided because of once having to give the terrible news about Frank, but she was always in fear that she might be raided, disgraced, and brought to court. The brothers used to tease her about being a favorite with the sergeant, and though pretending to resent this, she blushed and got very agitated and looked in all directions so as to avoid their insinuations. I wore a clean dress each day and, to enhance myself, a starched white collar which gave me, I thought, a plaintive look. I was forever plying them with more tea or another fried egg or relish. Michael would touch my wrist and say, "That the girl, that the girl," and I hoped that I would never have to go home. I even harbored a dream about being adopted by his mother, so that I would become his sister and shake hands with him, or even embrace, without any suggestion of shame or sin.

Each morning the oldest brother, William, filled the buggy with provisions in order to go up the country to buy and to sell. He used to coax me to go with him by telling me about the strange people he met. In one house three members of the family were mad and bayed like dogs, and the fourth, sane member had to throw buckets of water on them to calm them down. There was the house, or rather the hovel, where the hunchback, Della, lived, and she constantly invited him in for tea in the hope that he would propose to her. Each time when he refused, Della stamped her foot and said that the invitation wasn't meant anyhow. There was a mother and daughter who never stirred out of bed and who called to him to come upstairs, where he would find them in bed, wearing fancy bed jackets, with rouge and lipstick on them, consulting fashion catalogues.

"Do you ever score?" I heard his cousin Tom ask him one morning, and William put his finger to his lips and smiled as if there were sagas he could tell. But I would not be dragged to these places, because for one thing I had no interest in fields or hay sheds or lakes, and for another I wanted to remain in Michael's orbit and be ready at any moment should he summon me, or just bump into me and give me a sudden thrilling squeeze. He worked in the mill, which was a short distance across the garden. Sometimes I would convey him out there, and if the birds were gorging on the currant bushes, as they usually were, he would flap his hands and make a great to-do as he frightened them away.

"Be seeing you later, alligator," he always said, and lifted his cap once or twice to show that he was a gentleman. I then had to go back and help Peggy to wash the dishes, polish the range, and scrub the kitchen and the back kitchen. Later we made the beds. Making his bed was exciting but untoward. Peggy would flare up as she entered the room, then she would whip the bedclothes off and grumpily shake them out the window. In the yard below the geese cackled when she shook these bedclothes, and the gander hissed and raised his orange beak to defend his tribe.

"I can't wait to get to England," Peggy would say, and her version of life there seemed to envisage a world that did not include geese or the necessity to make beds. The room itself was like all the bedrooms, high-ceilinged, covered with garish carpet and unmatching furniture. There was the dark mahogany wardrobe with a long mirror that looked muddied over and gave back a very poor reflection of the self. There was the double bed with wooden headboard, and there was a cane chair beside the bed on which he flung clothes. His shoes, so big and so important, were laid inside the curb of the tiled fireplace, tan shoes well shone and with the shoe trees in them, his fawn coat on a hanger, swaying a little in the dark space of the wardrobe. There were, too, his various ties, the red-tasseled box in which were thrown the several love letters, his scapulars, his missal, and then, most nakedly of all, his pajamas in a heap at the end of the very tossed bed, causing Peggy to be incensed and to ask aloud if he played hurley in his sleep or what. Along the mantelpiece was the row of cups that he had won at hurley and beside them a framed photograph of his mother as a very young girl, with lips pouted, like a rosebud. I would touch the cups and beg of Peggy to tell me when and where each one had been awarded. They were tarnished, and I resolved that one day I would get silver dip and put such a shine on them that when he entered his room that night he would be greeted by the gleam of silver and would wonder who had done it and maybe would even find out.

Once the beds were done, I would then concoct an excuse to go over to the mill. Up to the moment I had yielded I would intend not to go, but then all of a sudden some frenzied need would take hold of me, and though despising myself for such weakness, I succumbed. Crossing the garden, humming some stupid ditty, I would already picture him, his face and jacket dusted over with white grain, his whole being smelling of it, his skin powdered and pale, a feature which made him look older but made his eyes shine like deep pools. I would hear the rush of the little river and see segments of it being splashed and tumbled in the spokes of the big wooden mossy mill wheel, and I would go in trying to appear casual.

"Any news?" he would say, and invariably he asked if the English folk had been to the shop yet. An Englishman and his son had come to the district to shoot and fish, and their accents were a source of mirth to us, as was their amazement about nature. They were most surprised by the fact that they had caught a rabbit, and brought it over to show it to people as if it were a trophy.

One day, however, I found him in a rage, and saw that he was hitting the wooden desk and calling Jock, the boy who helped him, the greatest idiot under the sun. Michael had addressed the bills to his customers and had put *Esquire* after each one, when Jock had come along and put *Mr.* before each name, and now thirty or forty envelopes would have to be readdressed. Despite his fury he had put his arm around me as usual and said what a pity that I couldn't work in the mill, so's he'd send Jock to a reformatory, where he belonged. I was basking in being so close to him when a beautiful older girl sauntered in, on the very flimsy excuse that she was looking for her father. This was Eileen, with blond hair, blue eyes, and great long black lashes, which she knowingly flaunted by repeated fluttering. She worked in Dublin but was home for a few days, and as she came down between the sacks, it was prodigal to see their interest in each other quicken. She walked with a sway and said that her father was supposed to have come with bags of corn for grinding but where on earth had he vanished to? Seeing his arm around me, she pretended to be very haughty and said, "Sorry," then turned on her heel and walked away. She wore a red jacket, a pleated skirt, and wedge-heeled canvas sandals with straps that laced up over her calves.

"What's the big hurry?" he called out to her.

"Have to see a man about a dog," she said, and she turned and smirked. He said that he had not known she was at home and might he ask how long would the parish have the pleasure of her exotic company.

"Until I get the wanderlust," she said, and announced that she might go to a hotel at the seaside for a weekend, as she heard they had singsongs.

"God, you must be rolling in it," he said.

"Correct," she said, and put out her arm to reveal the bone bangles that she wore.

"I suppose we're the country Mohawks," he said.

"You certainly don't know how to pamper a gal," she said, and implied that men in Dublin knew what it was all about. The peals of laughter that she let out were at once sweet and audacious.

"Do you live on the north side?" he said.

"Gosh, no, the south side," she said, and added that if one lived on the north side, one would be roused by the bawling of cattle two mornings a week as they were driven to the cattle market and herded into pens. "The north side is far too countrified," she said.

"So you're sitting pretty on the south side," he said with a sting. By now he had deserted me and was facing her, taking such stock of her as if every detail of her person intrigued him. Though they were saying caustic things, they were playful and reveled in each other's banter.

"Who's the little kid?" she said, looking back at me, and upon being told, she said that she knew my sister, had seen her at dances, and that my sister was full of herself.

"What are you up to tonight?" he asked.

"Fast work," she said, and he biffed her, and then they linked and went outside to confer. Standing next to Jock, who was scratching the *Mr.*

off each envelope, I felt foolish, felt outcast just like him. They stood in the doorway close together, and fired with curiosity, I hurried toward them and slipped out without even being noticed. There was a lorry parked to one side and I stood on the running board in order to spy on them. It was awful. His arm was around her waist and she was looking up at him, saying, "What do *you* think you're doing." He said he could do as he pleased, break her ribs if he felt like it.

"Just try, just you try," she said, and with both hands he appeared to mash her ribs as he circled her waist. A few flies droned around the lorry, as there were milk tanks on the back, and there was a smell of sour milk and metal. The driver's seat was torn and bits of spiral spring stuck out of it. I wondered whose lorry it was. Not having looked for a few minutes, I now allowed myself another glance at the bewitched pair. He was standing a little behind her; her pleated skirt was raised so that it came unevenly above her knees, and I could see the top of her legs, the lace of her slip, and her mounting excitement as she stood on tiptoe to accommodate herself to what he was doing. Also, she let out suggestive sounds and was laughing and wriggling until suddenly she became very matter-of-fact, pulled her skirt down, and said what did he think he was up to. Then she ran off, but he caught her and they had a little tug of war. He let go of her on the understanding that they would meet that night, and they made an appointment in the grounds of what had once been a demesne but was now gone to ruin.

By the time they met, and possibly just as he was resting their two bicycles, interlocking them against a tree, or spreading his overcoat on the grass, I was kneeling down to say the Rosary with his mother, whose voice throbbed with devotion. She had decided that night to offer up the Rosary for her dead son and her dead husband. The kitchen flagstones felt hard and grimy; it was as if grit was being ground into our knees as we recited endless Our Fathers, Hail Marys, and Glory Bes. I was thinking of the lovers with a curiosity that bordered on frenzy. I could picture the meeting place, the smell of grass, cows wheezing, their two faces almost featureless in the dark, and by not being able to see, their power of touch so overwhelmingly whetted that their hands reached out, and suddenly they clove together and dared to say each other's Christian name with a hectic urgency. I was thinking this while at the same time mouthing the prayers and hearing the mumbling of the men in the bar outside. I even knew the men who were there, and saw one old man to whom I had an aversion, because the porter froth made gold foam on his gray mustache. Mrs. Flynn was profligate that night with prayers and insisted that we do the Three Mysteries—the Joyful, Sorrowful, and Glorious. It was after ten o'-clock when we stood up, and we were both doubled over from the hours of kneeling.

She asked if as a reward I would like a "saussie," and she popped two sausages into the pan that was always lying on the side of the stove in case any of her sons became hungry. In no time the fat was hissing and she was prodding the sausages with a fork and telling them to hurry up, as there were two famished customers. Afterward she gave me little biscuits with colored icing and said that I could come for every holiday and stay for the entire length. Saying it, I think she believed that I would never grow up. I slept with her, and all that I recall of the bedroom is that it was damp, that the flowered wallpaper had become runny and disfigured, and that the feathers in the pillows used to dig into one's flesh. That night, perhaps exalted from so much praying, she did not insist that we go to sleep at once but allowed us to chat. Naturally I brought the subject around to her sons.

"Which of them do you prefer?" I asked.

"They're all the same in my eyes," she said in a very practical voice.

"But isn't Michael a great hurler?" I said, hoping that we could discuss him, hoping she would tell me what he was like as a baby, and as a little boy, what mischief he had done, and maybe even discuss his present behavior, especially his gallivanting.

She said that a gypsy came into the shop one day long ago and predicted that Michael would have a checkered life, and that she prayed hourly

408

that he would never take it into his head to go to England.

"He won't," I said, without any justification.

"Please God not," she said, and added that Michael was a softie with everybody. Little did she know that at that moment he was engaged in a tryst that would make her writhe.

"I think he is your favorite," I said.

"What a little imp you are," she said, and announced that we must go to sleep at once. But I knew that I wouldn't. I knew that I would stay awake until I heard him come up the stairs and go into his room, and that having heard him, I would experience some remote satisfaction, thinking, or rather hoping, that he had tired of Eileen and was now ours again. It was very late when he got back and my mood was dismal because of his whistling. A mad notion took hold of me to go and ask him if he wanted sausages, but mercifully I resisted.

I wondered which of the two girls he would smile at next day at Mass. As it happened, Eileen and his girl friend Moira were in the same seat, but not next to one another. Eileen was all in black, with a black mantilla that shrouded her face. I thought she looked ashamed, but I may have imagined it. Moira had a cardigan knitted in the blackberry stitch and a matching beret that was clapped on the side of her head and secured with a pearled hat pin. During the long sermon she kept turning around, probably to see where Michael was. He stood in the back of the church with the men, and like them skedaddled at the Last Gospel. The two girls came down the aisle very quietly and exchanged a word on the porch. Then Moira went on home with her parents, and Eileen cycled home alone.

At lunchtime Michael was very attentive to me, kept giving me more gravy and more roast potatoes, kept telling me to eat up. It was my last day, as I was leaving very early in the morning on the mail car. Perhaps he was nice to me for that reason, or else it was a silent bribe not to betray his secret. I had already accrued a gift of ten shillings and rosary beads from his mother; in the back of the crucifix was a little cavity containing a special relic.

As we were eating, their cousin Tom rushed into the kitchen and announced that he was taking me to the pictures that night. The brothers let out some hoots, whereupon he said that for two weeks I had helped in the kitchen, helped in the shop, and had had no diversion at all. To my dismay their mother applauded the idea and said what a shame that one of her sons hadn't shown such thought. I disliked Tom; he had a smile that was faintly indecent, and whenever a girl went by, he made licking sounds and gurgles. He had glaring red hair, pale skin with freckles, and often he wore his socks up over his trouser legs to emphasize his calves. His hands were the most revolting, being very white, and his fingers were like long white slugs. Despite the fact that I withered at being invited, he said that he would pick me up at six and that we would have a whale of a time. The cinema was three or four miles away and we were able to cycle. I dreaded cycling, as even in the daylight I had a tendency to wobble.

The Angelus was striking as he arrived in a green tweed suit with matching cap. He was unable to conceal his pleasure, and at once I saw his salaciousness from the way he touched the saddle of my bicycle and said oughtn't I to have a little cover on it, as it wasn't soft enough. "You demon," Michael said to him as we set off. The cycling was most unnerving; I bumped into him several times and found myself veering to the ditch whenever a car passed us. He said that had he known of my precariousness he would have put a cushion on the crossbar and conveyed me himself. I could not bear his voice and I could not bear his unctuousness, and what I disliked most of all was the way he kept saying my name, making it clear that he was attracted to me.

When we got to the cinema he linked me up the steps and led me into the foyer. It was a very luxurious place with a wide stairs, and the streams of light from the big chandelier made rainbow prisms on the red carpet. The stair handle had just been polished and it smelt of Brasso. Inside, he settled us into two seats in the second to last row, and once it became dark, he grasped my hand and began to squeeze it. I pretended not to know what was going on. His next ruse was to tickle the palm of my hand slowly with his fingers. A woman

411

had told me that if tickled on the palm of the hand, or behind the knees, one could become wanton and lose control. On the screen Lola Montez was engaged in the most strenuous and alarming scuffles as she tried to escape a villain. Her predicament was not unlike my own. Having attacked the palm of one hand, he then set out on the other, and finding me unwilling, if not to say recalcitrant, he told me to uncross my legs, but I wouldn't. I sealed them together and wound one foot around the other ankle so that I was like something stitched together. I strove to ignore him, and annoyed by this he leaned over and licked my ear and so revolted me that I let out a cry, causing people to turn around in amazement. Naturally he drew away, and when the man behind him thumped his shoulder, he muttered some abject apology about his sister (that was me) being very highly strung.

When we left the cinema he was livid. He said why do such a thing, why egg him on with ringlets and smiles and then make a holy show of him. I said sorry. What with the dark and the long cycle home, I realized that I was at his mercy. I feigned great interest in the plot of the film and began to question him about it, but he saw through this ruse and suddenly swerved his bicycle in front of mine and said, "Halt, halt." I knew what it presaged. He took both bicycles, slung them aside, then embraced me and said what a little tease I was, and then backed me toward a gateway. The gate rattled and shook under the impact of our joined bodies and from inside the field a cow let out a very lugubrious moan.

"I'm not going in there," I said.

"Not half," he said.

He said he had paid three and sixpence per seat and had had enough codology and wasn't taking any more. I summoned all the temerity I could and said how the priest would kill me and also Mrs. Flynn would kill me.

"They needn't know," he said.

"They would, they would," I said.

He was not going to be fobbed off with excuses.

"Have a heart!" he said as he began to kiss me, and inquire what color underclothes I wore.

"I love Michael, I love Michael," I said vehemently. Foolishly, I thought jealousy might quell his intentions.

"Hasn't he got Moira?" he said, and went on to outline how Michael was at that very moment in the loft above the mill, close to Moira, a rendezvous they kept most Sunday nights.

"That's a lie," I said.

"Is it!" he said, and boasted how Michael described Moira's arrival, her shyness, her chatter, then her capitulation as he removed her coat, her dress, her underclothes, and she lay there with not a stitch. As his advances were now rapid, I knew there was nothing for it but to have a fit. I started to shake all over, to scream, to say disjointed things, indeed to be so delirious that he slapped me on the face and said for Christ's sake to calm down, that no one was going to do anything to me. We could hear a car in the distance, and as its headlights came around the corner, I ran out and waved frantically. It was the vet, who slowed down, wound the window, and shouted, "What's up?"

"Nothing's up," Tom said, and added that I had a puncture but that he had mended it. When the car drove off he picked up his bicycle and said for a long time he had not had such a fiasco of an evening.

Ours was a silent and a sullen journey home. He cycled ahead of me and never once turned around to see if I followed. As we neared the village, he cycled on downhill, and I got off because my brakes were faulty. I felt full of shame and blunder and did not know what I would say if Mrs. Flynn or the brothers asked me if I had enjoyed myself. I felt disgraced and dearly wished that I could go home there and then.

Michael confronted me in the hall as I was hanging up my coat. He said had I seen a ghost or what, as I was white as a sheet. Soon he guessed.

"The pup, the blackguard," he said as he brought me into the kitchen. He put me in the big armchair, sat beside me, and started to stroke my hair, all the while iterating what injury he would do to Tom. Suddenly he kissed me, and this kiss being a comfort, he followed it with a shower of kisses, embraces, and fond fugitive words.

"I love you," I said bluntly.

"Ditto," he said. His voice and expression were quite different now, young and unguarded. I was seeing the man for whom Moria, Eileen, and a host of girls would tear one another's eyes out. We heard a stir and he drew back, stood up sharply, and opened the kitchen door very casually, while also winking at me.

"Who goes there?" he said in a stern voice, and then went into the well of the hall, but no one answered. He crossed over into the shop and all of a sudden the kitchen became dark, either because he had interfered with the mains or their electricity plant had gone wrong. I was like someone in a trance. I could feel him coming back by his soft quick steps and then by the glow of a cigarette. Just as I had once imagined the lure of his voice in the dark saying a name, he now said mine, and his arms reached out to me with a sweet, almost a childlike supplicatingness. What had been disgusting and repellent an hour before was now a transport, and there was nothing for it but to be glad; that wild and frightened gladness that comes from breaking out of one's lonely crust, and just as with the swimmer who first braves the depths, the fear is secondary to the sense of prodigal adventure. He said that he would get some cider and two glasses and that we could go over to the loft, where no one would bother us. Whatever he proposed I would have agreed to. We went out like thieves, and crossing the yard, he picked me up so's I wouldn't spoil my shoes.

In the morning he stuck his tousled head out of his bedroom door, and in front of his mother gave me a quick kiss, then whispered, "I'll be waiting for you." It was not true, but it was all I wanted to hear, and on the drive home, the blue misted hills, the cold lakes, the songs of the birds, and the shiny laurel hedges around the grand estates all seemed startlingly beautiful and energized, and it was as if they had just been inhabited by some new and invigorating pulse of life.

My Mistress

Laurie Colwin

My wife is precise, elegant, and well-dressed, but the sloppiness of my mistress knows few bounds. Apparently I am not the sort of man who acquires a stylish mistress—the mistresses in French movies who rendezvous at the cafés in expensive hotels and take their cigarette cases out of alligator handbags, or meet their lovers on bridges wearing dashing capes. My mistress greets me in a pair of worn corduroy trousers, once green and now no color at all, a gray sweater, an old shirt of her younger brother's which has a frayed collar, and a pair of very old, broken shoes with tassels, the backs of which are held together with electrical tape. The first time I saw these shoes I found them remarkable.

"What are those?" I said. "Why do you wear them?"

My mistress is a serious, often glum person, who likes to put as little inflection into a sentence as she can.

"They used to be quite nice," she said. "I wore them out. Now I use them for slippers. They are my house shoes."

This person's name is Josephine Delielle, nicknamed Billy. I am Francis Clemens, and no one but my mistress calls me Frank. The first time we went to bed, my mistress fixed me with an indifferent stare and said: "Isn't this nice. In bed with Frank and Billy."

My constant image of Billy is of her pushing her hair off her forehead with an expression of exasperation on her face. She frowns easily, often looks puzzled, and is frequently irritated. In movies men have mistresses who soothe and pet them, who are consoling, passionate, and ornamental. But I have a mistress who is mostly grumpy. Traditional things mean nothing to her. She does not flirt, cajole, or wear fancy underwear. She has taken to referring to me as her "little bit of fluff," or she calls me *her* mistress, as in the sentence: "Before you became my mistress I led a blameless life."

But in spite of this I am secure in her affections. I know she loves me—not that she would ever come right out and tell me. She prefers the oblique line of approach. She may say something like: "Being in love with you is making me a nervous wreck."

Here is a typical encounter. It is between two and three o'clock in the afternoon. I arrive and ring the doorbell. The Delielles, who seem to have a lot of money, live in a duplex apartment in an old town house. Billy opens the door. There I am, an older man in my tweed coat. My hands are cold.

I'd like to get them underneath her ratty sweater. She looks me up and down. She gives me her edition of a smile—a repressed smile that is half smirk, half grin.

Sometimes she gets her coat and we go for a bracing walk. Sometimes we go upstairs to her study. Billy is an economic historian who teaches two classes at the business school. She writes for a couple of highbrow journals. Her husband, Grey, is the resident economics genius at a think tank. They are one of those dashing couples, or at least they sound like one. I am no slouch either. For years I was an investment banker, and now I consult from my own home. I too write for a couple of highbrow journals. We have much in common, my mistress and I, or so it looks.

Billy's study is untidy. She likes to spread her papers out. Since her surroundings mean nothing to her, her work place is bare of ornament, a cheerless, dreary little space.

"What have you been doing all day?" she says.

I tell her. Breakfast with my wife, Vera; newspaper reading after Vera has gone to work; an hour or so on the telephone with clients; a walk to my local bookstore; more telephoning; a quick sandwich; her.

"You and I ought to go out to lunch some day," she says. "One should always take one's mistress out for lunch. We could go dutch, thereby taking both mistresses at once."

"I try to take you for lunch," I say. "But you don't like to be taken out for lunch."

"Huh," utters Billy. She stares at her bookcase as if looking for a misplaced volume and then she may give me a look that might translate into something tender such as: "If I gave you a couple of dollars, would you take your clothes off?"

Instead, I take her into my arms. Her words are my signal that Grey is out of town. Often he is not, and then I merely get to kiss my mistress which makes us both dizzy. To kiss her and know that we can go forward to what Billy tonelessly refers to as "the rapturous consummation" reminds me that in relief is joy.

After kissing for a few minutes, Billy closes the study door and we practically throw ourselves at one another. After the rapturous consummation has been achieved, during which I can look upon a mistress recognizable as such to me, my mistress will turn to me and in a voice full of the attempt to stifle emotion say something like: "Sometimes I don't understand how I got so fond of a beat-up old person such as you."

These are the joys adulterous love brings to me.

Billy is indifferent to a great many things: clothes, food, home decor. She wears neither perfume nor cologne. She uses what is used on infants: baby powder and Ivory soap. She hates to cook and will never present me with an interesting postcoital snack. Her snacking habits are those, I have often remarked, of a dyspeptic nineteenth-century English clubman. Billy will get up and present me with a mug of cold tea, a plate of hard wheat biscuits, or a squirt of tepid soda from the siphon on her desk. As she sits under her quilt nibbling those resistant biscuits, she reminds me of a creature from another universe—the solar system that contains the alien features of her real life: her past, her marriage, why I am in her life, what she thinks of me.

I drink my soda, put on my clothes, and unless Vera is out of town, I go home to dinner. If Vera and Grey are out of town at the same time, which happens every now and again, Billy and I go out to dinner, during the course of which she either falls asleep or looks as if she is about to. Then I take her home, go home myself, and have a large steadying drink.

I was not entirely a stranger to adulterous love when I met Billy. I have explained this to her. In all long marriages, I expound, there are certain lapses. The look on Billy's face as I lecture is one of either amusement or contempt or both. The dinner party you are invited to as an extra man when your wife is away, I tell her. You are asked to take the extra woman, whose husband is also away, home in a taxi. The divorced family friend who invites you in for a drink one night, and so on. These fallings into bed are the friendliest thing in the world, I add. I look at my mistress.

"I see," she says. "Just like patting a dog."

My affair with Billy, as she well knows, is nothing of the sort. I call her every morning. I see her almost every weekday afternoon. On the days she teaches, she calls me. We are as faithful as the Canada goose, more or less. She is an absolute fact of my life. When not at work, and when not with her, my thoughts rest upon the subject of her as easily as you might lay a hand on a child's head. I conduct a mental life with her when we are apart. Thinking about her is like entering a secret room to which only I have access.

I, too, am part of a dashing couple. My wife is an interior designer who has dozens of commissions and consults to practically everyone. Our two sons are grown up. One is a securities analyst and one is a journalist. What a lively table we must be, all of us together. So I tell my mistress. She gives me a baleful look.

"We can get plenty of swell types in for meals," she says.

I know this is true and I know that Billy, unlike my gregarious and party-giving wife, thinks that there is no hell more hellish than the hell of social life. She has made up a tuneless little chant, like a football cheer, to describe it. It goes:

> *They invited us*
> *We invited them*
> *They invited us*
> *We invited them*
> *They invited us*
> *We invited them*

Billy and I met at a reception to celebrate the twenty-fifth anniversary of one of the journals to which we are both contributors. We fell into a spirited conversation during which Billy asked me if this reception wasn't the most boring thing I had ever been to. I said it wasn't, by a long shot. Billy said: "I can't stand these things where you have to stand up and be civilized. People either yawn, itch, or drool when they get bored. Which do you do?"

I said I yawned.

"Huh," said Billy. "You don't look much like a drooler. Let's get out of here."

This particular interchange is always brought up when intentionality is discussed: Did she mean to pick me up? Did I look available? And so on. Out on the street we revealed that we were married and that both of our spouses were out of town. Having made this clear, we went out to dinner and talked shop.

After dinner Billy said why didn't I come have a drink or a cup of tea. I did not know what to make of this invitation. I remembered that the young are more casual about these things, and that a cup of tea probably meant a cup of tea. My reactions to this offer are also discussed when cause is under discussion: Did I want her to seduce me? Did I mean to seduce her? Did we know what would happen right from the start?

Of her house Billy said: "We don't have good taste or bad taste. We have no taste." Her living room had no style whatsoever, but it was comfortable enough. There was a portrait of what looked like an ancestor over the fireplace. Otherwise it was not a room that revealed a thing about its occupants except solidity, and a lack of decorative inspiration. Billy made us each a cup of tea. We continued our conversation, and when Billy began to look sleepy, I left.

After that, we made a pass at social life. We invited them for dinner, along with some financial types, a painter, and our sons and their lady friends. At this gathering Billy was mute, and Grey, a very clever fellow, chatted interestingly. Billy did not seem at all comfortable, but the rest of us had a fairly good time. Then they invited us, along with some financial types they knew and a music critic and his book designer wife. At this dinner, Billy looked tired. It was clear that cooking bothered her. She told me later that she was the sort who, when forced to entertain, did every little thing, like making and straining the veal stock. From the moment she entered the kitchen she looked longingly forward to the time when all the dishes would be clean and put away and the guests would all have gone home.

Then we invited them, but Grey had a bad cold and they had to cancel. After that, Billy and I ran into one another one day when we were both dropping off articles at the same journal and we had lunch. She said she was looking for an article of mine—we had been sending each other articles right from the start. Two days later, after rummaging around in my files, I found it. Since I was going to be in her neighborhood, I dropped it off. She wrote me a note about this article and I called her to discuss it further. This necessitated a lunch meeting. Then she said she was sending me a book I had said I wanted to read, and then I sent her a book, and so it went.

One evening I stopped by to have a chat with Billy and Grey. I had just taken Vera, who was off to California, to the airport. I decided to ring their bell unannounced, but when I got there it turned out that Grey was out of town, too. Had I secretly been hoping that this would be the case? Billy had been working in her study, and without thinking about it, she led me up the stairs. I followed her and at the door of her study, I kissed her. She kissed me right back and looked awful about it.

"Nothing but a kiss!" I said, rather frantically. My mistress was silent. "A friendly kiss," I said.

My mistress gave me the sort of look that is supposed to make your blood freeze, and said: "Is this the way you habitually kiss your friends?"

"It won't happen again," I said. "It was all a mistake."

Billy gave me a stare so bleak and hard that I had no choice but to kiss her again and again.

After all this time it is still impossible for me to figure out what was and is going on in Billy's life that has let me in it. She once remarked that in her opinion there is frequently too little kissing in marriage, through which frail pinprick a microscopic dot of light was thrown on the subject of her marriage—or was it? She is like a Red Indian and says nothing at all, nor does she ever slip.

I, however, do slip, and I am made aware of this by the grim, sidelong glance I am given. I once told Billy that, until I met her, I had never given kissing much thought—she is an insatiable kisser for an unsentimental person—and I was rewarded for this utterance by a well-raised eyebrow and a rather frightening look of registration.

From time to time I feel it is wise to tell Billy how well Vera and I get along.

"Swell," says Billy. "I'm thrilled for you."

"Well, it's true," I say.

"I'm sure it's true," says Billy. "I'm sure there's no reason in the world why you come to see me all the time. It's probably just an involuntary action, like sneezing."

"But you don't understand," I say. "Vera has men friends. I have women friends. The first principle of a good marriage is freedom."

"Oh, I see," says Billy. "You sleep with your other women friends in the morning and come over here in the afternoon. What a lot of stamina you have, for an older person."

One day this conversation had unexpected results. I said how well Vera and I got along, and Billy looked unadornedly hurt.

"God hates a mingy lover," she said. "Why don't you just say that you're in love with me and that it frightens you and have done with it?"

A lump rose in my throat.

"Of course, maybe you're not in love with me," said Billy in her flattest voice.

I said: "I *am* in love with you."

"Well, there you are," said Billy.

My curiosity about Grey is a huge, violent dog on a very tight leash. He is three years older than Billy, a somewhat sweet-looking boy with rumpled hair who looks as if he is working out problems in higher math as you talk to him. He wears wire-rimmed glasses and his shirttail hangs out. He has the body of a young boy and the air of a genius or someone constantly preoccupied by the intense pressure of a rarefied mental life. Together he and Billy look not so much like husband and wife as co-conspirators.

What are her feelings about him? I begin preliminary queries by hemming and hawing. "Umm," I say, "it's, um, it's a little hard for me to picture your life with Grey. I mean, it's hard to picture your everyday life."

"What you want to know is how often we sleep together and how much do I like it," says Billy.

Well, she has me there, because that is exactly what I want to know.

"Tell you what," says my mistress. "Since you're so forthcoming about *your* marriage, we'll write down all about our home lives on little slips of paper and then we'll exchange them. How's that?"

Well, she has me there, too. What we are doing in each other's lives is a well-tended mystery.

I know how she contrasts to my wife: my wife is affable, full of conversation, loves a dinner party, and is interested in clothes, food, home decor, and the issues of the day. She loves to entertain, is sought out in times of crisis by her numerous friends, and has a kind or original word for everyone. She is methodical, hardworking, and does not fall asleep in restaurants. How I contrast to Grey is another matter, a matter about which I know nothing. I am considerably older and perhaps I appeal to some father longing in my mistress. Billy says Grey is a genius—a thrilling quality but not one that has any real relevance to life with another person. He wishes, according to his wife, that he were the conductor of a symphony orchestra and for this reason he is given musical scores, tickets, and batons for his birthday. He has studied Russian and can sing Russian songs. He is passionately interested in the natural sciences and also wishes he were a forest ranger.

"He sounds so charming," I say, "that I can't imagine why you would want to know someone like me." Billy's response to this is pure silence.

I hunt for signs of him on Billy—jewelry, marks, phrases. I know that he reads astronomy books for pleasure, enjoys cross-country skiing, and likes to travel. Billy says she loves him, but she also says she loves to read the works of Cardinal Aidan Gasquet, the historian of monastic life.

"If you love him so much," I say, taking a page

from her book, "why are you hanging around with me?"

"Hanging around," repeats Billy in a bored monotone.

"Well?"

"I am large and contain multitudes," she says, quoting a line from Walt Whitman.

This particular conversation took place en route to a cottage in Vermont which I had rented for five days when both Grey and Vera happened to be out of town at the same time on business.

I remember clearly with what happy anticipation I presented the idea of this cottage to her.

"Guess what?" I said.

"You're pregnant," said Billy.

"I have rented a little cottage for us, in Vermont. For a week when Grey and Vera are away on their long trips. We can go there and watch the leaves turn."

"The leaves have already turned and fallen off," said Billy faintly. She looked away and didn't speak for some time.

"We don't have to go, Billy," I said. "I only sent the check yesterday. I can cancel it."

There appeared to be tears in my mistress' eyes.

"No," she said. "Don't do that. I'll split it with you."

"You don't seem pleased," I said.

"Being pleased doesn't strike me as the appropriate response to the idea of sneaking off to a love nest with your lover," said Billy.

"What *is* the appropriate response?" I said.

"Oh," Billy said, her voice now blithe, "sorrow, guilt, horror, anticipation."

Well, she can run but she can't hide. My mistress is given away from time to time by her own expressions. No matter how hard she tries to suppress the visible evidence of what she feels, she is not always successful. Her eyes turn color, becoming dark and rather smoky. This is as good as a plain declaration of love. Billy's mental life, her grumpiness, her irritability, her crotchets are like static that, from time to time, give way to a clear signal, just as you often hit a pure band of music on a car radio after turning the dial through a lot of chaotic squawk.

In French movies of a certain period, the lovers are seen leaving the woman's apartment or house. His car is parked on an attractive side street. She is carrying a leather valise and is wearing a silk scarf around her neck. He is carrying the wicker basket she has packed with their picnic lunch. They will have the sort of food lovers have for lunch in these movies: a roasted chicken, a bottle of champagne, and a goat cheese wrapped up in leaves. Needless to say, when Billy and I finally left to go to our love nest, no such sight presented itself to me. First of all, she met me around the corner from my garage after a number of squabbles about whose car to take. She was standing between a rent-a-car and an animal hospital, wearing an old skirt, her old jacket, and carrying a ratty canvas overnight bag. No lacy underwear would be drawn from it, I knew. My mistress buys her white cotton undergarments at the five-and-ten-cent store. She wears an old T-shirt of Grey's to sleep in, she tells me.

For lunch we had hamburgers—no romantic rural inn or picnic spot for us—at Hud's Burger Hut off the thruway.

As we drew closer to our destination, Billy began to fidget, reminding me that having her along was sometimes not unlike traveling with a small child.

In the town nearest our love nest we stopped and bought coffee, milk, sugar, and cornflakes. Because I am a domestic animal and not a mere savage, I remembered to buy bread, butter, cheese, salami, eggs, and a number of cans of tomato soup.

Billy surveyed these items with a raised eyebrow.

"This is the sort of stuff you buy when you intend to stay indoors and kick up a storm of passion," she said.

It was an off-year Election Day—congressional and Senate races were being run. We had both voted, in fact, before taking off. Our love nest had a radio which I instantly switched on to hear if there were any early returns while we gave the place a cursory glance and put the groceries away. Then we flung ourselves onto the unmade bed, for which I had thoughtfully remembered to pack sheets.

When our storm of passion had subsided, my mistress stared impassively at the ceiling.

"In bed with Frank and Billy," she intoned. "It was Election Day, and Frank and Billy were once again in bed. Election returns meant nothing to them. The future of their great nation was inconsequential, so busy were they flinging themselves at one another they could barely be expected to think for one second of any larger issues. The subjects to which these trained economists could have spoken, such as inflationary spirals or deficit budgeting, were as mere dust."

"Shut up, Billy," I said.

She did shut up. She put on my shirt and went off to the kitchen. When she returned she had two cups of coffee and a plate of toasted cheese on a tray. With the exception of her dinner party, this was the first meal I had ever had at her hands.

"I'm starving," she said, getting under the covers. We polished off our snack, propped up with pillows. I asked Billy if she might like a second cup of coffee and she gave me a look of remorse and desire that made my head spin.

"Maybe you wanted to go out to dinner," she said. "You like a proper dinner." Then she burst into tears. "I'm sorry," she said. These were words I had never heard her speak before.

"Sorry?" I said. "Sorry for what?"

"I didn't ask you what you wanted to do," my mistress said. "You might have wanted to take a walk, or go for a drive or look around the house or make the bed."

I stared at her.

"I don't want a second cup of coffee," Billy said. "Do you?"

I got her drift and did not get out of bed. The forthrightness of her desire for me melted my heart.

During this excursion, none of my expectations came to pass. We did not, for example, have long talks about our respective marriages or our future together or apart. We did not discover what our domestic life might be like. We lived like graduate students or mice and not like normal people at all. We kept odd hours and lived off sandwiches. We stayed in bed and were both glad when it rained. When the sun came out, we went for a walk and observed the bare and almost bare trees. From time to time I would switch on the radio to hear the latest election results and commentary.

"Because of this historic time," Billy said, "you will never be able to forget me. It is a rule of life that care must be taken in choosing whom one will be in bed with during Great Moments in History. You are now stuck, with me and this week of important congressional elections twined in your mind forever."

It was in the car on the way home that the subject of what we were doing together came up. It was twilight and we had both been silent.

"This is the end of the line," said Billy.

"What do you mean?" I said. "Do you mean you want to break this up?"

433

"No," said Billy. "It would be nice, though, wouldn't it?"

"No, it would not be nice," I said.

"I think it would," said Billy. "Then I wouldn't spend all my time wondering what we are doing together when I could be thinking about other things, like my dissertation."

"What do you think we are doing together?" I said.

"It's simple," said Billy. "Some people have dogs or kitty cats. You're my pet."

"Come on."

"Okay, you're right. Those are only child substitutes. You're my child substitute until I can make up my mind about having a child."

At this, my blood freezes. Whose child does she want to have?

Every now and then when overcome with tenderness—on those occasions naked, carried away, and looking at one another with sweetness in our eyes—my mistress and I smile dreamily and realized that if we dwelt together for more than a few days, in the real world and not in some love nest, we would soon learn to hate each other. It would never work. We both know it. She is too relentlessly dour, and too fond of silence. I prefer false cheer to no cheer and I like conversation over dinner no matter what. Furthermore we would never have proper meals and, although I cannot cook, I like to dine. I would soon resent her lack of interest in domestic arrangements and she would resent me for resenting her. Furthermore, Billy is a slob. She does not leave towels lying on the bathroom floor, but she throws them over the shower curtain rod any old way instead of folding them or hanging them properly so they can dry. It is things like this that squash out romance over a period of time.

As for Billy, she often sneers at me. She finds many of my opinions quaint. She thinks I am an old-time domestic fascist. She refers to me as "an old-style heterosexual throwback" or "old hetero" because I like to pay for dinner, open car doors, and often call her at night when Grey is out of town to make sure she is safe. The day the plumber came to fix a leak in her sink, I called several times.

"He's gone," Billy said. "And he left big, greasy paw prints all over me." She found this funny, I did not.

After a while, were we to cohabit, I believe I would be driven nuts and she would come to loathe me. My household is well run and well regulated. I like routine and I like things to go along smoothly. We employ a flawless person by the name of Mrs. Ivy Castle who has been flawlessly running our house for years. She is an excellent housekeeper and a marvelous cook. Our relations with her are formal.

The Delielles employ a feckless person called Mimi-Ann Browning who comes in once a week to push the dust around. Mimi-Ann hates routines and schedules, and is constantly changing the days of the people she works for. It is quite something to hear Billy on the telephone with her.

"Oh, Mimi-Ann," she will say. "Please don't switch me. I beg you. Grey's awful cousin is coming and the house is really disgusting. Please, Mimi. I'll do anything. I'll do your mother-in-law's tax return. I'll be your eternal slave. *Please.* Oh, thank you, Mimi-Ann. Thank you a million times."

Now why, I ask myself, does my mistress never speak to me like that?

In the sad twilight on the way home from our week together, I asked myself, as I am always asking myself: could I exist in some ugly flat with my cheerless mistress? I could not, as my mistress is always the first to point out.

She said that the small doses we got of one another made it possible for us to have a love affair but that a taste of ordinary life would do us in. She correctly pointed out that our only common interest was each other, since we had such vast differences of opinion on the subject of economics. Furthermore, we were not simply lovers, nor were we mere friends, and since we were not going to end up together, there was nothing for it.

I was silent.

"Face it," said my tireless mistress. "We have no raison d'être."

There was no disputing this.

I said: "If we have no raison d'être, Billy, then what are we to do?"

These conversations flare up like tropical

storms. The climate is always right for them. It is simply a question of when they will occur.

"Well?" I said.

"I don't know," said my mistress, who generally has a snappy answer for everything. A wave of fatherly affection and worry came over me. I said, in a voice so drenched with concern it caused my mistress to scowl like a child about to receive an injection: "Perhaps you should think about this more seriously, Billy. You and Grey are really just starting out. Vera and I have been married a long, long time. I think I am more a disruption in your life than you are in mine."

"Oh, really," said Billy.

"Perhaps we should see each other less," I said. "Perhaps we should part."

"Okay, let's part," said Billy. "You go first." Her face was set and I entertained myself with the notion that she was trying not to burst into tears. Then she said: "What are you going to do all day after we part?"

This was not a subject to which I wanted to give much thought.

"Isn't our raison d'être that we're fond of one another?" I said. "I'm awfully fond of you."

"Gee, that's interesting," Billy said. "Just last week you broke down and used the word 'love.' How quickly things change."

"You know what I mean."

"Whatever our status quos are," Billy said, "they are being maintained like mad."

This silenced me. Billy and I have the world

right in place. Nothing flutters, changes, or moves. Whatever is being preserved in our lives is safely preserved. It is quite true, as Billy, who believes in function, points out, that we are in each other's life for a reason, but neither of us will state the reason. Nevertheless, although there are some cases in which love is not a good or sufficient reason for anything, the fact is, love is undeniable.

Yes, love is undeniable and that is the tricky point. It is one of the sobering realizations of adult life that love is often not a propellant. Thus, in those romantic movies, the tender mistress stays married to her stuffy husband—the one with the mustache and the stiff tweeds—while the lover is seen walking through the countryside with his long-suffering wife and faithful dog. It often seems that the function of romance is to give people something romantic to think about.

The question is: if it is true, as my mistress says, that she is going to stay with Grey and I am going to stay with Vera, why is it that we are together every chance we get?

There was, of course, an explanation for this, and my indefatigable mistress came up with it, God bless her.

"It's an artistic impulse," she said. "It takes us out of reality and gives us an invented context all our own."

"Oh, I see," I said. "It's only art."

"Don't get in a huff," Billy said. "We're in a very unusual situation. It has to do with limited doting, restricted thrall, and situational adoration."

"Oh, how interesting," I said. "Are doting, thrall, and adoration things you actually feel for me?"

Naturally Billy would never deign to answer a leading question.

Every adult knows that facts must be faced. In adult life, it often seems that's all there is. Prior to our weekend together, the unguarded moments between us had been kept to a minimum. Now they came more frequently. That week together haunted us. It dogged our heels. It made us long for and dread—what an unfortunate combination!—each other.

One evening I revealed to her how I sometimes feel as I watch her walk up the stairs to the door of her house. I feel she is walking into her real and still fairly young life. She will leave me in the dust, I think. I think of all the things that have not yet happened to her, that have not yet gone wrong, and I think of her life with Grey, which is still fairly unlived.

One afternoon she told me how it makes her feel when she thinks of my family table—with Vera and our sons and their friends and girl friends, of our years of shared meals, of all that lived life. Billy described this feeling as a band around her head and a hot pressure in the area of her heart. I, of course, merely get a lump in my throat. Why do these admittings take place at twi-

439

light or at dusk, in the gloomiest light when everything looks dirty, eerie, faded, or inevitable?

Our conversation comes to a dead halt, like a
horse balking before a hurdle, on the issue of what
we want. I have tried my best to formulate what
it is I want from Billy, but I have not gotten very
far. Painful consideration has brought forth this
revelation: I want her not ever to stop being. This
is as close as grammar or reflection will allow.

One day the horse will jump over the hurdle
and the end will come. The door will close. Billy
will doubtless do the closing. She will decide she
wants a baby, or Grey will be offered an academic
post in London, or Billy will finish her dissertation
and get a job in Boston, and the Delielles will
move. Or perhaps Vera will come home one evening and say that she longs to live in Paris or San
Francisco, and we will move. What will happen
then?

Perhaps my mistress is right. A love affair is
like a work of art. The large store of reference and
jokes, the history of our friendship, our trip to
Vermont, our numberless phone calls, this edifice,
this monument, this civilization known only to
and constructed by the two of us will be—what
will it be? Billy once read me an article from one
of Grey's nature magazines about the last Coast
Salish Indian to speak Wintu. All the others of
his tribe were dead. That is how I would feel,
deprived of Billy.

The awful day will doubtless come. It is like
thinking about the inevitability of nuclear war.

440

But for now, I continue to ring her doorbell. Her greeting is delivered in a bored monotone. "Oh, it's you," she will say.

I will follow her upstairs to her study and there we will hurl ourselves at one another. I will reflect, as I always do, how very bare the setting for these encounters is. Not a picture on the wall, not an ornament. Even the quilt that keeps the chill off us on the couch is faded.

In one of her snootier moments, my mistress said to me: "My furnishings are interior. I care about what I think about."

As I gather her into my arms, I cannot help imagining all that interior furniture, those hard-edged things she thinks about, whatever is behind her silence, whatever, in fact, her real story is.

I imagine that some day she will turn to me and with some tone in her voice I have never heard before say: "We can't see each other any more." We will both know the end has come. But meanwhile she is right close by. After a fashion, she is mine. I watch her closely to catch the look of true love that every once in a while overtakes her. She knows I am watching, and she knows the effect her look has. "A baby could take candy from you," she says.

Our feelings have edges and spines and prickles like cactus, or porcupine. Our parting when it comes will not be simple, either. Depicted it would look like one of those medieval beasts that have fins, fur, scales, feathers, claws, wings, and horns. In a world apart from anyone else, we are

Frank and Billy, with no significance to anyone but the other. Oh, the terrible privacy and loneliness of love affairs!

Under the quilt with our arms interlocked, I look into my mistress' eyes. They are dark, and full of concealed feeling. If we hold each other close enough, that darkness is held at bay. The mission of the lover is, after all, to love. I can look at Billy and see clear back to the first time we met, to our hundreds of days together, to her throwing the towels over the shower curtain rod, to each of her gestures and intonations. She is the road I have traveled to her, and I am hers.

Oh, Billy! Oh, art! Oh, memory!

We Are Nighttime Travelers

Ethan Canin

Where are we going? Where, I might write, is this path leading us? Francine is asleep and I am standing downstairs in the kitchen with the door closed and the light on and a stack of mostly blank paper on the counter in front of me. My dentures are in a glass by the sink. I clean them with a tablet that bubbles in the water, and although they were clean already I just cleaned them again because the bubbles are agreeable and I thought their effervescence might excite me to action. By action, I mean I thought they might excite me to write. But words fail me.

This is a love story. However, its roots are tangled and involve a good bit of my life, and when I recall my life my mood turns sour and I am reminded that no man makes truly proper use of his time. We are blind and small-minded. We are dumb as snails and as frightened, full of vanity and misinformed about the importance of things. I'm an average man, without great deeds except maybe one, and that has been to love my wife.

I have been more or less faithful to Francine since I married her. There has been one transgression—leaning up against a closet wall with a red-haired purchasing agent at a sales meeting once in Minneapolis twenty years ago; but she was buying auto upholstery and I was selling it and in the eyes of judgment this may bear a key weight. Since then, though, I have ambled on this narrow path of life bound to one woman. This is a triumph and a regret. In our current state of affairs it is a regret because in life a man is either on the uphill or on the downhill, and if he isn't procreating he is on the downhill. It is a steep downhill indeed. These days I am tumbling, falling headlong among the scrub oaks and boulders, tearing my knees and abrading all the bony parts of the body. I have given myself to gravity.

Francine and I are married now forty-six years, and I would be a bamboozler to say that I have loved her for any more than half of these. Let us say that for the last year I haven't; let us say this for the last ten, even. Time has made torments of our small differences and tolerances of our passions. This is our state of affairs. Now I stand by myself in our kitchen in the middle of the night; now I lead a secret life. We wake at different hours now, sleep in different corners of the bed. We like different foods and different music, keep our clothing in different drawers, and if it can be said that either of us has aspirations, I believe that they are to a different bliss. Also, she is healthy and I ... . .or conversation—that feast of r son, that flow of the soul—our house is silent as the bone yard.

Last week we did talk. "Frank," she said one

444

evening at the table, "there is something I must tell you."

The New York game was on the radio, snow was falling outside, and the pot of tea she had brewed was steaming on the table between us. Her medicine and my medicine were in little paper cups at our places.

"Frank," she said, jiggling her cup, "what I must tell you is that someone was around the house last night."

I tilted my pills onto my hand. "Around the house?"

"Someone was at the window."

On my palm the pills were white, blue, beige, pink: Lasix, Diabinese, Slow-K, Lopressor. "What do you mean?"

She rolled her pills onto the tablecloth and fidgeted with them, made them into a line, then into a circle, then into a line again. I don't know her medicine so well. She's healthy, except for little things. "I mean," she said, "there was someone in the yard last night."

"How do you know?"

"Frank, will you really, please?"

"I'm asking how you know."

"I heard him," she said. She looked down. "I was sitting in the front room and I heard him outside the window."

"You heard him?"

"Yes."

"The front window?"

She got up and went to the sink. This is a trick of hers. At that distance I can't see her face.

"The front window is ten feet off the ground," I said.

"What I know is that there was a man out there last night, right outside the glass." She walked out of the kitchen.

"Let's check," I called after her. I walked into the living room, and when I got there she was looking out the window.

"What is it?"

She was peering out at an angle. All I could see was snow, blue-white.

"Footprints," she said.

I built the house we live in with my two hands. That was forty-nine years ago, when, in my foolishness and crude want of learning, everything I didn't know seemed like a promise. I learned to build a house and then I built one. There are copper fixtures on the pipes, sanded edges on the struts and queen posts. Now, a half-century later, the floors are flat as a billiard table but the man who laid them needs two hands to pick up a woodscrew. This is the diabetes. My feet are gone also. I look down at them and see two black shapes when I walk, things I can't feel. Black clubs. No connection with the ground. If I didn't look, I could go to sleep with my shoes on.

Life takes its toll, and soon the body gives up completely. But it gives up the parts first. This sugar in the blood: God says to me: "Frank

Manlius—codger, man of prevarication and half-truth—I shall take your life from you, as from all men. But first—" But first! Clouds in the eyeball, a heart that makes noise, feet cold as uncooked roast. And Francine, beauty that she was—now I see not much more than the dark line of her brow and the intersections of her body: mouth and nose, neck and shoulders. Her smells have changed over the years so that I don't know what's her own anymore and what's powder.

We have two children, but they're gone now too, with children of their own. We have a house, some furniture, small savings to speak of. How Francine spends her day I don't know. This is the sad truth, my confession. I am gone past nightfall. She wakes early with me and is awake when I return, but beyond this I know almost nothing of her life.

I myself spend my days at the aquarium. I've told Francine something else, of course, that I'm part of a volunteer service of retired men, that we spend our days setting young businesses afoot: "Immigrants," I told her early on, "newcomers to the land." I said it was difficult work. In the evenings I could invent stories, but I don't, and Francine doesn't ask.

I am home by nine or ten. Ticket stubs from the aquarium fill my coat pocket. Most of the day I watch the big sea animals—porpoises, sharks, a manatee—turn their saltwater loops. I come late morning and move a chair up close. They are waiting to eat then. Their bodies skim the cool glass, full of strange magnifications. I think, if it is possible, that they are beginning to know me: this man—hunched at the shoulder, cataractic of eye, breathing through water himself—this man who sits and watches. I do not pity them. At lunchtime I buy coffee and sit in one of the hotel lobbies or in the cafeteria next door, and I read poems. Browning, Whitman, Eliot. This is my secret. It is night when I return home. Francine is at the table, four feet across from my seat, the width of two dropleaves. Our medicine is in cups. There have been three Presidents since I held her in my arms.

The cafeteria moves the men along, old or young, who come to get away from the cold. A half-hour for a cup, they let me sit. Then the manager is at my table. He is nothing but polite. I buy a pastry then, something small. He knows me—I have seen him nearly every day for months now—and by his slight limp I know he is a man of mercy. But business is business.

"What are you reading?" he asks me as he wipes the table with a wet cloth. He touches the salt shaker, nudges the napkins in their holder. I know what this means.

"I'll take a cranberry roll," I say. He flicks the cloth and turns back to the counter.

This is what:

Shall I say, I have gone at dusk through narrow streets

448

And watched the smoke that rises from the pipes
Of lonely men in shirt-sleeves, leaning out of
   windows?

Through the magnifier glass the words come forward, huge, two by two. With spectacles, everything is twice enlarged. Still, though, I am slow to read it. In a half-hour I am finished, could not read more, even if I bought another roll. The boy at the register greets me, he smiles when I reach him. "What are you reading today?" he asks, counting out the change.

The books themselves are small and fit in the inside pockets of my coat. I put one in front of each breast, then walk back to see the fish some more. These are the fish I know: the gafftopsail pompano, sixgill shark, the starry flounder with its upturned eyes, queerly migrated. He rests half-submerged in sand. His scales are platey and flat-hued. Of everything upward he is wary, of the silvery seabass and the bluefin tuna that pass above him in the region of light and open water. For a life he lies on the bottom of the tank. I look at him. His eyes are dull. They are ugly and an aberration. Above us the bony fishes wheel at the tank's corners. I lean forward to the glass. *"Platichthys stellatus,"* I say to him. The caudal fin stirs. Sand moves and resettles, and I see the black and yellow stripes. "Flatfish," I whisper, "we are, you and I, observers of this life."

"A man on our lawn," I say a few nights later in bed.

"Not just that."

I breathe in, breathe out, look up at the ceiling. "What else?"

"When you were out last night he came back."

"He came back."

"Yes."

"What did he do?"

"Looked in at me."

Later, in the early night, when the lights of cars are still passing and the walked dogs still jingle their collar chains out front, I get up quickly from bed and step into the hall. I move fast because this is still possible in short bursts and with concentration. The bed sinks once, then rises. I am on the landing and then downstairs without Francine waking. I stay close to the staircase joists.

In the kitchen I take out my almost blank sheets and set them on the counter. I write standing up because I want to take more than an animal's pose. For me this is futile, but I stand anyway. The page will be blank when I finish. This I know. The dreams I compose are the dreams of others, remembered bits of verse. Songs of greater men than I. In months I have written few more than a hundred words. The pages are stacked, sheets of different sizes.

If I could

one says.

says another. I stand and shift them in and out. They are mostly blank, sheets from months of nights. But this doesn't bother me. What I have is patience.

Francine knows nothing of the poetry. She's a simple girl, toast and butter. I myself am hardly the man for it: forty years selling (anything—steel piping, heater elements, dried bananas). Didn't read a book except one on sales. Think victory, the book said. Think *sale*. It's a young man's bag of apples, though; young men in pants that nip at the waist. Ten years ago I left the Buick in the company lot and walked home, dye in my hair, cotton rectangles in the shoulders of my coat. Francine was in the house that afternoon also, the way she is now. When I retired we bought a camper and went on a trip. A traveling salesman retires, so he goes on a trip. Forty miles out of town the folly appeared to me, big as a balloon. To Francine, too. "Frank," she said in the middle of a bend, a prophet turning to me, the camper pushing sixty and rocking in the wind, trucks to our left and right big as trains—"Frank," she said, "these roads must be familiar to you."

So we sold the camper at a loss and a man who'd spent forty years at highway speed looked around for something to do before he died. The first poem I read was in a book on a table in a waiting room. My eyeglasses made half-sense of things.

451

THESE
are the desolate, dark weeks

I read

when nature in its barrenness
equals the stupidity of man.

Gloom, I thought, and nothing more, but then I reread the words, and suddenly there I was, hunched and wheezing, bald as a trout, and tears were in my eye. I don't know where they came from.

In the morning an officer visits. He has muscles, mustache, skin red from the cold. He leans against the door frame.

"Can you describe him?" he says.

"It's always dark," says Francine.

"Anything about him?"

"I'm an old woman. I can see that he wears glasses."

"What kind of glasses?"

"Black."

"Dark glasses?"

"Black glasses."

"At a particular time?"

"Always when Frank is away."

"Your husband has never been here when he's come?"

"Never."

"I see." He looks at me. This look can mean

452

several things, perhaps that he thinks Francine is imagining. "But never at a particular time?"

"No."

"Well," he says. Outside on the porch his partner is stamping his feet. "Well," he says again. "We'll have a look." He turns, replaces his cap, heads out to the snowy steps. The door closes. I hear him say something outside.

"Last night—" Francine says. She speaks in the dark. "Last night I heard him on the side of the house."

We are in bed. Outside, on the sill, snow has been building since morning.

"You heard the wind."

"Frank." She sits up, switches on the lamp, tilts her head toward the window. Through a ceiling and two walls I can hear the ticking of our kitchen clock.

"I heard him climbing," she says. She has wrapped her arms about her own waist. "He was on the house. I heard him. He went up the drainpipe." She shivers as she says this. "There was no wind. He went up the drainpipe and then I heard him on the porch roof."

"Houses make noise."

"I heard him. There's gravel there."

I imagine the sounds, amplified by hollow walls, rubber heels on timber. I don't say anything. There is an arm's length between us, cold sheet, a space uncrossed since I can remember.

"I have made the mistake in my life of not being

453

interested in enough people," she says then. "If I'd been interested in more people, I wouldn't be alone now."

"Nobody's alone," I say.

"I mean that if I'd made more of an effort with people I would have friends now. I would know the postman and the Giffords and the Kohlers, and we'd be together in this, all of us. We'd sit in each other's living rooms on rainy days and talk about the children. Instead we've kept to ourselves. Now I'm alone."

"You're not alone," I say.

"Yes, I am." She turns the light off and we are in the dark again. "You're alone, too."

My health has gotten worse. It's slow to set in at this age, not the violent shaking grip of death; instead—a slow leak, nothing more. A bicycle tire: rimless, thready, worn treadless already and now losing its fatness. A war of attrition. The tall camels of the spirit steering for the desert. One morning I realized I hadn't been warm in a year.

And there are other things that go, too. For instance, I recall with certainty that it was on the 23rd of April, 1945, that, despite German counteroffensives in the Ardennes, Eisenhower's men reached the Elbe; but I cannot remember whether I have visited the savings and loan this week. Also, I am unable to produce the name of my neighbor, though I greeted him yesterday in the street. And take, for example, this: I am at a loss to explain whole decades of my life. We have children and

454

photographs, and there is an understanding between Francine and me that bears the weight of nothing less than half a century, but when I gather my memories they seem to fill no more than an hour. Where has my life gone?

It has gone partway to shoddy accumulations. In my wallet are credit cards, a license ten years expired, twenty-three dollars in cash. There is a photograph but it depresses me to look at it, and a poem, half-copied and folded into the billfold. The leather is pocked and has taken on the curve of my thigh. The poem is from Walt Whitman. I copy only what I need.

But of all things to do last, poetry is a barren choice. Deciphering other men's riddles while the world is full of procreation and war. A man should go out swinging an axe. Instead, I shall go out in a coffee shop.

But how can any man leave this world with honor? Despite anything he does, it grows corrupt around him. It fills with locks and sirens. A man walks into a store now and the microwaves announce his entry; when he leaves, they make electronic peeks into his coat pockets, his trousers. Who doesn't feel like a thief? I see a policeman now, any policeman, and I feel a fright. And the things I have done wrong in my life haven't been crimes. Crimes of the heart perhaps, but nothing against the state. My soul may turn black but I can wear white trousers at any meeting of men. Have I loved my wife? At one time, yes—in rages and torrents. I've been covered by the pimples of ecstasy and have rooted in the mud of despair; and I've lived for months, for whole years now, as mindless of Francine as a tree of its mosses.

And this is what kills us, this mindlessness. We sit across the table now with our medicines between us, little balls and oblongs. We sit, sit. This has become our view of each other, a tableboard apart. We sit.

"Again?" I say.
"Last night."
We are at the table. Francine is making a twisting motion with her fingers. She coughs, brushes her cheek with her forearm, stands suddenly so that the table bumps and my medicines move in the cup.
"Francine," I say.
The half-light of dawn is showing me things outside the window: silhouettes, our maple, the eaves of our neighbor's garage. Francine moves and stands against the glass, hugging her shoulders.
"You're not telling me something," I say.
She sits and makes her pills into a circle again, then into a line. Then she is crying.
I come around the table, but she gets up before I reach her and leaves the kitchen. I stand there. In a moment I heard a drawer open in the living room. She moves things around, then shuts it again. When she returns she sits at the other side of the table. "Sit down," she says. She puts two

folded sheets of paper onto the table. "I wasn't hiding them," she says.

"What weren't you hiding?"

"These," she says. "He leaves them."

"He leaves them?"

"They say he loves me."

"Francine."

"They're inside the windows in the morning."
She picks one up, unfolds it. Then she reads:

Ah, I remember well (and how can I
But evermore remember well) when first

She pauses, squint-eyed, working her lips. It is a pause of only faint understanding. Then she continues:

Our flame began, when scarce we knew what was
The flame we felt.

When she finishes she refolds the paper precisely. "That's it," she says. "That's one of them."

At the aquarium I sit, circled by glass and, behind it, the senseless eyes of fish. I have never written a word of my own poetry but can recite the verse of others. This is the culmination of a life. *Coryphaena hippurus*, says the plaque on the dolphin's tank, words more beautiful than any of my own. The dolphin circles, circles, approaches with alarming speed, but takes no notice of, if he even sees, my hands. I wave them in front of his tank.

What must he think has become of the sea? He turns and his slippery proboscis nudges the glass. I am every part sore from life.

Ah, silver shrine, here will I take my rest
After so many hours of toil and quest,
A famished pilgrim—saved by miracle.

There is nothing noble for either of us here, nothing between us, and no miracles. I am better off drinking coffee. Any fluid refills the blood. The counter boy knows me and later at the café he pours the cup, most of a dollar's worth. Refills are free but my heart hurts if I drink more than one. It hurts no different from a bone, bruised or cracked. This amazes me.

Francine is amazed by other things. She is mystified, thrown beam ends by the romance. She reads me the poems now at breakfast, one by one. I sit. I roll my pills. "Another came last night," she says, and I see her eyebrows rise. "Another this morning." She reads them as if every word is a surprise. Her tongue touches teeth, shows between lips. These lips are dry. She reads:

Kiss me as if you made believe
You were not sure, this eve,
How my face, your flower, had pursed
Its petals up

That night she shows me the windowsill, second story, rimmed with snow, where she finds the poems. We open the glass. We lean into the air. There is ice below us, sheets of it on the trellis, needles hanging from the drainwork.

"Where do you find them?"

"Outside," she says. "Folded, on the lip."

"In the morning?"

"Always in the morning."

"The police should know about this."

"What will they be able to do?"

I step away from the sill. She leans out again, surveying her lands, which are the yard's-width spit of crusted ice along our neighbor's chain link and the three maples out front, now lost their leaves. She peers as if she expects this man to appear. An icy wind comes inside. "Think," she says. "Think. He could come from anywhere."

One night in February, a month after this began, she asks me to stay awake and stand guard until the morning. It is almost spring. The earth has reappeared in patches. During the day, at the borders of yards and driveways, I see glimpses of brown—though I know I could be mistaken. I come home early that night, before dusk, and when darkness falls I move a chair by the window downstairs. I draw apart the outer curtain and raise the shade. Francine brings me a pot of tea. She turns out the light and pauses next to me, and as she does, her hand on the chair's backbrace, I am so struck by the proximity of elements—of the night, of the teapot's heat, of the sound of water outside—that I consider speaking. I want to ask her what has become of us, what has made our breathed air so sorry now, and loveless. But the timing is wrong and in a moment she turns and climbs the stairs. I look out into the night. Later, I hear the closet shut, then our bed creak.

There is nothing to see outside, nothing to hear. This I know. I let hours pass. Behind the window I imagine fish moving down to greet me: broomtail grouper, surfperch, sturgeon with their prehistoric rows of scutes. It is almost impossible to see them. The night is full of shapes and bits of light. In it the moon rises, losing the colors of the horizon, so that by early morning it is high and pale. Frost has made a ring around it.

A ringed moon above, and I am thinking back on things. What have I regretted in my life? Plenty of things, mistakes enough to fill the car show-room, then a good deal of the back lot. I've been a man of gains and losses. What gains? My marriage, certainly, though it has been no knee-buckling windfall but more like a split decision in the end, a stock risen a few points since bought. I've certainly enjoyed certain things about the world, too. These are things gone over and over again by the writers and probably enjoyed by everybody who ever lived. Most of them involve air. Early morning air, air after a rainstorm, air through a car window. Sometimes I think the cerebrum is wasted and all we really need is the lower brain, which I've been told is what makes the lungs breathe and the heart beat and what lets us smell pleasant things. What about the poetry? That's another split decision, maybe going the other way if I really made a tally. It's made me melancholy in old age, sad when if I'd stuck with motor homes and the national league standings I don't think I would have been rooting around in regret and doubt at this point. Nothing wrong with sadness, but this is not the real thing—not the death of a child but the feelings of a college student reading *Don Quixote* on a warm afternoon before going out to the lake.

Now, with Francine upstairs, I wait for a night prowler. He will not appear. This I know, but the window glass is ill-blown and makes moving shadows anyway, shapes that change in the wind's rattle. I look out and despite myself am afraid.

Before me, the night unrolls. Now the tree leaves turn yellow in moonshine. By two or three, Francine sleeps, but I get up anyway and change into my coat and hat. The books weigh against my chest. I don gloves, scarf, galoshes. Then I climb the stairs and go into our bedroom, where she is sleeping. On the far side of the bed I see her white hair and beneath the blankets the uneven heave of her chest. I watch the bedcovers rise. She is probably dreaming at this moment. Though we have shared this bed for most of a lifetime I cannot guess what her dreams are about. I step next to her and touch the sheets where they lie across her neck.

"Wake up," I whisper. I touch her cheek, and her eyes open. I know this though I cannot really see them, just the darkness of their sockets.

"Is he there?"

461

"No."

"Then what's the matter?"

"Nothing's the matter," I say. "But I'd like to go for a walk."

"You've been outside," she says. "You saw him, didn't you?"

"I've been at the window."

"Did you see him?"

"No. There's no one there."

"Then why do you want to walk?" In a moment she is sitting aside the bed, her feet in slippers. "We don't ever walk," she says.

I am warm in all my clothing. "I know we don't," I answer. I turn my arms out, open my hands toward her. "But I would like to. I would like to walk in air that is so new and cold."

She peers up at me. "I haven't been drinking," I say. I bend at the waist, and though my head spins, I lean forward enough so that the effect is of a bow. "Will you come with me?" I whisper. "Will you be queen of this crystal night?" I recover from my bow, and when I look up again she has risen from the bed, and in another moment she has dressed herself in her wool robe and is walking ahead of me to the stairs.

Outside, the ice is treacherous. Snow has begun to fall and our galoshes squeak and slide, but we stay on the plowed walkway long enough to leave our block and enter a part of the neighborhood where I have never been. Ice hangs from the lamps. We pass unfamiliar houses and unfamiliar trees, street signs I have never seen, and as we walk the night begins to change. It is becoming liquor. The snow is banked on either side of the walk, plowed into hillocks at the corners. My hands are warming from the exertion. They are the hands of a younger man now, someone else's fingers in my gloves. They tingle. We take ten minutes to cover a block but as we move through this neighborhood my ardor mounts. A car approaches and I wave, a boatman's salute, because here we are together on these rare and empty seas. We are nighttime travelers. He flashes his headlamps as he passes, and this fills me to the gullet with celebration and bravery. The night sings to us. I am Bluebeard now, Lindbergh, Genghis Khan.

No, I am not.

I am an old man. My blood is dark from hypoxia, my breaths singsong from disease. It is only the frozen night that is splendid. In it we walk, stepping slowly, bent forward. We take steps the length of table forks. Francine holds my elbow.

I have mean secrets and small dreams, no plans greater than where to buy groceries and what rhymes to read next, and by the time we reach our porch again my foolishness has subsided. My knees and elbows ache. They ache with a mortal ache, tired flesh, the cartilage gone sandy with time. I don't have the heart for dreams. We undress in the hallway, ice is in the ends of our hair, our coats stiff from cold. Francine turns down the thermostat. Then we go upstairs and she gets into her side of the bed and I get into mine.

It is dark. We lie there for some time, and then,

before dawn, I know she is asleep. It is cold in our bedroom. As I listen to her breathing I know my life is coming to an end. I cannot warm myself. What I would like to tell my wife is this:

What the
imagination
seizes
as beauty must be truth. What holds you
to what you see of me is
that grasp alone.

But I do not say anything. Instead I roll in the bed, reach across, and touch her, and because she is surprised she turns to me.

When I kiss her the lips are dry, cracking against mine, unfamiliar as the ocean floor. But then the lips give. They part. I am inside her mouth, and there, still, hidden from the world, as if ruin had forgotten a part, it is wet—Lord! I have the feeling of a miracle. Her tongue comes forward. I do not know myself then, what man I am, who I lie with in embrace. I can barely remember her beauty. She touches my chest and I bite lightly on her lip, spread moisture to her cheek and then kiss there. She makes something like a sigh. "Frank," she says. "Frank." We are lost now in seas and deserts. My hand finds her fingers and grips them, bone and tendon, fragile things.

Sweet Talk

Stephanie Vaughn

Sometimes Sam and I loved each other more when we were angry. "Day," I called him, using the surname instead of Sam. "Day, Day, Day!" It drummed against the walls of the apartment like a distress signal.

"Ah, my beautiful lovebird," he said. "My sugar sweet bride."

For weeks I had been going through the trash trying to find out whether he had other women. Once I found half a ham sandwich with red marks that could have been lipstick. Or maybe catsup. This time I found five slender cigarette butts.

"Who smokes floral-embossed cigarettes?" I said. He had just come out of the shower, and droplets of water gleamed among the black hairs of his chest like tiny knife points. "Who's the heart-attack candidate you invite over when I'm out?" I held the butts beneath his nose like a small bouquet. He slapped them to the floor and we stopped speaking for three days. We moved through the apartment without touching, lay stiffly in separate furrows of the bed, desire blooming and withering between us like the invisible petals of a night-blooming cereus.

465

We finally made up while watching a chess tournament on television. Even though we wouldn't speak or make eye contact, we were sitting in front of the sofa moving pieces around a chess board as an announcer explained World Championship strategy to the viewing audience. Our shoulders touched but we pretended not to notice. Our knees touched, and our elbows. Then we both reached for the black bishop and our hands touched. We made love on the carpet and kept our eyes open so that we could look at each other defiantly.

We were living in California and had six university degrees between us and no employment. We lived on food stamps, job interviews and games.

"How many children did George Washington, the father of our country, have?"

"No white ones but lots of black ones."

"How much did he make when he was Commander of the Revolutionary Army?"

"He made a big to-do about refusing a salary but later presented the first Congress with a bill for a half million dollars."

"Who was the last slave-owning president?"

"Ulysses S. Grant."

We had always been good students.

It was a smoggy summer. I spent long hours in air-conditioned supermarkets, touching the cool cans, feeling the cold plastic stretched across packages of meat. Sam left the apartment for whole afternoons and evenings. He was in his car somewhere, opening it up on the freeway, or maybe just spending time with someone I didn't know. We were mysterious with each other about our absences. In August we decided to move east, where a friend said he could get us both jobs at an unaccredited community college. In the meantime, I had invented a lover. He was rich and wanted to take me to an Alpine hotel, where mauve flowers cascaded over the stone walls of a terrace. Sometimes we drank white wine and watched the icy peaks of mountains shimmer gold in the sunset. Sometimes we returned to our room carrying tiny ceramic mugs of schnapps which had been given to us, in the German fashion, as we paid for an expensive meal.

In the second week of August, I found a pair of red lace panties at the bottom of the kitchen trash.

I decided to tell Sam I had a lover. I made my lover into a tall, blue-eyed blond, a tennis player on the circuit, a Phi Beta Kappa from Stanford who had offers from the movies. It was the tall blond part that needled Sam, who was dark and stocky.

"Did you pick him up at the beach?" Sam said.

"Stop it," I said, knowing that it was a sure way to get him to ask more questions.

"Did you have your diaphragm in your purse?"

We were wrapping cups and saucers in newspaper and nesting them in the slots of packing boxes. "He was taller than you," I said, "but not as handsome."

Sam held a blue and white Dresden cup, my favorite wedding present, in front of my eyes. "You slut," he said, and let the cup drop to the floor.

"Very articulate," I said. "Some professor. The man of reason gets into an argument and he talks with broken cups. Thank you Alexander Dope."

That afternoon I failed the California drivers' test again. I made four right turns and drove over three of the four curbs. The highway patrolman pointed out that if I made one more mistake I was finished. I drove through a red light.

On the way back to the apartment complex, Sam squinted into the flatness of the expressway and would not talk to me. I put my blue-eyed lover behind the wheel. He rested a hand on my knee and smiled as he drove. He was driving me west, away from the Vista View Apartments, across the thin spine of mountains which separated our suburb from the sea. At the shore there would be seals frolicking among the rocks and starfish resting in tidal pools.

"How come you never take me to the ocean?" I said. "How come every time I want to go to the beach I have to call up a woman friend?"

"If you think you're going to Virginia with me," he said, "You're dreaming." He eased the car into our numbered space and put his head against the wheel. "Why did you have to do it?"

"I do not like cars," I said. "You know I have always been afraid of cars."

"Why did you have to sleep with that fag tennis

player?" His head was still against the wheel. I moved closer and put my arm around his shoulders.

"Sam, I didn't. I made it up."

"Don't try to get out of it."

"I didn't, Sam. I made it up." I tried to kiss him. He let me put my mouth against his, but his lips were unyielding. They felt like the skin of an orange. "I didn't, Sam. I made it up to hurt you." I kissed him again and his mouth warmed against mine. "I love you, Sam. Please let me go to Virginia."

"George Donner," I read from the guidebook, "was sixty-one years old and rich when he packed up his family and left Illinois to cross the Great Plains, the desert, and the mountains into California." We were driving through the Sierras, past steep slopes and the deep shade of an evergreen forest, toward the Donner Pass, where in 1846 the Donner family had been trapped by an early snowfall. Some of them died and the rest ate the corpses of their relatives and their Indian guides to survive.

"Where are the bones?" Sam said, as we strolled past glass cases at the Donner Pass Museum. The cases were full of wagon wheels and harnesses. Above us a recorded voice described the courageous and enterprising spirit of American pioneers. A man standing nearby with a young boy turned to scowl at Sam. Sam looked at him and said loudly, "Where are the bones of the people they ate?" The man took the boy by the hand and started for the door. Sam said, "You call this American history?" and the man turned and said, "Listen, mister, I can get your license number." We laughed about that as we descended into the plain of the Great Basin desert in Nevada. Every few miles one of us would say the line and the other one would chuckle, and I felt as if we had been married fifty years instead of five, and that everything had turned out okay.

Ten miles east of Reno I began to sneeze. My nose ran and my eyes watered, and I had to stop reading the guidebook.

"I can't do this anymore. I think I've got an allergy."

"You never had an allergy in your life." Sam's tone implied that I had purposefully got the allergy so that I could not read the guidebook. We were riding in a second-hand van, a lusterless, black shoebox of a vehicle, which Sam had bought for the trip with the money he got from the stereo, the TV, and his own beautifully overhauled and rebuilt little sports car.

"Turn on the radio," I said.

"The radio is broken."

It was a hot day, dry and gritty. On either side of the freeway, a sagebrush desert stretched toward the hunched profiles of brown mountains. The mountains were so far away—the only landmarks within three hundred miles—that they did not whap by the windows like signposts, they floated above the plain of dusty sage and gave us the sense that we were not going anywhere.

"Are you trying to kill us?" I said when the speedometer slid past ninety.

"Sam looked at the dash surprised and, I think, a little pleased that the van could do that much. "I'm getting hypnotized," he said. He thought about it for another mile and said, "If you had managed to get your license, you could do something on this trip besides blow snot into your hand."

"Don't you think we should call ahead to Elko for a motel room?"

"I might not want to stop at Elko."

"Sam, look at the map. You'll be tired when we get to Elko."

"I'll let you know when I'm tired."

We reached Elko at sundown, and Sam was tired. In the office of the Shangrila Motor Lodge we watched another couple get the last room. "I suppose you're going to be mad because I was right," I said.

"Just get in the van." We bought a sack of hamburgers and set out for Utah. Ahead of us a full moon rose, flat and yellow like a fifty-dollar gold piece, then lost its color as it rose higher. We entered the Utah salt flats, the dead floor of a dead ocean. The salt crystals glittered like snow under the white moon. My nose stopped running, and I felt suddenly lucid and calm.

"Has he been in any movies?" Sam said.

"Has who been in any movies?"

"The fag tennis player."

I had to think a moment before I recalled my phantom lover.

"He's not a fag."

"I thought you made him up."

"I did make him up but I didn't make up any fag."

A few minutes later he said, "You might at least sing something. You might at least try to keep me awake." I sang a few Beatles tunes, the Simon and Garfunkel, the Everly Brothers, and Elvis Presley. I worked my way back through my youth to a Girl Scout song I remembered as "Eye, Eye, Eye, Icky, Eye, Kai, A-nah." It was supposed to be sung around a campfire to remind the girls of their Indian heritage and the pleasures of surviving in the wilderness. "Ah woo, ah woo. Ah woo knee key chee," I sang. "I am now five years old," I said, and then I sang, "Home, Home on the Range," the song I remembered singing when I was a child going cross-country with my parents to visit some relatives. The only thing I remembered about that trip besides a lot of going to the bathroom in gas stations was that there were rules which made the traveling life simple. One was: do not hang over the edge of the front seat to talk to your mother or father. The other was: if you have to throw up, do it in the blue coffee can, the red one is full of cookies.

"It's just the jobs and money," I said. "It isn't us, is it?"

"I don't know," he said.

472

A day and a half later we crossed from Wyoming into Nebraska, the western edge of the Louisiana Purchase, which Thomas Jefferson had made so that we could all live in white, classical houses, and be farmers. Fifty miles later the corn began, hundreds of miles of it, singing green from horizon to horizon. We began to relax and I had the feeling that we had survived the test of American geography. I put away our guidebooks and took out the dictionary. Matachin, mastigophobia, matutolypea. I tried to find words Sam didn't know. He guessed all the definitions and was smug and happy behind the wheel. I reached over and put a hand on his knee. He looked at me and smiled. "Ah, my little buttercup," he said. "My sweet cream pie." I thought of my Alpine lover for the first time in a long while, and he was nothing more than mist over a distant mountain.

In a motel lobby near Omaha, we had to wait in line for twenty minutes behind three families. Sam put his arm around me and pulled a tennis ball out of his jacket. He bounced it on the thin carpet, tentatively, and when he saw it had enough spring, he dropped into an exaggerated basketball player's crouch and ran across the lobby. He whirled in front of the cigarette machine and passed the ball to me. I laughed and threw it back. Several people had turned to stare at us. Sam winked at them and dunked the ball through an imaginary net by the wall clock, then passed the ball back to me. I dribbled around a stack of suitcases and went for a lay-up by a hanging fern. I misjudged and knocked the plant to the floor. What surprised me was that the fronds were plastic but the dirt was real. There was a huge mound of it on the carpet. At the registration desk, the clerk told us the motel was already full and that he could not find our name on the advance reservation list.

"Nebraska sucks eggs," Sam said loudly as we carried our luggage to the door. We spent the night curled up on the hard front seat of the van like boulders. The bony parts of our bodies kept bumping as we turned and rolled to avoid the steering wheel and dash. In the morning, my knees and elbows felt worn away, like the peaks of old mountains. We hadn't touched each other sexually since California.

"So she had big ta-ta's," I said. "She had huge ta-ta's and a bad-breath problem." We had pushed on through the corn, across Iowa, Illinois and Indiana, and the old arguments rattled along with us, like the pots and pans in the back of the van.

"She was a model," he said. He was describing the proprietress of the slender cigarettes and red panties.

"In a couple of years she'll have gum disease," I said.

"She was a model and she had a degree in literature from Oxford."

I didn't believe him, of course, but I felt the

sting of his intention to hurt. "By the time she's forty she'll have emphysema."

"What would this trip be like without the melody of your voice," he said. It was dark, and taillights glowed on the road ahead of us like flecks of burning iron. I remembered how, when we were undergraduates attending different colleges, he used to write me letters which said keep your skirts down and your knees together, don't let anyone get near your crunch. We always amused each other with our language.

"I want a divorce," I said in a motel room in Columbus, Ohio. We were propped against pillows on separate double beds watching a local program on Woody Hayes, the Ohio State football coach. The announcer was saying, "And here in front of the locker room is the blue and gold mat that every player must step on as he goes to and from the field. Those numbers are the score of last year's loss to Michigan." And I was saying, "Are you listening? I said I want a divorce when we get to Virginia."

"I'm listening."

"Don't you want to know why I want a divorce?"

"No."

"Well, do you think it's a good idea or a bad idea?"

"I think it's a good idea."

"You do?"

"Yes."

The announcer said, "And that is why the night before the big game Woody will be showing his boys reruns of the films *Patton* and *Bullitt.*"

That night someone broke into the van and stole everything we owned except the suitcases we had with us in the motel room. They even stole the broken radio. We stood in front of the empty van and looked up and down the row of parked cars as if we expected to see another black van parked there, one with two pairs of skis and two tennis rackets slipped into the spaces between the boxes and the windows.

"I suppose you're going to say I'm the one who left the door unlocked," I said.

Sam sat on the curb. He sat on the curb and put his head into hands. "No," he said. "It was probably me."

The policeman who filled out the report tried to write "Miscellaneous Household Goods" on the clipboarded form, but I made him list everything I could remember, as the three of us sat on the curb—the skis and rackets, the chess set, a baseball bat, twelve boxes of books, two rugs which I had braided, an oak bed frame Sam had refinished. I inventoried the kitchen items: two bread cans, two cake pans, three skillets. I mentioned every fork and every measuring cup and every piece of bric-a-brac I could recall—the trash of our life, suddenly made valuable by the theft. When the policeman had left without giving us any hope of ever recovering our things, I told Sam

I was going to pack and shower. A half hour later when I came out with the suitcases, he was still on the curb, sitting in the full sun, his cotton shirt beginning to stain in wing shapes across his shoulder blades. I reached down to touch him and he flinched. It was a shock—feeling the tremble of his flesh, the vulnerability of it, and for the first time since California I tried to imagine what it was like driving with a woman who said she didn't want him, in a van he didn't like but had to buy in order to travel to a possible job on the other side of the continent, which might not be worth reaching.

On the last leg of the trip, Sam was agreeable and compliant. If I wanted to stop for coffee, he stopped immediately. If I wanted him to go slower in thick traffic, he eased his foot off the pedal without a look of regret or annoyance. I got out the dictionary. Operose, ophelimity, ophryitis. He said he'd never heard of any of those words. Which president died in a bathtub? He couldn't remember. I tried to sing to keep him company. He told me it wasn't necessary. I played a few tunes on a comb. He gazed pleasantly at the freeway, so pleasantly that I could have made him up. I could have invented him and put him on a mountainside terrace and set him going. "Sammy," I said, "that stuff wasn't much. I won't miss it."

"Good," he said.

About three a.m. green exit signs began to appear

announcing the past and the future: Colonial Williamsburg, Jamestown, Yorktown, Patrick Henry Airport. "Let's go to the beach," I said. "Let's just go all the way to the edge of the continent." It was a ludicrous idea.

"Sure. Why not."

He drove on past Newport News and over an arching bridge towards Virginia Beach. We arrived there just at dawn and found our way into a residential neighborhood full of small pastel houses and sandy lawns. "Could we just stop right here?" I said. I had an idea. I had a plan. He shrugged as if to say what the heck, I don't care and if you want to drive into the ocean that will be fine, too.

We were parked on a street that ran due east towards the water—I could see just a glimmer of ocean between two hotels about a mile away. "All right," I said, with the forced, brusque cheerfulness of a high school coach. "Let's get out and do some stretching exercises." Sam sat behind the wheel and watched me touch my toes. "Come on, Sammy. Let's get loose. We haven't done anything with our bodies since California." He yawned, got out of the van, and did a few arm rolls and toe touches. "All right now," I said. "Do you think a two-block advantage handicap is about right?" He had always given me a two-block advantage during our foot races in California. He yawned again. "How about a one-and-a-half-block lead, then?" He crossed his arms and leaned against the van, watching me. I couldn't tell whether he had nodded, but I said anyway, "I'll give you a wave when I'm ready." I walked down the middle of the street past houses which had towels hanging over porch rails and toys lying on front walks. Even a mile from the water, I smelled the salt and seaweed in the air. It made me feel light-headed and for a moment I tried to picture Sam and myself in one of those houses with tricycles and toilet trainers and small latched gates. We had never discussed having a child. When I turned to wave, he was still leaning against the van.

I started out in a jog, then picked up the pace, and hit what seemed to be about the quarter-mile mark doing a fast easy run. Ahead of me the square of water between the two hotels was undulating with gold. I listened for the sound of Sam's footsteps but heard only the soft taps of my own tennis shoes. The square spread into a rectangle and the sky above it fanned out in ribs of orange and purple silk. I was afraid to look back. I was afraid that if I turned to see him, Sam might recede irretrievably into the merciless gray of the western sky. I slowed down in case I had gone too fast and he wanted to catch up. I concentrated on the water and listened to the still, heavy air. By the time I reached the three-quarters mark, I realized that I was probably running alone.

I hadn't wanted to lose him.

I wondered whether he had waited by the van or was already headed for Newport News. I imagined him at a phone booth calling another woman collect in California, and then I realized that I didn't actually know whether there was another woman or not, but I hoped there was and that she was rich and would send him money. I had caught my second wind and was breathing easily. I looked towards the shore without seeing it and was sorry I hadn't measured the distance and thought to clock it, since now I was running against time and myself, and then I heard him—the unmistakable sound of a sprint and the heavy, whooping intake of his breath. He passed me just as we crossed the main street in front of the hotels, and he reached the water twenty feet ahead of me.

"Goddammit, Day," I said. "You were on the grass, weren't you?" We were walking along the hard, wet edge of the beach, breathing hard. "You were sneaking across those lawns. That's a form of cheating." I drummed his arm lightly with my fists pretending to beat him up. "I slowed down because I thought you weren't there." We leaned over from the waist, hands on our hips, breathing towards the sand. The water rolled up the berm near our feet and flickered like topaz.

"You were always a lousy loser," he said.

And I said, "You should talk."